ALL IN THE
APRIL MORNING

ALL IN THE APRIL MORNING

Jean Saunders

Pan Books

First published in Great Britain by
W. H. Allen & Co. Plc, 1989

This edition published 1997 by Pan Books
an imprint of Macmillan Publishers Ltd
25 Eccleston Place, London SW1W 9NF
and Basingstoke

Associated companies throughout the world

ISBN 0 330 37015 4

1 3 5 7 9 10 8 6 4 2

A CIP catalogue record for this book is available from
the British Library.

Typeset by AKM Asociates (UK) Ltd.
Printed and bound in Great Britain by
Mackays of Chatham PLC, Chatham, Kent

ALL IN THE
APRIL MORNING

Chapter 1

It seemed to Dermot O'Connell that he had lain awake for hours. Long before daybreak he had slid out of the warm bed, careful not to waken his sleeping wife, and peered through the bedroom window as if to seek inspiration.

The land-locked Bay lay far below, still and beautiful in the pre-dawn calm, where thin slivers of light made ghostly patterns on the pewter-coloured water. The long, ugly island of Alcatraz resembled a crouching, waiting monster. It occurred to Dermot uneasily that everything seemed to be waiting.

A feeling he couldn't explain made him edgy. This should be a good day, a happy day, yet something seemed wrong. In the distance a dog howled, as if in agreement with his sixth sense.

'Come back to bed, Dermot,' he heard Mavreen say sleepily. 'Surely 'tis not time to be up yet?'

'Hush now, darlin'. 'Tis just the fidgets in me legs bothering me,' he lied. 'There must be bad weather brewing.'

She sighed, the bed creaking again as she tried to settle more comfortably on the lumpy mattress. The Pendletons were grand folk all right, but they didn't believe in too many comforts for their paid help.

The frown on Dermot's rugged face deepened. Paid help indeed. It was a fine label to stick on a man. He had come to America on the emigration boat with such high hopes, bringing his family to the golden city of San Francisco, where there was work in plenty and a man could hold up his head instead of scratching a living in the peat bogs of Ireland.

7

It had been the brink of a new year, a new century, and Dermot had been buoyant with optimism. They would grow rich in America. His Mavreen would wear silk dresses and act the lady; his little daughters would grow up to be sought-after young ladies and marry well in their chosen land; and the coming baby, which Dermot prayed every night to the Holy Mary would be a boy, would be the spit of his daddy and make him proud. . .

Now the century was six years old and so was Michael, this very spring day that was dawning – April 18th, 1906. And whatever dreams they had brought from Ireland had evaporated quicker than the San Francisco sea-fog. There were few decent jobs to be had, and no peat bogs to be worked . . . only menial jobs that the O'Connells had always considered beneath them. It was Mavreen's quiet voice that had brought him to his senses when Dermot was ready to give up and admit defeat.

'Are the O'Connells incapable of cleaning other folks' mansions? Won't these Pendletons who are advertising have the best cook and general factotum that ever lived? See here, Dermot –'

Her voice had cracked a little as she held out the newspaper: ' "a married couple preferred, children accommodated." How many jobs will there be where we can all be together? We'll be living in a fine house on Nob Hill, and sure and we can always pretend it's ours!'

She had won him round as always, her wide blue eyes pleading with him to do this for all of them. The baby was still suckling, and Mavreen needed a settled home and proper nourishment. The two girls had clambered over their stocky bull of a father, his wee Kitty a little charmer at two years old, his beautiful eight-year-old Bridget already showing the promise of becoming a lovely Irish colleen.

'Oh, please Daddy,' the girls sang into his ear, their voices still lilting, still bringing a breath of the green hills and meadows of Ireland to his heart whenever he heard them, none of the brashness of the new American accent rubbing off on them yet. 'Can't we live in the big house? Can't we, Daddy?'

'All right then, me darlings,' he'd given in cheerily. 'We'll see about getting the job, and dance to the Pendletons' tune, and mebbe one day we'll have such a house for our very own!'

The girls squealed and clapped, and Mavreen bent her dark head to attend to the baby's needs, not letting her brave and desperate husband see her shadowed eyes.

Being no more than servants to wealthy Americans was so much less than their dream . . . but they couldn't let the little ones starve! What was the loss of a little pride compared with that?

'I don't want to dance to the Pendletons' tune!'

Not really understanding, it was as if Bridget's child's mind sensed the sorrow beneath the smiles, and her high spirits vanished.

Dermot's eyes softened as he looked at her, his darling. With those looks of hers, she'd survive, no matter what, the thought went through his mind.

'Come on then, love, and make a tune for us on your Daddy's fiddle instead.'

Her eyes shimmered for a moment at his gentle encouragement, knowing that no matter how she tried, she couldn't master the simple instrument the way her father could. What she did best was to accompany him in a pure sweet voice that Dermot said was like the sound of the angels. But he knew better than to belittle her attempts on the fiddle. He swung her round in the mean little shack by the wharf, teasing his defiant little love into smiles again.

'You'll make the sweetest music one of these days, my Bridget! I predict it!'

A fine lot he had accomplished for his family in six years, Dermot thought dismally now, as sounds of the early morning stirred the city to life, and San Francisco stretched and yawned and welcomed a new dawn. Precious little except for moving uptown from the hovels where the immigrants lived, to the mansion on Nob Hill. . .

But it was not their mansion, and no matter how they all play-acted, he sometimes caught the longing in Mavreen's

9

eyes as she watched the ladies preen in the big house, while she wore the plain clothes of an Irish cook. And Bridget was old enough now to suspect the uselessness of a man's dreams.

He had wanted so much more for them all. For his wife and his boy, and the two girls who must realise that despite their surroundings they were still poor, and would probably always be poor.

Michael was still too young to notice. Kitty was sometimes curious about the way the family was segregated from the real Americans. Dermot snorted. Real Americans indeed! They had arrived a generation before him, that was all. You only had to hear their names, the German, the Dutch, the Norwegian, to know it. And the elite from England, of course . . . his lips curled, feeling as ever a second-class citizen when compared with the English with their beautiful vowel sounds and carrying their noses in the air. Dermot had no patience with the English.

But Bridget . . . she was fourteen now, and becoming a real young lady, or could be, given the chance. Sometimes Dermot was uncomfortably aware that Bridget had begun to know he only had feet of clay. He was letting them down . . . and the one thing he prized above all was the love of his family. The two girls were as close as two sisters could be, for all the difference in their ages. He thanked God for that.

Dermot moved away from the bedroom window and shrugged into his working clothes as the chill of the morning sent a shiver through him. He shouldn't waste time day-dreaming.

It was five o'clock and he should be downstairs and raking out the fires and setting them for the day; throwing back the curtains and unlocking the doors so that when the grand Pendletons arrived downstairs it was to find the sun streaming through and the panorama of the city spread out below them.

It must be grand indeed to be rich and have minions to do such things for you, Dermot thought wistfully. He went nimbly down the long winding staircase to attend to his tasks, but somehow his mind was still on Bridget, his prettiest daughter.

10

She was more than pretty, he amended. She was already beautiful, and he hadn't missed the way some of the young buckos who called at the house eyed her up and down. Gentry or bakers' boys, the look was the same. And Bridget, with her sweet air of innocence, her long black hair and those enormous blue eyes she inherited from her mother, was just beginning to be aware of it. It wasn't Dermot's place to warn her. Mavreen must do it, and soon.

He gave a jump as a small cold hand touched his arm. He was in the drawing-room now and the curtains were pulled back into their day-time position. Outside the house, the front lawns sloped away, lush and cool, where trees and shrubs were bursting into their spring greenery. Beyond in the distance the Bay was shrouded in the early morning mist. It looked set fair for a corking day.

'What are you doing up, Michael? Sure and you almost scared the daylights out of me, creeping about the house like a little ghost!'

'Can I help you scrape the grates, Daddy?' The boy said eagerly. 'I won't get in the way, or let the muck get on the furniture.'

Dermot gave a small sigh. Such a tiny ambition for a healthy son of his. To scrape out fire-grates . . . his mind was surely full of gloom that morning. He made an effort to sound more cheerful.

'All right, boy. Just don't make too much noise and wake everybody up.'

'I couldn't sleep. The horses keep making noises. Mammie's still in bed, but the girls were fighting. I heard them creep out a while ago.'

Dermot wasn't a swearing man. If he had been he would have cursed then. Bridget had no right to be taking Kitty out of doors this early the way she often did. God knew rogues might be on the streets at this hour. Bridget always said defiantly that they never ventured far, just to the end of the garden to look down at the city and watch it awaken, like a sleeping camel.

Up here on Nob Hill they were on the hump, Kitty added gleefully, her imagination caught, and Bridget said loftily

11

that it was the right and proper place for the O'Connells to be. Oh yes, his Bridget wasn't going to be satisfied with her lot for ever, Dermot thought uneasily.

And he couldn't argue with Michael over the restlessness of the horses in the city. He had heard them too, snorting and whinnying, and making a disturbance long before dawn. Dermot shrugged, moving away from the long windows towards the elegant Adam fireplace.

This was the most splendid room at the Pendleton mansion, furnished with costly period pieces, fine paintings, and deep-pile rugs on the smooth blue Persian carpet. The kind of room it made you want to walk across on tip-toe for fear of disturbing anything. The O'Connells never came here in any footwear but the house shoes Mrs Pendleton provided for them.

In one corner of the room stood a huge grandfather clock, imported from England, and dominating the entire corner. It showed just after ten minutes past five. In the centre of the room above their heads was the most spectacular chandelier the O'Connells were ever likely to see, dazzling with crystal droplets, the eye-catching pride of the Pendletons whenever visitors came to stay.

To the side of the house stood the gleaming bronze-coloured Cadillac that Lincoln J. Pendleton had just purchased, 'half the width of the house and twice as long', Dermot had heard him laughingly tell an admiring acquaintance. And he wasn't so far wrong either. . .

The Cadillac had been used for the first time just last night when the Pendletons went to the Opera House to hear Enrico Caruso take the role of Don José in Bizet's Carmen. Bridget had reported these facts with breathless awe when the daughter of the house had carelessly mentioned it. Such news enchanted Bridget.

The Pendletons would be still sleeping upstairs while the workers began the day, easing them into their affluent life. Bridget had sighed with envy when she heard they were going to hear Caruso sing. Not that his girl had any grand aspirations to be an opera singer, thought Dermot, but she loved all sorts of music, from the old Irish tunes played on her daddy's fiddle, to the popular classics of the day played on Mrs Pendleton's phonograph.

'Mind you don't scuff that carpet now, Michael,' Dermot said sharply, as the boy moved eagerly across the room to the fireplace. They were no more than halfway across the vast soft carpet when a tinkling sound caught their ears at the same instant. It was too small a sound to be one of the Pendleton bells demanding service, Dermot thought . . . such a tiny, tinkling sound . . . but somewhere beneath it, somewhere so deep beneath their feet it was no more than a strange vibration, there was a rumbling noise, almost as if the earth was complaining. . .

In almost the same instant the noises gathered strength, and then there was a roaring sound, accompanied by a great heaving and sawing from side to side, as though the whole house had taken the sea-sickness. The floor rippled in front of them, the sheen of the pale blue carpet catching the first daylight like waves of the ocean, and Michael lost his balance and slid away from Dermot, screaming in terror. The gilt-framed pictures crashed from the walls, glass shattering in all directions. The keys of the grand piano reverberated discordantly as it appeared to leap in the air and settle in fragments.

Michael was somewhere beneath it. Michael was his beloved son, and yet in an instant, Dermot knew it hardly mattered. Above him ceilings cracked and fractured. Floors twisted and turned as if the very earth was eager to spew up the intrusive grandeur of the mansions on Nob Hill.

Directly above Dermot's head, the tinkling sound he had first heard shook and sang and became awesomely orchestrated in a glittering crystal symphony.

The hundred droplets of the costly chandelier rained down towards Dermot, even as he watched, fascinated. It was just as though he waited fatalistically for his neck to be speared, for veins and arteries to be pierced, and for the beautiful ruby-coloured blood to ruin Mrs Pendleton's elegant blue Persian carpet for ever.

The O'Connell girls were clambering on the ornate wrought

iron gates. Their mother would scold them if she knew, but no one else was about at so early an hour. The gas-lights on the streets were just fading, and the blue and golden morning was just beginning. Above them a pale crescent moon still threw delicious eerie shadows all around them. For the sisters, it was a moment to savour, a moment when all of San Francisco was theirs.

'One day I'll have a mansion like this for my very own,' Bridget declared, hugging her woollen shawl to her chest in the cool crisp air.

'Daddy says you'll have to find a rich man to marry you first, Bridget O'Connell!' Kitty pooh-poohed her. 'And who's going to look twice at an Irish maid-of-all-work?'

Bridget tossed her long black hair away from her neck, knowing she could afford to feel superior to her little sister. At fourteen years old, Bridget considered herself almost a woman, while Kitty was still a child. Despite her love for her sister, she sometimes felt generations older than Kitty, far more than the six years separating them.

'I shan't always be a maid-of-all-work, though,' she said. 'Why shouldn't I marry a rich man? Sure, and some of them are probably quite nice.'

Kitty giggled. Her Mammie sometimes said tartly that she hadn't seen one yet. The toffs who came to the Pendleton house were all stinking rich, so their daddy said, and they mostly ate off gold plates and threw them away afterwards. A fine one with words, was their daddy, and Kitty was never quite sure whether to believe him or not. Bridget said it was all made-up nonsense, but Bridget was the clever one, and if anyone was going to end up rich and famous, it would be her adored Bridget. . .

Bridget seated herself more comfortably on the gate just as it began to move. She started to ask Kitty if she was dreaming, but before she could even speak, the movements became a shudder and then a great twisting, and she saw Kitty being hurled to the ground. Then she lost her balance, thrown down and hitting the ground with a ferocity that rattled her bones, and she couldn't see anything for a minute because of the near-blinding dust all around her. It was choking her throat and clogging her eyes, and she was convinced that she must be going to die. . .

Terrified, Bridget realised that every bit of street that she could still see was rocking back and forth in huge rolling waves. She heard the frantic tolling of church bells, as if demons were pulling the ropes . . . but the warning came too late.

'Kitty, are you all right?'

Bridget's voice left her throat in a bellow, but by the time it reached the air, it was no more than a croak.

Kitty's answer was a thin screech. 'I don't know. I can't see you. I'm frightened, Bridget!'

Noise enveloped and deafened them. New sounds mingled with the old – grating metal, exploding masonry, screaming voices. Bridget could see the girders of buildings hanging crazily, then disintegrating. The walls of a house nearby crumbled like a pack of cards. The Pendleton mansion itself swayed dangerously. It was the most awesome thing Bridget had ever seen. It was a nightmare. She felt her sister's hand grapple hers.

'What's happening?' Kitty screamed.

Bridget's voice was so tight with fear she could hardly breathe, let alone talk. 'An earthquake, I think. Or somebody's blown up the street.'

She moved cautiously. Her head hurt. She touched her forehead and felt something sticky. Her fingers were red when she took them away. Her leg hurt too. She wrenched it from beneath the heavy iron gate that had fallen on her. A jagged piece of it was stuck in her ankle. Bridget bit her lips hard, trying not to cry as she pulled it out, ramming her hand over the cut for a few seconds to stop the sudden pain and gush of blood.

'There's blood, Bridget,' Kitty whimpered. 'I don't like it –'

· 'I don't like it much either,' Bridget muttered, doing her best not to cry out with the pain. But crying would only make Kitty more frightened, and the need to protect Kitty at all costs was uppermost in her thoughts. As Kitty's fingers clutched at her shoulder, she winced. Bridget realised that she hurt everywhere. There wasn't one bit of her that wasn't bruised or cut. She peered through the dust into her sister's small shocked face.

'Are you hurt, love?' She said hoarsely.

Suddenly Kitty couldn't stop crying. Her whole body shook. 'I don't know. I want Mammie and Daddy and Michael.'

At her words, there was a great lump in Bridget's throat. Kitty obviously hadn't realised all that had happened yet, and no wonder. Bridget was hardly able to take it all in herself. The word earthquake had come glibly to her lips, but she knew it had really happened.

'Can you move, Kitty? We'll be all right. Somebody will help us.'

She said it bravely, praying that somehow her mammie and daddy and brother had got out of the house. They would come rushing towards them soon, arms outstretched, thankful that they were all safe, all together, the way her family always strove to be.

Inside, she knew the reality would be nothing like that . . . but she wouldn't know, she refused to know . . . she had to keep praying, for Kitty's sake. . .

Her sister gave a sudden terrified shriek.

'Bridget, the house –'

Her voice was swallowed up as a second jolting earth movement threw bronze-coloured fragments high in the air, just recognisable as the Pendletons' coveted new Cadillac. A third and more violent quake showered earth and stones all over the girls and finally demolished the bits of the Pendleton mansion that still lurched drunkenly together.

Bridget threw herself over her sister, staving off the worst of the debris. Her heart beat so fast she was sure every breath must be her last. At any moment she expected to be buried alive. When she felt able to move a little, she spat out the dank taste of earth. It felt truly like the end of the world.

Bridget grabbed Kitty's icy hand.

'We've got to move,' she shouted in her sister's ear. 'We've got to find somebody to help us.'

It was hard to think. She was fourteen years old, orphaned

and homeless, with no time to weep or to search for her family. Her stomach clenched every time she thought of them now, cursing her vivid Irish imagination. They'd be buried beneath tons of rubble, cut to ribbons by falling masonry. . . Bridget hurried Kitty into the street where people were rushing about in a panic.

'You Irish girls get down to the waterfront,' a man who recognised them shouted. 'The priest will take care of you. Get down to safety before the gas starts exploding.'

'What did he mean, Bridget?' Kitty stuttered.

'Take no notice,' Bridget snapped. 'He doesn't know anything. But we'll find Father Malley like he says. He'll tell us what to do.'

Kitty began to cry. 'I want Mammie.'

'So do I, love.' Bridget swallowed as the image of her calm and lovely mother swam through her senses.

'All right. We'll look for them first. They may have got out of the house.'

She scrambled to her feet, pulling Kitty after her, knowing her sister wouldn't be satisfied unless they made a token search. They couldn't crouch in corners like frightened rabbits forever while the city collapsed all around them. They crawled over piles of masonry, dust clogging their lungs, and all the while knowing it was useless. No one could have survived the earthquake here unless they'd been outside like themselves.

They spent a long time pretending to each other, clambering over bricks and stones, trying to give each other hope. Finally Bridget registered a new and sickly smell drifting into her nostrils.

Gas! When the earthquake struck, the morning had barely begun for the rich folk. But for the servants of the rich, gas stoves would have been lit, fires turned on in bedrooms for the pampered, and all those hundreds of gas appliances would be vulnerable. A stray match near broken pipes, a billowing curtain catching light from a stove, and the whole city could go up in flames . . . and the O'Connell girls had spent more than an hour fruitlessly searching. . .

If Bridget had felt fear before, it was magnified a

hundredfold now. She knew they must get away. Moonlight had faded and daylight had begun, and she heard the scream of a fire engine as several lathering horses dragged the vehicle up one of San Francisco's tortuous hills.

Dimly, she recalled a conversation between her parents just a few weeks before. Dermot had flung the newspaper away from him in disgust.

'Wouldn't you think a city this size would have an adequate fire service? The first sniff of a fire, and we'll all up go like burnt kippers. Mark my words, none of the city officials will heed Fire Chief Sullivan's warning until 'tis too late!'

And now it had happened. Small fires had already begun to spring up around them. Through the diminishing dust, tongues of flame were already licking greedily wherever they could get hold. Everything would soon be furnace-hot, because the strong wind that blew in from the sea hills would fan the flames.

'Get home to your mother, you stupid girls,' a man's voice yelled at them. 'The water mains have cracked and there'll be precious little water to fight these fires once the gas starts exploding. Tell your parents to get you down to the wharf.'

Tears blinded Bridget's eyes. One glance back at the Pendleton mansion made her jerk her eyes away. Her head spun with pain and this stranger had no time to listen to her stuttering explanation that they had no parents any more. That their soft and beautiful mother was dead, along with their bright spark of an Irish father, and their small brother . . . on his sixth birthday too. The stranger wouldn't care, nor stop to listen. He was already rushing away to look to his own safety.

Wherever they looked, huge fissures split the streets. Lower down the undulating hills of the city, tram-lines writhed impotently. The girls clung to each other. At least they were clothed, Bridget thought with rising hysteria. Some of the folks starting to run past them now wore far less.

Portly men with grand moustaches resembled great lumbering whales in their nightshirts. Ladies with their hair still in curlers beneath frilled caps were uncaring how they appeared in their buttoned-up cambric nightgowns.

In his more raucous moments, Dermot O'Connell might have said it would be interesting to be a fly on the wall and see who came rushing out of whose bedroom in such an emergency. Bridget's throat ached, and it felt as if her heart broke to know she would never hear his nonsense again.

'Should we find the priest, Bridget?' Kitty stammered, as people began to jostle them.

'Yes,' Bridget answered hoarsely. It was something positive to do. Father Malley was a an old fusspot, but he'd take care of them. She held on to Kitty very tightly as they ran, trying to think coherently.

They still had each other, even though they were in a land far from their real home. Kitty barely remembered the green fields of Ireland, but Bridget did. And right now, with a nostalgia that almost knocked her sideways with the same force as the earthquake, she longed for it with a longing beyond anything she had felt in her fourteen years. Ireland and safety were all mixed up in her mind. And being safe was the thing that mattered most in the world, more than being rich or being loved.

In those moments, she believed it implicitly. And if God allowed them to come through this day unscathed, then she vowed to spend the rest of her life keeping herself and Kitty safe.

They raced through the debris of the streets. As long as they kept going downhill they would eventually come to the wharf. Away from Nob Hill, past block after block of smoking ruin, conscious of the glow that was ludicrously glorifying the remnants of the once-proud city of San Francisco as the fires quickly got out of control. As the fires gathered momentum, so did their feet, pushed and knocked by others just as panic-stricken.

Ahead of them they could see the gleaming waters of the Bay, the little shanty-towns of the immigrants, and the Catholic church where Father Malley held court, ensuring that the Irish never lost their faith, no matter what fate handed them.

'Don't worry, darling,' Bridget panted. 'I'll take care of

19

you now, and we're always going to stay together, I promise you that.'

If such a task was monumental, Bridget was determined on it. As determined as her daddy had been that this land of opportunity was to be their golden future. And if the taste in her mouth was bitter for already America had taken nearly everything which she loved, she kept the thought bottled up inside. Her shoulders squared, and her arm went protectively around her little sister as they sought out the priest who would help them.

Chapter 2

Father Malley cared for his flock with the benevolence of a loving shepherd. His congregation, all immigrant Irish, unwittingly responded to his gentle manner by never burdening their priest overmuch with the sins of the flesh.

Father Malley thought blissfully that he shielded his community, when in reality, they shielded him. Round-faced, with an air of a cherubic angel, he went serenely about his daily tasks, and as long as no major catastrophes occurred, he was more than content.

He'd awoken early that Wednesday morning, and was already dressed before it was properly daylight. A few minutes later he wondered if all the demons in hell were after him.

'Holy Mother of God!'

He crossed himself quickly, said three Hail Marys and rushed out of his small house, to gaze in horror at the disaster that had struck San Francisco.

'Sweet Jesus preserve us,' he said hoarsely, his words more of a blasphemy than a real appeal to heaven.

People from the shacks were pouring into the streets, men and women half-dressed or naked, in whatever state they had gone to their beds. In the seconds that it took him to gape around him, the earth erupted for a second and third time.

For a second he knew utter panic. Father Malley knew that now he must face his real Calling, no longer the gentle priest who listened politely to the little failings of mankind, but one who must deal with the wrath of God.

Voices clamoured at him. 'Tell us where to go, Father, to be safe.'

'The shacks are splintering about our heads –'

A woman's howl would haunt him for the rest of his life. 'My babby's dead! 'Tis a curse on us all for leaving Ireland. My babby – my babby –'.

''Tis the devil taking his toll, so it is.'

Father Malley found his voice.

'Keep calm, all of you,' he roared. His small church was still intact, as were some of the less vulnerable shacks. 'You women take the children to the church and stay there. The men will help me search for survivors. Anyone with medical experience, make yourselves known.'

He hid his revulsion grandly.

'Father, there's a child here without a leg,' he heard the voice of a rescuer. 'She'll not survive. Will you come to her, Father, and say your piece?'

He turned quickly, and held little Mary Dowdy's hand and intoned the last rites as he watched the colour slip out of her cheeks and the flesh turn waxen. He sighed sadly. However long he was a priest, he would never reconcile himself to the finality of death, especially that of a child. You were here and then you were gone. Nothing changed that. No talk of hereafters or places in heaven . . .

'Thank you Father,' he heard the rescuer say gratefully. 'I'll pass on your goodness to the child's mother. 'Twill comfort her, so it will.'

Father Malley moved on blindly. There were others to help, and for several hours he toiled and tugged at the remains of the poor shacks, until he was satisfied that down near the waterfront they had been comparatively lucky. Only three people had died, a dozen needed medical help, although many more were cut and scratched. All were shocked. But the

21

majority were alive. Praise be to God.

He straightened painfully after spending so long on hands and knees, almost surprised to find that it was daylight and well into the morning. With the rest of them he had toiled for hours without realising it. Hunger gnawed at him, but misery took away the desire for food. He welcomed the cool wind coming in fresh from the sea, clearing the dust and spiralling towards the hills. The sea air felt clean and good . . .

Even as he thought it, he saw the orange-red glow inland, and realised that the earthquake hadn't merely reduced the small wooden shacks to splinters. It had demolished mansions and missions, and torn the heart out of the city. And the wind whipped up the fires as if God's giant hand was stoking the flames.

He scrambled along the street, but long before he reached his church he wondered if he was being accosted by more human demons. Two pairs of running feet leapt at him. Two pairs of clinging arms enveloped him, and the cracked voice of Bridget O'Connell rang in his ear.

'Oh Father, we've searched and searched for you! The house has gone, and Mammie and Daddy and Michael have gone with it, and we didn't dare move for hours, but now the fires are starting, and there's gas, and 'tis exploding, and the men say they're going to blow up parts of the streets to stop the fires spreading –'

He spoke sharply to stop the flow of words as the younger girl started bawling loudly.

'Stop that wailing, Kitty, and you calm down, Bridget, and stop frightening your sister,' he ordered. 'You'll both come with me to the church until we see what's what. As for this talk of blowing up streets, I'm sure you're mistaken. Come now, you're cold.'

They weren't cold. They shivered from fear and bereavement and loss. They had nothing but the clothes they wore and were fortunate to have them. The priest saw their small lost faces and felt a deep pity for them.

'Come along, my dears,' he said more kindly, reverting at once from the ogre to the priest the community knew and revered. ''Tis God's Will to send us these tasks to overcome, and we must never question it.'

With these two children he was tall and strong. They looked up to him, and he wouldn't fail them. But in Bridget O'Connell's head at that moment a question ran, deep and searching.

God wouldn't do this. If God was love, then God wouldn't take everything from her. She was too indoctrinated in the faith to accept that, and too independent not to question. But she couldn't say such things aloud to the priest. She could just let the doubt fester, blaming instead man, since she couldn't blame God, and creating the first barrier in her mind against all of them.

By noon San Francisco was an inferno. The troops were called in, and all through the afternoon and night the Navy ferried people across the Bay to the safety of Oakland on the far shore. Dynamite blasting to stop the spread of fire was begun. Left to mostly inexperienced hands, it merely ignited more fires.

'I told you so, Father,' Bridget O'Connell said to the priest, when the news was reported. 'The man said they'd blow up the streets.'

Father Malley looked at the girl. She was too knowing for her age, he thought with some irritation. He preferred to deal with children rather than adolescents, and Bridget was growing up too fast. She was losing that air of coltish childhood that her sister Kitty hadn't even acquired yet. Young as she was, Bridget had a sexual quality about her that must be restrained.

'You need to learn proper respect, Bridget,' he snapped. Her blue eyes widened, not expecting this.

'I am respectful, Father!' She said. 'I only said I told you so, and so I did!'

'Well 'tis not a proper way to speak to a priest, and my first task is to find a family to care for you –'

'Couldn't we stay with you, Father Malley?' Kitty begged. 'I can dust, and Bridget can cook, and we could live with you for ever and ever –'

He smiled faintly. Couldn't she see that such a thing wasn't possible, despite his wish to do all he could for the lambs in his care? He was a single celibate man, and it wasn't seemly . . .

'No, you can't, Kitty,' he said more gently. 'You must be cared for by a woman, in the shelter of a proper family. I'll hear no more about it now.'

'You'll not separate us, will you?' Bridget said in sudden alarm. 'I'm to take care of Kitty, and 'tis what Mammie and Daddy would wish. She'll be afraid without me –'

'I never said anything about separating you, Bridget. I'll do what I can.'

She couldn't think properly. She pressed on as if she was a wound-up clock that couldn't be stopped. 'If we're not kept together, we'll run away, so we will!'

'*Bridget*!' Father Malley thundered, and at his tone, she was silenced at last.

Someone else claimed his attention and he turned gladly away. Kitty slipped her hand into Bridget's.

'You're so brave, Bridget. Have we upset Father Malley, do you think?'

She tried not to show how she quaked at her own daring. 'I don't expect so, love. He just has a terrible lot of things to do today.'

'What's to become of us? Is Daddy really dead? And Mammie and Michael too?' Her voice wavered, and Bridget grasped her small hands tightly.

'Now you listen to me, Kitty O'Connell,' she said fiercely. 'Sure and it's true that we'll never see any of them again. I'd be a liar if I told you otherwise, and it's something we've both got to face. But we're the lucky ones because we've still got each other, and nothing's going to change that. We've got to keep telling ourselves how lucky we are to have one another, Kitty.'

And their daddy, who had brought them to this bright new land, was just as dead as the rest of them, she thought as the salty tears threatened. Where was their luck now? Their daddy hadn't been able to keep them together, so what chance did Bridget have? She pushed the thought away before it scared her to death.

'They won't try to take me away from you, will they?' Kitty quivered, her eyes bright with tears.

24

'No they won't, and if they did, I wouldn't let them. You heard me tell the priest so, didn't you? Whatever else happens, we're going to stay together, Kitty, and I'll always keep you safe.'

She stroked the soft dark head, feeling the clamminess of the skin, and felt an overwhelming surge of love for her small trusting sister. Kitty was her responsibility now, and Bridget made a solemn vow to herself that she would never let her down. Her mammie and daddy would expect it of her, and she wouldn't let them down either. If this was the mission in life that God had entrusted to her, she sensed the importance of it.

'I'll always look after you, darling,' she repeated. 'I'll always be here when you need me.'

Kitty pressed her trembling lips to Bridget's cheek.

'I do love you, Bridget.'

'I love you too,' she said, choked.

They sat in a corner of the church and hugged each other, and tried to remember how lucky they were, because at least they still had one another.

Loud-hailers on the streets announced that soup kitchens were operating. And Mayor Schmitz gave orders that anyone found looting from any building would be shot immediately by the Federal Troops. Bridget was shocked that anyone would do such a thing, but presumably it didn't deter looters who had nothing else to lose.

In the early evening, Father Malley sought out the O'Connell girls.

'Mrs Dowdy will take you in. The poor woman's lost her child, but she'll give you girls a home for now.'

'How long is that going to be?' Bridget wanted to know.

Father Malley sighed. He remembered how this one was always questioning, never letting a thing go until she knew all the ins and outs. A quick, bright girl, like her father, with all the softness of her mother about to burst forth. . .

'Do you have any other relatives in America?' He parried, knowing the answer.

'We do not,' Bridget's gentle Irish lilt confirmed. 'Our

relatives are in Ireland, Father. Should we go to them? It would dearly please me to go home to Ireland.'

The idea had entered into her mind more than once since she and Kitty had been orphaned. They would be safe in Ireland, as far away as possible from this horrible place, where even the ground wasn't safe to walk on.

She spoke as though Ireland were a hop and a skip away, Father Malley thought. Did she have no idea at all of the distance between here and the Emerald Isle! He looked into the girl's trusting eyes, and knew that she did not.

'Who do you have there, child? Do you know their names and where they live?'

Bridget felt as though she groped through a maze. Her parents had spoken of them in the old days, when they first came to America, but lately it had been rare that the old country figured in the conversation. She had known with a child's wisdom that her daddy had been hurt by the way none of his folks had 'written to them after they'd emigrated, thinking they had got above themselves.

'There was our Aunt Maudie and Uncle Padraig, and our Grandma who said she was never going to speak to my daddy again if he took us all away. They didn't live in our village though.'

She stopped abruptly as Kitty snivelled beside her. None of them would ever speak to her daddy again now, but for Kitty's sake she had to be brave and not cry at the thought. Unconsciously, she used the fragile wee girl as her own prop.

'Was it your mother's family or your father's?'

'Daddy's. So they'll be O'Connells too!' The small bit of detective work cheered her.

'Did you know where they lived?'

She frowned, trying hard to concentrate on the blurred memories, but it was all so tantalising and vague. She wanted to remember it all, to keep the images of the past whole and beautiful, the ones she remembered and the ones her parents had described. They were all she had left now, yet for the moment they completely eluded her.

'Didn't Daddy say he once lived near Dublin?' Kitty sniffled. 'It had a funny name that was something like Dublin.

26

Dunde-something –'

'Kitty, you're right, so you are! It was a place called Dundemanagh!' Bridget hugged her with delight, and Father Malley sighed with relief.

'We'll see if we can find it on the map before we get too excited,' he said, 'and then you'll go to Mrs Dowdy's. You'll be a comfort to her.'

Bridget made herself deliberately numb to the events of the morning, thankful enough to let someone else do her thinking for her for a while. At his house, Father Malley found the map of what Dermot O'Connell always called 'the tipsy square shape of Ireland'. The priest sought for the village of Dundemanagh and eventually found it a little way inland from the east coast.

'There we have it, girls! And you think that's where your Uncle Padraig and your family live?'

'It might be,' Bridget said warily. She couldn't be that sure. Nothing seemed certain any more.

'I'll use the names you gave me and write tonight to see if they'll send money to get you home. I agree 'tis best for you, but meanwhile Mrs Dowdy will house you both.'

Bridget and Kitty exchanged glances. They didn't want to stay with Mrs Dowdy, whom they'd seen in church and who was a grumbling, tight-lipped woman, but no doubt it was wicked and ungrateful to say so. Especially when Father Malley kept saying it was their Catholic duty to help her through her grief, adding as an afterthought that Mrs Dowdy would help them through their own.

'The Dowdys will be missing their child, so you just do as you're told and be good girls, and I'll see you tomorrow.'

He pointed the way to Dowdys' shack, relieved to have dealt with them. He wrote the letter to the Dundemanagh O'Connells straight away, praying that they were the right ones, and in the right frame of mind to send money for two nieces they hardly knew.

'So you're the O'Connell girls.' They quickly learned that Mrs Dowdy usually made statements rather than asked questions.

'Yes, Mrs Dowdy,' they said together. They stood as close as possible, trying to make themselves invisible in the wooden shack with the constant damp smells from Mrs Dowdy's take-in washing and ironing.

'And you've lost your parents and your brother too.'

'Yes, Mrs Dowdy –'

'Well, God's taken from both of us, so we must do the best we can to console each other. The church has supplied second-hand clothing, and I've found a nightgown for you, Bridget. Kitty can have one of – Mary's.'

She faltered just briefly over the name. Other than that, no one would ever think her only child had died that morning. Seeing the shock in Bridget's eyes, the woman spoke briskly.

'Those who question God's Will are as evil as those who sin, Bridget O'Connell. You'd do well to remember that. Your folks and my Mary have gone to a better life. None should begrudge them that.'

'No, Mrs Dowdy.'

'Get you both to bed then. Behind the curtain in the parlour's the only space we have, so it must do for the two of you. Tomorrow, Bridget, you're to begin helping me with the take-in laundry. Folk still want clean sheets and fresh clothes, and I can use a helper. Good-night to you now.'

'Good-night, Mrs Dowdy.'

They looked at each other, took the night-clothes they were offered and crept behind the parlour curtain. They undressed with shaking hands and climbed onto the hard bed, to lie holding each other and trying desperately not to cry. They dozed fitfully in each other's arms, and now that they were partly relaxed, the nightmare of the morning was constantly relived in their minds. Despite each other's presence, each felt utterly alone and bereft.

Long into the night, Bridget felt Kitty silently sobbing against her, and as another dawn began to lighten the sky she whispered the same words, over and over, in a vibrant, determined voice.

'I'll always look after you, Kitty. Nobody's ever going to separate us. We're all we have left of the family now, and we're going to stay together for ever and ever. I'll keep you safe, I promise.'

'I know. We're lucky, aren't we, Bridget?'

'That we are, my little love. We're the lucky ones.'

And long after Kitty had finally fallen into an exhausted sleep, Bridget lay dry-eyed, staring up at an unfamiliar ceiling, wondering who was going to look after *her*. From upstairs, the occasional creak of bed and floorboards during the long night had made her wonder if Mrs Dowdy was turning into the flatulent Mr Dowdy's arms and weeping for her Mary too. Even Mrs Dowdy must have feelings, Bridget thought.

In the next weeks and months they haunted Father Malley's house to ask if there had been a letter from Ireland. They prayed in the church, twisting the rosary beads in their hands and being careful not to miss saying a single Hail Mary or to forget to light candles for Mary Dowdy as well as their own family. They went to confession and confessed every misdemeanour, large or small. They did all that they could to will Uncle Padraig O'Connell to write and send the money to take them to Ireland.

'It's becoming an obsession with you, Bridget,' Mrs Dowdy snapped after four months, when the people of San Francisco had begun to breathe again, and the outside world said that they must be made of a particularly stoical breed to build their city all over again.

Within two weeks, electricity had been restored, new tram-lines ordered and plans for rebuilding begun, and although many people still occupied tents in place of permanent homes, the optimism of the survivors was undaunted. And Bridget O'Connell discovered that she had inherited her daddy's optimism for her own future.

She tossed her hair at Mrs Dowdy's words, no longer subdued by the thought of being a substitute child for the woman, for there was nothing maternal about her. Bridget didn't like her, nor her never-ending grumbling to Bridget to get the clothes clean in the old wash-tub, making her scrub and scrub until her hands were red-raw to the elbows.

'I'm not obsessed. I just hate this city,' Bridget said

defensively. 'I can't wait to leave it. I shall never feel safe here again.'

Her sense of the dramatic constantly annoyed the sour-faced woman.

'You'd best confess your hate to Father Malley, my girl. 'Tis a sin to hate and well you know it.'

'It only applies if you hate people. It doesn't count if you hate things,' Bridget retorted.

From his chair near the fire-place, her husband snorted with amusement.

'She's got you there, Mrs Dowdy. She's got a clever tongue on her that beats yours.'

'And I'll thank you to get your backside off that chair and do some work, you idle bastard!'

Bridget gasped. Mrs Dowdy was an odd mixture of the saintly and the practical. She'd once observed waspishly to Bridget that her husband had been born on the wrong side of the blanket, so there was no disrespect in calling him a bastard, because that was exactly what he was. She turned on Bridget now.

'And you're to get that hair cut, or twist it into a bun like I told you. You're flaunting yourself to all and sundry, and inviting hot looks from the sailors at the waterfront. You should be ashamed.'

Bridget felt her cheeks burn.

'My daddy loved my hair, and I don't flaunt myself. I can't help looking the way I do –'

'Don't give me any lip, my girl. While you're under my roof, you'll behave in a proper manner, and not give that young sister of yours any wrong ideas –'

Bridget leapt to her feet. In the last four months she had grown in height and breadth. Her fifteenth birthday had come and gone, and she was almost a young woman, and Mrs Dowdy felt threatened by the anger in the girl's eyes.

'The only wrong thoughts my sister gets is what you put in her head. I'm keeping Kitty safe, and teaching her things my mammie would have wanted me to –'

'Such as putting words to music and wasting your time singing soft songs instead of learning to sew a fine seam for

30

your marriage-bed,' Mrs Dowdy sneered.

'Leave the girl alone, woman,' her husband grunted. 'Sure and you torment her from day 'til night with your whining.'

'And who's talking out of turn now, bastard? 'Tis my house, and for all the work you do in it, you might as well join the down-and-outs,' she rounded on him.

These two were stifling her, Bridget thought frantically. Her parents' marriage had been warm and companionable, but in this house it was more like a battle-field. It was something she never wanted. As for encouraging the sailors, she had felt dirty because of their catcalls and innuendoes, and she wanted none of that either . . .

'I'm never getting married,' Bridget's brittle, metallic voice stilled them both. 'There's no use in loving people, and having children. They're only taken away from you. You should know that!'

The shocked silence stretched on. Outside, the muffled sounds of the waterfront drifted through the open window, bringing with them a whiff of the sea. Mrs Dowdy was puce with rage and something else. George Dowdy cleared his throat awkwardly.

'Bridget, don't talk that way. One of these days you'll find a good man and want to be married. 'Tis the way of things. You'll think differently in a few years. You'll want children of your own –'

'I *won't*. For one thing, I don't ever want a man – doing things to me just to get children,' she said, her voice shrill and upset, because somehow it all seemed to focus on that. All the sly remarks from the women, and the troubled discussions between the Dowdys and the priest, because of Bridget O'Connell's undoubted sexuality, however innocent and unwanted.

She felt the sting of Mrs Dowdy's hand across her mouth.

'We don't want none of that talk in this house. It's just like I expected. Wash your mouth with soap, and then ask Father Malley to forgive you. What goes on between a man and woman in wedlock is blessed by the church, and 'tis not for the likes of you to defile it with your lewd remarks.'

31

'I didn't!' Bridget almost wept. 'I said it's something I don't want –'

'Go now, Bridget.' Mrs Dowdy thundered, and pushed her towards the door. Bridget stumbled through it, seeing nothing until she reached the church.

Father Malley knelt before the rows of lighted candles. The main part of the church was dim after the brightness outside, and for a moment all Bridget could see was the priest's grey head haloed by the light of the candles, his black cassock covering him like a shroud, and the incongruous soles of his shoes with a hole in each one. The sight of them made him appear human, encouraging Bridget to tip-toe near and tap him on the shoulder.

He gave a start, crossed himself, and stood up. Bridget O'Connell was as tall as himself now, looking him levelly in the eyes with her bright blue gaze, and clearly with more than a hint of trouble to spill out.

'What can I do for you, child?' He asked.

'Father, we can't stay there a minute more,' she burst out. 'I'll have to take Kitty away. I'm sure Mrs Dowdy's a good woman, but the two of us are always at daggers drawn, and I swear 'tis not always my fault –'

'Let me catch my breath so I can understand what's been going on, Bridget!' He spoke with a mildness meant to soothe and rebuke at the same time. 'What's happened now?'

'She struck me, Father, and for nothing, I swear –'

'It would be more seemly if you'd stop swearing in God's house. Anyway, leave it for the present, because I've something to tell you.'

Her eyes blazed.

'You've heard from my people in Ireland?'

'I've had a letter, Bridget –'

She almost jumped up and down, whether it was seemly or not. He propelled her towards the small side room, where he'd put the letter from her Aunt Maudie in Dundemanagh. He showed it to her and she read it quickly. And as he had expected, her eyes filled.

'Uncle Padraig's dead. And my Grandma too.'

Of course, she remembered them only vaguely. Her mammie and daddy hadn't been great ones for visiting. But there had been a boisterous uncle, red-faced and cheerful like her daddy, and a small, black-clad woman with a creased leathery face and eyes still blue and keen . . . they had been her people, and she was part of them . . .

'You'll see that your Aunt Maudie wishes you and Kitty well, Bridget,' the priest said unnecessarily, as if she couldn't read the words for herself. 'And if you can ever find your way to Dundemanagh, she'll be happy to welcome you. But there's no money for fares, girl, no money at all.'

Bridget wasn't illiterate like some of the Irish children who cared nothing for book-learning and bettering themselves. But right then, she wished she didn't have the ability to read the heartbreak in the letter.

Uncle Padraig had died not six months ago, and her Grandma had a stroke at the news, and now Aunt Maudie was alone and hardly able to make ends meet, except for a bit of sewing and cleaning. What it amounted to was that there was no help for Bridget and Kitty, unless they could pay for themselves to get to Dundemanagh, and pay for their keep when they got there. And that was like asking for the moon.

Bridget gave a harsh dry sob. She would never get out! She would stay here and wait, like all of them, for the next time the earth erupted . . . there was no sense or logic in her reasoning, just blind terror that seemed to snatch at her throat so that she could hardly breathe . . . she heard the priest's kindly voice.

'Bridget, I know how you must feel at this news, but there's still some hope –'

'What hope?' Her cracked voice indicated that there was none, and he thought quickly.

'The church has a network of families who take in young destitute girls to work in their homes. Sometimes the families will pay all expenses to find the right type of girl –'

'And the church will send us to Ireland?'

'Alas, no. Our funds hardly go that far. But there's a large Irish community in New York and I'll contact Father Rourke there. I'll ask if there's a suitable family willing to take you and Kitty in. It's the best I can do –'

'Where is New York, Father? Is it near to Ireland?'

'Nearer than San Francisco.' He prevaricated, not daring to tell her it was as far again . . .

She gave a shuddering breath and squared her shoulders. She was strong, Father Malley thought, with grudging admiration. It would probably be her salvation. That, and the almost obsessive need to care for her sister.

'Then that's what we'll do. We'll go to New York and work hard, and save the money to go to Ireland.'

'Bridget –'

She smiled crookedly. 'I know. I'm dreaming again. But dreams are all I've got, besides Kitty. And sometimes dreams come true, don't they?'

'Sometimes,' he agreed, having seen too much of the world to really believe it.

Chapter 3

Bridget knew it was more than just the thought of Ireland that was an obsession. It was also the burning need to get away from San Francisco, which to her seemed to symbolise all that was bad in the world.

She found it easy to forget the enchantment of the cable cars and the wistful hooting of the fog sirens in the Bay that had drifted right up to the Pendleton mansion on Nob Hill. She hated the sound now. It was mournful and depressing and funereal. She could forget the charm of the undulating hills of the city, and the excitement of the Chinatown that had disappeared under the rubble, and seeing all the important people who visited the Pendletons.

None of it existed any more. There was just the shell of the city to which Dermot O'Connell had brought his family so optimistically. Even more frightening than the structural damage was the fact that whole families could be wiped out in seconds as though they had never lived. The grand Pendletons had fared no better than her mammie and daddy and small brother . . .

'Why can't we stay here, Bridget?' Kitty asked curiously, when her sister continually besieged Father Malley for news from New York. 'It's not so bad, and Mrs Dowdy gives me nice clothes to wear –'

'They're not nice, you ninny,' Bridget said shortly, knowing that the worst of the horror had faded from Kitty's young mind, and the few months living in the noisy wharf area with the priest's protection had done a lot to restore the little girl's self-confidence.

'Do you want to spend the rest of your life wearing clothes that belonged to a dead girl?'

Kitty flinched, and Bridget felt guilty at her sharp words. She hugged the child, feeling more inadequate than usual, because when she was unhappy, Kitty was unhappy too, and there seemed no way she could lift herself out of the depression lately.

'I'm sorry, love but it's true. We have nothing of our own, and I want so much more for us. This isn't our home, and Mrs Dowdy only keeps us here on sufferance and because I'm cheap labour. You know it well enough, and when you're bigger she'll have you scrubbing for other folk too.'

'They're not all dead girl's clothes, are they?' Kitty ignored the last remarks and spoke fearfully, fingering the plaid skirt covered by the white apron she wore that day. Bridget looked down at her. She was a wide-eyed child, plumper now despite the privations, her dark hair curling softly about her shoulders.

'Oh, of course not. I was just teasing. The skirt came from the church, and was probably donated by some rich family. Anyway, you look pretty in anything you wear, my love, so you're to forget what I said.'

Into her head from nowhere came her daddy's voice at that moment, his brogue rich and uproarious after a bellyful of ale, and it was just as if he was standing by her shoulder.

'Ah, Bridget, me darlin', if you'd only put your brain in action before your mouth, there'd be less hurtful things coming out o' those ruby lips o' yours.'

Kitty touched her sister's arm, her voice wary.

'Why have your eyes gone all funny? They look all shiny like bits of blue glass. Are you crying, Bridget?'

She shook her head. 'Of course not. Crying's for babies. Didn't I tell you that?'

''Cepting when you're hurt, like when I fell and scratched my knee,' Kitty said dubiously. 'Then it's all right to cry a bit, isn't it?'

Bridget gave her a bear-hug, her voice muffled for a minute.

'Of course it is, darling.'

Kitty didn't deserve to live in the circumstances they did, and the vow Bridget had made to get them both out of there someday was as strong and positive as ever. It was just the execution of it that sometimes seemed as far away to her as Ireland.

'Some of the boys at the wharf have been whistling after you, Bridget,' Kitty remembered suddenly, thinking to please her sister. 'Some of the older girls at school said more than one of them was sweet on you.'

Bridget stopped walking at once, her eyes stormy.

'Those toe-rags! I wouldn't give them the time of day in a snowstorm, and I don't want you bandying my name with the likes of them, Kitty, you hear?'

'I only said what the other girls said –'

'Well, please don't. I don't care to be talked about in that way.'

Kitty gulped. There was no pleasing Bridget these days. 'But the girls said it was only to be expected, because you were the best-looking one for miles, and their mammies had said you'd be a fine catch for any man.'

Bridget stared at her sister. Kitty was nine years old now, always hanging around the older girls and the women who leaned over yard fences passing the time of day, and to Bridget's exasperation, she knew that Kitty was as bad a wee gossip as any of them.

'Well, you can just tell them from me that no man's going to catch Bridget O'Connell! I've made up my mind that I'm never going to get married and that's for certain sure!'

Kitty's eyes were round and wondering in her face.

'But what about having babies? Girls have to get married to have babies, so there. I know so. The others were talking about it –'

'If that's the kind of talk you're getting up to at that school, then you're to stop hanging around with those older girls,' Bridget snapped. 'Besides, nobody has to get married if they don't want to. Most of the women around here would be better off without their drink-swilling men, anyway. Men get tired of you and babies grow up and leave you. If you don't want to get hurt, you'll have none of it!'

'Mr Dowdy's not tired of Mrs Dowdy, is he?'

Bridget hooted. Months of living in the Dowdy shack had told her a good deal about the couple. His drinking and her nagging should have driven them apart years ago, and what use was a gold band on a woman's finger when two people lived in perpetual argument with one another? It might as well be a ring through the nose . . .

She was about to expand this theory when Father Malley came hurrying towards them, smiling as he saw the O'Connell sisters.

'I was coming to see you,' he greeted them, 'but you've saved me the trouble.'

'Is it good news?' Bridget asked at once.

'Wait until we get indoors at the house,' he chuckled. 'We'll have some tea.'

Once inside his house he bustled about putting the kettle on to boil and bringing out three cups and saucers, until Bridget felt as though she could have screamed. And yet there was a strange expectant calmness about her. She knew in her bones that she could afford to wait. If there was good news, it could only mean one thing. Soon, very soon, she and Kitty would leave San Francisco for ever, and never come back.

'I've heard from Father Rourke in New York, and he's found an Irish couple willing to take you in. Kitty will attend school, of course, but you, Bridget, will be expected to work in the house for Miss Finley. After school, Kitty will do any little chores that are required.'

37

'Oh –'

Bridget had expected to be bubbling over with tears of joy, but she could hardly speak. She had wanted this so much that the reality was almost an anti-climax. She had imagined these words so often . . .

'You'll go in the new year –'

The euphoria vanished. This wasn't how the scene should continue. She glared at the priest.

'Why not now? Why not next week?'

Father Malley sighed. Patience was not one of Bridget O'Connell's virtues.

'Because, my dear girl, Miss Finley and her brother will be travelling in Europe until the beginning of January.'

'They sound fearful grand, Father,' Kitty said nervously.

'They'll be charmed by your sweet self as soon as they look at you, no matter how grand, my dear,' he said graciously, wishing the older girl could be as pliant as this one.

'Bridget, just be glad there's a place for you both,' he said sternly. 'Father Rourke tells me that Mr Thomas Finley is in his middle years, owning his own tinned goods business, and his sister is a bit younger. You'll do well there, I'm sure.'

'Thank you. I don't mean to be ungrateful,' Bridget muttered, trying to stifle her disappointment.

'Will we go in a train, Father?' Kitty asked next.

'Yes, child. Some people I know will be travelling back to New York at the same time, and have offered to escort you on the train, and to take you to the Finleys in their own car when you arrive in New York. It's very kind of them to carry all your bits and pieces for you.'

Their bits and pieces could all be put in a paper bag, Bridget thought. And she couldn't help wondering if this Mr Finley really wanted them in his house if he couldn't be bothered to meet them at the railway station himself. She was sure she wasn't going to like him.

But it would be such a relief to get away from the Dowdys and the city of San Francisco that she wasn't even going to think about that.

Bridget spent every bit of spare time finding out about New

York. Sure, and it wasn't Ireland, but it was a whole step nearer than the west coast of the country! It was in the right direction. She cajoled Father Malley to lend her maps and pictures and any bits of information about their new home that he could find.

Kitty didn't seem in the least interested after the first desultory glances at all the brochures Bridget collected. But long before January and the final departure for the long journey east, Bridget knew enough to be excited about the splendid new city on the Hudson and East rivers, and the glorious green bronze Statue of Liberty in the middle of the ocean that heralded freedom for all.

'We'll have a much better life in New York, Kitty,' Bridget told her sister repeatedly. 'I just know that everything's going to be better from now on.'

It couldn't be worse. Nothing could be worse than the dreary existence with the Dowdys, except for the memories of that terrible morning in April.

One night in December when the Dowdys were out visiting friends, Bridget discovered the painful truth that Kitty didn't want the move as much as she did. For a long while now, instinct had been telling her it was best to get away as soon as possible, and instinct had been right.

Kitty had made new friends at the makeshift school near the Bay, and didn't want to leave them. She was in bed and snuffling beneath the bedclothes when Bridget asked her if she was getting a cold.

'No, I'm not. But why should you care if I did? You don't care about me. We always have to do just what you say,' the child said accusingly. 'You always think you know best, and you never even ask me what I want. Why can't we stay here instead of going to rotten old New York to live?'

Her words took Bridget's breath away for a few seconds, and she looked down at her in genuine astonishment.

'Kitty, you know very well that I'm doing this for you – for both of us,' she said, hiding the hurt. 'It's what Daddy would have wanted, for us to go back to Ireland.'

'New York's not Ireland,' Kitty shouted. 'And how do you know what Daddy would want? He's not here to tell us, is he?

39

And if he'd wanted it so much, he'd have taken us there himself.'

Bridget's mouth dropped open. Kitty never used to be so aggressive. She'd always been such an amiable child, but looking at her now, blue eyes flashing, Bridget could see the echo of herself in Kitty's flushed and furious face. She was working herself up into a real temper, and in a few years' time, Bridget guessed she was going to be a real little madam.

'I think Daddy might well have taken us all back to Ireland one day, love.' She held her own volatile temper in check with an effort. She frequently let fly with other people, but rarely with Kitty. If she was sometimes too soft with her, it was because all her sympathy, all her love, was concentrated on her sister, and she would never hear a word against her from anyone.

'Kitty,' she said quietly, when there was no answer. 'America wasn't all that Daddy expected it to be. You're too young to understand it all, but when you and Michael were in bed at the Pendleton house, I'd hear him and Mammie talking, and I know he sometimes regretted bringing us here.'

Kitty clearly never got the pang of misery that the mention of her parents and brother always sent coursing through Bridget's veins. Despite that, Bridget still felt the need to talk about them, to keep their memory alive for them both. Kitty glared at her belligerently.

'But I like it here. I like my friends –'

'You'll make new ones, darling. Mr Finley will be sending you to a nice school where there are other girls –'

'I shan't like them.'

'Of course you will –'

'No, I won't. I shall hate them all.'

She turned her back on Bridget, and lay so stiff and unyielding that Bridget felt a great stab of unease. She admitted that these last months Kitty had run wild with the girls from the shacks, and Bridget had been too busy with her own problems to notice the imperceptible change in her.

Kitty was growing up too, and asserting her own personality, and it was no longer as gentle and uncomplicated as it had once been. The environment on Nob Hill may have been a servile one for the O'Connells, but it had kept them far removed from the rougher elements of the immigrant community.

Bridget saw now that it wasn't only her own reddened skin that had suffered from the months they'd been forced to live in what was called shack-town. And the sooner they got away, the better. If anything was destined to confirm it to her more, it was the change she saw in Kitty, from the bright pretty child to a more sulky and discontented one.

Her mammie would have hated to see her daughters at loggerheads, and the sooner they moved in with a decent family, the better that would be too. Whatever Kitty thought, it was all for the best.

If it hadn't been for Father Rourke's pointed remarks that everyone must do their Catholic duty to help the poor people of San Francisco, Sheilagh Finley would never have let herself be persuaded to house the O'Connell sisters.

As it was, her brother Thomas had been the one to give in, and only then because he had become impatient with Father Rourke's bleating. He'd finally agreed to it, muttering caustically that he hoped it was going to ensure his place in heaven, which was another remark that didn't endear him to the saintly Father.

And now they were about to be saddled with two motherless girls from God knew what kind of background, who would most certainly disrupt the harmonious household.

Miss Sheilagh Finley had a fine way of dismissing the fact that things were rarely harmonious between her brother and herself. Never were two born of the same stock so different in looks and temperament. Her brother, fifty now if he was a day, though never admitting it, was florid and loud, given to wearing pale check suits and green neckties as if to emphasise the brash Irishman that he was.

'We've made the money, so why not spend it?' Thomas frequently snapped when she complained at his extravagances.

'*You've* made it, and you can just as easily lose it if you don't save something for a rainy day.'

41

'You're tighter'n a hen's arse sometimes, Sheilagh,' he'd snarl, gloating at the disgust on her prim face. 'I tell you there's plenty more where that came from. There ain't an American yet who'll do without his canned beans, and Finley's are the best. Can't you get it through that grey head of yours that we're rich, woman?'

'No, I can't. I still remember the old days when we had to scratch for a living –' she'd reply freezingly, launching into one of her favourite themes.

It was after such a fight that he'd gone hot-foot to his company lawyer and made his Will. And since his shrew of a sister was so determined to remain poor, skimping on clothes and items for the kitchen, and paying the servants a miserable salary, she could damn well stew in her own juice after he was gone. Thomas found a sweet irony in the thought.

It didn't really trouble him that soon there were going to be two more in the house. He doubted that the presence of two small girls was going to bother him overmuch, and it would be easy enough to keep them out of his way. His business was his life, and domestic problems could safely be left in the hands of his capable sister.

Thoughts of business put the smile back on his florid face. He'd got back from the trip to Europe a week after his sister, a trip of mixed business and pleasure, and one that had provided Finley's Canned Goods with a new and highly satisfactory contract with a German company.

Export or be damned was Thomas Finley's motto, and his roots were still too deeply embedded in countries on the other side of the water to be able to resist sending a few million cans across it when the opportunity arose.

The Smiths, the couple who escorted Bridget and Kitty on the long wearisome train journey across America were met at Grand Central Station by their son in his open-top car. The girls were too awed by the sight of it to say too much as they were all squashed inside with their small amount of luggage and the vast number of Smith valises.

The engine noise of the car was so loud and the roads so bumpy that there was little need to talk, for which Bridget was mightily thankful. Now they were actually here, there was none of that great and optimistic feeling of being one step nearer to Ireland that she had expected. It was a bit like Christmas Eve, when everything necessary had been done, and the great day still seemed an eternity away.

Here, everyone seemed to be rushing about like maniacs. The buildings were so high they must surely topple down, and there were strange smells that she didn't like and couldn't identify.

'Is it far to the Finleys' house, Ma'am?' She asked Mrs Smith.

The woman nodded. 'I'm afraid so, Bridget. It's a long way out of the city, of course. It's mostly businesses and offices here.'

Such a statement was beyond Bridget's understanding. How could a city be filled with businesses and offices? Did the people come here to work each day and leave it like a ghost town every night?

'Where is the Statue of Liberty, please?' She asked next. The car driver gave a loud guffaw.

'It's nowhere where you're going, honey. Didn't they tell you anything? You'll be living in New York State, in fruit-growing country, not New York City. The Finleys have one of the best houses for miles, so you'll do all right.'

Bridget gasped, feeling ridiculously betrayed. She hardly noticed where they travelled any more. She was sure Father Malley had told her they would be seeing this wondrous Statue in the ocean. He had definitely said she would see the boats that brought people to America and took them across to Ireland . . . how could they do that if they were living in fruit-growing country somewhere called upstate New York?

She huddled beside Kitty, glad that her sister had dropped off to sleep, unaware that anything might be wrong. Kitty wouldn't care anyway, Bridget thought, with the first real burst of annoyance against her sister. Kitty was still being difficult about leaving her friends behind. Bridget had vowed to love and care for Kitty, but sometimes the child made it awful hard . . . she chided herself quickly for the thought.

When the Smiths were deposited at their home, Bridget

thought she might doze off as well. But Marcus Smith wanted to talk.

'All rightie,' he said heartily. 'Now it's you two for the skylark.'

'I don't think we're going to like New York,' Bridget muttered as the car headed northwards.

He glanced back at her. She wasn't a bad-looker. Too young and gauche for a college graduate like himself, of course, but someday he'd take a bet that she'd gladden some guy's eyes.

'You can't say that until you've lived here awhile. The Finleys are O.K. people.'

'Do you know them, then?'

'I've met the brother,' he commented. 'He's not exactly top-drawer OK, but what Irish immigrant is? Hey sorry – I didn't mean that, honey. My tongue runs away with me sometimes.'

'Mine too,' Bridget said bitterly. 'And we're not exactly top-drawer OK either.'

'You're kinda young to be in charge of a kid like that, aren't you?' He said next. 'What happened to your parents? Do they always let you two travel about the country on your own?'

Bridget went dumb for a moment. Somehow you expected everybody to know. Somehow when something terrible happened, you never thought you'd have to tell it again in words, bringing back the pain as sharp as ever.

'They were killed in the earthquake.' She said in a rush, and saw the quick embarrassment in his eyes as he tried to cover his mistake.

'Say, I'm sorry. But that was a long while ago now, and you'll have a good life with the Finleys. They say the guy's loaded. Adopting you, is he?'

Bridget gave a brittle laugh. '*No*, he's not *adopting* us! He's taking us in to be his skivvies. Don't you know *anything* about us poor Irish?'

She was rude because it helped to hit out at somebody, and he was the only one available.

She heard his well-brought-up, college apology. She saw his reddened face, and was ashamed of her outburst. Her daddy wouldn't want her to behave like this towards a stranger.

'I'm sorry too – really I am,' she muttered.

'Forget it, or we'll spend the entire journey saying we're sorry to each other. What d'you think of the old boneshaker?'

She blinked before she realised he meant the car. Boneshaker was a good name for it, although it seemed very grand to Bridget. But long before they reached the Finley house, she felt as though every bone in her body was being mangled, and how Kitty could sleep through it all, heaven only knew.

'It's very nice,' she said, knowing it was what he wanted to hear.

'She is, isn't she?' He said enthusiastically, patting the dashboard as if congratulating an obedient pet. 'My dad bought her for me for my eighteenth birthday, and she's a doll.'

Bridget listened politely, knowing she was in a different world from the one she had just left. He spoke of this car as if it were a toy, and nobody that Bridget knew owned such a thing. The Pendletons' bronze-coloured Cadillac was part of another world too, a lovely, rose-coloured world where she'd been part of a family, and not the head of what was left of it. Sometimes the responsibility of it made her go cold inside. To take her mind off it, she forced herself to look around her at the country through which they were driving now.

Although the light was fading, she tried to take some interest in the vineyards and peach orchards. Roadside stalls were shut up for the night, on which presumably grapes and peaches would be offered for sale in the morning. Bridget's mouth watered. It seemed a very long way from Mrs Dowdy's mediocre cooking, and the soup kitchens provided by generous San Franciscans for the homeless immigrants.

Marcus realised she was becoming more silent as the journey went on. He was burning with curiosity, wondering if he dared ask this strange, beautiful girl what he wanted to know. Finally he thought, what the hell? Ask or stay dumb!

'Say, what was it like – being in an earthquake? We read about it in the papers, but I've never met anybody who actually experienced it. Was it truly horrific?'

Her lips felt as if they were made of lumps of ice. Yet inside, she was burning up with rage. It was ghoulish of him to ask, when she'd just told him she'd lost her parents in the earthquake. She met his eyes in the mirror, and guessed he was no more curious than a lot of people, and the words tumbled out.

'Terrifying's more like it. I never want to live through anything like it again.' She chewed her lip. She hadn't wanted to die either, and that had been the alternative.

'But how did it *feel*? Were houses really thrown up in the air before they collapsed like doll houses?'

His face came back into focus. 'Yes, they were, houses and cars and people,' she said harshly. 'It tore everything to bits, including my mammie and daddy and small brother. Now is there anything else you want to know?'

'Hey kid, I'm sorry. I didn't think. They said San Francisco was a beautiful city before –'

Sweet Jesus, didn't he know when to leave it alone! Bridget hardly ever blasphemed, but the words slid angrily through her mind at that moment.

'Perhaps it was. I only know I never want to see it again. I'll never go back.'

Marcus glanced at her taut figure in the back of his prized open-top. With all that pain in her darkened eyes, Bridget O'Connell wasn't just a pretty kid, she was beautiful. But he wished to God he'd never brought up the subject of the earthquake.

'You won't ever have to,' he reminded her. 'You'll be taken care of now.'

Bridget looked down at Kitty, sleeping exhaustedly in her arms.

'That's what happens to poor people, isn't it?' She said slowly, not really accepting until that moment that they *were* poor. 'You hope that other people will take care of you, otherwise –'

'We're here, kid.' Marcus Smith said with obvious relief in his voice.

The car was slowing down, and Bridget gasped as she saw the wide flat lawns on either side of a long driveway. At the end of it was a sprawling colonial house that was very grand indeed. It was as grand as the Pendleton house on Nob Hill, but she knew that that had never frightened her the way this house did. She had gone to live at the Pendletons' house when she was eight years old and had always been sheltered by her parents.

Now, she was the eldest O'Connell, and Kitty was in her charge, and she admitted freely that the thought was getting more nerve-racking every day.

'Nice, isn't it?' Marcus said, with the complacency of someone well used to money.

Bridget gathered up her pride. 'Oh yes, it's very grand. It's a bit like the house where we used to live in San Francisco.'

She saw his lips twitch.

'Oh yes? Pull the other one, Bridget O'Connell. What would a poor Irish girl like you be doing, living in a house like this?'

Her temper snapped. 'The same as I'm doing now,' she said smartly. 'Living on other folks' charity.'

He stopped the car with a jerk of the hand-brake, startling Kitty into wakefulness.

'I'll say one thing for you, honey. You've got a lot of pride. Watch out that it doesn't destroy you.'

She stared at him. What a daft thing to say. Pride was about the only thing she had left. She felt perilously near to tears as Kitty woke up with a start, looked about her and clung to her sister in a fright.

'I want to go back with Father Malley and Mrs Dowdy. I want to go home, Bridget –'

If anything was destined to put the fight back into Bridget O'Connell it was that.

'Well, I certainly don't! And this is home now, so stop your blubbing and we'll go and ring the doorbell and see if we're getting any supper tonight.'

She thanked Marcus Smith for his trouble, and after handing them their bags he left them to walk unsteadily towards the front door, stiff from the hours of travelling. After a few minutes they saw the shape of someone illuminated in the light behind the glass panel.

47

Kitty's hand crept inside her sister's. For a few sweet seconds, Bridget pretended everything was still the same, with the two of them against the whole world instead of growing more and more against each other.

Chapter 4

Miss Finley answered the door herself, curious to see these Irish sisters Thomas had inflicted on them. She inspected the girls briefly. Bridget inspected her back, relieved after all to find that she wasn't exactly a monster, even if she was thin and tight-lipped and what her daddy would have called 'a bit of a scrawny old bird' with her grey hair bunched into a knot at the back of her head. She didn't look at them unkindly, but there was little welcome in her face either.

'So you're the O'Connell girls, are you?' the woman said, the Irish brogue hardly discernible now among the cultivated New York twang.

'I daresay you'll be tired and hungry,' the woman went on. 'Carter will show you the kitchen, and you'll be given some food. The housekeeper will give you your duties in the morning. The child will start school next week when the new term begins and will be taken there each day by Carter. I hope you understand your good fortune in being taken into the house of a gentleman.'

'Yes, Miss Finley –'

'See that you remember it. But for our generosity, you'd be on the streets. You'll accompany us to church on Sundays and sit with the rest of the servants. The Finleys make a good showing on Sunday mornings to show the rest of the community that we're God-fearing Catholics. You've not lapsed in the faith, I hope?'

'No, Miss Finley!'

Sheilagh allowed them a thin smile. They seemed obedient enough, and she was just thankful that the older one seemed docile and the younger one wasn't crying. Only now did she admit to a feeling of apprehension in dealing with children, a situation she hadn't encountered before.

When she rang a bell a butler appeared from nowhere and motioned the girls to follow him. They were stunned into silence by his splendour, the regimented order of the house, the deep pile carpets, the luxurious furniture and the sweep of the grand staircase.

In the steamy kitchen the middle-aged housekeeper put up her feet after a long day, and two young maids chatted non-stop about gentlemen callers. In the huge grate a fire was roaring, and the scene was so homely and normal after the interminable journey and the stiffness of the last few minutes that the two newcomers clung to each other and simultaneously burst into tears.

'Here now, what's all this?' Mrs Harris said at once. 'We don't look that bad, do we?'

Her motherly arms went round both of them. Bridget was mortified with shame, while Kitty continued to sob noisily.

'I'm sorry. We're both so tired, and we didn't know what to expect –' Bridget gasped.

'Well, of course you didn't,' the woman said comfortably. 'And the first thing you saw was that stiff-neck Carter and the old trout herself. No wonder you felt like squawking.'

The maids giggled at the housekeeper's irreverence, and Bridget felt a smile tug at her lips. It was just like her daddy might have spoken. He too had the knack of bringing people down to size. Remembering him, her bottom lip trembled again, and Mrs Harris saw that briskness was the answer for these two.

'What d'you fancy to eat? You both need fattening up a bit by the looks of you. In that terrible earthquake, weren't you, and living on nothing but soup if the papers are to be believed, which of course they never are. How does a bit of cold chicken and hot homemade bread sound to you?'

'Wonderful,' Bridget said, realising that she was famished, as the woman paused for breath.

'Martha can get it for you. This here's Martha and Sally,

and I'm Mrs Harris, so sit down at the table and tell us your names.'

Bridget could see that Kitty was already charmed by Mrs Harris, a no-nonsense New Yorker, and when Bridget mumbled through the delicious cold chicken hunks and the hot bread oozing with butter, that she thought there would be all Irish servants here, Sally laughed derisively.

'Oh no. My lady takes a special delight in hiring American servants, so you two are honoured. It makes her feel superior to us white trash, see?'

'White trash?' Bridget echoed.

'Take no notice of her nonsense,' Mrs Harris said quickly. 'And you must form your own opinion of Miss Finley, of course –'

'What about Mr Finley?'

'He's a fair man,' she said firmly. 'You just keep your place, Bridget, and you'll be all right. He's a powerful man and thinks he owns half of New York state, which he may well do for all I know.'

For some reason, Bridget felt a shiver run through her. She didn't like the sound of one person having so much power, unless he was God. And his shrewish sister sounded real mean with her bigoted ideas. When they'd finished eating, she saw that Kitty was nearly asleep again.

'I think we'd better go to bed if you'll show us where to go, please,' Bridget said awkwardly.

Martha got up. 'I'll show you. It ain't the Ritz, but it's clean.'

Bridget and Kitty were to share a room. The Finleys didn't give huge rooms to servants, but it was adequate. Martha told them the best rooms were for house-guests and people who could be useful in business. Some of the folk who were entertained were scum of the earth, the maid said, but none of that mattered if Thomas Finley thought they could be of use to him.

Bridget hardly listened. Kitty was limp with fatigue, and fell asleep as soon as she struggled into her nightgown. Bridget followed her immediately and was asleep in minutes. This was the start of a new life, she remembered thinking drowsily. It was the start of the dream that would take them to Ireland one day, where the streets, if not exactly paved with gold, would at least be green and welcoming. The thought should have filled her with ecstasy, but she was just too tired . . .

They were awoken at five in the morning by someone knocking on the door and telling them to get up as there was work to be done.

'You can't lie in bed till all hours now that you're working girls,' Sally called out.

Bridget didn't bother saying that five in the morning was nothing new to her. Hadn't they done the same thing on Nob Hill? Hadn't she worked her guts out with the washing and ironing at Mrs Dowdy's? But some devil inside her made her resist the telling. Let the other girls go on wondering about them. They might be destitute, but they could still keep their dignity.

They dressed in the tidy clothes Miss Finley had put out for them, plain working clothes for Bridget, and a second-hand dress for Kitty that was clean and fresh and made her look less like the orphan that she was.

'You look less maggoty this morning,' Mrs Harris said when she saw them. 'You're to go directly to Mr Finley's study when you've had breakfast. He's off to his factories today and wants to see you before he leaves.'

She saw the fright in Kitty's eyes. 'He won't eat you, honey –'

'I don't want to see him, Bridget,' Kitty scowled.

'We've got to, haven't we? We can't live in his house and never see him, silly.'

'I don't want to live here. I want to go home –'

God, was she starting that song *again!*

Martha giggled. 'He might take a nibble or two out of you, honey. He's partial to soft-cuts –' she said, to be immediately hushed by Mrs Harris.

Bridget frowned, not liking the sound of this at all. Kitty grumbled all the way to the study where they were directed, but when they finally met Thomas Finley, he wasn't half as alarming as she had expected.

When they went into the book-lined room that smelled of old leather, Thomas Finley rose from his chair behind the large oak desk to look them over gravely.

Bridget's first impression was that he reminded her of one of the bawdy music-hall acts in newspaper pictures. Thomas Finley was large and broad, with mutton-chop whiskers in a florid face and tufty brown hair on top of his head.

The hair was so dense in colour that Bridget was sure it must be dyed, because it contrasted so starkly with the corrugated face. His suit was of a very loud check pattern of pale beige and green, and his fingers glittered with rings. He was in such complete contrast to his austere sister that Bridget and Kitty could only stand and stare at this comic vision.

'So you're our protégées, are you?'

They stared dumbly, not understanding the word. Thomas Finley's eyes were pale grey like his sister's, but that was the only similarity. Bridget didn't like his eyes. When he wanted to hide his feelings, they were completely devoid of expression. It was a weapon Thomas frequently used in business dealings.

'Do you have tongues in your heads?' His smile revealed uneven, discoloured teeth. He made no attempt to hide his own accent. It was strident and broad. He came to the front of the desk and perched on the edge, supremely self-confident, his patent leather two-tone shoes the latest thing, adding to the image of the showman.

'Yes, of course we do,' Bridget said.

'And you, child?'

'Yes Sir, Mr Finley,' Kitty stammered. He laughed, reaching forward to tickle her under the chin. He smelled of scent. Their daddy always said they should never trust a man who wore scent. He moved back and sat behind the desk again, his arms spread out as if he encompassed the world.

'Well now, you'll be going to school, Kitty, and I'll expect you to do your best and not be lazy. Schooling's a fine thing, and you'll learn your reading and your numbers and not let me down. That's right, isn't it?'

'Oh yes, Mr Finley,' Kitty muttered, the words reminding her of her old friends, and stirring up the resentment she felt towards Bridget. It might be a grand house, but she didn't feel at home, there. She was sure that she never would.

'Good. And your sister –' he paused, seeing the pulse beating in Bridget's white throat.

This one was was more than a child, he thought, and sure to God, but she'd be a real Irish beauty in a couple of years. And not ill-bred either, if his practised eyes knew anything. Her family may have been poor, but there was an air of breeding about Bridget O'Connell that had nothing to do with parentage, but more to do with herself. Instinct told him she was too good for the skivvying, or his name wasn't Thomas O'Flaherty Finley.

'You'll learn to wait on tables for now, Bridget,' Thomas said abruptly. 'You can tell Mrs Harris I said so. You'll be more decorative than those white trash girls who waste their time trying to catch every young bucko's eyes. You'll not be interested in young men yet, I hope?'

'That I am not, Mr Finley, nor likely to be.'

Bridget said it so fast, her blue eyes flashing, that it took Thomas by surprise.

Here was a novelty, he thought. A beauty who didn't care for men. No matter. His brain was seething ahead. When the time was right, he'd sell her off to the highest bidder. There'd be plenty of house-guests panting after this lovely Irish colleen.

His magnanimity in bringing these orphans to New York to pacify the priest's blatherings, could pay off after all. All he had to do was wait patiently for her to grow up.

Thomas Finley had no lascivious thoughts on his own account regarding Bridget O'Connell, though he revised his earlier views about her future with surprising speed. Bridget's looks were too classy for her to end up a servant. And if he hoped to marry her off to some wealthy American tycoon, which was his revised plan, she would do better to be seen as his ward, together with her sister.

'You can't mean it, Thomas!' Sheilagh was outraged when he told her. 'Father Rourke says the girls are from poor immigrant stock –'

53

'And where do *we* come from, my fine high-flying society hostess?' He said sarcastically. 'You find it easy to forget, but don't ever forget that 'tis my good fortune with the canning business that's made us rich. 'Tis the dollar that makes us acquaintances to be cultivated, not the fact that we have the Irish gift of the gab.'

Sheilagh Finley's lips compressed even tighter as he resorted to his favourite pastime of cutting her down whenever he thought she was getting too uppity. As always, his brogue broadened and his coarse tongue rasped.

'All the same,' she went on doggedly. 'You can't really intend to tell everyone that these two O'Connell girls are your *wards*?'

'Why not? Sure, and they're the most personable girls in the state. The priest will praise us and think us fine folk indeed!'

'But what of those tittle-tattling maids? Mrs Harris will be discreet and you never get a whisper out of Carter, but the maids will blab all over town –'

'No they won't,' he said calmly. 'I've got them new positions in Philadelphia. I'm packing them off with a small gratuity, and the new ones will accept from the start that Bridget and Kitty O'Connell are my wards.'

There was no changing his mind. He could always manipulate people, no matter how others raged and wept. It was a side of his nature that she found frightening. He might look bland enough, but he had a fine way of twisting events to suit himself.

And in a matter of weeks, she was forced to accept that the O'Connell girls now had status in the house. They were told to call the Finleys by their first names. Kitty was sent to a good day-school, and Bridget was allowed to attend a snooty finishing school upstate, coming home at weekends now to a bedroom of her own as if she was the daughter of the house.

Sheilagh resented every hair of the interloper's pretty head, and vowed that one day she'd find a way to get rid of her for good.

'Is he a fairy godfather, Bridget?' Kitty had said in bewilderment when they first heard the news.

'I think he must be.' Bridget was too excited at all that was happening to think about it too hard. She, who always questioned everything, was not questioning this at all, for fear it might all be a dream and she'd be waking up back in the dreary Dowdy shack after all . . . she hugged Kitty tight on that first morning when they knew what Thomas had in mind.

'Now say I wasn't right to keep on at Father Malley to get us away from San Francisco!' She demanded. 'Say that you don't think we've fallen on our feet at last, you ungrateful child!'

She laughed as she said it, for she truly felt as if she was in wonderland, and she couldn't understand why Kitty still wore her long face.

'I still can't see my friends, that's why,' Kitty sulked. 'These new girls will be all snobby and they'll hate me, I know. I shan't talk like them, and they'll all know each other –'

For once, Bridget lost her patience. 'Oh, for pity's sake! Did you want to be known as a poor Irish kid for the rest of your life? This is a great chance for us, Kitty, and I'm damned if I'm going to let you spoil it for us.'

'Don't swear,' Kitty said automatically. 'Mammie doesn't like you saying – what you said.'

For a few seconds they stared at each other without speaking, and then Bridget saw her sister's bottom lip tremble. She was instantly contrite. One minute they were standing glowering at each other, and the next they were in each other's arms, and Kitty was snuffling into Bridget's shoulder.

'I don't like it here, Bridget. I shan't see you any more when you're at your posh school all week. I'll miss you, and I miss Mammie and Daddy and Michael too.'

Bridget shushed her, feeling the sting of tears in her own eyes. Kitty so rarely mentioned their parents that if Bridget sometimes thought her callous, she put it down to the swiftness of childhood, when memories were short and good times as well as bad were soon obliterated. She'd been the one to try to keep their memories alive, when Kitty had seemed to forget so easily . . . but now she wondered how deep were the scars on Kitty's memory.

'Kitty, we mustn't try to push them out of our lives,' she said softly. 'They're still part of us, even if they're not here any more. We should talk about them and remember how they loved us, and how we loved them. The earthquake was a terrible thing, but we must try to remember our family as they were before –'

This was too much for Kitty. With the embarrassment of a nine-year-old, she wriggled out of Bridget's arms, and it was as if a curtain came down over her features.

'I don't want to talk about that old earthquake,' she said jerkily. 'I don't want to be here, and I don't want to go to any snobby school, so there.'

'Well, that's just silly. Everyone has to go to school,' Bridget snapped, and the close moments were gone as Kitty turned tail and ran out of the room to take refuge in the kitchen and Mrs Harris's sticky afternoon buns.

Bridget sighed heavily. She hadn't wanted this responsibility thrust on her, and it had seemed like a gift from heaven when Thomas had decided to make the O'Connell girls his wards. Good schools, an education, a decent home . . . who would have believed it possible a few short months ago. And Kitty was the most ungrateful child alive, she thought angrily.

Did she think it was so easy to blot out the nightmares of the earthquake? Perhaps it was, when you'd only been eight years old. It was infinitely more difficult when you were an impressionable adolescent, and the scenes were indelibly marked on your brain for ever more.

There were still nights when Bridget had terrible nightmares when she would awaken damp with sweat, and the room would seem to be rocking wildly in the grip of the earthquake, and she had to remind herself forcibly that because of the Finleys' generosity, she and Kitty were safe. That fact was still the most important thing in life, the one that restored her sanity in those moments.

*

Over the years, it dawned on Sheilagh gradually that Kitty was destined to be the wild one of the two. Bridget was enjoying every bit of freedom at the upstate school, and it was Kitty who flounced about, declaring that she hated her new school, and that nobody spoke to her. All this, despite the fact that she was often asked to other girls' homes for tea, and went with a defiant look on her face.

Sheilagh also found to her annoyance that in the O'Connells' background there were no skeletons to be raked out of cupboards, no illicit meetings with young men. As she left her teens and passed the age of twenty, Bridget continued to be cool and distant towards any male guests at the house, a fact that constantly annoyed Thomas, who wanted her to be at her most scintillating wherever a suitable beau appeared.

Towards Thomas himself, Bridget had never been more than cautiously friendly. She was wary of him, but she admitted that he took the the task of surrogate father seriously. He kept his arrogance under control at home, except when mounting concern over events in Europe got him frowning and blaspheming. Even then, his thoughts were usually how best to turn disasters to his own best advantage.

When Great Britain declared war on Germany in the August of 1914, he was scratchier than usual over the weekend newspapers with their blazing headlines.

'The Americans will go in next, you'll see,' he snapped. 'They'll not be done out of their bit of glory when the government thinks the time's right. And when they do, God knows what effect it will have on trade.'

Bridget found it difficult to hide her dislike of him at that moment. After the years at the elegant upstate school, she was far more self-assured than in the past, and ready to argue if she disagreed with him.

'Is that all you can think about? What of the young boys being sent to fight? Irish boys as well as English –'

His brows drew together. He'd aged considerably in the seven years since taking in these girls. His hair was still dyed the unnatural brown colour, and it sat even more incongruously above his raddled skin and sagging jowls.

'Since when did you begin to care about boys?' He sneered.

'I thought you'd taken a vow of purity!'

'War means senseless slaughter, and anybody with any sense cares about that!'

'God thins out the population by the occasional war, doesn't he?'

'That's a wicked thing to say. It's people who destroy each other, not God.'

'Oh yes? What about natural disasters then? It ain't people who cause volcanoes and earthquakes. Look what happened to your own family, and if that wasn't God's doing, I suppose you put it down to the devil, which is much the same thing.'

He saw her flinch and knew he shouldn't have mentioned the bloody earthquake. But the thing had happened a long time ago now, and it didn't make it any less real to try and block it out of your mind. He had no idea whether she did or not. At one time, he'd thought she brooded on it, but lately, as that sister of hers got flightier, she seemed harder, and not so introspective.

'I've got things to do,' she said distantly now, and Thomas knew it was her way of ending the conversation.

Watching her taut back as she marched out of the room, he knew he was right. She kept the memories in a closed box, but one day, Thomas guessed they would all come spilling out. There had to be a time of reckoning. Anyway, he had his own worries. This bloody war in Europe was going to affect everybody, and if America cut off trading relations with Germany . . .

Still, Thomas decided it was time something was done about Bridget. She was coming up to twenty-two years old now, and did very little other than escort Sheilagh on her fund-raising jaunts and look decorative at dinner parties. It was time she did something useful. Besides, it might stop her and that young madam of a sister of hers from squabbling when they got together. That early closeness seemed a thing of the past, and he'd overheard them enough times.

Bridget had some notion of going back to Ireland and taking Kitty with her. And Kitty, contrary as ever, suddenly decided she didn't want to go anywhere, least of all to be tagging along behind an older sister when she was having plenty of fun . . .

'I'm disappointed in you, Bridget,' he said shortly, the next time he had words with her.

'Why don't you tell me what it is you want of me?' she said, too angry to care what she said. He was always baiting her lately, and she didn't know why.

'I've brought plenty of young men to the house, and you persist in being rude to them –'

'I'm not rude. I've just no intention of being any man's plaything, and it's best to let them know how I feel from the start.'

He looked at her in annoyance.

'A man doesn't treat his wife as a plaything, my girl. Do you know how many fellows have asked to come courting you? What's wrong with you? That sister of yours gives them the glad eye, and her not sixteen yet, and not a patch on you for looks –'

'I'm not interested in men. It's not compulsory, is it?' She said, heavy with sarcasm. 'Plenty of women stay single. Your sister, for one. Are you suggesting there's something peculiar about her too?'

Her arguments always beat his. She was beginning to get on his nerves, and if it wasn't for upsetting his saintly image in making these girls his wards, he'd have Bridget out of his house and his life. But he still had another card to play.

'I know you're keen on music, Bridget. How'd you like to go to a singing Academy to have your voice properly trained?'

She gaped at him, unable to believe what she'd heard for a minute. 'Do you mean it?'

She could see that he did. Her eyes glowed, and even while he registered how stunning she was, the thought irritated him. Why the devil couldn't she look like this for the eligible young bucks he brought to the house, so he could get her off his hands for ever?

'When did I ever say anything I didn't mean?' He said roughly. 'I'll arrange it then.'

Impetuously, Bridget flung her arms around his neck, and kissed his cheek, because it was so much more than she had ever dreamed about. To be taught singing and music properly . . . Thomas Finley felt the pressure of her firm young breasts against his chest, and his heart leapt drunkenly for a minute. Her lips were soft against his old flesh, and something that was a mixture of disgust and desire surged inside him at their touch. God, he was old enough to be her father, and he wasn't normally roused to lust by nubile young women . . .

Bridget couldn't wait for Kitty to come home for the summer holiday, from Bridget's old boarding school which she now attended.

'Just wait till you hear the news!' Bridget said as soon as Kitty got indoors, hot and irritable from the car journey with the silent Carter, who doubled as chauffeur when required.

'What news?' Kitty said sulkily. 'All we hear in class is about that stupid war in Europe. I don't want to hear any more about it –'

'Not the war!' Bridget said impatiently, though she thought Kitty might have been a little less scathing. 'My news, ninny! I'm going to Connecticut at the end of the year to an Academy of Music to learn to sing properly!'

'God! It sounds so boring. You aren't going to be singing all day long, are you?'

'It won't just be singing. I'll be learning the theory of music, and the history of famous singers and musicians and composers, even an instrument if I want to.'

For a warm sweet moment, the image of her daddy playing a jig on his old fiddle came sharply to her mind. She could almost smell the warmth in the old cottage in Ireland where there had been hardly room to swing a cat, but more love than anywhere she had ever known. There was her daddy sawing away on the fiddle by the fireside where the peat burned steadily, and her mammie with her face flushed and happy as she foot-tapped away to the music. And herself, singing the tune in her high shrill childish voice that her daddy always said reminded him of the angels. Herself and her mammie and daddy in the old stone cottage, and the baby Kitty cooing in her swing-cot, before the great adventure that took them across the sea to America . . .

'Well, I think it sounds dull,' Kitty said crossly. 'And why have you got such a silly look on your face? You're not mooning over all that stuff about ever getting to Ireland, are you?'

Bridget was angered by the sneering words. People didn't stay the same, and this was not the same frightened Kitty who'd clung to her and wept so pitifully after their parents died. Kitty had changed . . . and Bridget knew that she had too. It was almost as if, in the growing up, there had been something of a role-reversal. It was Kitty who had the sharp tongue these days, while Bridget had undoubtedly mellowed a bit.

In two ways though, she would never change. She still cared for her sister and wanted to protect her and keep her safe. And yes, she still hoped one day to take them both to Ireland.

'What's wrong with dreams?' Bridget snapped.

'Dreams are for children, that's what's wrong with them. If you think you're ever going back to Ireland, you're stupid. Even if you ever got the money, you could go if you like, but I'm never going with you. I don't remember any of it. We're both more American than Irish now, and it's time you believed it.'

'Kitty! You don't mean that. You know it's been the one thing on my mind all these years!'

If she was the crying kind, she'd cry now, but she was damned if she was going to let this stiff-necked young girl have that to crow over.

'I do mean it,' Kitty snapped. 'Why should I live out your dreams anyway? If you were normal, you'd want to get married and have kids like everybody else, instead of getting all excited over a few singing lessons. My God, *singing lessons*! I outlived that stuff years ago. Don't you ever want to go out with a man? They're the ones who buy you things and treat you nice. Sometimes I think there's something wrong with you, Bridget!'

For once, Bridget was too stunned to answer as her worldly-wise sister tossed her long dark curls and stalked out of the room, swaying her hips like the latest movie-queen vamp.

Chapter 5

Kitty knew she was going to miss her friends dreadfully. Bridget was going off to her snooty Music Academy, and Kitty would be twiddling her thumbs at home for a while. She'd been one of a set of daring young ladies who spent money freely and had rip-roaring tales to tell of stolen meetings with young men. The girl with the wide blue eyes and pretty face was popular, and as the ward of a rich businessman she was readily accepted in the exclusive little cliques.

When Kitty and her friends finally left school, they vowed to keep in touch, and the elegant little cars that roared up to the house to collect her began to sport more than young girls. Sheilagh complained repeatedly to Thomas, on her account.

'Leave her be,' he growled. 'It's better to have one normal one than two icebergs.'

'You'll be singing a different tune if she brings trouble to the house,' Sheilagh snapped.

'We'll face that if it ever happens. You always did anticipate trouble, woman. We didn't do so badly in Father Rourke's books by bringing the girls here, did we?'

'That's not what I mean and you know it,' Sheilagh answered, but Thomas had already tired of her whining, and she was talking to thin air.

At that precise moment, Kitty was enjoying a picnic with girl-friends and college boys on the wooded banks of a lake. The girls were also aware of the attention of two men farther along the bank.

Kitty forgot them as one of the college boys put his arm around her waist, his fingers sliding upwards to tease her breast. She pushed them down with a laugh, but they slid back just as smoothly.

'Be nice to me, Kitty, in case I have to go away to war. Any decent American girl would give a guy something special to remember her by. What d'you say, honey?'

She giggled at his cheek. 'I'm Irish, *honey*, and good Irish girls don't give their favours so lightly.'

He held her against the tree trunk, enjoying the tease, and letting her know the feel of his body pressed against hers.

'Don't be stupid, Jake,' she mocked him. 'I'm not throwing away my principles for the sake of some old war that'll never happen.'

'It's already happened, honey,' he drawled. 'Don't you girls ever read the papers?'

'Well, it's not here. Anyway, you needn't worry. Your daddy won't let you go and be killed. He'll find ways of keeping you out of it.' She refused to take any of it seriously. Not the war, nor Jake's intentions.

'I might decide to go, anyway. Girls like men in uniforms, and then maybe you won't be so fussy.'

'I'm not fussy,' she said airily. 'I just don't want you messing about, that's all.'

She felt Jake's breath on her face. She didn't mind a few kisses. Kisses were fun. It was the way he rubbed himself up against her that she didn't like too much. And another guy, Lewis, had his arm around her back and his hand was squeezing her buttocks, and she didn't like that either. These idiots didn't know the meaning of romance. They had no finesse, the way a girl wanted finesse in a man . . . She twisted away, intending to tell them to go jump in the lake, like all the fast girls said these days.

The rest of the group had disappeared among the trees, and Kitty began to get annoyed, and yelled at the two boys to stop. And then without warning all three of them scattered, and she heard the crack of fists connecting with bone. Unbelievably, Kitty realised that the two brawny fellows from along the bank were throwing punches that had Jake and Lewis bloodied in seconds, and sent them racing away. It all happened so fast Kitty couldn't think straight.

'You want to get away from here, girlie?' The younger of the two rescuers said in a heavy accent.

'I'm all right,' she said. 'I'll find my friends.'

Even as she said it, she knew they wouldn't want to be found. Not if they were up to tricks in the woods . . .

'Your friends wait for you,' he said next, and she followed his gaze to where Jake and Lewis hung around on the edge of the lake. The minute these two left her, the college boys would take out their spite on her.

She looked uncertainly at the strangers. The younger of the two was very physical, and not particularly handsome. The other was positively pug-nosed.

'Where you want to go?' The spokesman said.

Kitty made up her mind. 'I'll get to the main road and call a cab,' she said haughtily.

'We take you. Come quick, before they catch you.'

Jake and Lewis were walking back, and without warning the stranger caught Kitty's hand and she found herself running between him and his friend. They reached a road, where an old van stood at the kerbside. .

'They won't find you now,' he said easily. 'You like to come for joy-ride?'

'No thanks. I have to get home,' she said quickly. 'I don't go joy-riding with strangers –'

'What strangers? I'm called Pieter. I'm a boxer, and Jan is my manager. Now we know each other, girlie.'

Kitty felt herself smile at the cheek of him. He smiled back, and he wasn't so bad. But joy-riding? Not likely. She wasn't that much of a fool . . .

The older man began talking quickly in a foreign tongue, and the first one answered him. They seemed to be arguing, and Kitty guessed by their glances that it was about her. It was suddenly flattering, and seconds later the older man swaggered off, hands deep in his pockets, and Pieter leaned against the van.

'Jan has business deal. Look, girlie, you still look shaky.

Joy-ride with me, then I show you my fight posters and we take tea, heh? Allow me to show Dutch hospitality. Trust me.'

His old Dutch charm was persuasive. And tea in one of the steamy bake-houses would be fun.

'Just half an hour then. And then you promise you'll get me a cab?'

'Of course. Trust me.' he said.

She got into the van and Pieter started the engine.

'You're not kidnapping me, are you?' She joked, to hide a sudden unease. 'I don't have any money, you know.'

'Who needs money? I make plenty money at the fights.'

'Do you really?' Kitty said, intrigued. She looked at his hands on the steering-wheel. They were large and powerful. No wonder Jake and Lewis had backed off fast.

'I go soon to the West Coast. Make big money there.'

'More than in Holland?'

Pieter laughed. 'Holland small country, and I have to leave quickly when my fight opponent got killed. America where the money is, heh?'

Her heart lurched alarmingly at his words. Did he mean he'd killed a man? He said it obliquely, but she knew he couldn't have meant anything else.

She tried to forget it as Pieter took her on a real joy-ride, showing her parts of the neighbourhood she'd never seen before.

When the car finally stopped, she saw that they were outside a tall building in a back street. It didn't look like a bake-house but Pieter said they'd have Dutch tea inside. She stepped inside a small sitting-room with thick lace curtains that kept the room dark.

'Is this where you live?' She asked. "I thought we were going to a bake-house –'

'I never said so, girlie.'

The voice was suddenly full of menace, and Kitty felt the beginnings of panic.

'I think I'd better go. I won't stay for tea. My guardian will be worried if I'm late –'

'Your guardian?' He sneered. 'Rich girl, are you?'

'No. Look, I said I don't have any money –'

'I don't want your money. This is what I want.'

He pulled her towards him so fast he knocked the breath out of her. Kitty took one look at his face and knew real terror for the first time in her life. She heard her own hoarse scream as his hands began to roam over every part of her, as immovable as iron bands.

More than two hours later, Kitty staggered into the street. She was numb with shock after the harsh spearing of her body. She had never known there could be so much pain. It enveloped her in the darkness outside the house.

She had no idea where she was. She stumbled through the narrow streets of miserable buildings, too dazed to take stock of her surroundings. Tattered newspapers snatched at her legs like tumbleweed. A scrawny cat twined itself around her ankles, the soft feel of it drying her throat as if it was the man's hand violating her flesh again.

She knew that no cabs would cruise this neighbourhood, and the Dutchman had thrown her out when he'd done with her.

At last she crept into an old shack and stayed there terrified all night. And only during the long sleepless hours did the full horror of what had happened catch up with her. She'd been raped, and by a self-confessed killer.

Bridget had never been so happy. The Connecticut Academy of Music was run on very genteel lines. Her room was pleasant, and she didn't have to share it. It looked out over green meadows, and stretching away as far as the eye could see were forests that everyone said were spectacularly beautiful in the fall when all the leaves turned colour. She anticipated seeing that. It was the end of April now. The hated date of the 18th had come and gone, and she loved her new life.

Her singing tutor was a mild-mannered Frenchman with grey-white hair. He was rotund and pink-faced and some of the students laughed at him behind his back. It didn't concern Bridget. Nothing mattered but that Monsieur Alphonse praised her singing, and that they got on well.

Predatory modern young women made him nervous, and Monsieur Alphonse saw that there was nothing of the predator in Bridget O'Connell. He was safe with her, as safe as she felt with him. It was strange how much she still welcomed the feeling of safety. She was twenty-two years old and the earthquake that had devastated her life was eight years ago, yet still it influenced her. The experience should have made her strong, and in many ways it had, yet she still wanted to cling to what was safe.

Monsieur Alphonse was quite happy to give his favourite extra tuition at the weekends when most of the other students pursued outside activities. Unless Bridget was due to go home on her monthly visit, she was quite content to remain behind and continue her studies. Theory she found particularly difficult, and she was perusing one of her manuals out of doors in the spring sunshine when she heard the rustle of skirts and turned her head enquiringly, half-annoyed at being interrupted.

She experienced a moment that was almost unlike any other. Almost . . . because in the same instant she realised she had felt like this once before. And what had happened then, she thought almost simultaneously with the surge of sick apprehension inside, was the earthquake.

'Kitty! What are you doing here!' The manual slid off her lap onto the sweet young grass as Bridget jumped to her feet at the sight of her sister.

She knew immediately that something was wrong. She had always known such things where Kitty was concerned. Why else would her sister have come all this way so unexpectedly? The thoughts whirled in her brain.

Kitty ran to her. Her cheeks were flushed, and whatever she had been about to say was totally forgotten as she burst into noisy tears at the sight of Bridget's astonished face. Without another word, Bridget held her in her arms, feeling the brittleness of her body, as if she was about to break.

'Bridget, you've got to help me.' Kitty gasped at last. 'I don't know what to do, and I didn't know who else to tell. Not the girls from St. Pat's. They'd think me a fool, or worse.

They'd probably be scandalised. I daren't go to Father Rourke. He'd excommunicate me for sure, and though the church doesn't mean all that much to me, I'm still terrified of it, Bridget, I am so!'

'Will you stop it!' Bridget gave her a little shake. 'Anybody would think you'd committed murder.'

She said it teasingly, hoping to bring a smile to Kitty's face. Expecting her caustic sister to tell her how ridiculous she was being, and to pooh-pooh her for thinking such a daft thing. One look at Kitty's terrified face, and she knew it was nothing simple that brought her here.

'Not me, *him*. He was a killer, and that makes it even worse. He said it was an accident, but I know he was capable of killing, Bridget. I think he enjoyed it –'

She whimpered as Bridget's hand struck her across the face. She was becoming hysterical, and the last thing Bridget wanted was for her to draw attention to the two of them out here in the grounds of the Academy.

'I haven't the slightest idea what you're talking about, but we'd better go inside to my room and then you can explain it all. I'll make some tea and I've a jam sponge in my cupboard. I must have known you were coming.'

She kept on talking, hoping to take away the blank look of horror on her sister's face. Bridget was becoming more alarmed by the second. Whatever Kitty had come here bursting to say, all the spirit seemed to have drained out of her.

Only when she had made the tea and cut them both a wedge of jam sponge, which Kitty made no attempt to touch, did Bridget kneel down beside her so that her face was level with her sister's. She took the restless hands in hers, and made them still.

'Darling, if you're not going to tell me what's happened, it was a waste of your time coming here,' she said gently. 'You know I'll do anything I can to help you. Haven't I always?'

Kitty's face suddenly became animated with a bitterness that made Bridget draw in her breath with surprise.

'You said we'd always be together. You promised you'd always take care of me –'

'So I have! How can you say any different? Didn't I insist that we'd stay together when Father Malley wanted to separate us in San Francisco? Didn't I keep on nagging him until he got us a family to take us here in New York, and haven't I always tried to take care of you, Kitty?' She was bruised more than she could say.

'If we'd stayed together, I wouldn't be in this mess now, would I!' The truth of it was written plain as day on her face, even without the nervous little touch of her hand on her belly. Bridget felt her head spin for a second.

'Holy mother of God, Kitty, you're not telling me you're pregnant?' She whispered.

Kitty gave a shrill laugh.

'That I am, sister dear, and the Holy Mother of God had nothing to do with it. It was a bastard of a man who did it. He raped me, so he did, and I thought I'd got the stink of him out of me from the number of times I scrubbed myself. But it's still in me. It's growing, day by day, and I want to be rid of it before it possesses me completely!'

Bridget shook her as her voice throbbed with terror.

'Who was it, Kitty? He must be made to marry you, though dear God, I don't know how we're going to explain it away to Thomas Finley, and you only sixteen years old –'

'Marry him!' Kitty shrieked. 'I'd never marry him if he was the last man on earth. He's a pig, and I never want to see him again. I'll never tell who he is, Bridget, so don't try to make me.'

'You said something about killing. What did you mean?'

Kitty laughed hoarsely.

'I can't tell you any more, but I'll tell you this. He was a prize-fighter and he told me he'd killed a man in a fight and he had to get away from his own country and come here. Do you think I'd want the child of a killer, Bridget? Don't you think I feel defiled enough without knowing what I'm carrying inside me? It would be a monster, which is why it mustn't be born. I've got to get rid of it, Bridget, and you've got to help me, for God's sake.'

'The child's innocent, Kitty –'

'It's a monster,' she shrieked.

69

'And if you kill it, you'll be as guilty as the man. It's a terrible sin to rid yourself of an unborn child, and against everything the church tells us –'

'Since when did you take so much notice of the church?' Kitty blazed, wrenching herself away from Bridget. 'You weren't so bloody pious when the earthquake took Mammie and Daddy and Michael away from us. I remember you saying the church was doing the devil's work in making us thank God for his mercy when He'd taken everything away from us. I thought I still had you, Bridget.'

'You do. You'll always have me,' she said huskily. 'So tell me what you want me to do, darling.'

Kitty went limp in her arms with relief. Her voice was muffled in Bridget's shoulder.

'Find somebody to take the thing away. A doctor – or a woman – people do these things, don't they?'

'An abortionist, you mean.' Bridget said the word deliberately. She saw Kitty flinch. 'How do you think I know such a person, or how to find one? They're not listed in the telephone book, Kitty. It's against the law.'

Kitty looked frightened now, her skin ashen where she had been flushed minutes before.

'But you must know somebody who can find a suitable woman. You could do it, Bridget, I know you could.'

'For pity's sake, I'm not God!'

She was momentarily irritated by Kitty's blind trust, and by the assumption that Bridget would take care of everything. It was too large a burden . . . too much to expect of anyone . . . she looked into the immature blue eyes, darkened by this new responsibility, and knew that whatever it took, she had to help. She was committed to help.

'We both need hot tea. It's supposed to be good for shock,' she said dryly, and saw the ghost of a smile around Kitty's pale lips. After a few minutes she clattered her cup onto her saucer, and looked straight into Kitty's eyes.

'There's only one person who can help us, and that's Thomas. He knows everybody. He has fingers in every pie, and he'll get us out of this mess.' Unconsciously, she included herself in it.

'No – I can't tell him!' Kitty stuttered. 'The shame would be too great, and he'd – he'd –'

'Kill you? No, he wouldn't, love. He might rant and rave a bit, but if this got out, his pride would be damaged. He'd do anything to keep up his status, and he'd not want it known that one of his wards was going to have a bastard. He'll help, believe me. I know him.'

'No, please, Bridget,' Kitty was weeping again. 'I can't tell him –'

'You won't have to. I'll tell him,' Bridget said calmly. 'We'll go home together this week-end, and you'll keep out of sight until I've spoken to him and got him to promise to make the arrangements. He'll do it, I know he will.'

Kitty bit her lips to stop them shaking. It wasn't Thomas Finley's shame, she thought resentfully, and she hated the thought of him knowing she had been so weak and foolish. But when Bridget spoke so sensibly, she knew there was no other way. Bridget would tell Thomas, and it would all be taken care of. Horribly embarrassed, she tried to voice her thanks with difficulty.

'Thank me when you're back to normal,' Bridget retorted. 'I hate to see you like this, instead of the self-confident American young lady you're supposed to be.'

'I don't feel very self-confident now,' Kitty muttered. 'I feel as if I've been kicked into the ground. Oh, Bridget, I do love you, really I do.'

She hugged Bridget fiercely.

'And was it all so awful – being with this man, love? It really was – rape – was it? No lies, now.'

Kitty moved away from her, her eyes dark with re-membering.

'It was the worst thing that ever happened to me, Bridget. It was like having a knife thrust inside me, again and again until I was so bruised and sore I was just one mass of pain.'

She leaned against her sister, and Bridget's eyes were vacant as they gazed into the wall. She was shocked at her sister's venomous voice. Not to want a man had been her own choice, yet there had been moments when Bridget wondered

71

if she was being very foolish in turning her back on something so fundamental.

Her own parents had shared a very loving relationship, but since their deaths, she had hardened her heart against love. She hadn't wanted it, nor sought it, pouring all her affection instead on this girl who was suffering so badly now because of lust. Lust, not love. It was all the same, she reminded herself, and the brief moment of doubt disappeared.

'Kitty, you're to stay here while I go and find the Principal and tell him I'm going home this weekend after all. I'll say my sister is ill, and that it might be necessary for me to stay away for a few days. If Thomas finds someone quickly, you'll want me around, I expect.'

'Oh yes –'

'There's something else you had better tell me,' Bridget went on carefully. 'I presume this didn't happen too long ago, so you're absolutely sure about it, are you?'

'I'm sure. I'm sick every morning, and I'm tender here,' she touched her breasts. 'I know it's true –' her voice rose in panic.

'All right.'

It was obvious there was no possible chance of Kitty wanting to see the man again. No question of a hasty marriage, or compensation for the child. Just to be rid of it as quickly and efficiently as possible.

It was one of the worst sins, but the circumstances overcame Bridget's revulsion. When you were personally involved, it was surprising how the sin became a necessity, she discovered. And in less than an hour they were on the train taking them away from Connecticut, travelling the last miles in a taxi-cab and recklessly spending the last of Bridget's monthly allowance on the fare.

Bridget faced Thomas Finley across the width of his desk. The moment of telling was here, and she quaked inside. Kitty was the one at fault, but Kitty would be a gibbering wreck if she had to tell Thomas herself. It was better this way . . .

'What d'you want, Bridget?' He scowled. 'I'm busy, and if you've summat to say, then say it and stop standing there like a hangdog.'

72

She sat down abruptly, because suddenly it felt as though her legs wouldn't hold her up.

'Yes, I've something to tell you and something to ask you,' she said in the clear King's English diction that always irritated him, even though he'd paid for her good education.

He looked at her sharply. He was able to assess a situation quickly, and knew at once that this was no mere plea for an increased dress allowance. This was something bigger.

'Nothing ever got solved for the want of telling, so out with it,' he said sourly.

Bridget's heart beat sickeningly at his uncompromising face.

'Promise to hear me out before you say anything –'

'Holy Mother of God, get on with it,' he roared.

Bridget blundered in. 'Kitty's got herself in trouble and won't name the man. You have to help us, Thomas. She wants to be rid of it. We know it's a mortal sin, but the man's disappeared anyway, and Kitty will probably kill herself if we don't get help. And it would be a disgrace to us all if it became known that one of your wards was carrying a bastard –'

She spoke so fast and stopped so quickly that his mouth was still in the act of falling open. He seemed speechless, and then his fist crashed onto the desk-top, making her flinch in fright.

'So you think to blackmail me into finding a quack doctor, do you? Is this my reward for taking you snivelling chits into my house and paying for your fancy schooling?'

'It's not like that!' Bridget screamed back. 'I'm asking for help, and since you profess to be so much of a Christian –'

She felt the slap of his hand against her cheek with his full weight behind it. She felt the room spin, but he wouldn't make her cry.

'Thomas, please listen. Kitty's desperate. She's ashamed and terrified, and she knows she's let you down –'

Bridget knew she was humbling herself in front of this lout. She loathed herself for doing it, but there seemed no other way.

He breathed so heavily she wondered if he was going to have a seizure. Beneath his check jacket and weskit she could see the rise and fall of his chest. He stared at the fiery Bridget

73

O'Connell as a new idea occurred to him at this turn of events.

'And what of you, my fine young innocent? Will you be bringing this kind of trouble to my door too?'

Bridget's chin lifted. 'Don't worry. I'm not so gullible as my sister, nor as young and foolish.'

He leaned back in his chair again, his eyes narrowed.

'And you expect me to find your sister an abortionist, is that it?'

She bit her lip. It sounded so brutal, but she realised now that Thomas was beginning to enjoy making her squirm. He'd never tried to touch her, saving her for better things, but now . . . she nodded dumbly.

'There'd be a price to pay, of course.'

She swallowed, not understanding. Was he mad? She had no money, only her precious savings. But she knew she'd give it all away for Kitty's sake, even the dream of Ireland . . . she heard Thomas give a low laugh.

'I don't want your piddling allowance back, if that's what you're thinking, Bridget,' he said softly.

'What then?' She stuttered, because deep inside, it was as if she already knew. She could see it in those piggy eyes that had suddenly filled with lust. He took one of her cold hands in his flabby ones, imprisoning it.

'*You*, of course. In return for helping Kitty, you'll marry me –'

'*No*! I won't – it's obscene –'

Almost hysterical, she could see that even her undisguised disgust at the thought was exciting him, and he spoke thickly.

'You'll either do it, or I'll wash my hands of the pair of you, girl. If you refuse me, Kitty will carry her brat, and you'll both be turned out immediately. So there's the choice. The good life in this house, or the streets for you both.'

She knew he meant every word. He could be as implacable as a mountain when he chose. She couldn't answer. She was too faint, too shocked. She saw him consult the almanac on his desk. Into her frenzied mind came the thought that it was the very end of April, and this was a day as torturous in its way as that other April morning.

'We'll marry in a week's time,' Thomas informed her. 'And

one week later, when you've been wedded and bedded, Kitty will be rid of her trouble. And with luck, you'll be on the way to carrying yours.'

The breath caught in Bridget's throat.

'You want a child?' She almost gagged at the thought.

'Children, Bridget. A man needs perpetuity, and you'll do your Catholic duty and provide one every year.'

She could still hear the sound of his laughter long after she rushed from the study with stinging eyes. The prospect was so appalling she almost preferred the streets. But she couldn't condemn Kitty to a life of shame, and she felt completely trapped.

In her own room she leaned against her door, head back, eyes closed, but the tears squeezed through and ran silently down her cheeks. She hadn't cried in years, but she cried now as if her heart would break.

Chapter 6

Kitty was horrified and adamant.

'I won't let you do it, Bridget. I'll marry him myself if I must.'

She shuddered at the thought, and Bridget gave a twisted smile.

'It's not you he wants, darling, it's me. In a way, I think I've always sensed it, despite all the men he's brought to the house to try and marry me off.'

'But you never wanted to get married at all!'

'People can change their minds, Kitty.'

It was essential that Kitty believed that she didn't find the idea as repellent as she did. Kitty was quite reckless enough to clear right out of the house in the belief that she was doing Bridget a favour, and heaven knew what would become of her then. Bridget daren't take that risk.

She tried hard not to picture the future. She tried to blot out the images of sleeping in the same bed as Thomas Finley, and of being submissive to anything he wanted of her. She, who had never submitted to a man in her life . . .

She closed her eyes as Kitty clung to her. It had to be all right. Plenty of women married for convenience and made a success of it. After years of rejecting the thought of marriage, Bridget felt additionally bitter that if it had to happen, it couldn't be to a man of her choice. To be pushed cold-bloodedly into marriage with Thomas Finley as the price for helping Kitty was humiliating and degrading.

She felt Kitty shaking against her, and knew that for her sister's sake, she must be strong. She put her arms on Kitty's shoulders and looked steadily into her eyes.

'You're not to worry about this, Kitty. I could just as easily have refused,' she lied. 'Anyway, Thomas is away for much of the time as you know, and at least I'll be in charge of the house.'

'You don't think Sheilagh will let you take over from her –'

'She won't be able to stop me. If I'm Thomas's wife, I'll be more important than flint-eyed Sheilagh. I'll be a rich man's wife. Didn't I always say if I married at all, I'd marry a rich man?'

She tried to sound cheerful, but the words fell dismally flat. It gave her no satisfaction, but she had to keep repeating the fact to herself to make it seem in any way real. She didn't care about her future position. The day she married Thomas Finley would be one of the worst days of her life, and yet . . . at least she would be Somebody. She'd have a real status in life for the first time, and until now, she hadn't even realised how important that was.

She still dreaded the thought of becoming a child-bearing machine. But there was always the hope that he wouldn't prove a virile man, whatever his intentions . . .

Unconsciously, Bridget began to invent her own future, because it was the only way she could go into this marriage and remain sane. And at last Kitty seemed uneasily convinced that it was what Bridget wanted.

'I'm still not happy about it, Bridget,' she said slowly. 'But as long as you've agreed to go ahead with it, I suppose it's all right. Better the devil you know, perhaps.'

The devil was right, Bridget thought grimly, as Kitty prattled on, gradually becoming less tense. Kitty was finding it surprisingly easy to forget that her stupidity had caused all this. As long as Bridget wasn't miserable about marrying the old goat, then it could do them both a lot of good. Kitty knew very well that she was weaker than her sister, and that Bridget accepted Kitty's failings and was over-protective because of it. She loved Bridget intensely for what she was doing, without having the wit to see that she was ruining her sister's life.

'We'll need new clothes for the wedding,' she said suddenly, putting her own troubles out of her mind, and thinking to brighten Bridget a little. 'Thomas is sure to buy us all new outfits. I'd like emerald green. They say it's unlucky, but I like it. What do you think Bridget? Would it suit me?'

Bridget looked at her flushed face, with most of the panic smoothed away now, and swallowed her instant fury at Kitty's ability to switch her mind from anything unpleasant. She bit back the harsh words she'd been tempted to say, because Kitty still had an ordeal to go through. And Kitty was the only person she loved in the world, and they had to support one another. She'd promised her sister that a long while ago.

'You'll look beautiful in emerald green,' she agreed thickly. 'I'll speak to Thomas about new outfits.'

Yes, they would both have new outfits. Why shouldn't he pay too? She was going to pay for the rest of her life.

Sheilagh Finley burst in on the two girls without knocking.

'Is it true?' She shouted.

'Is what true?' Bridget stood up, moving automatically in front of Kitty. She didn't know how much Thomas had told his sister. She prayed that it hadn't been necessary for him to gloat over Kitty before divulging his wedding plans.

Sheilagh looked fit to explode.

'My brother says you've trapped him into a promise of marriage, you young slut. Have you been tempting him into your bed at night?'

It was so far from the truth it was almost laughable. Bridget

77

heard Kitty gasp, and gripped her arm in warning.

'No one's trapped your brother, Miss Finley,' Bridget snapped. 'He's asked me to marry him and I've said yes. You might have the grace to wish me luck. You'll be my sister-in-law in a week's time, and I shall be the mistress in this house.'

Both girls could see that the older woman had never hated the Irish upstarts more. And this one in particular, who had all the looks that Sheilagh had never had, who looked at her so contemptuously . . . coming from poor stock, yet with all the poise of a lady.

Oh yes, she'd be an asset to Thomas, Sheilagh admitted furiously. She'd be a decorative butterfly to grace his table and warm his bed, and would no doubt produce hordes of Irish brats to scream through the house . . .

'Don't think I shall ever acknowledge you as any relative of mine, Miss,' she raged. 'I don't know how you got my brother to agree to marry you, but be sure that life will be anything but comfortable for you while I'm still living here.'

'Then perhaps you'd better find somewhere else to live,' Bridget said. She spoke calmly enough, though her legs were trembling at her own daring. She saw Sheilagh blanch for a second, and the moment was very sweet.

'Oh no! I don't know what Thomas promised you in his lustful moments, but you won't get rid of me that easily, Bridget O'Connell. This house is as much mine as my brother's, and you'll do well to remember it.'

The girls stared at the door for some seconds after Sheilagh Finley had banged it shut.

'Don't believe her,' Kitty said. 'A wife always has priority over a sister. He'll leave everything to you in his Will, and he's sure to die before you, because he's so old. Then you'll own Finley's Canned Goods, and that'll put the old witch in her place.'

Her words swam in and out of Bridget's head. The only ones that stuck were those glorious words 'He's sure to die before you . . .' It was a mortal sin to wish anyone dead, but if Thomas Finley dropped dead the day after Kitty had her abortion, she'd be fervently grateful to God. She didn't want riches. She just wanted to be rid of him.

'Forget about her, Kitty. We need to talk about more important things. Are you absolutely certain you want to go through with this?'

Kitty blinked, her mind still caught up with the possibility of Bridget being a business and property owner one day, and Bridget lost patience.

'For God's sake, you haven't forgotten why you came rushing to Connecticut to find me, have you?'

The sick feeling enveloped her again. Connecticut would be finished for her now. There would be no more voice training, no more musical interludes with Monsieur Alphonse, no more impromptu duets and choir practices with the other students, no more Academy.

Such frivolities were perfectly acceptable for his ward, but Thomas would never indulge his wife in such activities. And even if he did, the Academy wouldn't allow it. Married women weren't allowed in the curriculum.

'No, I haven't forgotten.'

Bridget came back to the sound of Kitty's strangled voice with a great effort.

'If I don't keep talking about it, I can pretend it hasn't happened. As for getting rid of it – I'm terrified at the thought of what they'll do to me. People die having abortions –'

Bridget forgot everything but the need to reassure her. She held her tight, feeling that old desire to keep Kitty safe. If her daddy were here now, he would expect it of her. The closeness of the family had always been important to Dermot and Mavreen O'Connell. Bridget owed it to them not to desert Kitty in any way now.

'You're not going to die. Thomas will get the best person possible, darling. I guarantee it.'

Thomas arranged the wedding for the first Friday in May. He had obtained a special licence, and Father Rourke was assured that there was no reason for a hasty marriage, other than the mutual wish to be together before Thomas got much older. He said this to the priest with a jocularity that Father Rourke didn't appreciate, and recklessly promised to go to confession before the great day, to appease the priest.

'You'd do better to appease your God, Mr Finley,' he spoke dryly.

'Oh, of course,' Thomas said hastily. 'Not that I've done anything to be ashamed of.'

'We've all done things to be ashamed of, my son,' the priest said piously.

Pompous turd, Thomas thought, and said a silent Hail Mary to compensate. Not that he had any intention of confessing any but trivial things. It was all priests required. A nice little run of minor faults to listen to, to while away the morning and give their saintly blessings to.

One of these days he'd like to run amok in Father Rourke's confessional, and give him the shock of his life. He went over the scene in his mind, chuckling to himself.

'The O'Connell sisters have been my downfall, Father. The younger one got pregnant by a person unknown and had the bastard aborted. The other tried to force me into helping them by offering herself into my bed, but being a good Catholic soul the only way I could agree to this was by marrying her. Now, who would you say is the real sinner, Father?'

He was still smiling at the thought of sending the priest into an early grave by such revelations when his sister came lathering into his study.

'I've just had a confrontation with your mistress, Thomas!' She stormed.

'Bridget is not my mistress,' he snapped. 'I'm marrying her because I choose to, and that's all there is to know –'

'But perhaps it's not all you know, brother dear,' she said triumphantly. 'Your flighty piece has just informed me that once she's married to you, she'll be the mistress of this house, and if I don't like it I can find somewhere else to live. She's nothing but a common gold-digger, so who's the clever one now?'

Thomas ruminated for a long while after she'd flounced out. For the first time he began to wonder if he'd underestimated Bridget O'Connell and that little sister of hers. Had they cooked up this little scheme between them, thinking to outsmart him?

He only had their word that Kitty was pregnant. He'd hardly spoken to the girl herself, because Bridget said she was too upset and ashamed to see him unless she had to. Kitty had barely whispered the facts to him, confirming what Bridget had told him, and insisting that she didn't know the man nor where to find him . . .

His eyes narrowed. All these years that Bridget had been so aloof from him and every other man . . . had that been a ploy too, waiting until the time seemed right to spring her little trap? Perhaps marrying him had been her goal all this time, and if it was, he was the one being manipulated.

He was cunning and devious enough to appreciate a master-plan when he saw one. But he was incensed at being taken for a fool. True or not, the O'Connell girls were going to pay dearly for their trouble. They might think he was acting the benefactor, but each of them was in for a rude awakening.

Kitty . . . he'd felt briefly sorry for the silly little baggage. He'd intended getting hold of a doctor for her who didn't mind a bit of illegal work on the side. Now, Kitty would get more than she bargained for, whether there was anything in her belly or not.

He knew of a woman nick-named Madame Lentil. 'Gets rid of unwanted brats as easy as shelling peas' was her proud boast, and never mind the agony of her patients as long as the job was done.

And as for Bridget . . . Bridget was going to get a bedding true to his boast. And a child in her belly every year until he was too old to crawl over her and had to be helped every bit of the way. His skin tingled at the thought.

But there were things to attend to first. Thomas became businesslike. He reached for the telephone and waited impatiently for the operator to connect him. His lawyer answered in his New York twang.

'Donaldson? Come out to the house this afternoon. Bring my latest Will, and a witness. There are more alterations to be made.''

He hung up without waiting for an answer. Let the fool of a man earn his keep. It was nobody's business but his own if he kept changing his mind over his money and possessions. If the lawyer didn't like the extra work involved, it didn't matter a damn to Thomas. He'd just get another lawyer.

The first Friday in May was warm and sunny. The garden of Finley House had never looked so beautiful, nor the flowers smelled so fragrant. Bridget had the strangest feeling as she stepped out of the house in her wedding finery, and into the car that would take her to church. Numbly, she felt that she'd never smell flowers with the same pleasure again. Never see the grass looking so green, or the sky so blue. After today, everything in her life would be changed.

She tried not to think at all as the car sped on its way. Kitty sat beside her, resplendent in emerald green. In a second car, Thomas and his sister and a male supporter, sat in silence.

The day after the wedding, to Bridget's relief, Thomas would be taking Sheilagh to visit a friend upstate for several weeks. Sheilagh would be away when Kitty was taken to Madame Lentil, and there would be no suspicious eyes on the girl while she recovered from the operation.

Sheilagh Finley was wishing she'd been strong enough to refuse to attend today's farce of a ceremony, but she hadn't dared.

Thomas spent the journey to church anticipating the end of the day, when Bridget O'Connell would finally be his.

And the supporter was thinking he could spend his time more usefully with his horses than going to church with this old fool who'd probably expire at the first sight of his unclothed young and lovely bride.

The ceremony was to be as brief as Father Rourke could be persuaded to make it. They had invited no guests, and Thomas wanted no fuss, for which Bridget was thankful. To her, this was no occasion for celebrating, but rather for mourning the loss of her self.

She felt Kitty's hand on hers as they neared the church.

'Are you all right, Bridget?' She asked cautiously, seeing her sister's frozen face.

'Of course I am.' She stared straight ahead.

'But are you quite happy about marrying Thomas?' Kitty persisted. Bridget turned to look at her.

82

'At this moment I'm perfectly happy,' she stated.

She bent the truth with amazing ease. It was so easy to put a completely different interpretation on words. At this moment she was perfectly happy . . . because she wasn't yet Thomas Finley's wife. She was still the same as she'd always been, and the nightmare hadn't yet begun.

And later, no one noticed the tears on her lashes as Thomas pushed the wedding-ring onto her slender finger. If they had, they would have thought it quite natural for a young bride to become emotional at such a time.

It was her wedding-night. Bridget shivered in the huge four-poster bed in Thomas Finley's bedroom. She'd never been in this room before. She'd been unaware of the dark furniture and ornate fireplace and the heavy lace drapes around the bed that could be released by a single pull on a cord, enveloping those inside the bed with a sense of claustrophobia.

To one side of the room, the bathroom was Thomas's pride and joy. The bath-tub and lavatory were heavily patterned with pink and yellow flowers. There was a wash-basin in the same ridiculous pattern, and clean towels and bars of soap everywhere.

'I don't have a fetish for cleanliness, Bridget,' he said, which instantly told Bridget that he did. 'But you will use the bathroom every night before we come to bed, and immediately after we've had connection.'

She felt somewhat hysterical. What of the times she had smelled him, when excitement made him almost rank? Presumably that didn't count. He wanted his wife clinically clean. Well, he needn't have any fears of her washing herself after – *connection*. She would be desperate to get the smell of him off her body.

She huddled down beneath the bedcovers, her nightgown pulled up to her throat. Her eyes were shut tight, her heart beating wildly as she heard Thomas's padding footsteps approach the bed. She squeezed her eyelids open a fraction. He stood by the bed, looking down at her with what she could only describe as a leer. He wore a striped nightshirt, and above it his face looked fat and old.

The bed dipped and creaked as he climbed onto it. Then with one swift movement he pulled the cord of the lace drapes and enclosed them both inside.

'You're overdressed, my dear,' he said hoarsely.

Before Bridget could say a word he had pulled the bedcovers away from her, and with both hands he ripped her nightgown from top to bottom, and pushed it away from her body. Bridget lay in terror, as if mesmerised by him.

He didn't speak. She could have borne it more, perhaps, if he had spoken. He merely looked at her, examining every part of her as if she was some fine new purchase. Which was exactly what she was . . . He looked first, and then he touched, humiliating her by his prodding, pudgy fingers. Hurting her . . .

'Why don't you just do it?' She burst out at last. 'Haven't you seen enough of me yet?'

It was as if he'd been waiting for her to goad him. He leaned back on his heels and tore the nightshirt over his head. Bridget could hardly bear to see him naked. He was large and gross and repulsive.

But she didn't have to see him for long. In seconds he was astride her, and now the real torment began. He thrust himself into her tender flesh, until she could hardly breathe for the pain of it. On and on and on, as ruthlessly as an animal . . . when at last he flopped away from her, leaving her hot with her own blood and his semen, she felt utter revulsion. And with it came the agony of knowing she was no longer Bridget O'Connell, but this evil devil's chattel to do with as he liked, any time he wished.

'Go and wash yourself,' he growled as soon as he could catch his breath. 'And then you'll change these sheets while I soak in the bathtub. Be quick about it. I need my sleep. And don't think you're about to die because of a bit of mess. It'll be better next time.'

He never told her he loved her, or spoke with any endearments. She didn't want his love, any more than she could ever give him back love. But any small word of comfort would have been preferable to this coldness, this knowledge that he was just using her to gratify his lust.

Bridget slid from the bed painfully. She moved towards the bathroom like a sleepwalker. She had never felt so utterly under someone else's control. She had no strength to weep, although when she saw herself in the bathroom mirror her eyes were swollen and her cheeks were streaked with tears she hadn't even noticed.

She dragged the torn nightgown across her bruised body. He had ravaged her breasts, and there were ugly marks on them. She was ashamed to see herself, and hated him because none of this was her shame. She washed and dried herself gently, and then went back to the bedroom to do her husband's bidding and change the sheets, but Thomas was already heavily asleep.

He lay sprawled on his back, everything about him loose and flaccid. The thing that had defiled her was limp and useless between his legs. As she stood uncertainly he gave an enormous fart, turned on his side and dragged the bedcovers around him.

Bridget shuddered, and crept away from the bed to the chaise longue. Silently she wrapped herself in one of the blankets and lay down carefully, praying that the throbbing tenderness would soon pass. Until the next time . . .

And then despair overcame her, and she spent the rest of the night trying to smother her sobs.

Kitty was anxious to see her sister the next morning. Thomas left early. Business wouldn't wait, he told Bridget briskly, as if the horror of the night had never happened.

'Bridget, are you all right?' Kitty said fearfully, seeing her sister's ashen face. 'You look awful. Was it very bad?'

It was on the tip of Bridget's tongue to pass it all off lightly. Why worry Kitty more than necessary? The girl was only sixteen . . . but then she remembered that Kitty was already more worldly-wise than she. Kitty had known the brutality of a man before Bridget.

She spoke without expression, 'He was an animal.'

Kitty was frightened. She'd never seen Bridget like this before. She looken beaten.

'Oh, Bridget, I know it was all my fault. I wish I'd never

told you anything. I wish I'd found somebody to take care of me without involving you. But yesterday you said you were happy, and I believed you –' she was accusing and defensive.

'Yesterday I *was* happy. Yesterday I hadn't been degraded by a man I loathe.'

There was no point in pretending any more. She was married to Thomas Finley for better or worse, and it was a sin to break a partnership that God had made sacred.

Kitty began to cry. For once, Bridget had no pity to waste on her. She needed it all for herself. All her dreams had vanished. She would never go back to Connecticut, and she would never go to Ireland.

'I know I'm to blame for it all,' Kitty sobbed. 'But not all men are animals. Daddy wasn't, and the priests aren't. Don't talk so, Bridget, please!'

Bridget's heart twisted.

'No, Daddy wasn't an animal. He did what he thought was best for us, and look where it got him and Mammie and Michael. And you can't compare the priests with real men, so we've only found one good man in the whole world. So don't talk to me of good men, for I've no time for any of them.'

And Bridget guessed that in a week from now, Kitty would be the last one to defend them. Kitty's ordeal was yet to come.

'It's time, love.'

Kitty opened her eyes fearfully. No matter how much she wanted to be rid of the child, she was dreading this day. And the teachings of the church that she'd hardly heeded for years, kept ringing in her head like a death-knell. She couldn't lose the sense of foreboding that everything was going to go wrong . . .

If only she had the courage, she'd refuse to go through with it. Not that she wanted the child. She was still a child herself, however grownup she pretended to be. But there was no going back. Bridget had made such a sacrifice for her in marrying Thomas, and she couldn't throw it all back in her face now. She had no choice any more.

Bridget looked as pale as herself. She never mentioned what really happened behind the closed doors of the room she shared with Thomas now, but a week of marriage hadn't put any bloom on her cheeks or happiness in her eyes.

'Come on, Kitty. Thomas will be ready soon, and you know how he gets when he's kept waiting. Get dressed, for pity's sake.'

'Bridget – you will stay with me, won't you? You won't leave me there alone?'

'Of course I'll stay.'

Kitty attempted a smile. 'Thank God the old witch has gone on a visit upstate. I couldn't bear having her watching me and trying to guess what's wrong when I take to my bed for a couple of days. That's all it will be, isn't it?'

'That's what Thomas said, and I'm sure he's right. In a few days you'll be as good as new.'

They heard him shouting for them to hurry up, and Bridget flinched. Didn't he have any understanding of Kitty's feelings today? But by now, she knew very well that he had no perception of women's feelings at all. The next minute he walked into Kitty's room without knocking, and the girl pulled the covers around herself angrily. He gave a sarcastic scowl.

'It's a bit late for all that nonsense, sweetmeat,' he said shortly. 'Anyway, 'tis not your soiled body I've come to gawp at, but to tell my wife some good news. We've got the commission to supply army units with canned beans. When this war hots up they'll want plenty overseas, and we'll be in clover. Now get a move on. I can't waste all day on this caper.'

He banged out of the room. The girls looked at each other wordlessly. There couldn't be a more insensitive man in the whole world, Bridget thought. She saw Kitty begin to shake, and held her close for a moment.

'He's such a bastard, Bridget,' she quavered. 'He doesn't care about me at all –'

Nor me, Bridget thought silently. But she couldn't waste time on tears. She tried to encourage Kitty into feeling more positive.

'At least he's organised today for us, and we must be thankful for that. Once the next few hours are over, you must forget it ever happened. You'll be just as you were before.'

Which was more than Bridget could. She tried not to let depression take hold of her, but it was virtually impossible. She had her own agonies to bear, and even her silly expectations were as nothing. She was no one of importance, despite her fine words about being the mistress of this house. Thomas Finley had effectively broken her spirit along with everything else.

They travelled into New York city in silence. They sat in the back of Thomas's car, trying not to look at his bullet-shaped head. They held hands, and Bridget knew that however much she wanted to help Kitty, in the end her little sister would have to go into that operating room alone. The car took them into a sleazy part of the city, where strange signs hung above doors in a language they couldn't read.

'We're on the edge of Chinatown,' Thomas said curtly. 'Madame Lentil's Chinese, but she speaks good English, and knows exactly what's to be done.'

He was about to make the usual joke that Madame Lentil did these jobs every day, as easy as shelling peas . . . but he noticed the misery in Bridget's eyes reflected in the driving mirror, and for once held his tongue.

Once at the place, he got out of the car and opened the rear door for the girls.

'I'll come back for you later. It's all paid for in advance, and there's a room to wait afterwards until you're collected.'

He spoke directly to Kitty for almost the first time. 'Your name is Miss Green for today. It seemed appropriate since you liked your new green dress so much.'

Bridget was furious at this callous treatment, but Kitty was too tense to notice. And then, unbelievably, Bridget heard her grovelling words to him.

'Thank you for all you've done, Thomas,' she whispered. She reached up and kissed his mottled cheek, and Bridget had to turn away in total disgust at the way he preened himself as he steered them towards the door of the building and then abandoned them.

Chapter 7

It was dim and musty inside the house, apart from a strong smell of incense. Glass ornaments hanging in the hallway jingled in the draught from the door.

For a breathless instant the sound reminded Bridget of something else, something long ago. In a San Francisco sea breeze the costly chandelier in the house on Nob Hill had made such small tinkling movements. They had always scared her small brother Michael, and her daddy had teased him saying it was only the angels playing their music . . .

Nothing could be more different than this hovel. She shivered, hoping it wasn't a bad omen. She saw that an uncarpeted flight of stairs led to an upper floor which looked completely dark and empty, and she wondered uncertainly what they were supposed to do. Damn Thomas for leaving them like this, she thought savagely. Damn him to hell and back . . .

Kitty clung to her sister.

'Bridget, I'm afraid,' she stuttered.

'I'm sure there's nothing to be afraid of, love,' she muttered, though she was just as frightened of this alien place. 'If you want to change your mind, say so now. We'll get through it somehow.'

An upstairs door opened, throwing a stream of light down the stairs. A woman peered downwards.

'Miss Green, please come up,' she said. 'The lady may come with you.'

They moved slowly. As they neared the woman, they could see that she was oriental. She wore a shapeless garment of blues and greens wound about her several times so that she resembled a parcel. Her feet were very small in black slippers. Her face lacked any emotion.

Kitty's heart palpitated with fear as the woman pointed to a small room and motioned Bridget to go into the adjoining one. The last glance Kitty gave her sister was one of complete terror, before the door closed behind her and the oriental woman.

Bridget waited in a poorly furnished room. There was a table with a few out-of-date newspapers, a chair, and a couch with an old blanket thrown on it. The window was so grimy she could hardly see out, and there was nothing to see when she tried. She couldn't concentrate on anything except what was happening behind that other door.

She heard occasional movements and sometimes there was whimpering and muttering voices. Once she heard Madame Lentil speak sharply and twice she heard Kitty scream out, but she clenched her hands, knowing there was nothing she could do until it was all over.

And then she could give Kitty all the love and tenderness she needed. Bridget's own bitterness vanished, and she only felt all the protectiveness of those other times, when the two of them had been so alone. Kitty needed her now, more than ever.

It seemed an eternity before the door slowly opened again, and Kitty shuffled into the room.

'Mother of God, what has she done to you?' Bridget whispered hoarsely.

Madame Lentil hovered behind the bent body and white-faced girl. She spoke to Bridget, as if Kitty no longer existed.

'She's bleeding heavily,' she rasped. 'It's not unusual, but she must lie flat on the couch now with her legs higher than her head. She must stay in bed for at least two days in that position. She will take these pills to make sure everything has come away. If anything goes wrong, I will deny I have ever seen you. You may stay here for one hour, no more. I have another person due.'

She went away, and Bridget hated her more than she had ever hated anyone. Even more than she hated Thomas

Finley, she hated this woman who had turned her bright, pretty sister into this shambling old woman.

Kitty shook so much she could hardly reach the couch. Bridget eased her onto it, where she lay totally exchausted. Her teeth chattered uncontrollably and her closed eyelids were waxen and blue.

Suddenly, Bridget was terribly afraid. She tucked the blanket round her sister as tightly as she could and held her limp hand, summoning up all the prayers she could remember.

'Bridget,' Kitty said in a reedy voice. 'Am I going to die?'

'Of course not,' Bridget said adamantly. 'The woman said you're bleeding a lot, but that's all. Once it stops, you'll feel much better.'

She understood none of the mechanics of abortion or childbirth. Now, she wished desperately she'd found some medical book in the penny library, to know if this situation was really normal or . . . She hardly dared think of the alternative. She mustn't think of it. Kitty couldn't die. She was young and strong . . .

'Did she hurt you very much, darling?' She leaned forward to smooth Kitty's pale brow, and recoiled in horror. The girl was as white as death, yet her forehead burned and was beaded with sweat. This wasn't normal, Bridget thought frantically. None of this was as it should be . . .

'I'm going to find Madame Lentil,' she said swiftly, half-rising. Kitty grasped her hand with a strength that surprised her.

'Don't leave me,' she shrieked. 'I won't let that bitch touch me again. Stay with me Bridget, and don't make me move, for pity's sake. It's like a fire in my belly –'

'All right,' Bridget soothed, seeing that it would only make things worse to get her agitated. They must remain where they were until Thomas Finley came to collect them. A boiling anger filled her because of Thomas. How could he have found this she-devil to perform the abortion? There must have been others available. Why this Chinese bitch?

The truth flashed through her brain. This was part of the punishment. This part was Kitty's which mercifully would be over in a few days . . . while Bridget's would continue for as long as she was shackled in marriage with their 'saviour'.

She stifled a sob. She still couldn't help thinking of her daddy and his dreams that had all come to nothing, like Bridget's. Dermot O'Connell's dreams had included a fine house for his wife and children, and to be able to hold up his head in his chosen land. The O'Connells were destined for greater things than the poor Irish immigrants who lived in shacks on the San Francisco waterfront . . . Dermot had always said so, Bridget thought bitterly, and all the dreams had turned to dust.

'Bridget, it hurts so bad,' Kitty gave a small shriek. In her parchment face, her eyes looked as black as coals. Bridget began to feel desperate. They seemed to have been here for hours, but she knew it couldn't be that long. *Where* in God's name was Thomas?

Her heart skipped a beat. Perhaps he had truly abandoned them. She had no idea where they were, except that it was Chinatown. She had no money to take a taxi-cab back to Finley House. Waves of panic swept through her, and she tried to appear calm for Kitty's sake. And then the door opened, and Thomas's portly frame filled the doorway.

'Is it finished?' He said.

Bridget nodded, hate in her eyes. Without warning, she remembered the feeling of joy at the chance to leave San Francisco and come to New York to these benefactors. It had seemed like a giant step towards Ireland . . . now, for the first time, she wished she'd remained where she was. Better still, that the earthquake had taken her and Kitty as well, and finished off the entire O'Connell family in one swallow.

'She's too ill to stand by herself,' she snapped as he waited for Kitty to stand. 'She'll have to be carried to the car.'

He strode into the room. Bridget could see how he pinched his nostrils together at the smell of blood, and something else. She couldn't identify the smell, but it was the worst she had known. Somewhere in her memory she recalled hearing someone mention a dreadful smell like this. She fancied it was Father Malley . . .

' 'tis the death-smell that one must pretend not to notice for

92

the poor victim's sake . . .'

The sickening recollections wouldn't seem to let go. She prayed that it wasn't the death-smell on Kitty. But if she didn't improve quickly, Thomas must get a proper doctor to her. Bridget would insist on it if she had to send for one herself.

She tucked the blanket firmly around Kitty. The girl trembled so much that Bridget had no intention of uncovering her. Let the Chinese hag buy another.

Thomas carried her with reasonable care down the stairs. They passed a young girl with an older woman on the way. All of them avoided looking at each other.

'Kitty will go straight to bed,' Thomas instructed as he drove back to the house. 'Mrs Harris has been told that she's had a fall and is under sedation and only wants her sister to attend to her, so neither she nor the maids are to go to Kitty's room. Any bedding that becomes soiled will be burnt.'

He was practical and efficient. Bridget wondered briefly why he hadn't just done the abortion himself and saved all this bother. She was sure he was capable enough. He was capable of anything.

'I'm so weary, Bridget,' Kitty whispered. 'The jolting makes the pain worse. I know I'm still bleeding. It can't be right.'

'Everything will feel better when you're in your own bed, love,' she said. 'And I shall sleep in your room for as long as you want me.'

She dared Thomas to object, but he said nothing. Truth to tell, he didn't like the look of the O'Connell girl either, and if anything happened, God knew how he was going to explain it all away to the priest and Sheilagh. Damn their eyes, Thomas thought savagely, for bringing this kind of trouble to his door.

Once they were back at Finley House, he carried Kitty straight to her own room. She lay exhausted in her own bed on clean white sheets. Bridget packed towels beneath her feet and legs to raise her as Madame Lentil had ordered. She was still as cold as death. Quickly, Bridget lit the fire in the grate and filled two stone water bottles with hot water to put in the bed. She gave the girl a sedative to help her sleep more peacefully.

'Don't go, Bridget,' Kitty whispered. 'I don't want to be alone –'

'I'll just go to the kitchen and get some fresh water for you to drink, that's all.'

'Don't make Thomas angry. He frightens me –'

She drifted into sleep, and Bridget sped down to the kitchen for the pitcher of water, and found the servants musing over Kitty's supposed accident.

'Is the poor love hurt bad, Mrs Finley?' The housekeeper said sympathetically.

Bridget started, and then realised the woman was addressing her. It was the first time she'd been called by that name. It seemed to symbolise the sacrifice made for this day. She licked her dry lips.

'She's badly shaken and bruised, all she needs is rest and quiet. I shall be nursing her and I'll send down if we need anything.'

'Very well, Mrs Finley. Perhaps the poor lamb could take some soup?'

To please her, Bridget took a jug of soup and two bowls and spoons with the water.

'I can't eat,' Kitty said, when Bridget tried to feed her. 'It will choke me if I try.'

Bridget couldn't eat it either. It was hot and nourishing, but the smell of it reminded her of the soup kitchens after the earthquake.

Bloody, *bloody* earthquake, she thought in sudden passion. Why must the memory of it burst into her brain when she was least expecting it? Sometimes she wondered if the memories would ever leave her.

She tip-toed to Kitty's bed. The girl was asleep again. She had lost a lot of blood. When Bridget had removed the distasteful blanket from her body and eased her into her own nightgown, the blood had gushed from Kitty, bright and frothy. The flood frightened her and Bridget had quickly packed her sister with towels.

Nobody came near them all that night. Bridget kept a silent vigil beside her sister, and while she moaned in her sleep, all the forgotten prayers came tumbling through Bridget's mind again. She prayed to God and to the Blessed Virgin, to every saint she had ever heard of, and a few more that she invented.

She must have dozed, for the sound of birdsong awoke her, and it was daylight outside. Sunlight streamed through the window-panes. It was going to be a bumper day . . . she turned to tell Kitty so, for a few sleep-drugged seconds forgetting the trauma of yesterday.

The instant she looked at Kitty, she knew. Kitty lay peacefully, her face no longer distorted with pain. She looked young and defenceless, her dark hair spread around her white face on the pillow. She looked like an angel.

Bridget knew she was going to vomit. The bulk of it filled her mouth and throat, and she rammed her fist into her mouth, forcing it down.

She seemed unable to breathe properly at the shock of it all. And then all the emotion was released in a great cry, and she laid her head beside her sister's on the pillow and wept. Her mind was in complete turmoil. She needed help here. Thomas must come and help her. Unthinkingly, she wrenched at the bell pull, and a maid came into the room a few minutes later, frozen in horror at what she saw.

'Clara, fetch Mr Finley at once.' Bridget almost snarled. 'It's urgent.'

'Yes, Miss – Ma'am –' the girl gasped, and ran from the room in a fright to do Bridget's bidding.

Later, bulging-eyed, she told Mrs Harris that she could swear that young Miss O'Connell was dead, and that it looked for all the world as if the older one was about to wrap her up and take her away, and wasn't going to let anybody else touch her . . .

'What's happened, Bridget?' Thomas strode into the room. 'Mother of God, has she snuffed it?'

Bridget looked up at him from her prone position on Kitty's bed. Her eyes were murderous.

'You bastard,' she said, slowly and deliberately. 'This is my sister you're speaking about, not a lump of butcher's meat. I blame you for this. You killed her –'

Thomas slammed the door shut, crossed the room and

pulled her away from Kitty's body, thrusting his hand across her mouth.

'We'll have none of that talk,' he hissed in her ear. 'Take hold of yourself. I'm sorry the girl's dead, but it won't help her to wallow over her. We must think what's to be done next.'

She stared in disbelief, pushing his hand away from her face.

'You know what's to be done. She must have the priest here to give her absolution. She must make her peace with God. She must have a decent burial and have her name recorded in the church's ledger. What else do you suggest? Pretend she never *existed*?'

Thomas seemed to realise at last that she was near to breaking-point.

'Don't fret. She'll have the priest,' he said swiftly. 'And a doctor too –'

'It's too late for that,' Bridget said bitterly.

'The doctor must certify the cause of death,' he snapped. 'I'll telephone Doctor Bauer right away. He'll give us a suitable certificate. He owes me a few favours.'

Bridget heard herself laugh incredulously. Somehow the incongruous thought filled her mind that this vast, generous, and beautiful country seemed to be filled with the worst of foreigners . . .

'A German, is he? We've had a Chinese abortionist and now some German quack is going to give a false death certificate. How many more unsavoury friends do you have? I thought we were on the verge of being at war with Germany. Are they still letting them into America, this free and wonderful golden country that spews up streets, and lets young girls die in agony –?'

He shook her so hard that it stopped the flow of words. His face came into her wild focus.

'Would you rather I sent for a regular physician and asked him to examine Kitty?' He said harshly. 'Would you rather she went to her grave with the stigma of dying from an illegal abortion? Would the priest still give her absolution? Think, Bridget, *think*.'

She couldn't think. Only that there was a need for more

lies. One lie on top of another . . . yes, this was all for Kitty's sake . . . but it was also for Thomas Finley's sake too. It mustn't ever be known that he'd arranged this illegal operation. He had his position to think about. And so did his wife. And what of Sheilagh Finley, who knew nothing as yet? She must be told the same lies as the rest. Bridget wilted, seeing there was no help for it.

'Send for your doctor, and the priest. Just get it over with.'

'Good girl.' He was clearly relieved. 'Straighten things up and get rid of those towels in the bed. Even an old fool of a priest will know that a girl who died from a fall didn't need her legs propped up. Stay where you are while I make a telephone call to Doctor Bauer, and I'll have some hot tea and brandy sent up to you. You'll drink it all, Bridget, do you understand?'

'Yes,' she moaned.

Just as long as somebody else took care of it all. She was too weary to think any more. All that she loved in the world was cold and still. All that Bridget ever cared about had gone. Nothing that Thomas Finley did from now on was ever going to hurt her as much as this. Nothing.

She tip-toed back to the bed, as if afraid of disturbing Kitty. She looked down at the girl's face, young and clean, and felt a deep shame wash over her.

'Forgive me, Kitty,' she whispered. 'I promised to keep you safe, and I failed. Just like Daddy failed to keep us all safe. I thought I was stronger than him, but I'm not. I'll never make promises I can't keep again.'

Bridget expected the next days and weeks to be sharply etched in her mind, but instead they were hazy, colourless days with no substance. Nothing came clearly into her focus, and she felt as though she lived in a vacuum. The pills Doctor Bauer constantly fed to her to ensure that she was numbed through the worst of the ordeal became a kind of lifeline. Even so, the enormity of Kitty's death and the emptiness it left behind was the only thing occupying her mind. There was no room for anything else.

If the rest of America was very much occupied with worry

about maintaining her neutrality in the war in Europe, it didn't affect Bridget Finley. She cared nothing for Thomas's frequent outbursts of rage at realising too late that to cash in on the fortunes of war, he should have turned his factory over to munitions.

'These newshounds print nothing but rubbish,' Thomas snapped to his wife and sister a few weeks after Kitty's death, when political arguments for entering the war were at their height.

'Don't get so worked up, Thomas,' Sheilagh said edgily. 'The government will make up its own mind, whatever we think, and it won't do us any good to be on bad terms with our neighbours because of this. Some of the German immigrants in Mayfield are very nice people.'

And some of them could lie and cheat. Doctor Bauer was one of them, Bridget thought, sickened at his well-told tale of how Kitty had fallen on railings and impaled herself. The imaginary injury had resulted in the massive internal bleeding that had killed her.

Sheilagh Finley, the priest and the servants had believed it all. Everything was conducted neatly and tidily, and in Thomas Finley's mind at least, it would soon be easy to forget that Kitty O'Connell ever existed.

'Are you all right, Bridget? You've hardly touched your dinner.'

She nodded at hearing Sheilagh's sharp voice. Sheilagh had been sent for immediately, and had returned from her visiting, shocked out of her resentment of the O'Connells. She had come home offering a small olive branch to her sorrowing sister-in-law, but for Bridget, it was too late. The woman had been her enemy for too long.

The Finleys simply didn't know how to be kind in the way that everyone else was kind. But by now Bridget's nerves were so brittle that she couldn't take much more kindness from anyone.

Sheilagh leaned forward and encouraged her to eat the delicious meal of roast beef. Thomas always took wine with his meals, and there were three glasses of red wine alongside the plates. The colour revolted Bridget, reminding her of blood.

'I don't want it. I'm tired. I think I'll go and lie down, Miss Finley.'

She stood up awkwardly, and the napkin in her hand caught the edge of her wine glass and tipped it over the white cloth. The stain spread quickly, and Bridget watched it in numb horror. Sheilagh's first reaction to snap at her, and to demand to know why she was suddenly so ridiculously formal with her, was stilled by the horrified expression in Bridget's eyes.

'You'd better see to her, Thomas,' Sheilagh said quickly. 'Give her one of her pills and let the doctor see her tomorrow.'

Thomas scraped back his chair. He knew very well that Bridget's attitude these days unnerved his sister. To Sheilagh, the girl would always be an Irish upstart, but now she had a strange almost ethereal beauty that to him was untouchable.

Since Kitty's death, Bridget had somehow put a shield between herself and reality, and it effectively put a stop to any relations between himself and his new bride as well, Thomas thought irritably. It would be like trying to bed a saint to lie with Bridget O'Connell right now, and there was no quicker way of shrinking a man's equipment.

She slept in Kitty's room all the time now, and that wasn't right either. But he didn't object. There was another little matter he didn't want to think about too much, anyway. His great plan of impregnating his wife every year was in danger of falling at the first post, since he'd discovered he wasn't quite as capable as he thought he was.

In the present circumstances, it didn't matter too much, but he had no intention of remaining celibate for ever. That was for priests, not for a healthy man like himself, and it wasn't why he had married Bridget O'Connell.

'We're going to take a trip,' Thomas announced a few weeks later. 'It will do you good.'

And perhaps on neutral ground, in an hotel where Bridget could hardly object to their sleeping together, they might resume marital relations. Thomas liked the sound of the old-fashioned phrase. It gave it more dignity than the wild thrashings that he inaugurated. He saw the sudden burst of life return to Bridget's face. She looked more animated than at any time since her sister's death.

'A trip? Oh, you must know there's only one place I long to see!'

'And where's that, girl?' He said indulgently, thinking himself a fine fellow to bring about this glow to a young woman's cheeks.

'Why, Ireland, of course!' She almost laughed at him for needing to ask such a question. Ireland would be green and beautiful in summer. Sure, and her mammie and daddy had always said so, with such memories in their eyes that had stirred her imagination . . .

Thomas gaped at her as if she had lost her senses.

'Are you quite mad, girl?' He said harshly. 'When I said a trip, I meant to Boston or Niagara, not halfway across the world into the middle of a war!'

'But Ireland's neutral –' she stammered.

'So's America, but that don't stop the Germans sinking any ships they see fit to,' he snapped. 'I thought you had more sense than to imagine I'd take you to Ireland. Perhaps when the war's over, I'll think about it.'

Her disappointment was acute, but she could see the sense in it, and felt stupid for not thinking it out for herself. But if only she had this to look forward to, she might yet be able to get through the days as his wife . . . and perhaps she could manage to forget the irony of marrying Thomas Finley – that it had all been for nothing. She had done it for Kitty, and Kitty was dead.

He thought nothing of making promises he had no intention of keeping. He'd left Ireland behind and didn't want to see it again. But if a promise brought a bit of a sparkle to Bridget's eyes again, so be it. He was tiring of a wife who had lain like a block of wood when he had the lust upon him. He was tired of hearing her weep for her sister, and the way she thought herself so superior to him, despite her poor background. Bridget O'Connell got above herself far too often.

'We'll go up to Niagara and see these waterfalls that people say are so Godamned marvellous.' He decided. 'We'll stay in an hotel for a few days and act like rich Yankees. What d'you say, Bridget?'

'If you say so,' she said. She didn't relish being anywhere alone with him, but her wishes didn't really come into it. If he said they were going to Niagara, they would go to Niagara. She had little interest in anything any more. She rarely went out of the house, except for yesterday.

He would be livid if he knew where she had been. She had gone to the church, and sat behind the confessional curtain and felt even guiltier because it was a long while since the last time she had been here like this.

'Bless me, Father, for I have sinned –' she had murmured.

Father Rourke felt an immense sorrow for this beautiful girl who had lost all purpose in life now that her young sister was gone. And after her family being struck down all those years ago too . . . Such tragedy in one family, he thought sorrowfully, and made the usual platitudes, before suddenly sitting up straighter at the words Bridget O'Connell Finley was saying.

'I don't love my husband, Father,' she said tremulously. 'I can't love him. He repulses me worse than anyone I've ever known. When he comes near me I want to retch. And when he touches me I want to tighten myself into a little ball so that he can't get in –'

Father Rourke recovered his breath and told her harshly to stop this blasphemy at once.

'You are committing a terrible sin, Bridget, to deny the union between a man and woman God has joined –'

His piety roused her into anger.

'God didn't join us. You did!' She accused him.

'I am the instrument of God –' he said, outraged.

'Did God tell you so Himself?' Bridget demanded.

She was astounded at her own daring, knowing she had appalled the priest. She tried to peer through the curtain to see him more clearly.

'Are you sick, Father?' she said, when he didn't answer.

'Only with sorrow for you, Bridget Finley,' he said with barely suppressed rage. 'I hardly know how to deal with such wickedness as to question God's work –'

She was fearfully defensive at that. 'I thought God had given us wits to think for ourselves. Besides, I only meant that He's the Mighty One, not mortal men –'

Father Rourke choked. 'I think you had best leave the confessional until you have taken control of yourself, Bridget Finley –'

'But I came for help! I want to know what to do about my marriage.'

He was relentless. 'The duty of a good Catholic wife is to obey her husband, Bridget,' he resorted to safe ground. 'You made your vows before God, and if you go against them, in deed or thought, you sin against God.'

'Thank you, Father.' She said dully. She sat with bowed head while he chanted on, and heard none of it. All she knew was that she was tied to Thomas Finley for life.

She stumbled out of the cool church into the brilliant summer sunlight outside, leaving the priest to pray for her. She was tied, and she had never even wanted a man. She was complete within herself. And yet, the honesty of it was, that she was not.

She was lonely. Since Kitty died, she had never been more lonely. And now Thomas wanted to take her away to Niagara to look at a lot of water, and to stay in an hotel where no doubt he intended to resume marital connection, and it was her solemn duty to obey . . .

Chapter 8

'Well? What do you have to say about it, Bridget?' Thomas said expansively, as if he had personally engineered the wonder and glory of Niagara Falls by himself. Bridget looked into the chasm of the horseshoe falls where the heaving cauldron of water evaporated in a white mist, and was suitably impressed.

'Very nice,' she murmured.

Thomas gave a great guffaw to cover his embarrassment at

this insipid response, particularly when a group of sightseers nearby was exclaiming in awe at the spectacle.

'Can't you be more enthusiastic?' Thomas hissed.

A young woman in the party alongside them overheard, and glanced sympathetically towards Bridget. For a second their glances met, and the other girl seemed to recognise the desperation in Bridget's eyes. She spoke impulsively.

'Forgive me for intruding, but aren't you and your father staying at the same hotel as us? I thought I saw you arrive this afternoon.'

Bridget went a fiery red, and daren't look at Thomas. She hardly needed to. The ends of his fingers on her arm were suddenly pincer-like against her skin.

'This is my husband,' she felt obliged to say quickly. 'We're Mr and Mrs Finley, and I believe we did see you and your family.'

The girl's colour matched Bridget's. She had moved a little distance away from her family, and the others hadn't heard, to Bridget's relief.

'Oh I say, what an appalling *gaffe*. Do please forgive me, Mrs Finley.'

'It's quite all right,' Thomas put in stiffly, but clearly furious at the mistake.

And Bridget relaxed. Yes, it was quite all right. It was more than all right. It was a natural mistake. This oaf looked more like her grandfather than her father. She gave the other girl a sweet smile.

'Please don't apologise, Miss – ?'

'Carson. Mary-Jo Carson. I'm here with my parents and my brother, and I say, I really am sorry for my mistake. It was an awful thing to do –'

'I assure you, it's perfectly all right, Miss Carson. Don't trouble yourself about it.'

Bridget put plenty of warmth into her voice. She liked the look of this pretty fair-haired girl, who was certainly a diversion from Thomas. And anything that took her away from his exclusive company was wonderful.

She could tell that he didn't like this little exchange. He was put out by the girl's assumption that Bridget must be here with her father. They hadn't been out a great deal since their marriage, because of Kitty's death, and this was a situation that hadn't arisen before. Bridget relished it. Far from being offended, she felt a perverse delight in making Thomas squirm.

'Since we're staying at the same hotel, Miss Carson, perhaps you and your family would join us in the hotel lounge this evening? I believe they have dancing and some entertainment. Just to show there's no ill-feeling at all.'

Mary-Jo's eyes lit up. 'What a lovely idea. I'll ask my parents at once. Please excuse me for a moment.'

Bridget was still smiling as the girl went off to catch up with her family. Thomas's voice was filled with anger as he wrenched Bridget's arm.

'What the devil did you do that for? We don't want these people joining us –'

'These damn Yankees?' Bridget asked archly. 'Is that what you were about to say? Wasn't it your idea for us to join the tourists?'

His puffball face darkened.

'Don't think you can make a fool of me, Bridget. As your husband, you'll obey me –'

'Yes, Daddy.' The word slipped out, incensing him even more. She didn't know why she'd said it. But he looked so much the irritated father, chastising a small child at that moment. She saw how it angered him, and kept it as a small reserve of annoyance to use on him in future.

It didn't feel wrong. He'd given her a home and comfort, but she had been cheated of something far more precious. He'd taken her youth and innocence. He'd stolen her dreams, and killed her sister. He was evil, and there was nothing too bad for him in Bridget's mind . . .

The Carsons were approaching. They were a middle-aged couple, Mary-Jo, who looked about Bridget's age; and the most gloriously handsome young man she had ever seen. The sun glinted through the rough waves of his fair hair, his skin was tanned, and he wore his casual holiday clothes with a fashionable elegance. Bridget's fleeting thought was that if Kitty were here now, she'd undoubtedly fall hook line and sinker for David Carson.

'We'd be very happy to join you this evening, Mrs Finley,' Mary-Jo said with undisguised pleasure.

'I believe we're town neighbours, Finley. Your name is familiar to me and I'm sure I've seen you in Mayfield. That is, if you're Thomas Finley of Finley's Canned Goods,' Gerald Carson added, the iron grey eyes that matched his thatch of hair thoughtful and interested.

'That I am, Sir.'

Bridget noted with embarrassment how Thomas preened himself at the recognition.

'Then I presume you are also a resident of Mayfield, so may I ask your business, since you seem to know mine?' He said, his voice having the merest edge to it.

Gerald Carson laughed genially. 'I'm afraid I know too much of the town's business, even though my family and I have only moved there in the past month. I've recently become manager of the Mayfield Banking Corporation, and am slowly getting round to meeting my most important clients. Now that we've met so informally, it would seem a good opportunity to invite you and your lovely wife to our next garden party at the beginning of August.'

Bridget felt her mouth curving into a smile, an occurrence that wasn't so frequent these days. The world wasn't *all* bad, even if the first thought that swam into her mind was how Kitty would have loved such an invitation . . .

David and Mary-Jo looked pleased at their father's words, and Mrs Carson seemed a most gracious woman as she endorsed them.

'That's most agreeable of you, Carson,' Thomas said. 'We shall be happy to accept, providing it doesn't clash with any other commitments.'

'Naturally,' Gerald Carson replied.

Bridget wished that Thomas could have been slightly readier with his acceptance, but it didn't matter. Since Kitty's death, she'd hardly gone outside the house, but she admitted now that this trip was probably doing her good, even though she had hated the thought of it. And meeting the Carsons took away the unwanted intimacy of being alone with Thomas so much. He was drawn into conversation with the older Carsons now, and Bridget felt as though a breath of fresh air was blowing through her lungs as David and Mary-Jo strolled along beside her.

Mary-Jo spoke enthusiastically. 'I'm so glad we've met you, Mrs Finley. We've so recently moved to Mayfield from Vermont, that I don't know anyone else there yet. It seems strange that we should meet someone from our new home-town up here. I believe it must be fate, don't you?'

'It couldn't be anything else.' David Carson put in. 'Unless you call it the most fantastic luck to meet up with such a beautiful girl.'

Mary-Jo laughed. 'You'd better remember that Mrs Finley's a married lady, David.'

'That's why it's safe to compliment her,' he grinned.

Bridget laughed too, exhilarated by the candid conversation of these two, and sensing at once that David Carson's easy tongue could flatter and mean nothing, which suited her admirably.

'I may be a married lady, but we must be all about the same age, so please call me Bridget. I'd like us to be friends. It would be nice to meet in Mayfield, and I shall look forward to your party very much.'

It would be good to have a woman friend, and something quite precious if it developed into a lasting friendship. Someone in whom she could confide, the way she once used to confide in her mammie, and then in Kitty . . .

'Bridget it is, then. And we're Mary-Jo and David. We must meet often in Mayfield, if you'd like that. And you really have forgiven me for mistaking Mr Finley for your father?' Mary-Jo said.

'There's nothing to forgive. To be honest, I sometimes think of him that way myself,' she said, which had them laughing like conspirators.

She didn't miss the fact that although she was Bridget to the younger Carsons, Thomas was still referred to as Mr Finley. She liked that. Whether Thomas noticed or not, Bridget felt it was a small way of establishing her independence. She didn't belong to Thomas utterly. She was still her own person.

She soon found that he thought very differently when they returned to the hotel. Both parties had only arrived at Niagara that day, and when they parted to go to their separate suites, they had arranged to meet in the lounge later that evening.

'I shall take a bath before I change for dinner, Thomas,' she said as they went inside their room.

'And then we'll take a rest and you can smile at me as seductively as you smiled at that young Yankee pup,' he said without expression.

She started. 'I was merely being polite, and nothing more. I thought you would expect it, especially since Mr Carson's a bank manager. I'd have thought his status in the town appealed to your mercenary mind,' she said daringly.

Thomas snorted. ' 'Tis my money that puts him where he is, so that makes him less impressive than me. You'd agree with that, I presume.'

'No, I wouldn't,' Bridget said, nettled. 'Mr Carson's an important man –'

'And so am I and don't you forget it. Be quick about that bath, Bridget. I intend to smoke a cigar for the moment and ponder on how Mr Gerald Carson can be of use to me.'

He could really be sickening at times, Bridget thought in disgust, in business matters as well as personal. Whenever he could, he used people.

Perhaps everyone did to some degree. Even Mary-Jo Carson and herself were going to use one another to rid themselves of loneliness. But that was different. That was a mutual need for friendship both had recognised.

The Finleys had an imposing suite at the hotel, with a large bedroom containing one double bed that had made Bridget's heart sink when she first saw it; an adjoining bathroom, and a small balcony overlooking the Falls and the Niagara River. The last thing Bridget wanted was for Thomas to consider this trip as some kind of belated honeymoon. It was what she dreaded the most. She was still in a state of shock over Kitty, and he must surely know that, and be considerate . . .

She knew her fears were justified when she came out of the

bathroom to find him lying on his back in the middle of the double bed, the bedclothes up to his neck, his eyes closed. She hesitated, pulling her bathrobe more tightly around her, thinking he was asleep. She prayed that he was. If she just relaxed for a while in one of the soft armchairs she could be dressed for dinner by the time he awoke . . . even as she thought it, his eyes opened.

'Come here to me, Bridget.'

His voice was soft and filled with meaning, and she shuddered. It had been weeks since he had tried to touch her, and she had successfully kept out of his reach by one means or another. Now, as she had always known, there was to be no escape. He threw back the bedclothes invitingly.

Beneath them he was naked. The rolls of flesh that were so pendulous when he stood upright, were now distributed sideways. The thing in the middle, to which Bridget could never refer in any other way, lay slack and inert, and she hoped desperately that it would remain so.

On the last few occasions, Thomas's attempted act had been ludicrously unsuccessful.

At her hesitation, his voice rasped.

'*Now*, Bridget.'

She flinched, untied the bathrobe with shaking fingers and crawled into the bed, inching as far from him as possible. She wore nothing beneath the robe, and she didn't miss the way his greedy eyes took in the shape of her body. And she belonged to him, in the eyes of the church and God. But God as well as herself must know that there was nothing sacred or wholesome about this marriage.

He pulled her nearer with rough hands, pinning her beneath the great mound of flesh. He liked her to be clean, but he wasn't so fussy himself. He hadn't bathed since driving from Mayfield to Niagara early that morning, and she had difficulty in not wrinkling her nose. As well as his body odour, he stank of stale tobacco smoke. He leaned over her, his great belly warm on her freshly washed skin, making her muscles contract instinctively.

'Why no smile on your face, girl?' He asked aggressively. 'The same smile you gave the Carson boy.'

She felt a sharp anger at the insinuation. 'You're not going to persist in this, are you, Thomas? I didn't encourage him, and I don't even think of him –'

'Ah, but I *want* you to,' he insisted. 'Put that grand imagination of yours to work, my girl, and imagine 'tis David Carson's firm young flesh against yours. Shut your eyes fast, and do as I say. I want that look on your face to tell me that you're thinking of a fine young lover who can fill your belly with fire, do you hear? If it takes all night, you'll do it.'

As she listened to him, her heart pounded in disgust. What devilment was this? She wasn't attracted sexually to David Carson, and didn't want to think of him at all . . . But the insidious voice kept repeating the words, telling her to think of David, to imagine him naked, to sense the touch of his hands on her body, his lips on her breasts . . . The evil devil was hypnotising her with lewd suggestions, his own hands and lips putting the movements to the words, and however much she fought against them, Bridget's senses were beginning to swim . . .

'That's it, my beauty.'

She heard Thomas give a hoarse pant, and realised that a small moan had escaped her lips. Suffused by the languorous heat from the bath and the soft insistence from his voice, she knew too late that she'd done just as he wanted. In her mind the weight above her was no longer that of her detested husband, but of a young, virile lover. Her own imagination had aroused her to ecstasy.

This was what he had intended . . . too late, she felt the thrust of the thing inside her. He had goaded her into this, in a way that was new and exciting to him, in order to obtain his own erection. It was shameful and terrible . . . and there was absolutely nothing she could do about it until his clumsy jerkings were over.

Once it was done, he rolled away from her as always and turned, snoring, into the pillow. And Bridget lay exhausted, tears trickling down her cheeks, staring unseeingly at the ceiling.

But slowly through the misery, came a new and unexpected realisation. She wasn't frigid. The man who had roused her to passion wasn't Thomas Finley, despite being held in his unwelcome grasp, nor David Carson. It had been no more than a fantasy lover, yet somehow she had been able to respond as if she was truly in a lover's embrace. The knowledge made her wonder tremulously if after all, there might be someone somewhere, whom she could truly love.

It would never be Thomas Finley. But as Kitty had said in her wise young desperation, he wouldn't live for ever. Bridget was still young and would surely outlive him and have a life of her own. And perhaps if destiny was kind to her, there might even be a love of her own too. It was an idea so gradual and new that she hardly dared believe it, in case it vanished like will-o'-the-wisp.

Bridget lay with her eyes shut for a long while, but she felt calmer now. The ironic thing was that she didn't feel anything for David Carson – in *that* way. He was handsome and amusing, and any girl would be proud to be seen on his arm, but because Thomas had forced her to think of him *in that way*, she knew she would be hot with embarrassment whenever she saw him again.

It was something else to damn her husband in her eyes, and she was still bemused as to how Thomas had made such a thing happen. If anyone had told her that another person could control her own thoughts and the actions of her body, she would have been appalled.

She felt him move out of the bed, and as he went to the bathroom he spoke to her as if nothing untoward had happened between them.

'Get ready for dinner, Bridget. Later we can join these new friends of yours if we must.'

She didn't move for a few minutes, and he spoke sharply again when he came back into the room. She moved as if in a dream, going to the bathroom to wash his smell from her body. Tears mingled with the hot water, realising that there was no escape from him, ever. She gave in to the inevitable, dried herself, dressed in one of the new frocks Thomas had bought her – a pretty creation in a bronze, watered silk, with yellow rosebuds around the neck and sleeves – and went to meet his approval.

The hotel was plush, with pink marble columns and dazzling chandeliers that reminded Bridget again of the Pendletons' mansion in San Francisco. Thomas didn't know anything about that. He'd never bothered to ask the O'Connell girls about their background. Bridget reminded herself that there must be thousands of hotels that had such costly chandeliers. Yet tonight seemed to be filled with ghosts.

After dinner, they retired to the hotel lounge, where there were soft armchairs in deep, brown velvet material, with little glass-topped coffee tables placed at intervals around the room. At one end there was a platform on which a three-piece ensemble played music at a discreet pitch.

Bridget saw Mary-Jo Carson waving to her from the far side of the room. Mary-Jo looked fetching in peacock blue, her mother elegant in navy with a rope of pearls around her neck. The Carson men rose to greet the new friends. Both were darkly handsome, one a younger version of the other. Bridget avoided looking at either of them for more than seconds, and sat beside Mary-Jo.

'We thought you weren't coming,' Mary-Jo said. 'We had dinner ages ago –'

'You must forgive my daughter, Mrs Finley,' Gerald Carson said genially, his smile embracing both girls, and it was obvious that Mary-Jo was the apple of his eye. 'She's frank to the point of rudeness at times –'

'Oh, please call me Bridget,' she said quickly. 'Too many people hide behind false politeness, and I like people to say what they mean, especially when they intend becoming friends.'

Gerald laughed. 'I see you two have found kindred spirits in one another, and I'm happy to hear it.'

Thomas didn't look terribly pleased at the sudden intimacy between these people and his wife, especially when it seemed to exclude him for a moment.

'Then I take it you've no objection to the brash Irish, like some of the Ya – Americans we've come across?' He said tartly.

Mrs Carson gave a laugh as elegant as her dress.

'We live in a democracy, Mr Finley. There aren't so many Americans who can boast true American blood if the truth were known. A vast number have their roots in some European country, and all are welcome here. America is big enough for all.'

For some reason her very generosity irritated him. Bridget could see it, and felt a little alarmed, hoping he wasn't going to upset these very nice people. He could be viciously aggressive when he chose, and he'd been drinking, which loosened his tongue still more.

'And those that didn't come from good Irish or German or Danish stock, probably came from the damn redskins,' Thomas said aggressively.

Bridget saw Mrs Carson go pink, and wished herself anywhere but here, with her florid-faced husband in his ridiculous circus-look suit.

'True enough, Mr Finley.' David Carson said. 'But good breeding will always show, no matter what a person's roots. If one researches into North American history, one sees just how instrumental the Indians were in developing this land that the immigrants take for granted.'

Bridget's admiration was immense. With one sentence, David had reduced her stupid, bungling husband to the insensitive man that he was. The Irish immigrant, boastfully trying to take on the best of American society. The Carsons might not have been the cream of it, but they certainly had style.

The wonder of it was that they didn't seem to take any offence at Thomas's crudely phrased insult. Or perhaps from someone like him, it simply didn't matter. David turned to her as the band struck up a dance tune.

'Would you care to dance, Bridget? That is, if Mr Finley doesn't object?'

'You go on and dance with the little lady, David. My feet just get themselves in a twist when I try, so I'll enjoy seeing you two young things.'

Bridget squirmed. She didn't particularly want to dance at all. Still less did she want Thomas watching her dance with

David Carson and guess at the embarrassment. But once David led her away from the rest, and they were swallowed up in the midst of other guests moving to the lively tune, she felt less awkward than she had expected.

'How the devil did you come to marry such a brute, Bridget?' He grinned, as forthright as his sister.

His words disarmed her and she shrugged.

'It seemed the right thing to do at the time,' she said mechanically.

'Do you love him?'

There was a ready reproof on her lips, but she knew instinctively she could be as candid as these two new friends. In no way did she feel threatened by David Carson, and after the earlier hour with Thomas, it was an extraordinary and wonderful feeling. Somehow she could dissociate herself from the traumatic experience Thomas had put her through because of this man.

'No, I don't love him.'

'Thank goodness you said so. I'd have felt disappointed in your good taste if you'd answered yes. You do look a bit like beauty and the beast, you know. Mary-Jo and I couldn't help remarking on it.'

'Do you discuss everybody in this way?' She laughed up at him.

'Only the people we like, and those we especially don't,' he said meaningly. 'And I'll leave you to guess in which category we put each of the Finleys!'

Bridget laughed again. He was a man, and she didn't care for them as a species, but she sensed that David Carson could be as good a friend to her as Mary-Jo, and she had been short of friends all her life.

When they rejoined the others, both were flushed from dancing, and Thomas remarked that they made a handsome couple. Bridget's eyes challenged him.

'Yes, we do, don't we? I caught sight of us in one of the long mirrors and was surprised at how well our steps matched.'

She saw him frown. This wasn't what he had expected. He wanted a deeper colouring of her cheeks, a look of humiliation, stammering and trembling, and he wasn't getting it. She felt a brief triumph.

This was clearly the way to offset his disgusting perversion – by appearing to enjoy the other man's presence. Just as long as he didn't then look around for another target. If he tired of the game, he might suggest that Bridget imagined herself in the arms of David's father, or the butler, or the man who cleaned the stables, or – the little burst of triumph faded, and she gave a small shiver.

'You can't be cold, Bridget!' Mary-Jo said, noticing. 'You look positively glowing. What a pity we didn't meet you a few weeks ago. You could have come with us to West Point to see David graduate, and make every other new officer jealous!'

Bridget turned to him in surprise. Whatever else she had imagined David Carson to be, it wasn't an Army Officer. He seemed too light-weight, too flippant . . . but she'd once heard someone remark that such men were exactly the right calibre to be officers. They kept cool under all circumstances, and didn't feel things too intensely when everyone around them was being carved up by the enemy. She'd thought nothing of the snippet of conversation before, but she remembered it now.

'Congratulations, David! I had no idea I was dancing with someone so important!'

He laughed. 'Tell me that when we go to war. I'm not sure I shall think myself such a swell then.'

'But I suppose you can't wait, can you?' She said, with sudden perception.

'You've discovered his guilty secret, Bridget. Mother doesn't want him to go to Europe, naturally, but what's the point of having an army career if there are no wars to fight?' Mary-Jo said lightly.

'And you're confident that America will soon be drawn into this one, are you, boy?' Thomas put in. 'I mean our war, of course.'

They all looked at him, and this time, David's grey eyes flashed with something approaching anger.

'*Your* war, Mr Finley? I presume you include yourself in that because of your Irish background, but no matter. All Americans will be called upon to enlist when it becomes necessary, and I think the time cannot be too far off now. Wilson can't dither for ever.'

'Please don't let's talk of war tonight, David,' his mother said quickly.

'We have to face facts, Mother. The war is happening, and we shall lose our country's self-respect if we don't act soon.'

'Not to mention the huge debt that America is owed by our overseas allies for increased imports,' his father, the bank manager, said dryly. 'If Britain loses the war to the Germans, then our assets will dwindle away, and the loss to American economy could be huge.'

'Well, if you men want to talk about the war, we shall talk about something else,' Mary-Jo said determinedly, and Bridget could see how she wanted to protect her gentle mother from all unpleasantness.

It wasn't altogether a good thing, Bridget thought. If David were sent to the front, he could be in danger. Mrs Carson couldn't bury her head in the sand then, and even officers weren't invincible.

A cold feeling ran through Bridget. A new friend had come into her life, and within minutes she was imagining the possibility of losing him. She shook off the unwelcome image as she heard Thomas's boastful voice.

'The war can do my business a powerful bit of good, Carson, as you'll discover when the old bank balance starts accelerating. An American army will be happy to live on baked beans, and I aim to supply 'em.'

'Anyway, Mary-Jo's right,' David added. 'Let's forget all this talk of war and just enjoy being here for these few days. When do you return to Mayfield, Bridget?'

Thomas answered for them both.

'We're staying for three days. I can't be away from my factories for longer than that. Got to keep applying the whip to let 'em know who's boss.' He reached out and caught Bridget's hand in his, blatantly caressing the palm with his fingers in full view of them all. 'Not that I wouldn't want to stay longer with my pretty bride. This is our delayed honeymoon, isn't it, sweetness?'

'Yes,' she had to reply, hot with embarrassment.

'Oh well,' Mary-Jo said practically. 'If Mr Finley's so busy at his factories, there's no reason why we shouldn't meet quite often, is there, Bridget? And when you come to the garden party in August, we can both meet more people quite informally. There will be lots of Daddy's clients, of course, so they'll be highly respectable.'

Except for the comic Finleys, Bridget thought. The silly young girl, whom everyone would be bound to think had married for money. And the grossly overweight husband, with his heavy insinuations about honeymoons and his insults about the heritage of his adopted country.

She caught the twinkle in Mary-Jo's eyes, and knew her friends meant her remark to be a shared joke between them, and felt immensely cheered.

And then, in unbelievably bad taste, she heard Thomas's smooth, oily voice.

'Why don't you get up and give us a song, Bridget?'

Chapter 9

Before she could stop him, Thomas was striding towards the stage in his loud check suit, and she could see a few amused guests glance his way. As if in a nightmare, she saw him speak to the leader of the ensemble, and they both looked at Bridget.

'Dear Lord, what does he think he's doing?' She whispered frantically. It would finish his social standing with the Carsons for certain. Gerald Carson wouldn't care to invite such an oaf to his home, and there might be some doubt as to whether he would want his daughter to be friends with the wife of such a man.

'Do you sing, Bridget?' David Carson asked. 'I'd be charmed to hear you.'

'Oh yes, Bridget. How marvellous to have a real singer in our midst!' Mary-Jo said excitedly.

Her throat felt full. They were being kind, smoothing

over a terrible moment as Thomas wove his way back to them between the tables. Perhaps the ensemble leader hadn't agreed to his suggestion, Bridget thought desperately, but in the next second, her hopes were dashed.

The leader tapped his baton on the side of his music-stand, and cleared his throat. As he began his announcement, Bridget was mesmerised by the way his Adam's apple rose and fell above his stiff white collar and black bow tie. The tails on his evening suit were so long he looked like a shortened penguin . . . She absorbed all these inconsequential facts as if they would make her forget what was really happening. And then she heard her name.

'Ladies and Gentlemen, we are fortunate in having a young lady among us who has been voice-trained at the Connecticut Academy of Music. I wonder if Miss Bridget Finley can be persuaded to give us a rendition?'

Bridget registered two things. The man had called her *Miss* Bridget Finley; and there was polite clapping from the other hotel guests. She could hardly sit there and refuse. It would look too awful and silly, and David and Mary-Jo were encouraging her enthusiastically.

With a savage glare at Thomas, she walked with head held high towards the stage. Her heart thumped. She had never done such a thing before. To sing at the Academy before Monsieur Alphonse was one thing. To sing with a group of her peers in the social evenings there was another. But to sing in public before she was ready . . .

She reached the stage, her palms slightly damp. And for the first time in a very long while, she seemed to hear the echo of someone else's voice in her head. It belonged to her father, Dermot O'Connell, as he played a wild tune on his fiddle for her to accompany him . . .

'Sure and Bridget, me darling, you've the voice of an angel, and someday the whole world will hear it and love you for it.'

The words had charmed her then, and sustained her now. She didn't really believe them, but they gave her the confidence she needed to whisper the name of a song to the ensemble and see them nod.

'Sing into the microphone, Miss Finley,' the leader

murmured. 'Stand a little way back from it as I did when I spoke, and your voice will be magnified for those at the back of the room.'

Bridget looked at the contraption nervously. She had never used a microphone, though there had been several at the Academy for special occasions. The musicians began to play her music, and she saw the expectant faces in the room in front of her, some still chattering, some politely waiting, and then it was as though all her nerves fell away, and common sense took over. If she didn't sing, then she was going to look very foolish standing here completely dumb.

The song was a gentle and poignant one, all about the moon and June, roses blossoming under a summer sky, and of a lost lover returning. She realised there was an extra quality instilled in her voice through the microphone's magic. The purity of her voice blended with the slight huskiness the song demanded, and she was conscious of nothing else but the song until it was ended.

Only then did the room come back into clear focus, and only then did she register the total silence, and the fact that other hotel guests had crowded the doorway of the room, rather than disturb those listening so attentively.

For a second, Bridget was unnerved by the silence, until it was broken by rapturous applause and shouts for an encore. And into her heart came the sheer wonder and glory of it all. Her daddy had been right all along. Her voice had brought pleasure, if not to the whole world, then at least to this small part of it. She could hardly believe it and turned uncertainly to the leader of the ensemble, who said they would play for her all night if she wished.

'Just two more songs then,' she said. 'I think that will be enough.'

It wasn't enough for the guests, but Bridget smilingly offered to sing again tomorrow night if required. It was clear from the applause that they wanted her. She went back to her seat with their praise ringing in her ears. For the first time in her life, she felt fêted and wanted, and more than a little drunk by it all.

'Congratulations, my dear,' said Mrs Carson warmly.

'Bridget, you were simply marvellous,' Mary-Jo exclaimed.

'You certainly were,' David echoed. 'You looked as though you were born to the stage. That's obviously where you should be, Bridget!'

Instead of being married to a disgusting old man, whose unpredictability was just about to assert itself.

'Ah, but I've no intention of letting my wife be ogled by all and sundry,' Thomas said lazily. 'Once was enough, and you should have consulted me before offering to sing again, my dear.'

She looked at him in astonishment. 'But it was your idea, Thomas. You made me do it.'

But he had never expected her to enjoy herself so much, she realised instantly. He had never expected her to show such poise, or to hold an audience captive, or to be a person in her own right. He had expected her to make a fool of herself. The slow fury began to boil up inside her.

'And I have every right to forbid a recurrence,' he continued, his voice light enough to be menacing.

David spoke belligerently, sensing the brittle tension between these two now.

'Surely you wouldn't forbid allowing your wife to give people so much pleasure?'

'David, what Mr Finley chooses to do is his family business, and not ours,' Gerald Carson spoke quickly as his wife and daughter exchanged glances.

'Your father is quite right.' Thomas looked unflinchingly at David. 'And if I say that my wife will not stand up in public for other men to leer at, then she will not. I've no wish to have a whore for a wife.'

Mrs Carson gasped. Her husband put his hand on her arm, but his face was dark with anger, his voice low and controlled.

'You forget where you are, Sir. You'd do better to confine such remarks to pool halls. And I think it best for my family to retire. Good-night, Bridget, my dear, and thank you once again for embellishing this evening.'

'Good-night,' she whispered, hardly able to credit how everything could be spoiled in an instant. Was her husband completely mad?

Mary-Jo leaned forward and kissed her quickly on the cheek, speaking softly so that Thomas couldn't hear.

'He's a pig, but he won't spoil our friendship, I promise you. I'll see you tomorrow.'

They left the hotel lounge in a little convoy of respectability. Bridget's eyes pricked as she watched them go. They were so normal, the way her own family would have been but for the earthquake. She felt her nerves jump. Was the memory of that terrible time always going to haunt her whenever something had occurred?

'I think we understand one another, Bridget,' Thomas said, as if nothing untoward had happened. This cruel unconcern for her feelings was his special gift, she thought bitterly. A gift from the devil.

'I shall never understand you,' she said.

He smiled. 'Then it's as well that we have the rest of our lives getting to know one another. I think we'll retire as well. We mustn't waste any more of our honeymoon on trivialities.'

She flashed him a look of pure hatred. 'Is that what you call this farce? And am I supposed to think of someone else the next time I'm trapped beneath you?'

He glanced around him. They were seated in a corner of the lounge, where the splendour of Niagara Falls could be seen through the large window. They were separated from other tables and the ensemble had struck up a bright tune again. Even so, Bridget's voice was shrill enough to carry.

'Do you want the entire hotel to know of our little pleasures?' He snapped.

She gave a laugh bordering on the hysterical.

'*Pleasures*? That disgusting performance?'

He looked at her through narrowed eyes. Then, as if remembering something else, he spoke suspiciously.

'You didn't fall for the pretty army officer's line, I trust.'

'Would it bother you if I did?'

She saw immediately that it would. It wasn't part of the plan. She was supposed to submit to his will, to profess an enjoyment in sexual activities that would enable him to perform the act. Without her co-operation, he was useless. Without her submission, he might even be impotent. If she

120

appeared to enjoy her enforced sexual fantasies, it might diminish him completely. She gave a small sigh, taunting him, and from his face she knew she was right. It was a weapon to use, if only a small one.

'He's very handsome, isn't he? I wish I could have been at West Point to see him graduate –'

Whatever Thomas might have answered was prevented by two people approaching their table. It was to Bridget that they spoke.

'Miss Finley, my husband and I do thank you for the pleasure you gave us in your singing tonight. Your songs were particular favourites of ours. I hope you and your father enjoy your stay here, and only wish we were staying longer to hear you again. Good-night to you both.'

'Good-night,' she murmured.

Thomas rounded on her when the couple went away.

'So. For the second time today I've heard you referred to as my daughter.'

It had been obvious to Bridget that the ensemble leader had regarded her that way too, since he had introduced her as Miss Finley. She was resentful at the accusation in Thomas's voice now, as if it was all her fault for being young. She was stung into answering.

'Well, you can hardly blame people for making the mistake. You took Kitty and me into your house as poor orphans until it suited you to let everyone think we were your wards. Trying to get your place in heaven, I've no doubt, but nobody forced you into marrying me.'

'No, they didn't. Ours was hardly a shot-gun affair, was it?' He sneered. 'But my other idea will soon stop any nonsensical notions of this singing lark.'

'What idea?' She was always suspicious when he got that calculating look in his eyes.

'I told you I want children. It's not too late for me to have a son to perpetuate the business, my girl. Finley and Son, Canned Goods, sounds mighty impressive. With my brains and your looks, he'll be a broth of a boy, so we'll waste no more time.'

She looked at him in horror as he got up and pulled her to

her feet. She had put the idea of bearing Thomas Finley's child right out of her mind in her anxiety for her sister. Saving Kitty had been her only concern, and the consequences of this marriage had never gone farther than that. Seeing the lascivious look in his eyes now, she shuddered visibly. And seeing it, he merely gloated at her, knowing he had her at his mercy – providing he could do the necessary.

It was a complete failure. He tried to perform the same trick on her, but it didn't work. She was ready for it now, and stared blankly into his eyes while she thought of everyday, mundane things, and refused to let her body be controlled by his mind. She was stronger than he, and eventually he rolled away from her in an impotent fury.

'Never mind,' he growled. 'There'll be plenty of other nights, and we're leaving here in the morning. I'm not having you making cow eyes at that young Carson pup.'

'Don't be ridiculous,' she began, and then held her tongue. Let him think she was taken with the dashing David Carson if it dampened his desire. Her husband was extraordinarily perverted. He actually wanted her to feel sexually aroused by another man, but only if Thomas himself produced the feeling.

She was elated that tonight her will had been stronger than his.

'You'll allow me time to say good-bye to the Carsons, I suppose? Or will you imagine I'm about to be seduced every time a man looks at me?'

'You'll do just as I say,' he snapped.

'Oh, yes, I forgot that you bought and paid for me, with my sister's life,' Bridget said, the words beginning to choke her.

She felt a stinging slap across her face. She felt tears swimming in her eyes as Thomas turned away from her and wallowed beneath the bedclothes like a beached whale.

'I'd advise you to remember it then. You're bought and paid for,' he snapped, and began snoring immediately.

Bridget lay sleepless for a long while, trying to shut out the odious presence of the man beside her. She was thankful to be cutting the trip short, except that she would miss the new friendship between her and the young Carsons.

She was determined to see Mary-Jo again, whatever Thomas said. He couldn't physically tie her down, and there would be plenty of opportunities for them to meet and talk. And at least she would take away with her the memory of one magical night within sight of Niagara Falls when she had felt like a star.

While her husband snored and snorted beside her, Bridget relived those moments. The stirring of ambition inside her was a new and emotional experience, with the realisation that for a little while, she had been somebody. Not just plain Bridget O'Connell, nor Thomas Finley's wife, but Somebody.

They left Niagara early the next morning. The Carsons hadn't come down to breakfast. If Thomas thought to make Bridget feel penned in by him, he had failed. She had tasted a brief moment of independence, despite the fact that he had forced it on her for his own amusement, expecting to see her flounder. She still glowed at the thought. So much so, that when Sheilagh Finley showed surprise at their early home-coming, she couldn't resist crowing a little. That small taste of success had given her more self-assurance than anything in her life so far.

'I was sorry to leave, but you know how Thomas frets over his business,' she said. 'But I had a wonderful evening. I sang on a stage and everyone applauded –'

'What!' Sheilagh Finley stared in disbelief. 'Surely Thomas didn't allow it?'

Bridget laughed. 'Thomas suggested it. I daresay he wanted to prove that his money hadn't been wasted in sending me to the Academy.'

'Well, really!'

Her look told Bridget that she considered singing on a stage in public was the worst kind of depravity. Bridget could tell her of more kinds . . . but she was enjoying Sheilagh's discomfiture too much to let such thoughts disturb her. Perhaps Sheilagh was speculating on whether her new sister-in-law was set on a stage career for the future, and just how much it would undermine her own status in this small town.

'Don't worry, sister dear,' Bridget said tartly, knowing how the term would annoy Sheilagh. 'I've been ordered not to sing in public again. Still, it was very enjoyable while it lasted.'

The words gave her a pang. Her daddy always said she had been born to sing, and now she knew it was so. She pushed the sweet memory out of her mind as Sheilagh continued to glare at her.

'Have you heard of a family called Carson, Sheilagh?' She asked next. 'Mr Carson is the new manager of the Mayfield Bank, and he's asked Thomas and me to his garden party at the beginning of August.'

She saw the other woman's mouth drop open. Bridget was really enjoying this. Sheilagh was obviously wondering just how this upstart could have wangled such an invitation.

'I don't know them,' Sheilagh snapped. 'The invitation was on account of Thomas, I suppose –'

'Oh no,' Bridget assured her. 'Mr Carson's son and daughter are friends of mine, and because of our friendship the invitation extends to Thomas as well as me.'

It was stretching the truth, but she was still smiling at Sheilagh's face as she left her to go to her bedroom. She still used Kitty's old room, insisting that it was hygienic to do so, and that it was the way the best families behaved. And every time Thomas attempted to force himself on her in the next few weeks, she blotted out his image, and thought instead of the joy of singing, and nothing else.

The telephone was the most wonderful instrument. When it rang on Friday morning two weeks later, no one was in the house but Bridget, and she answered it cautiously, knowing it would be a call for Thomas or his sister.

'Bridget, is that you?' A delighted voice said at the other end of the line. A voice with a bright New England accent with the strange flat vowel sounds that Bridget recognised at once.

'Mary-Jo!' She said joyfully. 'How wonderful. When did you get back?'

'Two days ago. I was going to call right away, but there was such a pile of mail to answer. Also I had to help Mother write out the invitations for the garden party, and you know how busy that keeps you!'

'Yes, of course,' said Bridget, who had no idea of the busy life for someone as far up in the social scale as Mary-Jo Carson obviously was.

Her initial excitement at hearing Mary-Jo's voice was tempered now, remembering the embarrassment of their last minutes together at Niagara.

'Bridget, are you well? I was worried when I heard that you'd checked out of the hotel, though Mother said perhaps you'd decided to extend your trip elsewhere.'

'Oh, everything's fine, really. Thomas just decided we'd been away long enough. Business, you know,' she added vaguely.

'After one day?' Mary-Jo said. 'I don't believe it!'

Bridget had forgotten the frankness of her new friend. And why shouldn't she be just as frank? There was no one around to hear. She gave a short laugh.

'Good! That was just the official story.'

'What's the unofficial one? Or shouldn't I ask?'

For a second, Bridget wished she had the nerve to spill out everything here and now.

'No, you shouldn't, I suppose,' she answered. 'Not with me being a married lady, and you still a delicate flower!'

'Untouched by human hand, you mean?' Bridget could hear the grin in Mary-Jo's voice. 'Well perhaps, but we won't go into that now, either. I do want to see you, Bridget. Can you come to tea on Monday afternoon? Mother will be out and David's gone back to his unit. Do say yes!'

'Of course, yes! It sounds wonderful. Tell me the address and I'll be there.'

'The house is called The Cedars on Lemmington Avenue. Any cab-driver knows the way. Come about three, then we can have a good old gossip.'

'All right. I'll see you then.'

She was still smiling when she put the telephone back on its hook. She had a friend and she was invited to tea. She wasn't in the Carsons' black books because of her uncouth husband,

and Mary-Jo had told her glibly to take a cab, as though it was something Bridget O'Connell Finley did every day of the week. And so she would if she wanted to, she thought. Her husband had money, so why shouldn't she use some of it to do as she chose?

She told the Finleys about the phone call while they were eating dinner that evening.

'And you managed to answer it without getting tongue-tied, did you?' Thomas said crushingly.

'Why shouldn't I? I'm not a complete idiot.'

She was no longer so afraid of him. He had trapped her into marriage because of Kitty, but after all that had happened, she felt she owed him nothing. She still missed Kitty so much, and Mary-Jo's friendship could mean a great deal to her. Thomas Finley mustn't be allowed to spoil that.

'What did the Carson girl want?' He asked next.

'I don't know that you have any more right to enquire about my private telephone calls than to open my letters – if I had any,' she amended, which annoyingly took all the sting out of her words, and made Thomas guffaw.

'Don't bother telling me then. Female chit-chat is of no interest to me.'

'She's asked me to tea on Monday afternoon, and I'd like to take a cab.' Bridget spoke quickly, remembering that she'd have to order one and she'd need some money . . .

Sheilagh's eyebrows rose. 'Taxi-cabs cost money. How far is it? Couldn't you walk?'

Without meaning to, she helped Bridget's cause.

'My wife doesn't need to walk anywhere in this town,' Thomas said curtly. 'Look up the number of a cab-owner in the book, and I'll leave you some money to pay for it.'

Sheilagh was bored with all this talk of people she didn't know.

'Thomas, a letter came for you this morning with some sort of seal on it. It's in your study.'

'Why the devil didn't you tell me this before?' He roared, all thoughts of his wife's activities forgotten. He slammed out of the drawing-room to return a few minutes later. He kept the contents of the letter to himself, but it was obvious that he wasn't pleased. He took a slurp of tea, and spluttered it back into the cup, to Bridget's disgust.

'God damn this muck! When will they learn to make decent tea in this country? Go and see to it, Bridget.'

'Let your sister see to it. She's the housekeeper here, not me.'

For a few seconds no one spoke, and Bridget wondered if she'd really said the words. From the dull red fury in Sheilagh's face, she knew that she had.

'You learn fast for a slut,' Thomas grunted. 'But you're right. Do as your mistress tells you, Sheilagh.'

Bridget was nearly quelled by this, but it was too late to back down now.

'I'll take my tea in my bedroom,' she said. 'Please see that it's sent up to me.'

'Anything else – Madam?'

'Not for now,' Bridget said, and swept out.

She related the incident to Mary-Jo on Monday afternoon. She had got over her awe of the house in Lemmington Avenue by then, and also her first hesitance at seeing Mary-Jo again in her own surroundings. And an easy friendship was quickly established between them.

'She sounds hateful,' Mary-Jo said in sympathy. 'Just like her brother. Bridget, forgive my frankness, but I can't understand how you could have married him. You're so beautiful, and you could have had any man you wanted.'

'But the truth of it is, I didn't want any of them. I never intended getting married at all.'

'Not ever?'

'Not ever.'

Mary-Jo looked puzzled. 'I must confess, I don't understand that at all. I thought every girl wanted to be married, but if that was how you felt, why did you do it, Bridget? He didn't *blackmail* you into it, did he?'

She said it teasingly, and then saw the look on Bridget's face. She spoke quickly.

'Look, if you'd rather not say, please don't. I know I'm prying, and it's my worst fault –'

Bridget felt her heart begin to thud. 'I never thought I'd tell anyone, but somehow I need to say it, Mary-Jo. It's like a terrible weight on my mind, and if you're prepared to listen –'

'Isn't that what friends are for? And I *am* your friend, Bridget. Whatever you tell me will go no farther than these four walls.'

Bridget knew instinctively that she could trust this bright, good-natured girl. She spoke stumblingly at first, but gradually it all came out. All about the horror of the earthquake, and her mammie and daddy and little Michael and the Pendletons' house where the O'Connells had been servants, and Father Malley and the Dowdys and their child who had died, and about Kitty. Most of all, about Kitty.

'You must have loved her very much,' Mary-Jo said at last, when the torrent of words ended.

'She was all I had left. So you see, I had to do everything I could for her. I promised I'd always look after her and keep her safe, and that meant marrying Thomas Finley, since that was the condition he put on getting rid of Kitty's child,' she said bitterly.

Mary-Jo put her arm around Bridget's shoulders and squeezed it.

'She must have known how much you loved her. She knows it now, anyway.'

Bridget looked at her through salty tears.

'You're not Catholic, are you, Mary-Jo?'

'No. But that doesn't mean I don't think there's probably something waiting for us somewhere after we die,' she said. 'Otherwise, what's the point of it all? And when Thomas Finley dies, you can have the last laugh by marrying somebody really gorgeous, and he'll be burning in hell while you enjoy his money, and he won't be able to do a thing about it.'

Bridget laughed, in spite of herself.

'You're wicked!'

'I know. But seriously, Bridget, you aren't really anti-men, are you?'

'Yes, I am,' she said vehemently.

'My brother took quite a shine to you –'

'No, he didn't,' Bridget grinned. 'I think David and I could be good friends, but neither of us would want more than that. We both sensed it.'

'Perhaps. Anyway, friends are what we choose. We're stuck with our relatives.' She clapped her hands to her mouth. 'Oh Lord, I've done it again, haven't I? Don't you have anyone of your own left in the world, Bridget? I can't imagine what it must be like to have no one.'

'I have some people in Ireland. One day I shall go there. That's my dream.'

'And you may have children one day too. They'd be yours, wouldn't they? You'd carry them, and you could simply discount old Thomas's part in them.'

She said it so easily that it was just as easy for Bridget to agree, even though the thought of carrying Thomas Finley's child was so distasteful to her. With Mary-Jo, the world seemed a happier place, and if ever she did conceive, she would do exactly as Mary-Jo suggested. She'd simply forget Thomas Finley's part in it, and think of it as some kind of divine conception, and hope that God would forgive her for the sacrilege.

'You hinted that you had a beau. Is it a secret?' Bridget said, quickly switching her thoughts.

Mary-Jo laughed. 'No secret! I've been sort of engaged for years. Our families intended us for one another, but Charlie and I had no intention of living out their dreams. That is, until we found our dreams were the same as theirs.'

'You mean, you really do love each other?'

'Bridget, such a thing isn't impossible! People do fall in love and taste the forbidden fruit, and it can be truly wonderful.'

For this straight-talking girl to hide behind the euphemistic biblical phrase told Bridget that she really did love her Charlie. It made Bridget feel oddly alone. She should be happy for Mary-Jo, yet it only seemed to emphasise her own lack of love. She took refuge in being crisp and businesslike.

'Well, I decided long ago that I'd never love anyone ever again. They're all taken away from you, and it's just not worth the pain of it.'

Mary-Jo looked shocked. 'But that's a terrible way to

think. Losing all your family must have been heartbreaking, but we all have to die in the end, darling, and how you can think of wasting your life by denying yourself the love of a man –'

'I do have a man, Mary-Jo.'

The bitterness in Bridget's voice said more than the words. They looked at each other, and remembering Thomas Finley, neither could find anything else to say.

Chapter 10

'Where does Charlie live, Mary-Jo?' Bridget said, to cover the small embarrassment between them.

'His family still lives in Vermont, but he graduated at West Point with David. You'll meet him at the garden party.'

'When are you getting married?' She was asking all the questions now, and Mary-Jo decided not to probe any deeper into this strange and beautiful girl's mind.

'We thought about next Christmas, but Charlie says that if we go to war, he doesn't want me tied to him before he goes overseas. That's the way men think, but if the worst happened there's nothing I'd want more than to know I belonged to Charlie.'

She curled up on the sofa, her legs tucked under her, and for a moment Bridget envied her secure and happy future. She spoke cautiously to her friend.

'Do you believe America will go to war?'

'I don't see how we can avoid it. Your husband's too old to go, and so is my father, but David and Charlie will go like a shot. They wouldn't even need to enlist, since they're already officers, and the new untrained recruits would need leaders like them.'

She spoke with pride and no trace of fear. Bridget wondered how she herself would feel if it was her brother Michael going off to war all those thousands of miles away. She realised she hadn't thought about him so much for a long while as she had just recently.

If he'd lived, he would be fifteen years old now, and probably longing to wear a uniform. He'd be as handsome as her daddy had been, with blue Irish eyes and waving black hair, and all the girls would be sighing over him . . . No, she wouldn't be at all as anxious to send her soldier brother off to war as this confident girl from Vermont.

'Let's have some more tea, Bridget. Cook has some fresh cream cakes in the kitchen. Why don't we go there and have some?'

And then she might be able to stop imagining how a nearly adult Michael might have looked, and knowing that if he'd survived, he would be the one man in the world able to tear at her heart-strings.

The Carson garden party was to be a grand affair. Once he realised how important it was to be, Thomas Finley spoke of his new friends expansively. He wasted no time in telling acquaintances how he and Gerald Carson had shared a trip to Niagara Falls. By the day of the garden party, any unfortunate listeners might have thought the two men were closer than peas in a pod.

'Will you listen to him?" Bridget said in exasperation on the blazing hot day of the event as he rambled on.

She and Mary-Jo strolled into the refreshment marquee, installed overnight, for some lemon cordial. The garden party was a tremendous success. The Carsons were generous people, the house was simply magnificent, and Mayfield opened its heart to them the way the Carsons opened their home to the town.

Bridget and Mary-Jo looked cool and summery in ankle-length voile frocks of peach and mauve respectively, tied at the waist with a satin sash, and each wore a straw hat with matching streamers to keep off the harshest rays of the sun. Any thoughts of a war somewhere in Europe could not have been further from their minds, and most of the guests seemed determined to keep it that way. If such carefree days were numbered, then they were intent on making the most of them.

Bridget kept as far away from Thomas as she could, though

131

it was impossible to miss the sound of his raucous voice occasionally.

'Most of the guests will be just the same,' Mary-Jo groaned. 'Daddy's list of invitations was very uninspiring, and I wish David and Charlie would arrive. They promised to bring some more officers with them to liven things up.'

She avoided Bridget's eyes. She knew Bridget would be very annoyed if she'd heard the telephone conversation Mary-Jo had had with her brother a week ago.

'For pity's sake, David, bring somebody really cracking. You and Bridget don't seem set for the grand affair, but she needs cheering up after her sister died of that awful accident. See who you can find.'

Mary-Jo kept the truth about Kitty's death a secret between her and Bridget. And then there were signs of new arrivals at the marquee in the grounds of The Cedars.

'At last,' Mary-Jo said with relief. 'Come and meet Charlie, Bridget.'

Charles, or Charlie Keating, was the most aristocratic young man Bridget had ever seen. He wore his officer's uniform with an easy grace, and it was obvious to Bridget from the way he and Mary-Jo looked at one another, that this was going to be a marriage made in heaven, regardless of the manoeuvrings of parents. Charlie was so splendid that he unnerved Bridget a little, but he was extremely gallant too. West Point officers were blessed with more than military training, she discovered.

David made the introductions. There were six officers in all, and apart from himself, all were tall, dark and handsome, causing quite a stir among the Mayfield matrons with eligible daughters. But it was Mary-Jo and her friend who met them first. The names tripped easily off David's tongue, and Bridget was sure she wouldn't remember half of them.

Toby Amery . . . Peter Braceby . . . Louis-Philipe Trenchmont . . . Austen Hamilton . . .

Bridget felt strong fingers curl around hers as she took the hand of the last man to be introduced, and her heart jolted. The eyes smiling down at her were blue and friendly if a little guarded, and although it was just a normal greeting, a *frisson*

132

of something akin to panic gripped her.

Momentarily, she felt totally disorientated. It was just as if the ghost of her brother Michael were looking into her eyes in the shape and form of Austen Hamilton . . . the Michael who had never lived to be a man . . . the Michael who might have been. It was difficult not to look at the man and feel pain, and she averted her eyes from him as he seemed to stare at her with a small frown between his brows. Probably because he didn't usually get such a reaction from a woman, Bridget thought dryly. Probably because with his dark good looks, he expected every woman for miles around to fall instantly in love with him . . .

'We've just heard the greatest news,' David Carson was saying.

Bridget was not listening. She was watching the young officer who was now walking away from her. She couldn't seem to get his name out of her mind, for all that she hoped he'd stay well away from her. Austen Hamilton . . . it was a name rich with history, or splendid with old money . . . it reminded her of the exciting new motorcars filling the city streets and causing havoc among the sedate residents . . . and yes, it was a beautiful name . . . and the fact that she registered it so irritated her very much indeed. Austen Hamilton might resemble her imagined grown-up brother, but he was still a man, and Bridget wanted nothing to do with men.

'What news is that?' Mary-Jo said, hanging on to the arm of her beloved with the special freedom permissible to a betrothed couple.

'We've all been given our commissions at last.'

Mary-Jo groaned. 'Is that good news? It all depends where they're sending Charlie as to whether I agree with you or not!'

Bridget remembered the first time she had met David Carson, thinking him light and superficial, and then suspected a stronger character beneath the gloss. She still suspected it, but there was no doubt that to David Carson and his fellow officers here, a military career was a glorious way to exist, whether or not they were ever battle-scarred. It was all part of the game . . .

133

'Don't keep us in suspense,' Mary-Jo said impatiently. 'At least I know you're not being sent to France, since we're not in there yet.'

Being 'in there' was the latest jargon among the younger New Yorkers. David grinned, glancing at one of his companions.

'More's the pity, eh? Louis still has family in Paris, and his choice would be to get in there right away and stick a bayonet where it hurts the Jerries most.'

'Louis, how awful for you,' Bridget said, above the laughter greeting David's remark. 'You must be very worried about your family.'

'Yes,' he said in his first-generation American accent. 'My elderly relatives refuse to come to America where they would be safe. It can't be long now before the Germans reach Paris, and the old men are just too weak to resist.' He shrugged with Gallic expressiveness.

In an instant the mood of the small group had changed. The war in Europe was suddenly in their midst, because this clean-cut officer with the sallow skin of the French had personal ties with the German invasion of his homeland.

'Louis, I'm so sorry,' Mary-Jo said.

'I'm sorry for letting such gloomy thoughts spoil this day, and you haven't even heard our great news yet!'

'Of course. Your commissions,' Mary-Jo said quickly, her clasp on Charlie's arm tightening a little.

It may have been great news for the boys, but Bridget could see that she didn't really relish being told that her Charlie was being sent to some faraway place, despite her pride in him.

'Louis got the worst of it,' David said sympathetically. 'He's only going to Washington, but there's always a chance for him to be in on the ground floor when the real action comes. Peter and Toby are for the Canal Zone, and Charles, Austen and myself are staying together. We've been assigned to General Pershing's command, though our exact whereabouts are hush-hush at present. With any luck, it'll be on the Mexican border. There's always trouble brewing with the Mexes.'

'Honestly, David, you make it sound as if fighting is fun,'

Mary-Jo said, more crossly than Bridget had heard her speak to him before. Mary-Jo too, was realising that whether they were fighting the Mexes or the Germans, war was dangerous and evil, and men who were still boys could be killed . . .

'Are you young things going to have your heads stuck together in this corner all afternoon?' They heard the re-proachful voice of Mary-Jo's mother. 'Come and meet the rest of the guests and mingle a bit. Everyone wants to meet the dashing young officers, and Mary-Jo, you should know better than to keep them all to yourself!'

Her daughter laughed, linking her arms in those of Charlie and David now, with the others in tow behind. She was a pretty butterfly with an admiring escort. Bridget watched them go with a smile, and just for a second she was shut out of the group, until she realised there was one officer still standing behind her. She turned slowly.

'Hello,' Austen Hamilton said.

'Shouldn't you be with the others? I'm sure some of the Mayfield Mamas will be dying to meet you.'

'That's why I prefer to stay and talk to you,' he said calmly. 'Especially if that's a wedding ring you're wearing on your finger.'

Bridget looked at him warily. This was a strange way for a young man to speak. It was obvious he wasn't one of the flirty breed of young officers who thought they had the gift of instant attraction to every swooning female. But then, she wasn't one of the usual swooning females either.

'You're very observant, Captain Hamilton.'

'And you're very beautiful, Mrs Finley. But just because I've told you so, you needn't be afraid that I'm making a pass at you.'

'I didn't think any such thing.' For some reason the very fact that he admitted it so coolly began to annoy her. Shielded by her status as a married woman, she challenged more boldly than usual.

'Don't you like women, Captain Hamilton?'

He laughed, and it was a rich, warm sound. His face, long and angular and normally handsome, became even more so when he laughed.

'I like women well enough,' he said casually. 'But I've seen enough friends caught up in the marriage trap not to want to become embroiled in the same situation just yet.'

The words left her speechless for a moment, but not for long.

'How very arrogant you are!' Bridget burst out. 'I never heard anything so arrogant in my life. I'll ask you to excuse me, please –'

She felt the touch of his hand on her arm as she was about to stalk away. His fingers were long and sensitive, and since people were coming their way she could hardly snatch her arm from his grasp. She realised how very frankly they had been speaking to one another. They were strangers, and yet they had somehow sparked off an instant rapport with one another that went beyond the usual platitudes strangers exchanged. It was more personal. It was simply streets ahead of the normal conventionalities, as if they had taken a gigantic leap into a kind of intimate friendship, and it sudddenly alarmed Bridget to know it.

'God, Bridget, I'm sorry if I've offended you. It wasn't my intention. I thought I could say what I felt without having to dress things up. There aren't many people you feel comfortable enough to do that with, and I had the feeling you wouldn't be so prissy as some of the women at this shindy. And now I suppose I've offended you again, so I had better offer you my apologies.'

She supposed it was a compliment. She also noticed how easily he slipped into the use of her first name. It was on the tip of her tongue to object, but he'd probably class her as one of 'the prissy young things' if she did, and since she was far from that, she ignored the familiarity. Besides, she admitted that he interested her. A dashing young officer who wasn't chasing women . . . there were few of them, if all that Mary-Jo had told her was correct. And he certainly wasn't one of the nancy-boys . . . Without knowing why she was so certain, Bridget would have staked her life on the fact that Captain Austen Hamilton was normal in every way . . . so he was intriguing. He was definitely intriguing.

*

136

'Will you take a walk around the garden with me, just to prove that you've forgiven me?' He said, clearly not prepared to let her go just yet.

'I haven't said I've forgiven you yet,' she returned smartly, at which she saw a small grin pull at the corners of his mouth. He had a very nice mouth, she thought. The kind of mouth that Michael would have had . . .

'Why do you keep staring at me?' Austen demanded.

Bridget gave a small sigh. Somehow she had the feeling that no one ever got away with anything with Austen Hamilton. If something bothered him, he wanted to know the reason, and would worry away until he got satisfactory answers. She glanced into his eyes, intending to fob him off with some frivolous comment about every girl being flattered by the attentions of an officer, when something stopped her. This was a man who demanded the truth, and got it.

'If you really want to know, you remind me of someone,' she said.

'Someone special?'

'My brother – but it's a long and complicated story,' and she only told it to very few people.

'We have plenty of time,' Austen said.

Out of the corner of her eye she saw Thomas holding court with a small group of bemused gentlemen. He was red-faced and excitable, and no doubt looking to the main chance to produce a few extra dollars.

Austen followed her glance and saw her hesitation.

'Your father?' He said, the way everyone did.

'My husband,' she answered, her eyes daring him to make any snide comment.

'Then you have my condolences,' he said gravely.

For a startled second, Bridget stared at him in amazement, and then she had to bite her lips to stop herself laughing. He was outrageous. He was impossibly arrogant, and yet he was like no one she had ever met before. He had the look of Michael as Michael might have been, and yet Austen Hamilton was essentially himself.

'Shall we take that walk?' He asked, and without answering, she fell into step beside him and walked in the fragrant

137

gardens towards the rose bower, where the scent of the full red blooms was powerful and heady.

'Have you been married long?' He asked.

'Only a few months.'

Already it seemed like an eternity. She glanced at him sideways. She waited for the beautiful, meaningless, flirtatious line that so many other gallants might have said. 'Then I'm a few months too late' . . . She didn't want him to say it. It would ruin the opinion of him already forming in her mind. That here was a special man, who deserved a special woman in his life, and who apparently was in no hurry to find one. And that made him extra-special.

'And now you're regretting it,' he stated.

Bridget spoke coolly, while her heartbeat quickened. It was as if he knew her too well already.

'I don't know what you base such an opinion on, Captain Hamilton. My personal life is none of your affair – or has David Carson said anything to you – ?'

She was suddenly aghast. Surely David wouldn't have been indiscreet enough to reveal the awfulness of that night at the hotel at Niagara Falls when Thomas had made such a spectacle of himself?

'David Carson only told me that you were a beautiful woman, and I hardly needed anyone to tell me that. And my name is Austen. Are you always so formal with your friends?'

Bridget laughed uncertainly. She rarely felt at a disadvantage with anyone these days, but this man unnerved her a bit. She admitted to her surprise that she was enjoying the cut and thrust of their conversation. It made the blood flow more swiftly in her veins, but she challenged his last remark.

'We're hardly friends, yet, Captain Hamilton. I don't know you. We've only just met, and after today, we'll probably never meet again –'

'If I thought that, it would be my loss. Still,' he gave a mock sigh. 'I believed you to be an intelligent young lady.'

She stopped walking, exasperated.

'Just what is that supposed to mean? You do talk in riddles, Austen –' his name was on her lips before she could stop it, and she chewed her lip in annoyance.

'It means that I don't believe in wasting time on trivialities, and I suspected that you were of the same opinion. If two people like one another and intend to be friends, they may as well begin by being honest with one another. And my guess is that you didn't marry for love.'

'Are you suggesting that I married for money?' She said furiously, freely agreeing that they had gone too far to pretend politeness any more. If she stood back for a moment and listened to herself and this stranger, she knew she would think of it as the most extraordinary conversation she had ever had.

'I doubt that. You're not a gold-digger. There had to be another reason, but I suspect this is not the time for you to tell me of it.'

Bridget felt a shiver run through her. He saw too much, or guessed too much.

'If you don't mind, Captain Hamilton, I'd like to rejoin my friends,' she said deliberately. 'My husband will be wondering where I am, and likes me by his side on these occasions.'

If she sounded pompous and stuffy, she didn't care. If he thought she was reacting like a frightened virgin at this unusual approach – she didn't care about that either. She suddenly needed to live by her own code. She needed to feel safe . . . and she certainly didn't feel safe with this man.

He'd as good as told her he wasn't looking for marriage, nor presumably an affair, since he'd made no attempt to flatter her with pretty speeches. He'd practically insulted her . . . But Bridget was honest with herself too, and all her instincts told her she had met someone who could mean something in her life. And that really scared her. It scared her half to death.

'Then I think I had better return you to your husband, Mrs Finley,' she heard Austen say gravely.

She glanced into his eyes again for a moment, and they were no longer Michael's eyes, but the eyes of a virile and powerful young man. She realised she had felt more alive in this brief time spent with him than ever in her life before. And he was about to let her go, to return her to Thomas, her jailer . . .

'Thank you. It's best,' she said, her voice steady.

They walked together in silence, and beyond them the sounds of the garden party seemed to float all around them, as if they came from another dimension. They moved towards the sounds, and Bridget knew that once she was swallowed up in them, Austen Hamilton would be lost to her for ever. And she hadn't said all that she wanted to say to him yet. Their conversation had barely begun, and it would probably take a lifetime to say all that they needed to say. She took fright at the force of her own thoughts, and as they reached the end of the rose bower, she moved slightly away from the officer.

'Wait a moment, Bridget,' Austen said.

Before she could guess what he intended, he picked two crimson rosebuds. He tucked one discreetly in the neckline of her frock, and her skin tingled where his fingers touched her soft flesh. The scent of the roses drifted into her nostrils, and involuntarily she touched the flower. Her fingers touched a thorn, and a small drop of blood appeared. She brushed aside the *frisson* of fear, thinking of it as a bad omen, as Austen tucked the second rosebud in the button-hole of his jacket.

'Before the rosebuds die, I hope our friendship will be established,' he said. 'I very much want to see you and talk to you again.'

'I'm married, Austen –' *And you know nothing about me. You don't know all the terrible things I've done. Lying about my sister's death. Being forced to give in to a blackmailing husband. Wishing him dead . . .*

'And I swore never to let a woman come between me and my career, but circumstances sometimes have a habit of overpowering our own intentions. Don't you believe in destiny?'

Whatever she might have answered was stopped by the appearance of Mary-Jo looking for Bridget. Her eyes widened a moment as she saw the matching rosebuds, but she spoke lightly.

'Did you pick that one for me, Austen? Whether you did or not, it might be more discreet if I tucked one in my frock too. Unless you want to give me yours, Bridget, since Austen and I are old friends – ?' She added teasingly.

'No – I'd like to keep it. The scent is so heavenly,' Bridget

140

said quickly. She pushed away from her mind the confused thought that whether or not she ever saw him again, she would press her rosebud in a book and remember Austen Hamilton.

He telephoned her the next morning. Thomas was out, and Bridget had become used to answering the telephone now. She felt her heart give a tremendous jolt when she recognised the voice. It was so clear, that he was instantly beside her.

'I've been thinking about you all night,' he said without preamble.

Bridget felt her heart beat more strongly. She didn't dare believe the implication of what she was hearing, and took refuge in jocularity.

'That's ridiculous. You'd be half-dead from lack of sleep.'

'I am. That's why I want to see you. I hate unfinished conversations and we left too many things unanswered. You wouldn't want to send me into battle with pegs holding up my eyelids, would you, Bridget?'

'That's blackmail,' she accused him. 'I didn't take you for a man who resorted to such ploys to persuade a woman to meet you.'

In the brief silence that followed, when she was aware of the sound of his breathing and her own, Bridget knew that she was accepting a second meeting. In her head, she knew she should refuse. She was already married. She was tied to a man she loathed . . . but in her heart she knew she had already discovered a sense of empathy with this man.

It was something she had never anticipated. She remembered reading somewhere that when a stony-hearted woman found her soulmate, nothing could stand in their way, because the gods had decreed it . . . She physically shivered, because suddenly it was as though she was no longer herself at all. Not the calm, capable woman she had always believed herself to be, who had always rejected love . . . and even at that thought, she told herself severely that Austen Hamilton had said nothing about love. If he had, on so short an acquaintance, she would certainly have rebuffed him.

He was speaking again, in that rich voice that seemed to be making her toes curl. 'Then I'll tell you the truth. I want to see you again for the simple reason that I can't stop thinking about you. You said we don't know each other, and that's what's wrong. I want to know you, Bridget. Give me the chance – please.'

She ran her tongue around her dry lips.

'What do you suggest?' She registered that her own voice was husky.

Hadn't he said he wasn't interested in marriage? Marriage between them was out of the question anyway. She was a Catholic, and her church forbade divorce. So what did he expect of her? And was it more than she was prepared to give? *Anything* was more than she was prepared to give . . .

'I have two weeks' leave. The others all have their own pursuits, and folks hereabouts, so I don't care to encroach on them too much. My family home is away in Idaho, by the way. Mary-Jo tells me you're alone a lot, and it would give me a great deal of pleasure to share some time with you. Besides, I have to get something straight in my own mind, and you're the only one who can help me with it.'

'And what's that?' She asked suspiciously.

Austen laughed. She liked the sound of it so much. It was completely different from Thomas's guttural smirking. It was fresh and young and endearing.

'If I told you right now, we'd have nothing left to talk about, would we? So what do you say, Bridget? Will you share some of your time with me?'

Her mind cleared a little. He wasn't demanding the impossible. He was only asking for a little of her time.

'Yes,' she said, ignoring the way her heart was jumping, because suddenly the vista of sharing time with this beautiful man was the most desirable thing in her life. It wasn't love. She didn't believe in love at first sight. She didn't even believe in love, except for other people.

But she was too honest not to admit that she was drawn to Austen Hamilton. Like a moth to a flame . . . and if she didn't agree to see him during these two weeks, she might never see him again.

'There's a little park quite near to Mary-Jo's house,' she went on in a rush. 'You understand that it would hardly be proper for me to say I'm going out alone to meet an officer, Captain Hamilton –'

'Of course.' He picked up the message at once. 'You will officially be calling on your friend Mary-Jo, but instead, you and I will continue our interrupted conversation in the park. I know the place. There's a lattice-work gazebo in the centre of it, if I remember correctly. I shall wait for you there at around three o'clock this-afternoon.'

She was flustered again. Bridget Finley, who *never* got flustered by the attentions of a young man, was all thumbs as she stammered that she'd be there, and replaced the telephone receiver carefully on its cradle.

She wasn't just going to meet a young man that afternoon. She was meeting him clandestinely, and there was a wild excitement deep in her veins because of it. Because of *him*. And the shivering inside her wasn't due to cold or fear or even guilt, but to something more primitive that, as yet, Bridget didn't even want to consider.

She continued staring for long minutes at the panorama of the gardens through the long windows, and saw none of it. If she'd felt sensible enough to analyse her feelings at that moment, she knew that the only coherent thing to enter it was the wanton thrill of knowing that Austen Hamilton wanted to see her again. That, and the fragrance of roses that seemed to be filling her senses.

Chapter 11

The feeling of unreality was still with Bridget as she prepared to leave the house that afternoon. She had changed her clothes a dozen times, and told herself how foolish she was being. She was behaving more like Kitty than herself . . . and the sweet memory of her sister sent her into even more confusion. Was this how Kitty had felt, all those reckless times she had fallen in love . . . ?

The way the word kept infiltrating into her mind alarmed

Bridget even more, and she wondered even now, whether she should simply fail to turn up in the park . . . but she knew it would take more than wild horses to keep her away. She was too intrigued by the man, and by her own bewildering feelings.

And seeing Austen Hamilton again, away from the colour of the garden party, might put him into a proper perspective. He was merely a dashing young officer, and she was a married woman. Those were the two things she must keep uppermost in her mind.

It wasn't as though men hadn't made passes at her before. They had, plenty of times. And always she had frozen them off by a caustic word or a frigid look, before and after marriage. She had had her chances, but she had never taken them, or wanted them, until . . .

He was at the park before her. She saw him standing in the lattice-work gazebo, with the sun slanting through on him. He looked – he looked simply stunning, Bridget finally admitted. And when he heard her approach and turned towards her, he merely held out both hands to her in greeting, and she reached out and felt his fingertips meet hers.

'I prayed that you wouldn't change your mind,' Austen said gravely, and the flippant retort vanished from her mind.

'I should have done,' she said, almost inaudibly.

He drew her to one of the bench seats in the gazebo, his hand still lightly holding hers. In the sunlight his eyes were very blue. It struck Bridget that in colouring they were extraordinarily similar. He with his blue eyes and dark hair that matched that of the Irish O'Connells.

'You've made me very angry, Bridget,' he said, startling her. This was obviously to be no seduction scene, whatever she might have thought.

'In what way?'

'You've come between me and my good intentions. You're going to think me very selfish, but would it horrify you to know I've asked you to meet me as a kind of exorcism, to try and prove that you're not as beautiful and desirable as I remembered from yesterday?'

Bridget's heart thudded. She gave a quick smile. For some

reason it was beyond her to make light of this, and the coincidence was too vital . . .

'It wouldn't horrify me at all. I came here for the same reason –' she blushed immediately, realising what she had said. 'Dear heaven, don't take that literally, Captain Hamilton. I didn't mean I thought you were desirable – nor beautiful – and now I know I've made it even worse! Can we please begin all over again – ?'

He laughed softly, and this time his hand covered her own more firmly. 'There's nothing I'd like more. I think we both understand one another, Bridget –'

She pulled her hand away. 'No, we don't. I don't understand why I've made you so angry, and I – I must confess I no longer understand myself. I shouldn't be here at all –'

'But you are here, and so am I. And what are we going to do about it?'

Her sister Kitty might have brazened it out, delighting in egging him on to a meaningless flirtation. Bridget was totally incapable of encouraging such a thing. If this was to mean anything at all, she knew in her heart that it had to mean everything. And she was still torn between loyalty to her wedding vows, and the undoubted way this stranger was breaking down all her carefully nurtured reserves. If there had been ice around her heart all these years, then Austen Hamilton had the power to melt it all.

'Will you believe me when I say that I've never approached a married woman in this way before, Bridget?'

She nodded slowly, believing him because she wanted to trust him so much.

'Will you tell me one thing honestly?' He persisted. 'Why *did* you agree to come here?'

'I told you,' she said. 'The same as you – to exorcise my feelings –'

Austen's mouth was unsmiling. She studied the shape of it and felt that she would recognise it blindfold among a hundred other mouths. Was this how love affected you . . . ?

'Then we both admit that we have feelings for each other,' he stated.

'We can't. How can we? Until yesterday we were strangers.'

'And you must have thought me very brash. I was covering up how much the sight of you affected me, Bridget. I had sworn to dedicate my life to being a good officer, with no entanglements, and then you came along.'

'Is that how you think of women, as entanglements?'

'I choose not to think too deeply about women at all, except as dance partners. I don't mean to be disrespectful, but I've seen how beautiful women can disrupt a man's thinking. They come between him and his duty.' She could hear the anger and frustration in his voice again.

'What arrogance!' Bridget said, just as angrily, because it seemed as if he both wanted and resented her for just being what she was.

They looked at once another, and simultaneously, they began to laugh. And without quite knowing how it happened, she was in his arms, and breathing in the scent of his uniform and tasting his mouth, and drowning in an embrace such as she had never known before.

When reason caught up with her, she struggled out of his arms, and sat a foot away from him as if she had been stung by a hornet.

'That should never have happened,' she said, her voice shaky.

'Then perhaps we'd better part at once, because I shan't trust myself not to let it happen again. Is that what you want? Is it, my lovely Bridget?'

She closed her eyes swiftly, seeing a future without him. Seeing the madness in continuing this – this affair – because in Bridget's mind, that was what it was, or soon would be. A scandalous affair that had already begun.

Married women did not meet officers in lonely parks. Good Catholic wives didn't entertain the thought of unfaithfulness. But the unfaithfulness was already there. It had happened, whether it was physical or not. And she knew instinctively that her life would never be the same again, because she had glimpsed and recognised the fact that she was not as frigid as she had always believed.

146

She could feel love, and even if she had only met Austen yesterday, it didn't matter. She felt as though she had always known him; in her heart and soul she had known him, and she couldn't bear to lose him now.

'So we go on,' Austen said quietly, as if she had spoken, and she knew that all her feelings must be mirrored in her eyes.

'I'm unused to intrigue, Austen,' she murmured in embarrassment. 'I have no experience outside my marriage –'

'Do you think I don't know that? I only have to look at you, Bridget, and your face tells me everything. But don't ever be afraid of me. We have two weeks before my leave is over, and that's all the time in the world. We have no need to rush anything. I'll court you, my love.'

Hot stinging tears rushed behind Bridget's eyes at the sweet phrase. Courtship was destined to end in marriage, but for her and Austen there could be no such fulfilment. If anything, the thought served to make her realise even more what she had missed in her life. Tied to an old man who taunted her, when somewhere in the world there had been Austen Hamilton. And he had arrived too late . . .

'Tell me about your husband,' Austen said. 'I can't think it's a happy marriage, and that makes me grieve for you.'

'Does it? Forgive me if I sound naive, but I thought that when a man was attracted towards a married woman, he'd want the marriage to be unhappy –' she floundered.

'To further his own cause, you mean,' Austen finished for her. 'Yes, my love, you know little about men. We can be as diverse as women, and if we love someone, we don't like to see them unhappy.'

Bridget held her breath. Was he saying that he loved her? When he waited for her to speak, she did so haltingly.

'I don't love my husband, but I made my vows before God and the priest. I'm torn between what I know is right and what the world sees as wrong.'

'Can I tell you how it looks to an outside observer?' He said, his arm sliding around her shoulders.

'Please do,' Bridget said feverishly.

'I see an oafish old man whose beautiful young wife has stark misery in her eyes whenever she looks at him or speaks of

147

him. I don't know how he persuaded you to marry him, Bridget, but do you honestly believe you owe him your loyalty?'

She gave a little sigh and involuntarily leaned her head against his shoulder. It felt so good to feel cherished, to feel that someone cared about her.

'I owe him nothing,' she said in a low voice. 'He took from me all that I had left, and my dearest wish would be that I never had to see him again as long as I live.'

She could hardly believe she had really said the words. And to a stranger . . . but this was a stranger who had suddenly become more of a confidant than anyone she had known before. She felt she could tell him anything and he would understand. It was the first time in her life she had felt that way about a man, and it made him very special to her.

Bridget became aware of laughter coming from one of the pathways in the park, and as several people strolled past the gazebo she moved discreetly away from Austen on the bench seat. They had had the place to themselves for some while, and now there were intruders into their solitude. She hated them for breaking into their seclusion.

'I think I must go home,' she said reluctantly.

'Then I'm afraid I shall have to let you go,' Austen said. 'Tell me, do you ever go to the theatre with your friend Mary-Jo? Tomorrow night, perhaps?'

'I never have, but I suppose –'

'And instead of going to the theatre, you and I will hire a car and drive far away from Mayfield and have supper at a small country inn. Would Mary-Jo approve?'

Bridget's skin tingled at the daring idea. Thomas would never think of contacting Mary-Jo to check up on her movements. It would be a perfect arrangement, and Mary-Jo would certainly cooperate. The last of her inhibitions vanished. She longed to see Austen Hamilton again. And if two weeks were all they had, then she would see him every possible minute of them.

'I'll arrange it with Mary-Jo,' she said in a breathless voice. 'My husband is frequently away and cares nothing about what I do with my time. And taking supper at a country inn sounds wonderful.'

'Good. Take a taxi to Mary-Jo's house and ask the driver to drop you at the gates at seven o'clock, and I'll be waiting with the hired car.'

She felt suddenly nervous. 'You sound as if you've done this kind of thing before!'

Austen took her hand in his and fondled it in his palm. He looked deep into her eyes.

'I assure you that I have not. I'm surprising myself, because it's all so easy to make devious plans when you want to be with someone so much.'

'Austen –'

He leaned forward and kissed her mouth, tracing the soft curves of it with his finger as if to imprint the memory of it in his mind.

'I doubt if you'd believe me if I said I love you, Bridget. You'd say it's too soon and we don't really know each other and all the rest of the conventional arguments. So I won't say it, but I think you know it all the same.'

Yes, she knew it. Instinct told her it was true. Glorious, magical instinct, and she silently blessed the day of Mary-Jo's garden party for sending Austen Hamilton into her life.

'Tell me properly when we know each other a little better,' she said, knowing she could afford to wait, because they had all the time in the world . . .

Mary-Jo was enchanted. Bridget had called straight round at The Cedars after she and Austen parted.

'Of course I'll stand cover for you, Bridget, any time you like! I'll even go to the theatre tomorrow night, to be on the safe side. I couldn't be more thrilled for you, and Austen's such a darling. He doesn't usually bother much with girls. David said it's because he comes from a military family, and they have a tradition that career comes first and marriage much later. He's a brilliant officer, but an even more gorgeous man. You *are* lucky.'

'Then you don't think I'm being very wicked?'

Mary-Jo hugged her, seeing her need for approval.

'Darling, you deserve every bit of happiness after all that's happened to you. No, I don't think you're wicked. I think you and Austen should take this chance and to blazes with bloated old Thomas!'

Bridget felt suddenly as reckless as her friend.

'Tell me, do you think it's possible to fall in love with someone when you've only seen them a couple of times? I ask in a purely impersonal way, of course –'

Mary-Jo's eyes shone with warm affection as she looked at Bridget.

'There was nothing impersonal about your face when you came here this afternoon. You were absolutely glowing, and if I didn't already know you were in love with Austen Hamilton, I'd have known it then.'

'You already knew – ?'

'I knew it yesterday, but you had to discover it for yourself, didn't you? I'm so glad, darling, so terribly glad for you. It must compensate for all the awful things that you've gone through.'

Bridget looked down at her hands and felt them tremble.

'You know, I never even knew what it was like before. Being in love and loving someone so much you want to be with them all the time. Even wanting to say his name as often as possible because it brings him near to you.'

'Just avoid saying it too much at home, Bridget,' Mary-Jo warned. 'Old Thomas isn't daft, and you don't want him getting suspicious. You'll have to say you're spending more time with me in the next few weeks.'

And as Austen had said, it was surprisingly easy to find ways of being together. That next day when Bridget was supposed to be at the theatre they drove through the sweet-scented orchards of the area, where the fruit hung heavy on trees and bushes, and the bees sang a harmonious song to summer. They drove into the country, to a white-painted inn, where the landlord served them with a candlelit supper, and was clearly charmed by the sight of the handsome young officer and his lovely companion. And Bridget gazed into Austen's eyes through the haze of candlelight, and knew that she had never been truly alive before meeting him.

They drank red wine, heady and sweet, and she felt her head spin. And she didn't want it to be so. She wanted to keep every memory sharp in her mind, to bring out on the bad days and remember . . .

'What are you thinking?' Austen asked.

'Just that I wish I could hold this moment for ever and never lose the magic of it,' she said honestly.

His hand reached for hers.

'You owe me yours now,' she said. 'A thought for a thought.'

'I was thinking that I want far more than mere moments with you. I want you always. And right now I don't want this night to end, because I know I'll have to return you to –'

'Don't say it,' Bridget said quickly. 'Don't bring his name into our lovely evening.'

As long as they didn't mention him he didn't exist. Nothing existed for them but each other, and she desperately wanted to keep it that way. However hazardous the future, today was theirs and theirs alone.

'Bridget, this isn't enough. I thought it was, but I know I want more. I want all of you. Do you understand what I'm saying?' He took his hand away, as if to convey to her that he had no intention of forcing her into anything.

And yes, she understood. And yes, she wanted it too. She wanted to feel his young body merging with hers, to be part of his flesh and to know that he was part of hers. She wanted him with a wild and unexpected flame of desire that took her breath away.

'I know what you mean,' she mumbled.

He looked at her flushed face. 'And I ask too much,' he said slowly. 'I can see it in your eyes. And I promise I'll try not to rush things. I'll keep a tight rein on my emotions –'

'But not too tight,' Bridget said tremblingly. 'Women have feelings too, Austen.'

He said nothing for a moment, and then –

'You know I love you, don't you?'

'And I you. I know it's madness, but I know how I feel, and I do love you, Austen.'

151

'Tell me you feel the same in three days' time,' he said unexpectedly.

'What do you mean?'

He spoke abruptly. 'I'm going to visit some friends, and I'll be away for three days. It's a sudden decision, but it's for both our sakes. If we both feel the same when I come back, then my Bridget, I think we shall have moved into a different phase.'

'Three days!'

She shouldn't have spoken so involuntarily. Nor with the disappointment so obvious in her voice and her eyes. She gave her feelings away, to Austen and to herself.

'If you look at me like that when I came back, I'm not sure I shall be able to keep control of myself, Bridget,' he said, and this time it was his voice that was unsteady. 'But I think it's best that we give ourselves this time apart.'

'But we've only just met –'

. . . and we've only just found each other, out of all the world . . .

'Dearest, I do have to see these people. I promised my parents. They're old family friends, and they'd be hurt if I didn't say hello.'

She couldn't beg him to stay, even though the words brimmed on her lips. Bridget was staggered by the force of her own feelings for this man, whom she hardly knew, and about whom she wanted to know everything. There was so much to say and discover about one another. They only had two weeks, and now that was to be sliced away . . . without thinking, she reached across the table and caught at Austen's hand.

'Promise me you'll get back quickly, and telephone me right away.'

'It will be the first thing I do,' he said, and they both knew that these three days were only going to be a respite after all. It wouldn't change anything. Austen busied himself in pouring more wine for them both, and spoke more casually.

'I've been staying with a buddy here in Mayfield, but I think I'll rent a room somewhere when I come back. It will be more convenient.'

'Yes,' Bridget said. She looked away, aware of the pulse beating in her throat, aware of what he was offering and she was accepting. They parted that night as friends, but knowing they were destined to be lovers.

Austen had been gone for the longest two days of Bridget's life when Thomas Finley came storming into his dining-room in time for the evening meal. For a second Bridget's heart leapt, wondering if he could have heard something, wondering if his wrath was directed against her . . . the next second she discovered that it wasn't.

'Blasted officialdom,' he bellowed. 'All this blarney over allowing consignments of beans to cross the Atlantic, and now they're insisting I go to Washington for talks. Lot of fuss and nonsense –'

'You know you enjoy it, Thomas,' his sister said tartly. 'It makes you feel important to be called to Washington and rub shoulders with the bigwigs. You'll socialise with some of the best people!'

He allowed a grin to slide from his lips. Sheilagh knew him too well. He glanced at his wife, silently breaking bread and keeping her eyes lowered.

'And what of you, me darling?' He said sarcastically. 'What do you say to your husband being away for a week?'

'A week?' Bridget stared, her thoughts jumbled.

He guffawed. 'Well now, I do believe you're going to miss me. I'm sorry I can't take you with me, Bridget, but this is men's business, and you'll just have to find other playmates while I'm away. The Carson girl will oblige, I'm sure.'

'Don't worry about me, Thomas –'

'I shan't,' he said rudely. 'I'll be too busy with more important matters.'

And far too busy to notice the glow in the eyes of his young wife as she contemplated a whole week without her loathsome husband, and a week when she'd be free to make the most of the time with someone else . . .

Austen telephoned the minute he got back, giving her the address of the house where he'd rented a room.

'We could have a quiet supper here tonight, or we could behave properly and go to a theatre out of town.'

Bridget knew exactly what he was offering, and for once she

was listening to her heart instead of her head.

'I'm not much of a theatre person,' she said. 'The tickets would be wasted on me. I can be with you about seven o'clock, Austen.'

'Will it be all right at home?'

'Perfectly.'

She hung up slowly. As yet, she hadn't told him her husband was away. As yet, she didn't know where this evening was going to end. She merely told Sheilagh Finley she was seeing Mary-Jo that evening, knowing that Sheilagh would be in bed long before Bridget was expected back.

And long before then, she had melted in her lover's arms, all pretence of this being mere friendship at an end. One look at Austen's face told her all she wanted to know. He had missed and wanted her as much as she had missed and wanted him. She entered the room he had rented, and a new era of her life began.

In his arms she learned the ecstasy of love at last. She discovered the real glory of a man's flesh against her own, the power and the gentleness, and the joy of giving and receiving pleasure. She was herself at last, but even more than that, she was Austen Hamilton's woman. In a mystical way she felt more wife to him than ever she had done to Thomas Finley, and she was totally alive for the first time since the earthquake took nearly everything away from her.

'God, but I love you,' Austen spoke roughly against the soft white skin of her breasts. 'I never believed I could love anyone so much, my dearest girl.'

'Nor I you,' Bridget whispered. 'I never thought myself capable of loving anyone, but you've shown me a different world, Austen.'

'A world that I want to share with you always,' he said, and felt her shiver in his arms. He looked into the aroused dark pools of her eyes gently. 'Don't be alarmed, my love. I know your beliefs are unshakeable, but we can still dream. And your husband won't live for ever, please God. If it's blasphemous to say so, then I hope your God will look kindly on us and forgive me for it.'

'I've had the same thoughts,' she admitted softly. 'But

never more so than now that we've found one another.'

'And when it happens, no matter how long it takes, we'll be together for always. We have to believe that, Bridget. Believe in a happy-ever-after for us.'

'I will,' she said fervently. 'I must.'

From then on, they shared every minute that they could in the small room on the outskirts of the town. Mary-Jo was their cover, and Thomas was too involved with meetings at his factories after his return from Washington to spare any time on his wife's activities. And then Austen's two weeks' leave were over, and Bridget was bereft. And still Thomas noticed nothing, not even the letters that were delivered through Mary-Jo, and tucked beneath Bridget's pillow to be read over and over again.

Austen was sent to Texas, with David and Charlie. Their darling boys were still together, and it made a special bond between Bridget and Mary-Jo. Both felt now that they were bound by more than friendship, and it was enough to put added stars in Bridget's eyes. And there was Christmas to look forward to.

The officers had Christmas leave. By then the air was crisply cold and snowy, and there was to be a big party at The Cedars. The Finleys were invited, but Sheilagh preferred to visit her own friends, to Bridget's relief. Then, to her glorious and guilty delight, Thomas got an attack of gout and decided to stay at home, insisting tetchily that Bridget must make an appearance at The Cedars to represent him.

'I'll take my pills and probably sleep for two days until the pain's gone,' he snapped. 'You'll manage to enjoy yourself, I daresay. Young David Carson can escort you to and from the house, or you can stay overnight with the Carson girl if the weather worsens. You won't disturb me.'

'Thank you, Thomas,' she said carefully. 'I'll probably stay with Mary-Jo. The roads are getting treacherous, and it's hardly fair to drag David away from his own party.'

'Suit yourself then,' he replied, and gave himself up to his pills and his brandy, a mixture that might be lethal, but certainly dulled the pain.

Bridget could hardly believe it. She was going to the Carsons' party alone, and she wasn't expected back that night. And Austen would be there ... during the evening she was persuaded to sing, and she chose just one song that had significance for only two people. 'A Rose Within My Memory Box'. She sang it in a husky voice, and if she kept her eyes averted from Austen Hamilton for most of the time, it was only because she was certain that if she looked at him, everyone must surely guess ...

The party was a great success, and afterwards ... she and Austen left the house in the crisp, crunching snow in a hired car. They slipped and slid up the steps of the old house to the same rented room as before, where a fire crackled in the hearth, and there was a deep pile rug in front of it.

· They undressed each other, finding delight in every touch, every caress.

'I've missed you so much,' Austen said. 'I never thought three months could be so long –'

'And having to pretend at the party that we were no more than good friends, when all the time –'

'When all the time I was burning to hold you in my arms and feel your body next to mine, and to blazes with all the pretence,' Austen finished.

They were so in tune, in thought, mind and body. Completely naked, they slid to the soft fireside rug with one accord, seeking and giving pleasure, wanting nothing more than this. Just to be together, to make glorious uninhibited love ... and to wake up in the morning still warmed by each other's arms.

'I'm not dreaming, am I?' Bridget said drowsily, not even remembering how they found themselves in the big bed, snuggling down together. 'This is real, isn't it, my love? You're here with me?'

'Now and always,' Austen said huskily. 'If not in body, then always in spirit, my Bridget.'

They discovered that making love in the chill of a December morning could be just as exciting. The embers of last night's fire had died, but love burned brightly in that small room, and each believed that everything they did brought them one step nearer to the heaven they sought.

Chapter 12

April 1906, when the earthquake had struck San Francisco, had been the most terrible time in Bridget's life. She had vowed then that she would never allow herself to love someone, because to love someone only meant heartache in the end.

Selfishly, she had sought to guard herself against that heartache, and she shuddered now, knowing that had she continued to do so, she would have denied herself the ecstasy she had found with Austen.

Neither would she have believed, in that time of acute misery, that a decade later she was to hold a glorious secret, spectacular enough to obliterate everything bad that had gone before.

It was at the end of January that Bridget first suspected something was amiss. Her monthly cycle failed to arrive at its usual time, and her breasts began to feel full and heavy and to tingle when she brushed against them.

She had prayed that she wouldn't have to bear Thomas Finley's child, and when he made his unwelcome visits to her room, she bit her lips and refused to acknowledge what was happening. But he hadn't been responsible for what was happening now.

Bridget knew with a glorious certainty that if she was pregnant, it would be Austen's child. It would have been conceived on Christmas night, and with the curious simplicity of her belief, Bridget was certain that God and the Holy Virgin had blessed their union, with or without the ties of marriage.

It was not without guilt that she knew she must pretend to Thomas Finley that the child was his, and that when it was born, she must persuade him' that the child was either premature or late . . . even so, the guilt was twofold.

157

Thomas would gloat at his accomplishment . . . and Austen would be denied the joy of bringing up his own son.

But Bridget also knew that there was no way her marriage could be dissolved without bringing disgrace on herself and more importantly on Austen. And she was as fiercely proud of his military position as his own family, and would do nothing to threaten it.

At first she said nothing to anyone of her suspicions, but eventually the news was too much for her to keep to herself. She dared not write to Austen yet, and besides, the news was best kept for telling him in person, the next time he had leave, which he would naturally want to spend in Mayfield . . . but she had to tell someone . . .

'Bridget, how wonderful!' Mary-Jo said, her eyes shining. 'And I must say you seem more pleased about it than I expected. You look absolutely glowing, but I always thought you didn't want a child –'

'I didn't want Thomas Finley's child,' Bridget replied, and at the steady look she gave her friend, Mary-Jo drew in her breath.

'You mean — oh, Bridget, you mean it's Austen's – ?'

Bridget gave a secret smile.

'It's mine and Austen's and I can't tell you what it means to me. To have something of his, here beneath my heart, something that we've created with our love –'

She pressed the softness of her belly, not yet showing any signs of pregnancy, but where the baby already grew and thrived. Bridget was as sure of that as she was of breathing.

'What are you going to do?' Mary-Jo asked, not seeing the future as clearly as Bridget.

She spread her hands. 'What I have to do. Thomas must believe that the child is his, but Austen and I will know the truth. And when it becomes possible we'll be married and he'll be able to formally adopt the child. It will be a Hamilton then, as it has every right to be.'

She sounded so confident that Mary-Jo didn't have it in her heart to show her doubts. It wasn't that she didn't trust Austen. She knew him for an honourable man, and it was obvious that he and Bridget were truly in love.

But it all seemed so hazardous, and quite alarming to see how being in love had changed Bridget from being a somewhat cynical young woman into someone quite besotted. Mary-Jo prayed that everything would turn out as well as her friend expected.

'Have you seen the doctor yet, Bridget?'

'Not yet. I shall go in another month, and then I suppose I shall have to break the news to Thomas.' She spoke reluctantly, suppressing a shudder at the thought of his reaction. 'He'll be quite stupid about it, of course. He'll think himself no end of a clever fellow, and I shall have to suffer it all.'

'And you're sure he'll believe it's his child? I mean, you and he – you have – you know what I'm trying to say –' Mary-Jo began delicately.

Bridget laughed shortly. 'Yes, I do and we have. I had to make sure of that, so that he'd believe it was his child. Don't despise me for it, Mary-Jo, but I couldn't see any other way.'

'Of course I don't despise you,' Mary-Jo gave her a hug. 'I just pray you'll be able to carry it through. He's not completely brainless, is he?'

'No, but he's become very forgetful lately. He habitually drinks brandy with his pills, despite the doctor's warning that it's dangerous. He certainly doesn't remember how many times he's come to my bedroom in the last few months. And he wants a child so badly, I'm sure he won't think to question when it happened.'

But as the weeks passed, Bridget knew she couldn't put off the telling for too long. It was probably her imagination, but both Thomas and Sheilagh seemed to look at her quizzically from time to time. It was just as if they knew she had a secret, and neither liked to be on the outside looking in.

. Bridget made an appointment to see the family doctor at the end of February, and had the pregnancy confirmed. That evening, she told Thomas. To her absolute horror he burst into noisy tears. He was barely sixty years old, but his blubbering face was that of a senile old man, Bridget thought, fighting to hide her disgust as he clawed her to him and held her fast.

'Ah, Bridget, me darling, sure and I never thought 'twas going to happen at all! I know I've been a randy old sod at times, but I hope you'll forgive me for it, and God knows it'll be the happiest day of me life when I hold me own Irish boyo in me arms –'

She twisted out of his cloying embrace.

'There's something else you must know, Thomas,' she said in a shrill voice. 'Doctor Sawyer was very insistent that we're not to continue doing anything in bed until well after the child is born. It could endanger the child, and neither of us would want that, would we? You will remember what I'm saying, won't you, Thomas? Unless you want to put the child at risk –'

He shook his head vigorously, moving back a step as if even to touch her would put the child in mortal danger.

'No, no, of course not. We'll do whatever you say, dearest,' he blathered. 'I'm just delirious at the thought of having a son, and for knowing that the Finley name will survive in this country. It's been my dream, and now it's coming true, thanks be to the Blessed Virgin.'

The Finley name will survive with the child for just as long as you do, Bridget thought hysterically. Just until Austen and I can give him his rightful name of Hamilton, you old goat . . .

She took refuge in silent derision, realising now that the ordeal of telling him had been much more unnerving than she had expected.

It had been inspirational to ask Doctor Sawyer about the child being at risk if Thomas continued his heaving performances in bed. She chose her words carefully and said them with great embarrassment, but it left the doctor under no illusions that the act was violent and hurtful to her, and then it was easy to persuade him to say what she wanted to hear. It was essential to have him say it, should Thomas himself ever question his marital rights.

She wondered if Thomas might even be secretly pleased that he wasn't expected to perform for some months. He had frequent difficulties lately, which only accentuated his pathetic attempts in the bed of his young wife.

*

Bridget ached to tell Austen that they were expecting a child. If only he could get leave soon ... she wrote to him regularly, but she couldn't have letters from him delivered to the house.

She only had news of him through Mary-Jo. His letters to her were out of date by the time they reached her, enclosed in David Carson's to his sister, and then transferred to Bridget. It wasn't satisfactory, but it was the only way they felt able to communicate safely.

To fill in the empty days without Austen, Bridget tried to keep up with world events. The newspapers were constantly filled with dire warnings that America was on the brink of war, but they had been saying it for so long now that people began to take them less seriously. All the fighting between the European nations seemed to be happening in France, and France was far away.

But there was turmoil of a different kind in Ireland, and it began to arouse the patriotism of loyal Irish immigrants living on American soil. Even such braggarts as Thomas Finley. The newspaper reports were written by salacious journalists who made the most of the Easter blood-spilling.

'They don't call it that, of course,' Thomas roared, purple-faced. 'The Easter Rising they call it, which some would probably call blasphemous, but seems as good a name as any for it. Listen to this – ''a group of extremists seized the centre of Dublin and proclaimed an Irish Republic'' – and about time too! ''The bitter street fighting lasted four days, and at the end of it only one of the new republic's leaders was spared execution, namely Eamon de Valera.'' Good for him. Ireland for the Irish, I say!'

Bridget felt utter disgust at his gloating voice.

'If you feel so strongly about it, why aren't you back there, helping to make Ireland prosperous?'

'Don't talk so daft, girl. You know nothing about business or politics,' he snapped. 'This de Valera fellow can thank God or the devil that he was born in America. According to the paper his father was Spanish and his mother Irish, so he's got plenty of spunk in him, and I reckon he's capable of great things.'

'How can you be so tolerant, when hundreds were killed in

the fighting, if all that's said in the paper is true!' Bridget persisted, shocked at the thought of so much Irish blood being spilled by their own countrymen.

Thomas looked at her with a superior sneer. 'Because independence is everybody's dream, you ninny, but I don't expect a mere girl to understand such things –'

'I'm twenty-four years old, Thomas, and hardly a girl any longer –'

'No. You're soon to be the mother of my child, and I think you had better remember that and calm yourself, Bridget,' he said sharply. 'We don't want to bring on any accidents.'

'I could say the same to you,' she went on, just as tart. 'Getting yourself mixed up in street brawling in Mayfield is hardly a dignified way for the owner of Finley's Canned Goods to behave!'

His eyes narrowed, and for a few seconds he looked taken aback.

'So you heard about that, did you?'

Sheilagh Finley came into the room in time to hear the last heated remarks and added her own ten cents' worth.

'We could hardly avoid it, since it was reported in the local newspaper! I know you chose not to tell your wife or myself, Thomas, but we can both read! We're not illiterate,' she said, heavy with sarcasm. 'Irishmen fighting their own is shameful enough, but Irishmen fighting Americans on their own soil is just plain lunacy. You can't possibly hope to win such a majority –'

'Will you bloody women stick to your embroidery and leave men's business to men!' Thomas bellowed, blundering out of the room in a fury. Sheilagh turned on Bridget, incensed at the way she'd egged Thomas on to such apoplexy.

'He's right in many ways, Bridget, and you shouldn't upset him so. We all owe something to our homeland. You left Ireland when you were a tiny child, and can have no feelings for it the way older people have, but the least you can do is to respect loyalty when you see it.'

'Loyalty!' Bridget began to laugh. 'You have a very misplaced loyalty to your own brother, Sheilagh. All he's interested in is whether or not he'll sell a few more cans of beans, and how to turn any situation to his own advantage. He should be careful who he upsets among his American friends, instead of professing this stupid loyalty to a country he turned his back on.'

Mary-Jo came to see Bridget unexpectedly in the middle of March. One look at her friend's ashen face, and Bridget knew something was terribly wrong.

'What is it?' Bridget said, filled with dread.

'Don't worry, it's none of our boys,' Mary-Jo said quickly. 'But there was a telephone call from David last night. He's terribly upset. Something ghastly has happened to General Pershing's family –'

For a shameful second, Bridget could only feel relief that it was nothing to do with Austen – or David or Charlie. And then she was overcome with remorse at her own guilty relief as Mary-Jo babbled on incoherently. Mary-Jo rarely babbled, which meant that this news was affecting her very badly.

'For God's sake sit down and talk more slowly, Mary-Jo. I can't understand a thing you're saying.'

They sat down together on the sofa, holding hands, and Bridget could feel the other girl's trembling.

'General Pershing arrived at El Paso to join his troops, and that's where David and Charlie and Austen are right now, Bridget. I still don't know the whole story, but while they were there General Pershing got news that his poor wife and three little daughters had been burned to death in San Francisco. Only his son survived, and I just – I just can't stop thinking about it –'

She sat silently weeping, and it was some minutes before she recovered enough from her own imagery of it all to register the stark horror in Bridget's blue eyes. Bridget sat rigid, too numb to speak. In her mind, it was the holocaust of the earthquake all over again. And worse than that – it was a portent of doom . . . she felt Mary-Jo shaking her, and she felt her teeth chatter.

'Oh God, Bridget, don't look like that. Oh, I wish I hadn't come and told you. Darling, it's not *Austen*. Nothing's happened to him, or to any of our boys. They're all right – at least for now –' she trailed away uncertainly.

'What do you mean – for now?' Bridget felt the voice being dragged out of her. She didn't want to ask. She didn't want to know, but masochistically, she *had* to know.

Mary-Jo was frightened, seeing the way Bridget's face looked so white and marbled. Bridget was in a vulnerable and delicate state of health, and if anything happened to Austen . . .

'Tell me, Mary-Jo,' Bridget said.

The words rushed out. 'David says that General Pershing's taking troops into Mexico to try and capture Pancho Villa.'

'The revolutionary,' Bridget breathed, knowing of his reputation. 'And that includes Austen?'

'And David and Charlie. They'll all be together like the three musketeers. That's what David said, and he sounded cheerful enough about it. I'm sure they'll make their own luck, darling,' Mary-Jo spoke with optimistic desperation.

They looked at one another, and out of nowhere Bridget heard herself laugh, a shrill, bitter sound that seemed to echo around the room.

'Do you know what's really stupid, Mary-Jo? All this time I've been frantic that if America goes to war Austen will be sent to France to be killed. And all the time, the bloody Mexes have been there sitting it out, just waiting to get at him –'

She felt Mary-Jo shaking her.

'Stop it, Bridget, for God's sake. You frighten me when you talk like that!'

But she didn't need Bridget's predictions to frighten her. She was terrified enough for the safety of her three best boys, and the days that followed were something of a nightmare. News filtered through so slowly. There were victories and defeats on both sides, but Pershing's army was by far the stronger, and finally had no real difficulty in overcoming the Mexes. Both girls relaxed a mite, even though details of American casualties were abysmally slow in being reported. And until they knew for certain that their boys were safely back on American soil again . . .

When it came, the news was all the more horrific because all three names were reported in the newspaper casualty list at the same time. Not the actual details . . . the details came later from Louis, whom Bridget had met at the Carson garden party, and who thought that Mary-Jo and that nice friend of hers would want to know the full facts before her brother was sent home from a field hospital somewhere in Texas.

Through Louis, they learned that David Carson had a badly gashed leg that fortunately hadn't needed amputation as had been feared at first; that Charlie Keating had had his knee shot up, and was disabled enough to be due for an honourable discharge; and that Austen Hamilton had had the top of his head blown off.

It was difficult to find out more details. Bridget had no rights as far as Captain Hamilton was concerned, and she was too shocked to even think properly. She told Thomas she had to spend time with Mary-Jo because the girl was so distraught at hearing the fate of her brother and his friends. In reality, Mary-Jo was the only person she could bear to be with.

'David managed to speak to me on the telephone again,' Mary-Jo told her a few days later, in the hushed tones people used when talking to the bereaved. 'They're sending Austen home to his family in Idaho, and he's going to be given a military funeral. It's what his family want for him, Bridget –'

'All nice and tidy,' Bridget said in a brittle voice. 'The battle-hero will be suitably honoured, but in the end he's still just as dead –'

'Darling, you have to accept it,' Mary-Jo said gently.

'Do I? Do you know what really gets to me, Mary-Jo? All those people who loved him – his parents and sisters, all weeping over his memory, and trying to be brave and proud when they drape the Stars and Stripes over his casket, and lower him into the ground. And none of them knowing that somewhere in Mayfield, away in New York State, part of him still lives.' Her voice caught on a sob as she pressed her hands protectively over her rounded belly. 'And I can never tell them –'

Her face contorted at the image of it all. She would know the day and the hour, and in spirit she would be there, somewhere in a small town in Idaho, where all that was left of her love would be buried.

'Bridget, do you ever wonder if you should tell his family about the baby?' Mary-Jo said uncertainly. 'It may comfort them, and put things right for you –'

'How can I tell them!' Bridget raged, quick to turn from despair to anger. 'You must be mad to suggest such a thing! If I'd been Austen's wife –' the sweet misery of knowing such a thing would never be possible now, overcame her, and she couldn't speak for a minute. 'But I'm not and never will be, and he'll never know that I was carrying his son. And it may comfort his family, but there's no one left to comfort *me*!'

'Oh Bridget, I'm so sorry,' Mary-Jo whispered, seeing her anguish.

'I'm sorry too. Didn't I always tell you it ended like this for me?' The brittleness was back again, the breathing deep and painful.

'Everything I love is taken away from me. All I have now is this.' She covered the swell of the baby with her hands again. Her thoughts switched again. 'Will you find out Austen's family address for me, Mary-Jo?'

She looked bewildered. 'But I thought –'

'There's one thing I have to do. Austen will understand.'

If Mary-Jo thought her mind was turning, so be it. But she obtained the address for her, and Bridget took a bus-ride to another town especially to order a huge wreath of expensive red roses to be sent packed in ice to Idaho in time for the funeral. She didn't attach a card. There was no need. Austen would know who sent them.

'I don't know what's wrong with you lately, Bridget,' Thomas said tetchily several weeks later. 'I know you've had an upset because of the Carson girl's brother and fiancé being wounded. And some other young fellow got killed as well, didn't he? But that's no reason for you to move about the house like a ghost. You'll do yourself and the child no good at all, and I mean to send you to Doctor Sawyer to give you a tonic. You'll do as I say now.'

She looked at him listlessly. She didn't care what happened to herself, but there was the child to think about. Austen's child. She had to keep strong for their son. She murmured that she'd do as Thomas said and see the doctor tomorrow. He looked at her sharply.

'I suppose you've heard that the Carsons are leaving Mayfield shortly? I see that you have, and I suppose that's another reason for the glum face these days.'

'Mary-Jo told me,' she said with an effort.

Mary-Jo had tried to keep it from her as long as she could, but in the end it had to be told. Her father had been offered the branch managership of his old bank in Vermont, and as it happened it suited Mary-Jo very well.

She and Charlie Keating had grown up in the same small town, and now that Charlie was discharged from the army, he too wanted to go back to his family home where there were career opportunities waiting for him in his father's business. They would all be leaving, and although it wasn't all that distant, to Bridget Vermont seemed as far away as the moon.

Mary-Jo and Charlie were making tentative plans for their marriage, but that too was something kept secret from Bridget. It was too cruel to talk about wedding plans when Bridget was still suffering her loss so badly. Once David was discharged from the Texas field hospital, he would have a brief leave and then return to his army unit, and The Cedars was about to be put up for sale.

It was a bright April morning when Bridget finally felt able to take a short walk in the park where she and Austen had met so long ago. She was thankful there were very few people in the park. She didn't want people, but for some reason she had felt compelled to come here today, to smell the freshness of the early spring in upstate New York, and to remember . . .

'. . . I doubt if you'd believe me if I said I love you, Bridget. You'd say it's too soon and we don't really know each other and all the rest of the conventional arguments. So I won't say it, but I think you know it just the same . . .'

Did she really hear his beloved voice saying the words, or was it merely a sighing of the breeze through the network of young trees? And her own, answering . . .

'. . . Tell me properly when we know each other a little better . . .' . . . and remembering how she had been so joyous at the time, thinking that they had all the time in the world . . . and now she had nothing. She looked up at the latticework gazebo with brimming eyes, willing Austen's image to come to her, just once more . . . to be with her just once more, to feel him and touch him and love him . . . and there was nothing.

'Damn you, Austen,' she sobbed in a low, broken voice. 'Damn you for making me love you so much, and leaving me alone. How can I go on without you?'

She leaned back against the white latticework, exhausted. She was so tired. She slept badly these days, and the baby frequently lay awkwardly against a nerve, making her jerk awake. It was pressing on her now, making her feel uncomfortably heavy. It was sending little shooting shafts of pain through her abdomen, and she had to sit down for a few minutes, her legs suddenly weak.

She closed her eyes, shutting out the sun. Was this the darkness Austen had experienced, when the sunlight was lost to him for ever . . .? She seemed filled with morbid thoughts today. She couldn't rid herself of them, and this idea of coming to the park probably hadn't been such a good one after all. It would be best if she went home.

Standing up was an effort, and she couldn't get her balance for a minute. She put out a hand to steady herself and missed the railing. The small pains in her belly were more persistent, and even before she went hurtling down the steps of the gazebo, Bridget already knew what was happening. Even if the fall didn't accelerate it, it was inevitable. She should have known it. It was April, and all that she had left was about to be taken from her.

Chapter 13

'It was my child too, and you don't see me bleating about it the whole time,' Thomas Finley said irritably. 'It's three months now, Bridget, and it's time you pulled yourself together. We've done it once, and we can always do it again,

168

but for God's sake, stop that endless *crying*!'

She wished she had the nerve to scream the truth at him. It wasn't his child that she had lost. It was hers and Austen's. Hers and her lover's . . . Three months ago. Spring had become summer and she had never noticed it. The awful lethargy wouldn't leave her. She received letters nearly every day from Mary-Jo, who had gone to live in Vermont and begged Bridget to recover in time for her wedding to Charlie Keating early in September. Her letters always tried to be bright and funny, to cheer Bridget up.

'Charlie's being so brave, and is determined to walk with just a stick at the wedding, and David says he'll try not to limp on the day or the groom and his best man will look like bookends. I do so want you to be my matron of honour if you can bear it, Bridget,' Mary-Jo wrote. 'But if you can't, then please just be there. It won't be the same without you, darling.'

Every word twisted Bridget's heart. Every word seemed to evoke a different meaning from the one Mary-Jo intended. She didn't mean to hurt . . . it would be the very last thing she meant . . . but no, she didn't think she could bear to be matron of honour. And how could she even bear to be there, when Austen wasn't? And nothing would ever be the same without Austen, either . . .

'You'd better stir yourself soon,' Thomas went on relentlessly, seeing her stare unseeingly at Mary-Jo's latest letter. 'We'll stay at an hotel for a few days when the Carson girl gets married. I want to take a look at some prime building sites in the area with a view to expanding. I've no intention of moving house, mind, so don't get your hopes up. Winters in Vermont can be colder'n hell, so I'm told, but business not being all it could be at present, we'll have a look-see.'

Bridget didn't care what he did, with his business or himself, as long as he didn't bother her. So far he hadn't, and she had insisted on sleeping permanently in separate rooms since the miscarriage, because she would only keep him awake at night with her crying . . . but an hotel room in Vermont reminded her only too well of Niagara Falls when she had first met the Carsons, and it couldn't be too long before Thomas would insist on his rights. He had expected to have a son in the fall, and he was eager for another.

She finally wrote to Mary-Jo, explaining that it was more than she could do to stand up beside her and be matron of honour, but that of course she wouldn't miss her wedding for anything. She and Thomas would be staying over.

'You must come and visit with us, Bridget dear,' Mrs Carson said over the telephone wire. 'There's no reason for you to stay at an hotel –'

'It's very kind of you, but it's what Thomas would prefer, Mrs Carson. He has business to see to, and keeps some odd hours –'

'Then if he's out during the day, you're to spend some time with me, my dear. Mary-Jo will be away on her honeymoon, and I won't hear of you being in a miserable hotel room all alone.'

'All right. Thank you.'

She waited, hearing the muffled exchange of voices in the background until Mary-Jo's cheerful voice came back on the line again.

'Mother will love taking you around in her new car, Bridget. She wants to show it off, and your visit will give her a lovely excuse. She'll be missing me, so you can be her daughter for a few days.'

'That's nice,' Bridget said politely.

She hung up carefully when they had run out of things to say. She didn't want to go to Vermont. She didn't want to hear the wedding music begin in the church of Mary-Jo's choice, and to stand up with the rest of the congregation and see Mary-Jo come walking down the aisle on Mr Carson's arm, pale and ethereal and reminding her of the way it should have been for Austen and herself. She didn't want to stay in an hotel, and have to sleep beside Thomas, grown fatter and more gross this past year. She didn't want to see David and Charlie and remember that there had once been three musketeers and now there were only two . . . she didn't want them to be embarrassed because of her, knowing they were alive and Austen was dead . . . she didn't want the familiar ache of loneliness to start all over again.

They left Mayfield in Thomas's sleek smooth car. Sheilagh hadn't been sent an invitation, because she was nothing to the Carsons. When they reached the New England countryside the trees were as fiery-red and flame-gold and brilliantly beautiful as everyone always said, and Bridget wished she could be as enthusiastic about them as she was meant to be. She was still numb inside, missing Austen. Missing their baby. But she wouldn't let Mary-Jo down. She couldn't face being matron of honour, but she wouldn't be a grouch either.

They checked into their hotel on the night before the wedding, when there was to be a small party at the Carson home. The hotel was a facsimile of the one at Niagara Falls, except that it didn't have a balcony. There was nothing to look at here but trees, anyway, she thought irreverently.

Bridget dressed without caring how she looked, knowing she was thinner than before the miscarriage, and that the Carsons were probably going to be shocked at the change in her. As it happened, slenderness suited her, fining down her cheek-bones and putting alluring hollows into her neck, and in the slim-fitting green frock she made a willowy picture. Mary-Jo hugged her at once, holding her at arm's length, with the shine of tears in her eyes.

'Oh, I've missed you, Bridget! How are you, darling? How are you really? Your letters tell me nothing.'

'I'm all right. I'm surviving,' she said.

'But that's all?' Mary-Jo queried.

'Isn't that enough? It's better than nothing.'

'Come and see the wedding-gifts. They're all laid out in the drawing-room, and Mother's showing them off to some aunts and cousins from out of town. We had a wonderful wedding-shower last week, and I really wish you could have been here. You could have met all my old schoolfriends from Vermont High, and I know you would have loved it. What do you think of the new house, by the way? Not bad, is it? It used to belong to some eccentric professor of art, which explains the rather elaborate iron-work on the stairs. He was into sculpture in a big way.'

Bridget suddenly realised that Mary-Jo was talking too fast. She was saying too much, because there was really

171

nothing much to say. In the five months since they had left town, their relationship had changed. They were no longer the inseparables they had been in Mayfield. In letters, they could still open their hearts to one another, but face to face, there was an indefinable barrier between them. Each knew too much about the other for comfort, and without the continuity of companionship, they had drifted apart without even knowing it. Mary-Jo had her old circle of girlfriends, and had been drawn back to them as though she had never been away. Bridget still had no one.

Mrs Carson was worried by Bridget's appearance and said as much to Thomas. She didn't like the man, but he was Bridget's husband, and therefore deserved courtesy.

'She felt the loss of the child very deeply,' he said. 'I never realised how much she wanted a baby, but I daresay the best thing is to have another as soon as possible.'

'You're probably right,' Mrs Carson said, deciding to steer the talk away from the subject with this type of man, before it got rather too indelicate. 'I propose taking Bridget around the country while you're busy, Mr Finley, with your approval. I'm sure that fresh air and different scenery will revive her a good deal.'

'Fine, fine,' he said heartily. 'And tomorrow's the big day for your little lady?'

'It is.' She gave a tight smile. The phrase was patronising in the extreme, and she turned thankfully as more guests arrived for the evening's party, and she could hand Thomas Finley over to someone else. She looked around to see that Bridget was all right, and found her gazing at a bowl of full-blown red roses on a side table, drinking in their perfume as if she were intoxicated by them.

'Bridget dear, David's just arrived. Will you come and say hello to him?'

'Of course.' She moved away from the roses, their scent lingering on her fingers where she had touched the petals. It was perfectly natural for roses to fill the house, but somehow it was as though Austen was there with her, and she felt calmer than at any time since that dreadful day when she had heard the news.

She thought that she would even be able to face tomorrow more easily now. It was Mary-Jo's wedding, at which she had confidently expected to be the matron of honour, and for Austen to be Charlie's second supporter, but none of it was meant to be. But she wasn't going to spoil it all by sad looks, and she greeted David with kisses and smiles, and he said how well she looked, and that she could pass for a model in a smart society magazine any day with her new slim-line figure.

'I'm not sure that you should be saying such things to an old married lady!' She teased him.

'Ah, but you're an old friend, so that cancels out the impropriety,' he said. 'Anyway, when did you and I take any notice of that old conventional nonsense?'

'Never,' she admitted, thinking how nice he was, and what a shame it was she couldn't have fallen in love with him after all. But they were simply the best of friends, as near to being brother and sister as two unrelated people could be, and when he asked how she was feeling, she didn't need to prevaricate with him, not even as she'd done with Mary-Jo. They sat in a corner of the room and looked out at the September evening, ablaze with the first glory of the New England fall.

'I miss him terribly,' she said blankly. 'I think I shall always miss him, but it gets less painful as the weeks go by. It doesn't get easier, just less painful. Sometimes I wish it didn't. It's as if I need the pain, David, because without it I shall feel guilty at starting to live my life again when Austen's not here. Does that make any sense?'

He was gentle, not rushing her. 'Of course it does. And losing the baby? Are you over that?'

'No.' She looked at him. 'I might have been, but – you knew it was his, didn't you?'

'I guessed. I was so sorry, Bridget, so devastated by it all. You can't know –'

He stopped, his mouth twitching for a second, and she saw how it must have been for him too, with one friend killed and the other maimed, and he the one to come out of it tolerably unscathed. His was a strange guilt too. She put her hand in his for a moment.

'It certainly makes you grow up the hard way, doesn't it?' She said finally.

'I'll tell you what. Let's make a pact to be each other's prop for tomorrow,' David said. 'Every time one of us feels panicky, we'll look at each other and remind ourselves that there's somebody who understands. What do you say?'

'I say you're a good friend, David,' she said. 'All right. You're my prop and I'm yours.'

Mary-Jo's wedding-day was as wonderful and emotional and chaotic as any other wedding-day, yet everything fell into place. So that when the beautiful golden-haired bride appeared on her father's arm, with the handsome bridegroom – made even more charismatic by the heavy stick on which he leaned – awaiting her at the altar, Bridget was grateful for the secret wink the best man managed to throw her way. Dearest David, her prop . . .

It was only later, when the honeymooners had been sent away with tin cans rattling beneath their car and rice thrown all over them, that Bridget realised she had lost her best friend. While she had been the married one, it had made no difference to the closeness between her and Mary-Jo. But all that was changed now. Mary-Jo had married for love, and she and Charlie would have a closeness that no one else could or should, divide.

Her nerves were even more brittle when Thomas tried to coax her into some intimate caresses in the hotel bedroom that night, with stupidly arch comments about a wedding making a man randy, she turned on him with loathing.

'Can't you see I can't stand you near me?' She said. 'Mary-Jo's wedding only reminded me of the way it happened for me, and I'm not proud of it.'

'Would you rather I let it slip to certain people just why you married me? How do you think Sheilagh would take it? Or the pious Father Rourke – ?'

'You wouldn't tell them. I know you wouldn't! It would condemn you for taking Kitty to an abortionist. You'd be arrested.'

It sounded sweet, except that she was perfectly sure he'd drag her along as an accessory. And how could she be sure that he wouldn't tell people in such a way that he would come out of it completely exonerated? Leaving her the guilty one. Even as she thought it, she saw his leer, and his words echoed her thoughts.

'You'd better be nice to me when I want you to, Bridget, or else you'll never know just when the story will come out, will you? And I want you tonight.'

He stopped bantering and became aggressive, and she knew it was useless. He owned her body and soul, and she had to submit. The blackmail went on . . .

One thing she could be thankful for was that she didn't seem particularly fertile. That, and the fact that during the following months, through that year and into the next, Thomas's amorous attempts had been either infrequent or didn't come to fruition. She could be thankful that his business was fluctuating. While American millionaires were created by those canny enough to cash in on munitions work for war, the prosperity of Finley's Canned Goods hadn't kept up with expectations. Any anxieties kept his sex drive abysmally low, to Bridget's relief.

He followed the progress of British and French activities keenly through the newspapers. In December of 1916 there was an election, in which Lloyd George became Prime Minister, replacing Asquith. In America, Woodrow Wilson was re-elected President, partly because of his avowed intention to keep America out of the war in Europe.

'The bastards!' Thomas raged, reading the latest news in early February of 1917. 'The bloody Jerries have started submarine warfare. That'll be it. We'll be in it up to our necks now, and the sooner I get my factories turned over to making shells the better.'

'Is that all you can think of?' Bridget said in disgust, her thoughts immediately going to David Carson and the anxiety his family would be feeling.

'Any man with sense thinks of number one first, and to hell with the rest,' he still scanned the blazing headlines. He swore loudly, and both Bridget and Sheilagh knew there was more to come.

' 'Tis the beginning of it all.' He stabbed a finger at the

newsprint. 'Wilson's severed diplomatic relations with Germany. The staff of the American Embassy in Berlin are to be sent home. The bloke writing this piece says that most of the Americans there have been under suspicion and surveillance for months.' He crunched the newspaper in his hand. 'They tell you nothing until 'tis too late to do anything about it –'

'What would you do, anyway?' Bridget said scornfully, grown bolder now than when she was an immature frightened girl. 'You've waited too long already, and you had plenty of chances to turn your factory over to munitions. You just wouldn't spend the money.'

'You can be bloody sure I'm not leaving it behind for you to spend, me darling!'

'I don't want your money. I don't want anything of yours –'

'Mother of God, can't we ever have a bit of peace around here?' Sheilagh joined in, red-faced. 'The two of you go on like a couple of Dublin fish-wives, so you do.'

Bridget flounced out of the room. She hated the two of them. She put a telephone call through to Mary-Jo, anxious to know how soon David would be affected by the news, but there was no reply. She felt frustrated and alone, and somehow this war that was no concern of hers took on greater importance in her mind. Her friends were going to be sent overseas to fight, and overseas meant Britain and France, and Ireland was part of it all. Neutral, perhaps, but still caught in the crossfire, since presumably her young men had enlisted too, in the peculiar burst of patriotism that was inherent in all men. Conscription had come to Britain a year ago. Soon it would surely be America's turn.

She went up to her own room, got out paper, pen and ink, and began a letter to a stranger.

'Dear Aunt Maudie,' she began, 'I hope that you'll remember me. I'm Bridget O'Connell – only I'm Bridget Finley now, and have been married to an Irishman called Thomas Finley for a year and nine months –' she experienced a small stab of surprise. So long . . . 'We live in New York State and Thomas owns a company called Finley's Canned Goods which cans and markets beans. Americans are very fond of beans, Aunt Maudie.

'I'm sorry to tell you that my darling sister Kitty is dead. She had a bad fall and died just after my marriage.'

The paper blurred as she wrote the words, and she dashed the tears away.

'It seems so likely that America is about to enter into this terrible war now, and I felt a great urge to be in contact with someone of my own over there. My dearest wish is still to come to Ireland someday. I still remember how softly my Daddy spoke of the green meadows and know how he missed it.

'It would make me very happy if you would write to me, Aunt Maudie. It would be a link with the place I think of as home. Your loving niece, Bridget O'Connell Finley.'

She stared at the words. They were stilted, but she couldn't think of any other way of saying what she felt, other than becoming maudlin. And this woman was still a stranger, despite the blood ties between them.

Bridget heard Thomas's car engine roar into action, and the wheels skid as he drove much too fast out of the drive. She went to his study and rummaged for a stamp, putting on several to cover the postage rate to Ireland, having no idea of the right amount. She went to the mailing-box and slipped the letter inside, and only then did she realise how tense she felt. But if only Aunt Maudie would reply, she would feel she had someone of her own who cared for her at last. And why she hadn't done this before, she couldn't think. Or yes, she could. Before, there had been Kitty, and then Mary-Jo, and Austen . . .

She realised something else too. People were out on the streets in Mayfield and there was an air of tension in the air – so brittle, it almost crackled. She realised it wasn't only Thomas Finley who was agitated by the crisis in Washington and the seriousness of the situation, but everyone else too.

'Mrs Finley,' someone called to her. 'Will you join the Ladies' Support Group we're organising?'

'What's it all about?' she said warily. She had been alone too long. She wasn't a joiner, and this group of well-dressed American matrons who were suddenly looking at her so eagerly made her nervous.

'Why, my dear, we aim to do everything we can to make the lot of our boys easier when they go in there,' a lady with stiffly waved hair said gushingly. 'We aim to meet at Mrs Turvey's home for a start, where we'll knit socks or roll bandages and write to our boys – just signed from an American lady, as a gesture of goodwill and hope – and bake cakes and cookies to send in food parcels from back home, or do whatever else we can get organised. We shall alert the Red Cross that we're available and register ourselves forthwith. Will you join us?'

Bridget was taken aback by this show of almost farcical enthusiasm. This was the new cause. Women of America arise and knit! She swallowed her own surge of sarcasm, as she saw that these were well-meaning women, however ludicrous they appeared standing on the streets of Mayfield as if their hen parties could win a war that had men drowning in mud and their own excrement. But perhaps none of these society dames ever read the reports from the British newspapers that reached Finley House . . .

'Yes,' she heard herself say huskily. 'Yes, I'll join you, if you'll have me.'

'Wonderful,' Mrs Turvey said joyfully. 'The more the merrier. We'll be in touch, my dear, as soon as things are properly organised.'

She excused herself and walked back to Finley House. She was part of a group. How odd that it took a war – or the imminence of a war – to give her something that had always eluded her. And all of America now, it seemed, was anxious for their boys to get the order to go in there and sort out the Jerries once and for all. To those already trained and keen for military service, like David Carson, it had been a long time coming.

In March the Germans sank American merchant vessels with a heavy loss of life.

'They're goading us,' Thomas almost screamed. 'Why doesn't the damn-fool government retaliate?'

It was April 6th, 1917, before Congress finally formalised a state of hostilities between the United States of America and the Central Powers.

'Why does everything bad in my life happen in April?' Bridget said to the ladies of the Ladies Support Group at one of their organised meetings that now took place on Monday and Thursday afternoons. At Mrs Turvey's suggestion, they had all sat silently for a few moments, sending up prayers for the dear boys who would soon be going overseas.

'That's a very profound thing to say, Mrs Finley,' her hostess said encouragingly over the clacking of the knitting needles. 'Would you care to enlarge on that for us, or is it too painful?'

Bridget looked at her smiling face with the over-rouged powdery skin. She heard the momentary pause in the knitting needles as the rest of them hoped for a tasty bit of tittle-tattle from this beautiful and slightly mysterious girl amongst them, who seemed more respectable than her circus-turn of a husband. Bridget knew by now that any small morsel that slipped out here would soon be bandied about the whole town.

'I'm sorry, I was thinking aloud. My parents died in April a long time ago, and I once had a bad fall in April, and the things just connected in my mind, that's all.'

She knew she was right when she saw the slight disappointment on their faces, quickly replaced by sympathy on her parents' account. She had no intention of telling them anything personal. Ladies they might call themselves, but right old gossips they most certainly were.

For a few minutes, bent industriously over the frustrating knitting that she could never get right, she imagined their shocked faces if she had come out with the truth of it all.

My darling Mammie and Daddy and brother Michael were squashed to death in a lovely mansion on Nob Hill in San Francisco in the earthquake of 1906 that none of you probably remember.

My sister Kitty got pregnant by some bum, and the price I had to pay for Thomas Finley to help us get the child aborted was to marry him. But Kitty died after the abortion, so it was all for nothing, and I'm tied to a fat stinking pig that I hate.

I met my lover soon afterwards and we had a few glorious weeks together one wonderful Christmas, before he was sent

179

to fight the Mexes under General Pershing. I was carrying his child when I heard that he'd had his head blown off, and then I lost our child, and that was in April too. So the matter of America going to war in April seems to fit my pattern nicely, so it does –

'Mrs Finley – Bridget – are you feeling unwell? You seem to be breathing so harshly. Can I get you some iced water?'

Bridget blinked, looking up quickly into the eyes of one of the younger ladies, and realised she had been totally wrapped up in remembering for a few nightmarish minutes. Iced water – the American panacea for all ills, just like hot sweet tea was for the British . . .

'Thank you, yes. I was just feeling a little faint, that's all.'

She saw the ladies glance at one another, and knew immediately that they wondered if there was a baby expected here. God, she prayed that there was not. Sweet Mother of God, anything but that, Bridget prayed fervently. The discomfort passed and she breathed easily again.

She waited impatiently for a letter to come from Ireland. Her own must have reached Dundemanagh by now, and her Aunt Maudie would surely not refuse to write back? It was just like the time she had been waiting for a letter in San Francisco, when the news had been so bad. Then it was her Uncle Padraig and Grandma who were both dead, and her Aunt Maudie had been kind but firm, and said there was no money for a boat passage, but she and Kitty would be welcome enough if they came . . . providing they could keep themselves . . . she wasn't even asking for that now. Just to have someone of her own to communicate with. It wasn't much for anyone to ask.

In August, Thomas toyed with the long envelope for some minutes before tossing it to her over the breakfast table. By then, she had given up hope that anyone from Ireland was ever going to bother writing to someone they didn't know, and cared less about. By then too, she knew to her horror, that she was pregnant.

'Who's writing to you from overseas?' He demanded. 'And with an Irish postmark too, by all the saints.'

Bridget snatched it up, her heart pounding with joy. Aunt

Maudie had written. She had so. At last!

'It must be from my Aunt, and I'll take it up to my room to read alone, if you don't mind,' she said.

'Please yourself. I'm in a hurry to be off, anyway.'

She didn't see him go. She took the letter upstairs, eager to open the envelope. She didn't recall her Aunt's writing, but it looked stronger than she would have expected from someone who must be a frail old lady by now.

'My Dear Mrs Finley,' the letter began formally, making her blink.

'This is a difficult letter for me to write, since I have to tell you that your Aunt, Mrs Maudie O'Connell, passed on several years ago. I took over the cottage when she died and bought a bit of land nearby. Since there are no other living O'Connells, Mrs Finley, I decided I must open your letter and that it should be answered.

'I'm very sorry to give you this news, as your letter did seem such a plea for news of Ireland. I presume you emigrated from here some years ago, and are missing home badly. Forgive me if I'm wrong, but I know nothing of your family affairs, having come here from England to recuperate after being discharged from the army. I was at the Somme, but you won't want to hear about that.

'We're all very thankful to have American destroyers based here at Queenstown. Not least, the young Irish girls, who go wild over the sailors in their uniforms. For them too, it's probably one of the bright spots of a war.

'Again, my regrets at giving you sad news. Yours most sincerely, Ralph Brett.'

Bridget sat with head bowed, after she finished reading. Her last link with Ireland had gone, yet here, miraculously, was another one. She wept for the Aunt she had never known, but when the tears were done, she reached for paper and pen once more, and began writing immediately.

'Dear Mr Brett,

'It was so very kind of you to write to me and tell me of my Aunt's death. I feel I have lost someone close, even though I never actually knew her. My parents brought me to America when I was so young that all my impressions are hazy, and I would love to hear yours. And you're quite wrong to think I would not be interested in hearing about the Somme, if you don't think it presumptuous of me to ask . . .'

Chapter 14

Thomas insisted on putting a small notice in the newspaper. Births, Marriages and Deaths columns were still local news, even though every page carried news of heroic deeds by American doughboys in France, until one might think that they alone were winning the war. He brought the paper upstairs to Bridget, and put it on her bed, folded prominently at the right page. There it was.

'On April 10th, 1918, to Bridget and Thomas O'Flaherty Finley, a daughter, Cassandra Mavreen.'

Bridget stared at the notice. It made it all official. The child had been born, after the worst day and night of pain she had ever known; after months of wishing it away, of begging the Holy Virgin to rid her of the child, uncaring of the blasphemy of it; after remembering cautionary tales from the more racy Academy girls, and drinking half a bottle of Gin and sitting in a hot bath until her skin was wrinkled and red-raw and her head reeling with drunken fantasies. But still the child had been born. It had wanted to be born. It was Thomas Finley's daughter, and it usurped the one child she had wanted so desperately, born of her love for Austen Hamilton. That child had died before it had been given life, and Bridget had no love to spare for another.

'Sure and she's the spittin' image of her Daddy!' Thomas chortled, poking and prodding the infant in the wicker crib beside Bridget's bed.

If anything was designed to alienate Bridget from her daughter further, apart from the thoughtlessness of being born in April, it was that. In fact, it was totally untrue. The child didn't resemble Thomas at all. She was Bridget in miniature, perfectly featured, black of hair, with dazzling blue eyes and a small curving mouth.

'Leave her alone, can't you?' Bridget said irritably. 'She'll want feeding again, and I want my rest.'

'But I like to watch you feeding her, me darling. It does these old eyes good to see her snuggling up to those goodies of yours. At least it keeps you home now, instead of sitting with those waffling do-gooder women.'

She looked at him in disgust.

'And what did *you* do in the war, Daddy?'

'Eh?' He said blankly.

'Oh, never mind,' Bridget said wearily, as Cassandra screeched more loudly. 'Give her to me, or I'll never get any peace. And leave me alone while I'm feeding her, please. I'm not putting on a peep-show.'

He was ready to argue, but Bridget simply folded her arms and let the child lie on her back screaming, waving her small fists in the air and getting redder and redder, until he gave in and went away. Only then did she pick up her screaming daughter, open her nightgown and put the child to her swollen breast.

She looked down at the dark head sucking furiously, and felt nothing. There was no great surge of mother-love, no growing closeness, nothing. Cassandra was Thomas Finley's child, even though she had been named after Bridget's own mother, Mavreen Cassandra O'Connell . . . such a lovely, flowing name Bridget had always thought it. And now there was Cassandra Mavreen Finley, whom they were going to call Cassie for short, and it didn't seem the same at all.

After the newspaper announcement and some telephone calls that Thomas made, the bedroom was soon filled with cards and flowers. They came from the Ladies' Support Group, and from Mary-Jo and Charlie, who excitedly scribbled a note to say that Mary-Jo was expecting. They came from Mary-Jo's parents, and separately from David, with a strange little drawing of a stick alongside the words 'Well Done'.

'What's this supposed to mean?' Thomas turned the card this way and that, trying to decode a message that only Bridget understood.

'Nothing. David just likes scribbling, and I daresay the pen slipped.'

Only she knew that it was a crude sketch of a crutch, or a prop. He was telling her that he was still her prop, if ever she needed him . . . and she was still marvelling that she had so many friends after all. Marvelling, and touched.

The priest had come to see her, and made the usual noises and gesticulations, and it had all meant nothing to Bridget. She intended to let this child make up her own mind whether or not she joined in the ritual of church-going. She would take her just as often as was necessary to abate the wrath of Father Rourke, but that was all. She had a new determination, and she meant to stick to it. She'd done what Thomas wanted and produced a child, even though it was a girl and not the boy he'd have preferred. But the old fool seemed to go practically stupid over the event.

'I think I might retire from business now,' he said expansively, when Cassie was three months old, and Bridget was beginning to wonder whether she would ever regain her slender shape again. Certainly the curves were more attractive than her gaunt figure after Austen died, but curves weren't terribly fashionable, and besides, they alerted a certain gleam in Thomas's eyes . . .

'Retire! What do you mean, retire?'

She watched him on hands and knees as Cassie lay gurgling on her back on a rug in the drawing-room. He still wore his outrageously loud suits, and his great backside seemed to fill one corner of the room, shiny from sitting in the green check trousers.

He twisted his face towards her. Where he leaned downwards, the jowls hung loose and flabby, the flesh scarlet. His eyes watered often these days, and he never failed to repel Bridget whenever she looked at him.

'I'm selling the business. Selling up so I can spend all my time with this wee charmer –'

'What? But you can't! You'd be bored silly sitting around here all the time –'

And I'd go out of my mind, having more of your company forced on me . . .

Thomas sat back on his heels, the green check material stretched tight over his knees, his waistcoat bunched up around his great paunch.

'What's the good of making money if you can't enjoy it? Besides, I'm bored with trailing round factories every day, and it's all settled. I've seen Donaldson and made all the legal arrangements. I'm being bought out as from the beginning of September.'

'All settled? Without ever consulting me, or breathing a word of all this? How long have you known you were going to sell out?' She raged.

He stood up, scooping the child in his arms as though she was a doll. It was how he thought of her. An exquisite little angel-doll, his pet, his darling.

'Since when did I have to consult with you about anything? The business is mine, not yours, Bridget, and since when have you shown any interest in me or my affairs? If you'd ever been a proper wife to me, it might have been different, but you haven't, not ever. Not once have you come to me willingly, and don't think I ever forget it.'

She looked at him numbly. She had always thought him the most insensitive of men, and this sudden appeal to her senses, if that was what it was, only aroused the deepest suspicion in her.

'So what do you intend to do?' She said at last.

'I intend to make myself so indispensable to my little daughter, that 'tis me she turns to, not you. She depends on you now, Bridget, because she's tiny and helpless, but I intend to take her love away from you, just by always being here. She's mine, and I aim to keep her mine.'

Bridget wanted to laugh out loud at the triumphant look in his eyes. He thought he was doing her such ill, but in reality, he did her the greatest favour. Of course the child was his. He could have her. She meant nothing to Bridget, except that she was indeed helpless and her own instincts meant that she would care for her as a good mother. But never a loving one. That much was beyond her.

'It'll be something else to tell your fancy-man in Ireland, won't it?' Thomas crowed now, as he swung Cassie to and fro in his arms and tried to coax a smile from her.

'Ralph is not my fancy-man. Don't be so ridiculous, Thomas. You read his letters. You know he's just an interesting man who tells me about Ireland, and first-hand accounts of the war –'

'Second-hand, you mean. He's not been in it, since he got shot up at the Somme, has he?'

'He's nearer to it than you are, and you profess to know all that's going on.'

'Only because I choose to keep my mind active, darling,' he said expansively, and because secretly he had a job to keep his thoughts on more than one thing at a time these day, so it didn't do to let himself stagnate mentally, especially now he had little Cassie to raise.

'Anyway, now that our boys are in there, it'll all be over soon,' Thomas said.

'Our boys now, is it? Have you switched your loyalties from the Irish roughs around here to the doughboys then?'

'There's no sense in antagonising people when you've got to live among them –'

Bridget laughed incredulously. 'You're a fine one to talk. You change opinions like Cassie changes her diapers. I've heard about your brawls, and at your age and in your position too. You just make yourself look ridiculous.'

He glared at her, while Cassie squirmed at the sudden tightening of his embrace.

'Watch your tongue, woman. What I do is my business.'

She stuck her chin in the air. 'Perhaps I should follow my own inclinations as well, then, since we seem to be set in opposite directions. Should I apply for a music-hall position, maybe? I can still sing a ditty that's more interesting than nursery songs.'

'You will not. My wife stays at home,' Thomas growled. 'You can forget all that singing nonsense, except for singing the child to sleep.'

Truth to tell, she'd nearly forgotten it anyway. After Austen died, it seemed as though the fire of ambition had died along with that of passion. She felt that her life was completely sterile. She hated her husband, felt nothing for her child, and her sister-in-law merely tolerated them both. It was somehow terrible and tragic, but that was simply the way it was.

She had lost touch with Mary-Jo again, who was now an infrequent letter-writer, and had her own life to lead. David wrote occasionally from France, but only the letters from Ralph Brett in Ireland did anything to put a spark of animation back in her eyes.

Her fancy-man indeed . . . she remembered Thomas's crude words as he took Cassie out into the garden to push her around in her baby-carriage. Nothing could be farther from the truth. There was friendship and nothing more in the letters that passed between them, but through Ralph, Bridget felt she knew her own Ireland better than ever before. Through him, she knew its soft green summers and cold snowy winters, the babble of the waterfalls running down from the hills in the spring thaw, the more domestic details of Dundemanagh and the white-washed cottage where O'Connells had once lived, and the patch of land that Ralph had cultivated until it was a modestly successful market garden.

'Everybody's growing what they can now, of course, Bridget,' his letters told her. 'We've all got used to food shortages, but there's nothing like cutting your own cabbage in the morning when the dew's still on it, and snapping open your own peas from the pod. And all this, from a Londoner, born and bred!

'I find it continually fascinating to realise how a person can adapt to a new environment and find that this is where he belongs after all. While I'd never say that our soldiers in France enjoy what they're doing – God forbid such stupidity on my part – but even they adapt. I know this from my own experience. One even became used to living in the trenches, and in breathing other men's smells. One got used to treading over dead comrades, because the need to survive made it imperative.

'If anybody had told me any of this before the war, I'd have laughed in their faces. I was an out-and-out townie, and probably a pompous ass, but now I'm quite the country squire – in a small way.'

Bridget lost herself in his letters. Thomas had quickly become bored with Ralph's obviously sophisticated and educated views, and rarely bothered to do more than skim the letters now. But to Bridget they had become a lifeline between her present world and another, more alluring one. They said the grass was always greener on the other side, and to her, there was still no grass greener than Ireland's. She had quickly become aware that Ralph was quite an intellectual, and her mind was keen enough to match his most astute observations. But any thought of romance between them never entered her head, and Thomas's tactless comments only damned him more in her estimation, because he had no comprehension of mere friendship between a man and a woman.

It was odd, really. She had two very dear menfriends. David, and Ralph. The one she hadn't seen for eighteen months, since Mary-Jo's wedding, and the other she had never met. Yet each of them meant more to her than her own husband, and she rejoiced that neither of them wanted more from her than she could give. She could never love again. She had loved once, and that was for ever.

Thomas read out the name from the published list of war casualties at the end of August.

'Here, listen to this. Lieutenant David Carson. Killed in Action in St. Mihiel, France. D'you suppose it's the same one? Didn't you tell me he was promoted to Lieutenant in Pershing's army – ?'

Bridget wasn't listening any more. She was rushing to the telephone. Her shaking fingers gripped the instrument as she almost begged the operator to connect her to the Carson home in Vermont. After an agonising wait, Mrs Carson answered calmly, speaking with immense quiet pride in her voice as she confirmed that it was true. Their dearest David had been killed in the service of his hero, General Pershing, but they had been told that David was to be awarded a posthumous medal for gallantry, and they had had a personal letter from General Pershing himself to say how exemplary David's conduct had been in the face of the enemy.

Bridget didn't know what to say to this distant woman who

seemed prouder of the fact that she would shortly possess a cold piece of metal with a ribbon attached, than in realising that she would never hold her son in her arms again.

'I'm so sorry, Mrs Carson,' she gasped. 'So sorry. Please tell Mr Carson and Mary-Jo and Charlie how very sorry I am. I shall miss David terribly.'

To herself, the platitudes sounded glib and false, but they seemed to please Mrs Carson, who said she would certainly pass on all Bridget's messages, and added that she hoped that Mr Finley and little Cassandra were thriving. Bridget hung up, telling herself that shock affected different people in different ways. Some couldn't always cry at first. Mrs Carson obviously couldn't. But Bridget could. She wept for her friend, her prop, the second of the three musketeers. Now there was only one, and he would be comforting Mary-Jo. Nobody needed her.

It was clear that the Armistice was going to be signed soon. When it finally happened, on November 11th, America rejoiced with the rest of the world. There were street parties for the children and wilder ones for the grown-ups, and ticker-tape rejoicings in New York city. The paper-flag manufacturers of miniature Stars and Stripes on sticks did a roaring trade. And Cassie Finley crawled across the drawing-room carpet for the very first time.

'Did you see that, Bridget? Did you see my little angel?' Thomas wheezed, crawling after her . . .

'You make the child out to be something of a phenomenon, Thomas,' Bridget said in exasperation at his antics. 'She's only crawling, for God's sake.'

'And you've swallowed a bloody dictionary since you started writing to your Englishman,' he growled.

Bridget appealed to Sheilagh, complacently watching her brother cavorting on all fours.

'Don't you think he's going soft in the head? The child will be completely spoiled if he doesn't stop coddling her like this.'

'It'll compensate for what she doesn't get from her mother,' Sheilagh said dryly.

Bridget flushed. 'She's fed and clothed and kept warm. It's

all a child needs at that age.'

She needed love too, Bridget thought guiltily, and at least Thomas gave her love, even if it was sometimes sickening to watch him prancing with her like a great mammoth. Since he'd sold the business, he was home all the time, and Bridget kept out of his way as much as she could. She'd taken to reading more, discovering the classics, and found a new delight in sharing her discoveries with Ralph Brett, who was as well-read as any university professor.

What Thomas had done with the proceeds of the business, Bridget never knew. He was as close as a clam on the subject, and she only knew that he and Donaldson, the lawyer, had been closeted for hours in the study to discuss all the legalities of it. His only stipulation had been that the new owners should retain the name of Finley's Canned Goods, and the new owners were only too happy to comply, since it was a name well-known in the trade.

Ralph's letter after hearing of David's death was unexpectedly bitter. Ralph's interpretation was that war was a total waste of life and energy, producing less glory than shame.

'What have we finally achieved, except to be left with a lot of maimed and broken men, and crushed cities to be rebuilt? Or should we suspect that this is the way some Divine Power sees fit to make us restock this world? It has even been termed as some Almighty method of controlling the population. Is this the God who purports to love all His children? I confess, Bridget, I find those who believe in such a God as being of simple intelligence, though living in this Catholic community, I keep my feelings very much to myself! And now, I suppose, you'll dissociate yourself from me for being the wicked agnostic that I am.'

She did not. She considered that a man who questioned things, even the very basics of religion, showed a far healthier attitude to life than an elderly lump of a man who spent his days on his hands and knees cooing baby-talk to a child.

'Will you read what the man's written now, for God's sake! Sure, and he's living in cloud-cuckoo land,' Thomas sniggered when he glanced through that particular letter. 'Some

Almighty plan indeed. I don't know know why you bother to answer such trash.'

But he didn't forbid her, and if he had, she would have ignored him. And coming from a man who never set foot inside a church now, his opinions about religion were less than nothing to her.

So she continued to have her intellectual contact with a man who was her friend. She felt that she knew more about him than her own husband. She knew when his vegetable crop did badly, causing him some anxiety for several months, and when he got a contract to supply a big English wholesaler, which cheered him enormously. She knew his likes and dislikes, and began hearing about friends coming to visit him from England, now that the war was over. Such normality was something to take for granted, instead of being a faraway goal.

In return she told him something of America, since everyone on that side of the Atlantic seemed interested. She never mentioned San Francisco, only the Eastern side of the country, Mayfield and New York State, the beautiful woods and colours of New England, her time at the Connecticut Academy of Music, the breathtaking panorama of Niagara Falls, and Mary-Jo's little boy, who had been born on the first Christmas Day after the Armistice.

And eventually, after several years of letter-writing, when Bridget felt she could almost write a book about him, Ralph told her about Alma.

'It's strange how you can see a person quite often in the village, and never think of her as anything more than a friend until you realise there might be something more. Alma came to Ireland for a holiday after her parents died, and loved it so much, she decided to stay. We discovered she was slightly acquainted with an old chum of mine in London – I may have mentioned him to you – Harry Ashworth. He's a horse-enthusiast, and has his finger in a lot of pies. This gave us a talking-point, of course. Last week when we met again at a charity village dance for war victims, I seemed to see her in a different light. There's no more to it than that yet, but what a lark it would be if I found my soulmate at last at the ripe old age of thirty! Now write and tell me what you think!'

Bridget wasn't sure quite how she felt at this news. Thrilled for Ralph, who deserved the best. Slightly miffed that this Alma was obviously going to be closer to her friend than Bridget ever could. Somewhat surprised at the description of the friend, Harry Ashworth, whom Ralph had definitely never mentioned before, who sounded a bit of a Jack-the-lad, and not the sort of chum she'd have expected for Ralph.

Thomas had long given up bothering to look at Ralph's letters. He had degenerated into a kind of bumbling fun-figure, to whom even Sheilagh hardly spoke any more. Cassie, nearly four years old, adored her overindulgent father and treated Bridget with the politeness of a well-behaved little visitor. She threw her arms around Thomas and received his noisy wet kisses every night before she was tucked up in bed. She pecked Bridget dutifully on the side of the cheek that was offered her.

Thomas and Bridget maintained separate rooms, and once in a while he came stumblingly to her, demanding his marital rights, and it was usually when he was the worse for drink. She suffered it in silence, because he was still stronger than she, and always ready for a physical fight if she refused him. But it was as abominable to her as ever.

In the years following the end of the war, Ralph had written to her of disturbing developments in Ireland. After the 1918 elections, there was an independent Irish parliament, the Dail Eireann, and Eamon de Valera had lived up to Thomas's prophecy, and now controlled a new Irish government. It was meant to be a peaceful government, levying its own taxes and emerging peaceably from British rule. The Irish Republican Army had different ideas, and a new and frightening kind of guerrilla warfare began against the British.

'It doesn't affect us here in the south,' Ralph wrote. 'But it's very sad to see a country divided against itself. And no-side in a civil war ever came out of it with honour.'

His words were proved true in 1920, when he told her how the new British unit of fighting men, the Black and Tans, wrought as many atrocities as the IRA. In 1921, Lloyd

George abandoned hope of controlling the situation, and in January 1922, the Irish Free State was created, allowing Ulster to remain part of the United Kingdom.

Bridget followed the news in the American newspapers which reported in screaming headlines for the benefit of the large Irish immigrant population, whipping each faction into a frenzy, about events taking place in a country which most of them would never see again.

Thomas Finley was stepping out with the best of them that evening. He might be well into his sixties, but he could still march and swagger and shout and hold a blazing torch, and his blood ran faster at the thought of being in at the confrontation in Mayfield's town square. It was all unofficial, of course, but everyone knew it was going to happen. Mayfield was the largest town in the area, and word had spread that those for and against the Dail were clashing tonight. Most of them didn't know the half of what they were fighting for, but they were all Irish and ready to blather until dawn if need be, and if a few trees got burned and town statues cracked in the process, it was all part and parcel of the riot.

Thomas was exhilarated by the sheer size of the crowds. It was a good turn-out. Ireland could be proud of its sons. The fact that no one in Ireland even knew what was happening here was of little importance. They cared, and that was the main thing. Thomas threw himself into the crowd brandishing his torch in the air as the bellowing from both sides completely demolished any sense or reasoning. Nobody knew what was going on, except that there were two sides arguing, and when the verbalising was exhausted, there was only one way to settle an argument.

He was somewhere in the middle of it, trying to get his breath, when he felt somebody knock his feet from under him. He went down so heavily he was completely winded for a minute. He couldn't get up. Men were trampling over him, toppling to join him, and he was trying desperately to tell them to let him up, to let him breathe . . . his torch had been flung down in front of him, and he suddenly realised it was beneath him, and there were other torches surrounding him, the tar on them still glowing, still burning, and it would take more than the weight of his body to put them out.

He scrabbled in the ungainly heap on the ground, trying to get away from the burning, and the stench of his own scorched clothes was in his nostrils, his own flesh . . . the flames touched his wild hair and filled his eyes, and sweet Mother of God, but it was drying out their sockets, and the pain was excruciating. Through it, he heard somebody yelling that there were men injured here, and to throw buckets of water over them for the love of Christ . . .

It wasn't just himself then, he thought incongruously as he tried to see through the red mist of pain. Not just himself that was going to die before he had the chance to see his little Cassie grow from a child to a woman. She was the last thing on his mind as the flames took hold, and the screams of his compatriots were in his head as the redness of the flames turned to blackness, and then to nothing at all.

Bridget heard the hammering on the front door as she was trying to pacify Cassie, who wanted none of her, but only her Daddy after she awoke from a bad dream. Still with Cassie in her arms, she ran downstairs, without waiting for the servants to answer. She gaped at the distraught, dirt-streaked faces greeting her.

'Missus, 'tis terrible bad news we're bringing you and several others this night,' the spokesman croaked in a rich Irish brogue. ' 'Tis your man that's been burned to death in the brawling 'n the square, so it is, and they're bringing him home to you now. The priest has been sent for, and will be doing all the rounds shortly –'

The men scattered as a blackened hulk was carried carefully on a makeshift stretcher into the house. It was only just recognisable as Thomas Finley by the tattered check suit and the wedding-ring hanging loosely on the bones of a skinless finger. Sheilagh Finley rushed down the stairs in rag curlers and dressing-gown, ramming her fist into her mouth to stop herself from retching at the sight of her brother's corpse. Then Cassie began screeching with terror as the men brought the body further into the house and looked at

Bridget, awaiting instructions.

'Get that – that *thing* – out of my house,' she heard herself scream. 'Take it to the priest's house and let him dispose of it. Just take it away – *now*.'

The men looked apprehensively at Bridget and then at the terrified child, and began to back away with their burden.

'All right, Missus. 'Tis upsetting the child, and Father Rourke will know what to do. You see to the child, and we'll see to Thomas Finley.'

The door closed behind them. Bridget stood stock still for a moment, still clutching Cassie. Wickedly, she felt a wild desire to dance and sing. Upsetting the child, was it? But that hadn't been her first consideration when she'd seen the realisation of all her wishes. Thomas Finley was dead, and she was free . . . only then did she realise that Cassie was crying uncontrollably in her arms, and when she tried to comfort the child, it was too late. Cassie screamed anew and fought with all her small strength against her.

Chapter 15

They sat opposite one another like two black crows. Bridget couldn't resist the irreverent thought. Both she and Sheilagh wore sombre funereal clothes, when Bridget would have much preferred wearing scarlet, or white, as they did in India at a burial. Only in *her* case, she would do it for sheer joy. She hadn't dared, of course. And what did it matter? If Thomas Finley was somewhere in the beyond looking down at her, she hoped he was perfectly aware of her hypocrisy. They had buried him two weeks ago, and now they sat in the drawing-room of Finley House while the servants took Cassie for an afternoon walk, and waited for Donaldson to tell them how Thomas's estate had been divided.

The lawyer cleared his throat, and it was clear to Bridget that he didn't relish the task ahead of him. He probably expected Sheilagh to throw a tantrum, because as Thomas's wife, Bridget would now own everything. She had earned it, she thought grimly. By all that was holy, she had earned it. She had been bound to the man for seven years, and they were the worst years of her life. Only two other times in her life meant anything more. The earthquake had been the worst . . . and loving Austen had been the best.

Bridget watched, fascinated, as the lawyer untied the pink ribbon binding the legal document together. What a fuss, to dispose of a man's possessions. Why did he not get on with it? she listened politely as he began to read, and then sat up straighter, hardly able to take in what Donaldson was saying in a voice heavy with apology now. Her breath became more laboured in her chest, and as for Sheilagh . . .

'*No*!' The other woman screeched. 'You lie! Thomas would never have made such a Will. I'm his only sister –'

The lawyer was stiffly dignified, well used to these outbursts at such a time. 'I'm very sorry, Miss Finley, but the Will is legal and binding. In fact, it was witnessed by two doctors who examined your brother immediately after he'd made this final Will, and each attested to his sane and sober state of mind.'

'He was never sane!' Bridget stormed at him now. 'He was the wickedest old bastard that ever lived, and this just proves it. Leaving me practically penniless –'

For once, the two women completely united in their hatred of Thomas Finley, and their disbelief in what he had done.

'Ladies, please.' Donaldson tried once again to pacify them. 'Allow me to read the contents once more. Very often, the full meaning fails to penetrate when the recipients are distressed –'

'It penetrates all right,' Bridget muttered. 'He's somewhere up there laughing at us –'

'He's more likely rotting in hell down below,' Sheilagh retorted. 'I hope he burns slowly.'

Donaldson looked slightly shocked at this. Such refined ladies . . . but such an upset could make harridans of them all. And in all honesty, he could hardly blame them. He'd tried to make Finley change his mind a hundred times, but the old devil had been adamant. He began to read, regardless of the glowering faces opposite him, taking refuge in the legal document. It was brief and cold.

'I, Thomas O'Flaherty Finley, being of sane mind, do hereby bequeath the following.

To my wife, Bridget O'Connell Finley, the sum of five hundred dollars.

To my sister, Sheilagh Finley, the sum of five hundred dollars.

To both of them, the right to live in the house known as Finley House, all bills and upkeep to be paid out of the residue of my estate, such arrangements to be calculated by my lawyer and accountant. If one or either of them should leave Finley House to live elsewhere, the right to return is forfeited. If either should remarry, the same rule applies.

To my daughter, Cassandra Mavreen Finley, the sum of ten thousand dollars, to be held in trust until she is twenty-five years old, an age when silly young girls become responsible women.

The rest of my estate, being mainly the proceeds from the sale of Finley's Canned Goods, I bequeath to whatever charities my lawyer and accountant choose.'

Donaldson looked up, to meet the still seething faces. But in Bridget's there was a glimmer of ironic laughter. The old devil indeed. He had made sure his beloved Cassie got the best of it, while she and Sheilagh lived on charity and a pittance, and were tied to each other for as long as they wanted a roof over their heads, an arrangement that Thomas would know very well was anathema to them both.

'You'll see to it that there's enough money for food and clothing, I presume, Mr Donaldson?' She asked sarcastically. For the first time he looked uncomfortable at her clear blue gaze.

'Mrs Finley, I'm truly sorry,' he said more gently. 'Of course, there will be sufficient funds for your comfort, and it will all come from a central fund from my chambers. I'm sure it was not Mr Finley's wish to see you walking about Mayfield in rags.'

He tried to make light of it, but failed miserably. To the two women, that was exactly what Thomas had intended. To keep them, if not poor, then still tied to him even beyond the grave. Dependent on him for every nickel and cent. Bridget rose to her feet. She held out her hand to the lawyer, and he had to admire her composure.

'Thank you, Mr Donaldson. Will you come into the drawing-room and take a glass of sherry before you leave?'

'Can we afford it?' Sheilagh said snidely.

Bridget smiled sweetly at her. She was recovering more quickly than the older woman.

'Mr Donaldson is my guest, Sheilagh, as well as our legal adviser, and is entitled to a little courtesy.'

She managed to underline the 'my' with just enough emphasis to remind her sister-in-law that Bridget was still the lady of the house, and Sheilagh had better not forget it.

And what was so different? She had never been rich. All that she had had through the guardianship and then marriage with Thomas Finley, had been on borrowed time. Bridget had always felt that. This house had never really been home.

And if she left it now, she would never be able to come back. The brief thought came into her head and went out again. She needed to be sensible and not to make any rash movements. There wasn't just herself to consider. There was Cassie. Thomas Finley's daughter who would be rich by the time she was twenty-five years old, when ten thousand dollars would surely have accumulated enough interest to seem like a fortune. She spoke quickly to Mr Donaldson.

'Cassie's money will be invested wisely, I trust? I know nothing of such things –'

She did know that the lawyer was one to be trusted, and he nodded at once.

'I've already discussed some possibilities with Mr Bevis, the accountant, and we have some cast-iron ideas. Also, I require you to approve the charities to which the bulk of the estate is bequeathed. Perhaps you could come to my office in a month's time, Mrs Finley? It might be less emotional there. I'll arrange for a taxi-cab to bring you into the city.'

'Thank you. That would be best.'

Anywhere away from Sheilagh's accusing eyes. Bridget

could almost read her mind. If it wasn't for the O'Connells, none of this would have happened. She would still be housekeeping for her brother, and everything would have gone naturally to her. Instead of which, both she and Bridget were as good as paupers, and only the child benefited.

It was impossible to comfort Cassie when her dearest, doting, unbelievably stupid father died. But to the child he hadn't been stupid. He'd been a knight in shining armour, a prince, a glorious larger-than-life figure of great fun, an endearing circus clown, the one who gave her all the love she needed. Bridget, overcome with guilt at hearing Cassie cry pitifully night after night in her luxurious little room, found that her every attempt to console her was rejected. She had never wanted Cassie, and now Cassie simply didn't want her.

She was shocked at the knowledge. The child was not quite four years old, and yet there was a wisdom in her eyes that disconcerted Bridget. She had given her daughter the attention she would give to a stray animal – just enough to keep it from suffering but with no warmth in the attention – and now she was reaping back what she had sown. Cassie was wounded by her father's death in a way that went deeper than Bridget could imagine. The one she loved best in all the world had been taken from her, and the one she didn't want tried to take her in her arms and tell her clumsily that she understood all about that, only too well . . . but it was too late. Cassie's affections turned inwards, to her rag dolls, to her childish drawing, to books, occasionally to the sympathetic maids, to anything but her mother. And after a while, Bridget gave up trying, and their relationship remained as static as before.

A month later, a taxi-cab took her to the palatial chambers of Donaldson and Partners in New York City. In all the years since she had come east, Bridget had only once been into the city. Thomas hadn't wanted his wards corrupted by what he called all the wickedness there, and he had never cared to take her there after they were married. The city held her spellbound. Such tall buildings, such straight streets and avenues, such an oasis of green they called Central Park with the horse-drawn buggies lining up to take people for rides.

The taxi-driver was amused by the frequent expressions of awe from this elegantly dressed young woman in the slim-fitting brown coat with the fur collar framing her face. Beneath the cloche hat the blue eyes were wide and luminous, the glimpses of hair dark and luxurious. She was a good-looker, the taxi-driver thought. Better'n some of the old well-to-do dinks he drove around, so steeped in scent he almost needed to fumigate his cab afterwards.

'Ain't you seen the city before, Lady?' He looked back at Bridget through the driving mirror.

'No, never,' she said. She gave him a sudden smile that startled him. Yes, a real beauty, this one. 'You must think I'm a real country bumpkin.'

'Naw,' he said frankly. 'Tell you what. I could give you a tour of the city if you like. The legal eagle said he was picking up the tab, and I was to take you anywheres you wanted to go today.'

'Did he?' Bridget said. The ride wasn't doing her stomach a lot of good. The taxi wasn't the best of vehicles, but the driver was chirpy and it was good to have a friendly face around. He was small and monkey-like, but she sensed his respectability. She made up her mind.

'My business shouldn't take more than half an hour. Will you wait for me and then give me a little tour? I may as well see something while I'm here.'

'Sure thing. The name's Walt, by the way.'

They drew up outside the tall building with the mass of business names on a huge brass plaque inside the foyer. Walt seemed very experienced in such places, and leapt out of the cab to point her in the right direction. She had to go up in an elevator, which frightened her to death, and she held her bag so tightly that her hands were clammy when she got out on the eighth floor in a crush of other people who all seemed to know where they were going. She was dizzy at the height, and relieved when she suddenly saw the names of Donaldson and Partners, Attorneys at Law, on one of the doors. She turned the handle cautiously and went inside.

Half an hour later, Bridget came out, bemused at all the legal jargon. She was hardly any wiser than before, except to know the long list of charitable organisations who were going to benefit from Thomas Finley's bequests, and would have his name on their registers as one of their benefactors. She knew where Cassie's money was to be invested, and it all seemed very satisfactory, and all she wanted now was to get out of the tall, oppressive building and into some fresh air. Walt was waiting outside. He leapt to attention as soon as he saw her.

'Go all right, did it, Lady?' He said, knowing nothing of her business, but ushering her into the back of the cab. 'Best to keep away from lawyers, I always say, and you do look a bit greenish. How about a first stop near the river, and a cup of tea at a stand-up refreshment bar?'

He looked at Bridget dubiously. 'Maybe you wouldn't care for it, though. It ain't the best place in town –'

'It sounds wonderful,' she said faintly. She could have told him she hadn't been too proud to line up at soup kitchens in San Francisco, a lifetime ago . . . she leaned back against the cab, and wondered why the interview with Donaldson had really taken it out of her. But she began to revive with Walt's cheerful chatter, and with the sight of the East River suddenly coming into view, with small ships ploughing through the waters, alongside several stately ocean-going liners. And some distance away, seemingly in the middle of the ocean, something spectacular that stirred her memory.

'Oh – isn't that –' she breathed. Walt chuckled.

'I knew you'd be impressed. That's Lady Liberty – the Statue of Liberty to give it the rightful name. Ain't she something? She's made of bronze, you know, and was given to America by the French.'

Walt warmed to his theme now, clearly well-used to being an unofficial tourist guide.

'This here bit we've been driving through is Manhattan, where Spanish explorers first landed in 1524 or thereabouts. The Dutch came in 1609 and called the town New Amsterdam. Fifty years or so later the British came and took over. We're a mixture, but I guess we're all Americans. Do you know we took in more'n a million immigrants during 1914? It all slowed down because of the war, but they're on the up and up again now.'

'What's your background, Walt?'

He chuckled. 'Swedish. That's a laugh ain't it? I wouldn't know a Swede from a turnip, if it came and hit me in the mouth.'

It was obviously one of his party-pieces for rich tourists. But by now they had arrived at a wooden shack where several dishevelled-looking drivers were drinking tea. Walt looked at her.

'OK? You wanna get out and stretch your legs, pardon my . . .'

'Yes. I want to breathe in the sea air.' She said quickly, really beginning to feel quite peculiar. The day had been more stressful than she had realised, and it felt good to stand at the water's edge and watch those great ocean-going ships with far-off destinations, and the smaller craft, busily going back and forth to what Walt told her was Liberty Island, and farther on to Staten Island. It was all bustle and activity, the gulls wheeling overhead, the ships' sirens hooting in farewell to New York, and Bridget was exhilarated by it all, her hands warmed by the great mug of strong tea Walt handed her. They watched it all for ten minutes or so, until the tea was gone, and Bridget felt she'd had enough history lessons for one day.

'They'll be off to Ireland or France or somewhere,' Walt said sagely. 'You're Irish, ain't you, Lady?'

'Yes,' she said, suddenly turning to him and giving him another of those dazzling smiles. For what was to stop her going to Ireland too? There was nothing, now. She had five hundred dollars, and if that wasn't enough for the fare for herself and Cassie, then she'd damn well beg a passage from the Captain and offer to sing for her supper.

The thought slipped away from her uncertainly. She didn't want to sing in public, not any more. The ambition had faded with Austen's death. Her songs had been for him. She didn't want to sing of Roses in Picardy, which had become one of her favourites, and see the nostalgic look on some other war hero's face. She didn't want to arouse emotion in any other man, ever again.

'Are you all right, Lady? You don't look so good –'

She heard Walt's concerned voice, and nodded quickly. Her head spun a little as she did so.

'I think I'd better be getting back home, Walt,' she said regretfully.

'Don't you wanna drive through Chinatown?' He asked, then took another look at her face. 'Well, maybe another time. If you need a cab any time, just call my number and ask for me, OK?'

'OK,' she said.

She reported the day's happenings at Donaldson's chambers to Sheilagh, who sat with pursed lips. It didn't matter to her now what was happening to her brother's money. None of it was coming to her, and if she could wash her hands of any association with Bridget O'Connell, the happier she would be. Cassie had been in the charge of the maids all day, who considered this a soft option to cleaning brasses and polishing beeswax into the furniture. The child was playing in her room now, with Ethel dozing in a chair by the window, jumping up guiltily as Bridget entered the room.

'All right, Ethel, you can go now,' Bridget said. The girl bobbed and scuttled out. Bridget looked at her daughter. Her dark head was bent industriously over a piece of paper, on which she was scrawling a crude picture of a large man in a vivid green suit. It was obviously meant to be Thomas. Bridget felt a pang of pity for the child, and complimented her on the drawing.

'That's very nice, Cassie –'

'No it's not. It's horrid.' She said at once, crunched the drawing up in her hand, and hurled it across the room. The action alarmed Bridget. It was almost violent. She was tempted to ask Cassie how she would feel about going on a big ship across the ocean, but decided against it. The answer would be no, and more than that, it would be blabbed all over the house, and Bridget intended telling no one what she intended. If she even intended it . . . It was not something to be decided on the spur of the moment.

But it was hardly that, she thought, as she sat near the window looking out at the gardens, with the spring flowers just bursting into blossom. It had been a dream for sixteen years, since she was fourteen years old and had vowed to look after Kitty. Sixteen years ago, she thought with a shock, and now she was thirty years old and somehow her youth seemed to have slipped away from her without her really noticing it. She realised Cassie had been talking to her for some minutes.

'I want my tea, Mammie,' she said petulantly. 'Can I go to the kitchen? Ethel said there might be chocolate cookies and lemonade. Can I, please?'

'Yes. Yes, Cassie, of course you can.'

She was wrapped up in her own thoughts, and she hardly noticed the resentful little glare her daughter gave her. Cassie resented everything. Her mother, her father's death, her stiff-necked aunt. Poor little Cassie, Bridget thought, to be so resentful. Poor Bridget, to have got so much less out of life than she had once wanted. But it wasn't too late. It musn't be too late.

She spent the evening in Thomas's study, poring over maps and finding addresses and writing everything down in a notebook. She had the five hundred dollars in a bank account, and presumably it would be no problem for her to draw it all out if she told the bank manager it was for some special purchase. A good thing it wasn't still Mary-Jo's father who was the Mayfield bank manager, or he might have been more curious than a stranger, she thought thankfully. Until now, she had had nothing to do with banks.

That afternoon, Walt had driven her along the river and shown her the terminus of the ocean-going liners, since she had shown such interest. She knew she could always call him to take her and Cassie there, although she wondered if it was really wise to contact Walt. She intended leaving this house as anonymously as she had entered it, and Walt had been employed for today by Donaldson . . . but what did it matter if they checked up on her movements after she had gone? By then, she would be somewhere on the Atlantic Ocean, and beyond their reach. It was a heady thought.

When Bridget got out of bed the next morning, she felt her head spin, and only just reached the bathroom before she was violently sick. She clung to the basin for endless minutes, knowing she should have seen this coming. The lethargy these past weeks; the ease with which she'd been able to detach herself from everything going on around her; the dizzy feeling and the threatening nausea in yesterday's taxi ride. She should have recognised the symptoms. Her monthly functions were always erratic, but all the other signs pointed to only one thing. She was pregnant.

She sat down abruptly on the side of her bed, her mind whirling. She sat there for a very long while. This pregnancy was the third. The first had been joyful, wonderful, because it had been Austen's child, and in time Bridget had known that she and Austen would be together, raising the child as their own. It would have been as inevitable as breathing.

The second time had been as repellent to her as if she'd been carrying a monster, despite the fact that the baby girl born to her had been delicate and as unlike Thomas Finley as chalk from cheese, and bore all the signs of growing into a beautiful woman.

This time . . . Bridget felt her hand move protectively to her abdomen, and it was as though a strange fierce love began to consume her. This child was hers and hers alone . . . the words slid into her mind before she could stop them. Thomas Finley was dead, and the fact that he had fathered the child growing inside her meant less than nothing to Bridget. He hadn't lived to see it, he could have no claim to it. No man would be involved in its upbringing.

To compare it with the immaculate conception would be blasphemous, but to Bridget, the event was no less miraculous. She had been given someone of her own to love at last. And even more than that, the means to take her secret with her to Ireland. This child would be born in Ireland. The beautiful simplicity of it all brought tears to her eyes. If there was ever a great plan to everyone's life, this surely was the culmination of hers.

She made her plans carefully. It was easy enough to check with the daily newspaper listings the dates and times of the ocean-going ships and to find out when she and Cassie could leave for Ireland. It was to coincide with one of Sheilagh's visits to her friends. She made the booking by telephone, and

205

said she would collect the tickets on the day of sailing, promising to pay in cash, and ignoring the sceptical voice at the other end of the wire.

She had given her name as Mrs Finley, but hung up before she was asked for an address or telephone number. Cassie would travel at a minimal price to cover her food, and would share her mother's cabin. They would both travel in the cheapest class, to conserve as much of her five hundred dollars as possible. It was almost all Bridget had in the world, but when she reached Ireland and found her way to Dundemanagh, she was confident that Ralph Brett would assist her in any way he could.

As well as Thomas's pittance, she still had a little money of her own, from the time she had begun saving to go to Ireland . . . but it had seemed such an impossible dream that the urge to save hadn't continued. She knew she would have to find work and accommodation, but if it meant she had to scrub floors or take in washing, she would do it. It would all be worth it for her dream to be realised, and for the child to be born in Ireland. A Christmas child . . . could there be anything more wonderful?

The glow she felt at doing something positive for herself at last, took away much of the discomfort and morning sickness she felt in the next few weeks. Everything in her life was coming together, and if Sheilagh looked at her pale face suspiciously at times, she ignored the woman completely. And on a fine May morning, when Sheilagh had left the house, Bridget packed everything she and Cassie needed in two suitcases, and told the child they were going on a little trip.

'Why?' Cassie pulled a face. 'I wanted to play with my dolls today.'

'You can bring your dolls with you,' Bridget said impatiently. 'All of them. Put them all into a bag.'

Cassie looked at her in astonishment. 'Are we going to sleep somewhere else?' She said.

'Yes, we are. We'll have a good time –'

'For ever and ever?' Cassie persisted. She was very bright, and for a second Bridget hesitated, unsure whether or not this would be good news to Cassie. She didn't want to cope with floods of tears. And Walt would be here with the taxi in a very short while now.

'We'll see,' Bridget said vaguely. 'Just get ready now, love, and be a good girl.'

Cassie did as she was told, bundling her dolls into a bag with infuriating slowness. But at last all was ready, and with relief Bridget saw Walt's familiar cab drawing up outside the front door. She hurried Cassie downstairs. There was a small pile of mail on the table inside the front door, waiting to be sorted. She flipped through it quickly. One letter was from Ralph that she stuffed into her bag to read later.

Thankfully, there was no one about to see them go, and Walt cheered Cassie up at once, teasing her about her family of dolls, and looking questioningly at Bridget. She gave the instructions, seeing his eyes widen. He didn't speak for a minute until the engine was running again and the cab began to move.

'Leaving for good, then, are you?' He said, as they swung out of the driveway of Finley House. Bridget never looked back once. The house held no good memories for her. But at his words, Cassie swivelled round on the seat and looked at the house with fright in her eyes.

'Where are we going, Mammie?' She stammered before Bridget could answer.

'We're going on a big ship, Cassie. We'll sleep in a small cabin every night for several weeks, and we'll meet plenty of other nice people all going to Ireland.'

Cassie's eyes overflowed at once.

'I don't want to go to – where you said!' She howled. 'I want to go *home*.'

'We are going home, love,' Bridget said in an edgy voice. 'Ireland is home.'

Cassie sobbed silently all the way to the ocean terminus. Walt stayed with her while Bridget collected the tickets and paid over the passage money, wondering about this beautiful woman who seemed to have no real idea about money at all. He had brought her all this distance from upstate New York, and she obviously had no idea of the cost.

And he was still wondering what kind of crazy fool he was,

supposedly a hard-neck New York cabbie, to be telling her not to worry about his fare, and that Donaldson would see to it . . . knowing full well it was going to be a loss for the week as far as he was concerned. He must be going soft in the head, to be doing this for a stranger and her kid . . . Bridget thanked Walt profusely, and pushed the reluctant Cassie up the gangplank of the ship. The journey home had begun. The dream was within her grasp.

It didn't feel very dreamlike to be squashed in the tiny cabin with the rebellious Cassie. The child continued to sulk, no matter how much Bridget coaxed her into believing that their new life would be much better than the old. To Cassie, before her father's death, life had already been wonderful. And she was still missing him dreadfully. Bridget reminded herself of that every time she became exasperated with the child.

'Let's go up on deck and watch as the ship sails, Cassie,' she said persuasively. 'It'll be less hot up there.' And hopefully, neither of them would feel sick . . .

Cassie allowed herself to be moved about with bad grace. Bridget sighed. She had been pliable enough with Thomas, but with herself, and even with Sheilagh, she had been awkward and difficult, and Bridget could see stormy days ahead, in their cabin if nowhere else. She prayed it would be nowhere else . . .

On deck, everyone crowded near the rails to see the coastline of New York receding gradually. The sirens hooted, and Bridget felt a surge of elation that at last, at long last, she was leaving this adopted country behind. The ship slid past the beautiful Statue of Liberty, so close that she almost felt she could touch it, and even Cassie stared curiously, in awe of the carved green bronze of the lady, so huge, close to . . .

'Isn't she lovely, *ma petite?* She's gracious indeed, just like the lady I presume is your Maman. It *is* Bridget O'Connell, isn't it?'

At the words, Bridget gaped in disbelief. She knew the voice, and the accent, and the dear, familiar rotundity of the man. The one out of all the world, perhaps, that she was grateful to see at this moment, when all of this was so alien to her, and when she began to realise uneasily how useful it was to have a man's shoulders to lean on.

'Monsieur Alphonse!' She gasped. 'Oh, I can't tell you how glad I am to see you!'

She fell on his neck, while Cassie looked on even more resentfully at her undemonstrative mother hugging this strange man with the pink face and almost-white hair.

Chapter 16

'I can't believe it's you!' Bridget gasped.

'Nor I you,' he said delightedly. 'A lot of – how do you say – water – has obviously gone under the bridge since we got a brief note from your guardian to say you weren't coming back to the Academy. We have plenty of time to talk about it now, Bridget, and for me to make the acquaintance of this little one.'

So much to say . . . so much to tell, and not to tell . . .

Bridget hugged his arm with tears at the back of her eyes, thinking how uncomplicated his life must be. She had always suspected he was unaffected by sex in any shape or form, and it would seem to be a very blissful state to be in. No highs, but no traumas either.

The passengers were leaving the decks now and finding their way about the ship, which was their home for the next few weeks. Monsieur Alphonse suggested they went to the salon for some lemonade and buns, his eyes twinkling at Cassie, who suddenly decided he wasn't so bad after all.

'And what of your singing, *chèrie?*' He asked, when they had exchanged as many confidences as each permitted.

Bridget gave a small laugh. 'A career that ended before it began,' she said lightly. 'I married and had a child, and there seemed no room for anything else.'

'But this need not be!' He said, appalled. 'When there's such a voice inside you, it must be heard, Bridget.'

She glanced to where Cassie was charming a couple of

stick-thin elderly women passengers with her favourite doll.

'There's also something else inside me,' she said quietly. 'I'm expecting another child, so I want to take things easily on this trip.'

'Then you will allow me to act as your protector,' he said at once, knowing now of her circumstances, and more than a little curious at her apparent lack of feeling at her husband's recent death.

'Thank you, Monsieur Alphonse,' she said, with the smile that he remembered.

'All the same,' he added, before they parted to rest before dinner that evening. 'There's no need to think a career is beyond you, just because you have children. Don't deny the world what you have to offer, Bridget.'

A fine thing it would be if she neglected Cassie still more while she pursued a musical career, Bridget thought wryly. And the coming baby . . . she felt a possessiveness new to her . . . she certainly wouldn't want to leave him to a nurse's attentions. She almost laughed at the thought. Bridget O'Connell's children left in the care of a nurse, indeed. As if she had money to pay for such things!

Cassie was already asleep on one of the narrow beds, when Bridget remembered Ralph's letter. It seemed like a good luck charm for it to arrive just as she was leaving for Ireland. A kind of welcome home . . . she had a smile on her lips as she opened the envelope and took out the pages inside, fewer than usual.

'My dear Bridget,' she read. 'My news this time will come as a surprise to you, though it shouldn't if you've been correctly reading all the signs in my recent letters. I'll stop prevaricating and just tell you simply, my dear, that Alma and I were married very quietly several weeks ago, and we have just come back from England, where we spent our honeymoon. It was good to see London again and to call on various old friends, but we're more than happy now to be back in our own cottage in Dundemanagh. I know you'll wish us both all the luck in the world.

Now, how are you, my dear? I trust that Thomas left you comfortably off, and that poor little Cassie doesn't pine for too long. I'm sure that she won't, with your loving care. We've known one another too long through our letters for me to be false and say that you'll be missing him. It will be a relief more than anything else, for you to be free again. I hope one day that you'll find a man you can love, and that you'll eventually be as content as Alma and myself.

My fondest regards, Ralph.'

The letter didn't say anything about discontinuing their association. It said nothing about a change in his feelings for Bridget, which had always been of the highest platonic friendship, as hers were for him. Yes, she had always known that this was coming. He was clearly destined to marry Alma . . . Yet, inexplicably, she felt betrayed. If only he had waited, so that she could have felt able to run to her friend as she had intended, for solace, for comfort, for reassurance that there was still a place for her somewhere in the world. For years, she had believed that her place was in Dundemanagh. And now?

Bridget drew a shuddering breath. She would still go there, of course. There was nowhere else to go. And Ralph would still give her support and advice . . . but it was no longer the advice of a single man. He was married, half of a couple, and inevitably it changed everything. She suddenly realised she was weeping, and seconds later that Cassie was awake and watching her.

'Mammie?' The child whispered. 'Do you feel bad?'

She slid off the bed and tottered towards Bridget, not having her sea-legs yet. Bridget sat up at once, dashing the tears away and forcing a smile.

'Mammie feels fine,' she said brightly. 'Let's get you washed and get a comb through that untidy hair, or we'll be late for our first dinner on the ship.'

Even as she said the words, it was almost as though she was standing back and watching herself and despising herself for the fool that she was. As though she could see into the future, and wonder if, years later, she would look back on that moment, when she hauled the comb through Cassie's long tangle of hair, hard enough to make her squeal, and realise she had lost a precious opportunity.

She could have taken her daughter in her arms for the very

first time that Cassie had been ready to comfort Bridget in her childish way, and felt a *frisson* of closeness that might have grown into love. As it was, Bridget closed her heart to such a weakness, and the moment was lost.

Monsieur Alphonse treated her like a mother hen with a chick and insisted that she now call him by his first name. If it amused the other passengers, neither of them noticed or cared. Cassie was pampered by the elderly American ladies vacationing in Europe, now that travel was freely open to everyone again. In the evenings, there was always a variety of entertainment in the salons, and one night there was to be a talent contest with a first prize of a hundred dollars.

'You must enter, Bridget,' Alphonse urged her. 'You will win easily, and the money will be useful for buying trinkets for the little one,' he added delicately.

'Oh, I couldn't –' she protested.

'Then I will enter your name for you,' he said calmly. 'I refuse to allow you to let my teachings go to waste. It is an insult to me!'

The ladies were seated alongside them on the deckchairs, enjoying the sea breezes on deck, and listening to Cassie's childish chatter.

'What is it that you do, Bridget?' Mrs Leydon said eagerly, her friend, Mrs Schuster, just as keen to know.

'Well, I sing a little –'

'She sings like an angel!' Monsieur Alphonse rolled his eyes with Gallic expresssiveness at her understatement.

'Then we insist that you enter too, honey,' Mrs Schuster said. 'And little Cassie may sit with us while you perform.'

'I've nothing suitable to wear – and my hair –'

The matrons swept all that aside. 'You let us take care of that. Come to our cabin and take your pick of a dozen cocktail gowns in our baggage that are much too frivolous for us old dames,' she said inelegantly. 'As for your hair, it could certainly do with some re-styling, but there's a hairdresser on board, honey, so go get yourself dolled up and knock 'em dead!'

Bridget was carried along by their enthusiasm, and a sliver

of excitement ran through her. Why not? It was all for a lark, as Ralph would say. And if the hundred dollars prize did come her way, she could certainly use it.

The talent contest was a huge success. There was a winsome child of five or six singing about a dead dog, and a juggler who dropped his clubs more often than not; there was a conjuror, and a banjo player, and a pianist who played Mozart very heavy-handedly; there was a bass baritone who gave a solemn rendition, and a ladies' duo who gave a high-pitched version of the Barcarolle from the Tales of Hoffmann. And there was Bridget.

'Mammie looks funny,' Cassie whispered, as Bridget gave the small ensemble the nod that she was ready to begin.

'No, she doesn't, *chérie*.' Alphonse chided her softly. 'She looks as she was always meant to look.'

The American ladies agreed. They had persuaded Bridget to borrow a cocktail gown in shimmering blue chiffon, a loose-fitting tubular affair in the latest fashion that Mrs Leydon had purchased in New York, knowing she would probably never wear it, but unable to resist it.

It suited Bridget to perfection, as did the new hairstyle. Her long black tresses that she had worn coiled and pinned, had been shorn into the latest bob, and the effect was stunning. But no more so than the voice that soared through the elegant ship's salon, and from the first pure notes there was no doubt who would be the winner of the talent contest.

The voice was more assured than when she sang at Thomas Finley's insistence at Niagara. There was maturity and strength in it now; nor was Bridget an immature girl wanting to please an audience. As the notes rose and fell, she knew she was really singing to please herself. At the end, the applause was deafening. Bridget's cheeks were flushed, her eyes shining, as she bowed time and again before she was allowed to sit down, clutching the precious winner's envelope in her hand.

Alphonse nodded in quiet satisfaction, in stark contrast to the effusiveness of their travelling companions. Cassie looked uneasily at the beautiful stranger who was her mother, her face was more animated than she had ever seen it in her life.

'Honey, you're wasting your life, going to some Irish backwater,' Mrs Schuster said frankly. 'Your name should be up in lights.'

Bridget laughed. 'That's not for me,' she told her. 'I thought it was, once, but now I have my daughter, and I'll be happy to live a quiet life.'

'You could earn more money in a single night as a singer than picking potatoes or whatever it is you intend to do in Ireland,' Alphonse put in slyly.

'I'm not going to pick potatoes,' she grinned. 'And money isn't everything.'

She wondered if it was really *her* saying those words. Ideally, it was true, of course, but there wasn't much you could do without money, all the same. She looked up as the ship's entertainments officer approached their table in the salon, where the evening's dancing was just beginning.

'May I speak privately with you for a moment, Mrs Finley? I shan't keep you long from your friends.'

'Of course.' She moved with the man to a nearby vacant table, and ten minutes later she came back with a startled expression on her face, thinking ruefully how quickly her own high-flown philosophy had been blown out of the porthole.

'What is it, Bridget?' Alphonse said.

'Well, I don't quite know how it happened, but I've agreed to sing for half an hour each evening for the rest of the voyage, and I'm going to be paid for it. That's a turn-up, isn't it? What on earth am I going to wear?'

The ladies laughed while they congratulated her, and said she wasn't to worry about that. They'd take care of it, and she was to have the pick of their wardrobes. They clearly saw her as their protégée, and were enjoying it immensely. And even while she thanked them in some embarrassment, Bridget met Alphonse's eyes above the rim of her glass, and didn't know what to think.

It wasn't what she had intended at all. She hadn't wanted to sing in public again, but there was an exhilaration about it that she couldn't deny. A feeling of oneness with the music

214

that she had never felt at any other time in her life. At least – only once.

She realised it was almost like the oneness she had shared with Austen Hamilton. The same glory inside, the same mystical completeness. It was strange that she should have put her singing aside because of him, and now she felt herself drawing closer to his memory because of it. Strange, and wonderful, and somehow, right.

'Mammie, are you going to sing every night?' Cassie was saying in her petulant voice.

'Yes, I am, darling! And you'll be my very important daughter, and sit at the very front table with Uncle Alphonse and Mrs Leydon and Mrs Schuster to listen to me.'

She glowed, leaning forward to give Cassie a hug. And realising that the child was stiff in her arms.

'I don't want you to sing,' she scowled.

'Why on earth not?' Bridget said. But even as the ladies laughed at her silliness, and Alphonse began expounding on what a marvellous pupil Bridget had been at the Academy, she knew the answer. In Cassie's childish mind, the mother who had never really been a mother to her, was moving even farther away from her.

Bridget had found something tonight that could bring back all the vitality she had never shared with her daughter. Cassie was too young to have it all explained in words, but the feeling of neglect was instilled deep inside her all the same. And helplessly, there seemed no way that Bridget could reach her.

By the end of the voyage, everyone knew Bridget's name and no one clinked wine glasses or called for a steward or left the salon while Bridget Finley sang for her half-hour spot. She was somewhat out of touch as far as the latest tunes were concerned, but the ensemble was only too ready to help her out, and they had a brief practice every morning while she learned the new melodies, and if she had to refer to the music sheet in the evenings from time to time, nobody worried, as long as she sang.

The ladies insisted that she keep several of the cocktail gowns for the sheer pleasure she had given them, and for the delightful Cassie's company. Alphonse was going on to

Bordeaux when the ship sailed from Dublin via Southampton, and hugged her with tears in his eyes as the great ship tied up carefully at its first port of call, and gave her an address where she could write to him if she ever felt the need.

Many of the passengers wanted to shake her hand and wish her well, and such adulation was new to Bridget. It might have turned her head, if it hadn't been for Cassie's troubled eyes. The child felt left out, but no matter how much Bridget tried to include her, she hung back sullenly, and in the end people tended to ignore her. Despite the usual impatience with her, Bridget was concerned about Cassie, but the chance to earn money so unexpectedly, and in doing something she loved, had been irresistible. But she was under no illusion that it had been a chance in a lifetime, and now it was over.

Once they were in Dundemanagh, there would be time for Bridget to try and sort out the problems of her disturbed little daughter. She had no idea how she would do it. She wanted to help Cassie, but there was still no feeling of love in her heart for the child. It was wrong, and she knew it, but she just couldn't help it. Unwittingly, she was putting a heavy responsibility onto Dundemanagh, as if just being there was going to solve everything.

It was impossible to get a taxi-cab to take them so far from the city. Dublin wasn't New York, where anything could be bought. Dublin was slower, less frenetic, more *Irish*. Bridget stepped out onto Irish soil for the first time since childhood, and could have wept. The emotion was exactly as she had expected. In her mind were all the lovely images of her Mammie and Daddy, and Kitty and Michael, just as they were so long ago before that terrible April morning sixteen years ago. A close, loving family, who would be glad that she had come home . . .

'Is it a taxi-cab for Dundemanagh you're wanting, missus?' A deep Irish voice said beside her as she clutched Cassie's hand and looked around uncertainly, after approaching several drivers in vain.

'Oh, yes, please! I've no idea how far it is, but can you help me?'

The grizzled farmer looked her over. He wore rough

corduroys and dung-spattered leggings halfway up his legs. His hair was as unruly as if it had never seen a comb, and although Bridget felt a bit wary, he seemed her only chance.

'American, are you?' He said easily.

She gave a short laugh. 'Me? Oh no. I'm as Irish as you are —'

'Pull the other one, missus. Anyways, if you don't mind a quiet ride, I'll take you to Dundemanagh in my trap. You and the little 'un. You'll be willing to pay for the privilege, no doubt?'

'Oh yes, of course,' Bridget said hastily.

The privilege was riding in an uncomfortable farm cart smelling none too sweet, for fifteen miles or so, while every bone in her body felt as if it would be black and blue . . . but it was a leisurely ride that Cassie seemed to enjoy, huddled up close to a great shaggy dog in the back. And all the while, the driver, Eamonn, prattled on about the countryside they were passing through.

And what struck Bridget the most, was the incongruity that in America everyone knew at once that she was Irish. Here in Ireland, the first person to speak to her took her for an American. Cassie had the American twang, of course, but she hadn't realised just how much of it had rubbed off on her over the years. She gave up pondering about it, and simply absorbed the sights and smells of this green land that was where she belonged.

'You're wanting the old O'Connell place, you said?' Eamonn enquired. 'There's new people living there now, missus.'

'I know. I just thought you might have known it by its old name.'

'Oh aye,' Eamonn said sagely. 'Good-living family, the O'Connells. The old lady died a while back, and that was the end of 'em. Though there was some tale about a branch of 'em going to America many years ago.'

'They did. I'm the last of them,' Bridget said, with a pang, and then a small swell of pride as he looked at her in astonishment.

'Is that so? You're an O'Connell, then? Well, bless my

boots and stop the rot,' Eamonn said colourfully.

They finally arrived at Dundemanagh. Bridget couldn't identify with the place at all. Her parents had lived far from here, and she couldn't remember that either. But because of family ties, this place was part of her past. She thanked Eamonn for his trouble and paid him more than he asked for, which was probably too much anyway, and stepped down gratefully, flexing her aching muscles. Cassie stood with her thumb in her mouth, sucking furiously, which often precipitated a crying fit, when the farm cart had trundled off, leaving a trail of dust behind it. There was utter silence for a few minutes.

Ahead of them, surrounded by fields of green, and the regimented rows of plants that Ralph obviously tended well, was a white-painted cottage with smoke curling from the chimney, even though it was the beginning of June now. The cottage was much bigger than Bridget had imagined, which cheered her, hoping desperately that Ralph and Alma would offer them hospitality at least for a short time until they could find a place of their own.

The money she had earned on the ship had swelled their assets a little, and the thought of it restored some of the confidence that was rapidly leaving her. She should have written to Ralph. She should have warned him she was coming. She had no idea what her welcome would be . . . or that of his new bride . . . they might not want a strange woman and child arriving unannounced on their doorstep so soon after their wedding . . . would she . . . ?

The thoughts flitted through her head and filled her with growing alarm. Added to that, she suddenly felt exhausted. The voyage, the exhilaration of her success, the joy of meeting Alphonse again, all evaporated, and all she was aware of was the child at her side, growing red-faced with fright or temper, and the child inside her who chose that moment to kick her for the very first time.

'Mammie, I want to go home,' Cassie said in a wavering voice.

Bridget's momentary wave of faintness at the movement of

218

the baby made her sharp.

'This is home now, Cassie, and you'll just have to get used to it,' she snapped. 'We'll go and knock at the door and see if anyone's home, and you be polite now; and don't go snuffling the whole time.'

What she would do if no one was there, Bridget didn't dare to guess. She hadn't thought that far. She hadn't thought it through at all . . . They neared the front door of the cottage, their feet crunching on the rough surface of the ground.

The suitcases in Bridget's hands began to feel as if they weighed a ton, and her heart was beating very fast as the front door suddenly opened and a thin, dark man looked at her enquiringly. A man with a small moustache and a woollen pullover worn over casual working trousers, a pipe held in one hand giving him a very solid-looking air.

Bridget opened her mouth to speak, and the thinnest croak emerged. 'Ralph? It is Ralph, isn't it?'

She saw the light of recognition come into his eyes. They had never met, but he knew her instantly, if only by the voice that he too, heard as American.

'Good God, Bridget! What the devil are you doing here? And little Cassie! Come inside at once. You look completely done in.'

She didn't hear anything beyond what was to her the sweetest welcome in the world. All her bones seemed to dissolve into jelly, and she folded into a heap at Ralph Brett's feet.

A long while later the four of them were sitting cosily around the peat fire that took Bridget instantly back to other days more piquantly than anything else so far. The interior of the cottage was warm with domesticity, and the antique bits of furniture that Ralph said had belonged to her Aunt and were sold with the cottage. There was herself now, with her feet on a footstool; Cassie tucking into homemade bread and preserves as if she were starving; Ralph, still amazed and concerned at Bridget coming all this way without telling him, and Alma.

Alma was tall and skinny, and the way Bridget expected

every well-bred English girl to look, big-boned and attractive in a slightly horsy, masculine way. And although friendly enough, clearly a little wary of Bridget, who didn't blame her at all. She apologised for the tenth time.

'I really am sorry for landing on you both like this. It was stupid of me not to write first, but impetuosity was always one of my faults. I could never wait for anything. It always had to happen tomorrow, if not yesterday.'

Alma smiled politely at her attempt at a joke. She asked Bridget where she and Cassie were staying while they were in Ireland. Bridget looked at her blankly.

'While we're here? But we've come to stay, Alma. This is our home from now on.'

She saw Ralph and Alma glance at one another, and it was Alma who spoke purposefully.

'Well then, we'd better get this poppet bedded down for the night, if she's finished scoffing, hadn't we? It's long past your bed-time, isn't it, Cassie? Do you want to come upstairs with me and see a real Irish cottage bedroom? You can see all the fields for miles around –'

Cassie went out trustingly with her new friend, without a backward glance at her mother, and Bridget felt choked as she looked at Ralph.

'What must you think of me? I never read your last letter until I was on the ship, and to impose on you and Alma like this –'

'Don't be ridiculous, Bridget,' he said gently. 'We're your friends, and where else would you go, if not to friends? But to be practical. You did let someone know where you were going, I suppose?'

She looked at him blankly. 'I didn't see the need. I shall never go back!'

'But haven't you forgotten Cassie's trust fund, my dear? You must let the lawyer know that she's alive and well. You can't avoid that responsibility.'

He must think her even more foolish for not thinking of it herself. Of course Donaldson must be informed. He had told Bridget she would receive annual statements on the investments made on Cassie's behalf. He must be given a forwarding address.

'I'll write to the lawyer,' she said humbly. She hesitated. 'Ralph, I've something else to tell you. I'm expecting another child. I've a little money to last me a wee while, but I must find work to support the three of us, and somewhere of my own to live. I don't mean to be dependent on anyone.'

He saw the spark of pride in her eyes and admired her for it. She was every bit as strong as he had always imagined she would be. He would never confess it to either of them, but it was Bridget O'Connell's own brand of strength he had seen in Alma, the first time they met.

His wife came down the twisting staircase as Bridget finished speaking. Was it her imagination, Bridget wondered, or was there more warmth in the other girl's smile now?

'There's absolutely no need to think of that immediately, Bridget. We've more than enough room for you and Cassie to stay here until you get yourself sorted, and Ralph and I will get our thinking caps on to decide how we can best be of help.'

She linked arms with her husband, and the little gesture told Bridget firmly that these two were a united pair, and no matter how attractive and alluring this stranger from America, nothing was going to disrupt the harmony of their marital state. But Alma was nothing if not determined. If Ralph's friend needed a home and stability, then she would do all she could to help out.

'What about Harry's place?' she said much later that evening, when confidences had been exchanged, and they had heard all about the singing sensation on the ship, and learned just as quickly that Bridget had no intention of exploiting her success.

Certainly not while she was still carrying the baby, whose future seemed to mean so much to her. In Alma's innocence, she assumed it was to cherish the memory of her late husband, and Ralph, who knew the truth of it, didn't bother to enlighten her.

'I don't know,' Ralph ruminated. 'He's always muttering about pensioning off that housekeeper of his and installing someone younger. It might suit Bridget, I suppose. There'd be plenty of room for the children –'

They carried on as if she wasn't there, while Bridget thought uneasily that the only Harry who had ever been mentioned to her was the disreputable-sounding English chum of Ralph's, Harry somebody-or-other who was a horse-enthusiast and had his finger in a lot of pies. Bridget hadn't thought he sounded too savoury a character.

She cleared her throat, and the Bretts both looked at her as if suddenly realising she was still there.

'I'm sorry, Bridget, you must think us awfully rude,' Ralph said at once.

'No – it's all right. I'm just wondering if this Harry is the friend you mentioned once before. Some sort of horse-dealer – ?'

Alma's peal of laughter echoed round the thick walls of the cottage. Her face was scarlet with merriment when she finally managed to speak.

'Oh, that's really rich, that is! Old Harry will scream with laughter when I tell him –'

'Then please don't!' Bridget said in alarm, realising she must have made some terrible mistake.

'She won't, I promise you,' Ralph said firmly, though the corners of his mouth were twitching as well. 'The truth is, Bridget, Harry is Lord Harry Ashworth, and he has a place in the country here where he breeds racehorses. His estate is in England, but he spends a few weeks in Ireland every couple of months, buying and selling horses, so I suppose you could call him a horse-dealer –'

He couldn't contain his laughter any longer, and this time Bridget joined in. Lord Harry Ashworth indeed! Why hadn't Ralph ever told her more about the man! She still didn't like him, anyway. He sounded elderly and too terribly pompous and English-country-squire for words.

But if he really did want a housekeeper for this place of his in the country, where she could bring up her children in the peace and tranquillity of Ireland . . .

222

Chapter 17

Alma was clearly enjoying herself at being an indulgent
pseudo-auntie for Cassie. And as Cassie's birthday had been
in April, Alma decided they would have a pretend birthday
party for her in the middle of July. Privately, she considered
that they were still getting over the exhaustion of uprooting
themselves, however wanted it had been on Bridget's part.
Alma's arrangements coincided with a letter from Harry
Ashworth to say he was coming over to his property and
would be calling on his old friends.

Which led Alma to urge her husband to reply promptly,
suggesting Bridget as his housekeeper, knowing full well that
the elderly Mrs Green didn't want to stay on much longer.
She made sure that Harry would arrive in time for the party.
It would be a useful way of letting them all size one another up
informally, Alma told Ralph, highly pleased with her ingenuity, but for the time being keeping Harry's proposed visit
to themselves.

Life in the country suited Cassie, who had lost much of the
pallor in her cheeks now. She was slowly getting over the
death of her father, but she was a solitary child and preferred
the company of her dolls to people. The country suited
Bridget too, and seeing no real threat in the visit, Alma had
told her she was welcome to remain with her and Ralph until
after the baby was born.

Then, it would be time to move on. It was what Bridget
wanted, and she was pretty sure it was what Alma wanted too.
It was generosity enough to allow her and Cassie to stay so
long.

*

The pretend-birthday was hot and sunny, and Cassie squealed with delight at the gifts showered on her. A toy dog that barked when his tummy was pushed; a new book of nursery rhymes; a party frock to wear at the important tea that was to be set out of doors in the summer sunshine.

The expensive car pulled up at the gate of the cottage in the middle of the afternoon, and Alma called from upstairs to say she'd be down in a minute, and saying in mock surprise that it was Harry Ashworth. Bridget squinted her eyes against the sunlight to see this old friend of Ralph's. The baby she carried was still five months away, but sometimes it pressed heavily on her side, as it did today, and she leaned against the wall for support, the soft lines of the convenient tubular dress fashion concealing the pregnancy well so far.

She felt a mild shock as she saw the tall lean figure of Lord Harry Ashworth approaching. For some reason, she had expected someone elderly, or dour, or at the very least, rakish. He was none of these. He was good-looking in a clean, aristocratic way, probably not yet forty years old, with springy brown hair and eyes that were a deeper brown. He carried a cardboard box beneath his arm.

The thought of keeping house for such a man made Bridget instantly revise all the luxurious thoughts she'd had about the opportunity. It might be better for him to stick with his elderly housekeeper, not one whose very presence in his house might cause talk! Her own haphazard thoughts made Bridget unnecessarily curt when Ralph came hurrying round from the back of the house and she was introduced properly.

'So this is the elusive singing star I've heard so much about,' he greeted her, his handshake firm and warm.

'If that's what Ralph's told you, he's given you a false impression,' she said tartly, irritated that he knew so much.

'Oh, I'd say you were definitely a star, even if I didn't know you. You have that kind of aura.'

Bridget was suspicious of compliments from strangers. But she reminded herself that yes, she *did* want his employment.

'Thank you, Sir, my Lord – I'm sorry, but I have no idea how I should address you. We have some grand houses in New York, but not too many Lords.'

He laughed easily, glancing at Ralph. 'The name's Harry. I thought you knew that. You don't need to worry about anything else. And where's the un-birthday girl? I've brought her something special.'

'Oh, there was no need –' Bridget was even more annoyed. This stranger didn't have to bring Cassie anything just because he happened to arrive at the cottage today. Then she realised that he must have known all about Alma's party, or he wouldn't have come prepared . . . her eyes glinted, wishing her friends hadn't done this, especially without telling her.

Cassie had been upstairs with Alma, wanting the new auntie to dress her in the party frock in lemon and peach spotted voile. Bridget bit back any further retorts as she saw the shyness fade from Cassie's eyes when Harry Ashworth crouched down to Cassie's level and opened the box he carried. He took out a replica of a racehorse made from pale grey velvet and held it out to the child. It was just as if he knew how Cassie would love the sensual feel of the fabric as she held it to her face, and let the softness of the velvet caress her skin. Bridget spoke sharply.

'Cassie, say thank you to – to –'

'Uncle Harry,' he supplied.

'Thank you, Uncle Harry,' Cassie said joyfully, and before Bridget could guess her intention, she had moved forward, thrown her arms around his neck and kissed him. Bridget was stunned. Cassie had never made such a show of affection to anyone except her father.

'This is a very special horse. Shall I tell you why?' Harry said, still smiling.

'Yes,' she said curiously.

'Because he belongs to me. The real one, I mean. His name's Smokey Sam.'

Cassie's eyes were growing rounder by the minute at all this information.

'Can I see him?' She said eagerly.

Bridget broke in, half annoyed at all the attention this stranger was giving her daughter, and even more at her uninhibited response. 'Cassie, of course not. Don't ask such forward questions.'

The swift disappointment on Cassie's face at this was replaced almost at once as Harry Ashworth said he thought it was most likely that she would see Smokey Sam very soon.

'I thought you and your mother might like to come and see my house tomorrow morning, if it's convenient, and you can tell me how you like it. And you can see Smokey Sam and the other horses too, of course.'

It was obvious to Bridget that this invitation was really an informal interview to see if each of them suited the other. Presumably Alma or Ralph had made all the approaches on her behalf. It was probably all going to be wonderful . . . but things had had a habit of becoming un-wonderful so often in her life that she couldn't allow herself to get too excited about it. Not yet. And not like Cassie, who was running round in circles now, bouncing the toy horse along the grass and ignoring all her other gifts.

'I'll run you over to Harry's place in the car,' Ralph was saying now.

'There's no need. I'll come and fetch Bridget and Cassie myself. About eleven, shall we say? You can stay for a bite of lunch and I'll bring you back in the afternoon.'

'Don't you have things to do?' Bridget said inanely, with the feeling that she was being swept towards something she wasn't sure she wanted after all.

'Yes.' Harry Ashworth said, his smile teasing her. 'I have to hire a new housekeeper.'

Promptly at eleven o'clock the next morning, the sleek black car pulled up outside the cottage again. Bridget hadn't slept well. The baby seemed to be lying on a nerve, and her erratic dreams were beset by images of a wealthy gigolo luring her into his clutches by enticing her daughter with gifts of sweets and toys. Lord Harry Ashworth didn't remotely resemble such a man . . . but Bridget's inborn suspicion of men went too deep for her to trust him completely on such short acquaintance.

In fact, his best recommendation was that he was Ralph's friend. She smiled wryly at the thought. Harry caught the smile as they drove away from the cottage, with Cassie clutching the velvet horse tightly in the back seat and breathing down their necks.

'That's better. I began to wonder if you ever smiled, Bridget.'

She bristled at once. 'Of course I do, when I'm pleased, or when something amuses me.'

'And what amused you just now?' He was canny enough to guess it was her second choice rather than the first.

'I was wondering how you and Ralph met,' she hedged. 'He's mentioned you occasionally, but he never said how you came to know each other.'

'The usual ways. The same university, the same regiment, even being treated in the same field hospital in France for a time. After the war we still kept in touch, especially when he found his retreat in Dundemanagh, and discovered my place was so near.'

'Oh.'

Bridget hardly knew what to say. In her experience, none of these things amounted to 'the usual ways' of getting to know each other. These were people of a different class, almost a different race . . .

'Are we nearly there, Uncle Harry?' Cassie's plaintive voice came from the back.

'Nearly, sweetheart. Look over there, through the trees. Those low buildings are the stables.'

In five minutes they could see the house as they drove slowly around the grounds where half a dozen valuable horses were being exercised by young lads. Bridget had expected the house to be magnificent, but it was a simple cottage, not much larger than Ralph's. It was the land around it and the livestock that was worth thousands. She let out a long breath at the sight of the cottage. Harry grinned at her.

'Disappointed? You expected a mansion, perhaps?'

'I'm relieved,' she said candidly. 'I didn't fancy the thought of being caretaker for a stately home!'

They exchanged steady glances, and each knew that Bridget was going to take the job.

'If you come to England, you must promise not to be overawed by my other place then,' he said.

She laughed. 'I hardly think that's likely – my going to England, I mean!'

'Did you ever think you'd come here?'

She considered that honestly. 'No.' She said finally. 'It was a dream that I never really thought would come true.'

'Then think of going to England as another possibility. You've travelled this far – why balk at a few more miles across the Irish Sea?'

'Because I've nothing to go to England for,' she retorted, and he laughed back.

'I like your style, Mrs Finley! A man knows exactly where he is with you. It might scare some off, but it doesn't scare me.'

'That wasn't my intention. To scare you off. Nor to encourage you. I mean – oh God, I don't know what I mean! You're confusing me now.'

She went scarlet, but to her relief he seemed to take no notice, pulled the car to a halt outside the cottage and turned to lift Cassie out of the back.

'Can we see the real Smokey Sam yet?' She demanded impatiently. 'Can I touch him?'

'Soon,' Harry promised. 'First, I want you both to see my house and to say hello to Mrs Green.'

'And don't sulk!'

Harry and Bridget said the same words simultaneously as the child's lower lip stuck out mutinously. Bridget began to smile, and heard Harry's answering chuckle, and even Cassie sensed that something funny had occurred and trotted towards the cottage door quite amicably. She tried to read the carved wooden sign above the door.

'Ros – something – what does it say, Mammie?'

'Rosewall Cottage, love.' Why couldn't it have been anything but that? Anything without a rose in the name that would always remind her of Austen, when she was doing quite well in keeping her emotions in check. Never forgetting him, for that was an impossibility, but coming to terms with the fact that she was never going to see him again . . .

'Ghosts?' Harry Ashworth said quietly, seeing the change of expression on her face.

'None that I can't keep in their place,' Bridget said tightly, and stepped inside the cottage.

An elderly woman came towards them, leaning heavily on a stick, smiling a welcome as Harry introduced them all to one another.

'Sure, and 'tis glad I am to see you both,' Mrs Green said at once. 'Lord Harry's told me all about you, and 'twould seem an ideal situation for you and the child – and the other one that's on the way. When is it, my dear?'

So Ralph and Alma had spread that bit of news as well! Bridget recalled her daddy saying long ago that everyone knew everyone else's business in the villages in Ireland, and nobody minded at all, since it saved folk the bother of repeating things ten times over.

'Around Christmas,' she said.

Harry encouraged them to sit down companionably in the cosy sitting-room. Mrs Green joined them and said she'd make them all a cup of tea in a minute. Clearly there was no thought of class distinction here.

'Mrs Green's happy to stay on until the new year, Bridget, but then she wants to go and live with her sister.' Harry said easily. 'It'll probably be best for you to remain with Ralph and Alma until then, anyway. Will that suit you?'

'Oh, yes. Of course.' She said hastily.

She'd assumed the job was available right away, and now she was glad that it wasn't. Everything was changing so quickly, and this gave her a breathing-space. It also gave her a settled home with the Bretts while she waited for the birth of her child, good friends around her, and security for Cassie.

'You'll tell me what the duties are here?' She enquired, when Mrs Green went off to the kitchen, and this began to feel like the oddest kind of interview.

Harry nodded. 'The very simplest. You'll treat the cottage as your own home, which it will be. All that's needed is for someone to live here to keep the place aired and clean, and to cater for me when I come over from England. The stable-lads and grooms are all local and trustworthy and require nothing from you, except their wages every Friday, which are delivered by a bank messenger in a sealed envelope containing the dozen packets. Mr Fletcher, my trainer, is in charge of the men and will give you any assistance you require. You'll have a housekeeping allowance, and a personal salary. It couldn't be simpler.'

She guessed at once that it had been made this simple on Mrs Green's behalf. It occurred to her that Lord Harry Ashworth was a very kind man. The rich could afford to be kind, the cynical part of her said. But they didn't need to be, all the same.

'I feel as if I shall be getting all the benefits,' she said slowly. 'A beautiful cottage, a home for my children, the freedom of the country –' the wonder of it all brought the sting of tears to her eyes. It was so much more than Bridget O'Connell had ever envisaged for herself.

'Nonsense,' Harry said. 'Leaving the cottage in the care of someone like you is doing *me* the favour. It's time Mrs Green retired, and she'll be glad to hand over to someone who's obviously going to love the place.'

Yes, she was, Bridget thought, with a lift of her heart. She began to look around the cottage with fresh eyes, seeing the solidly built fireplace with its inglenook, and the thick stone walls, and the window-seat with its fresh bowl of flowers, and the twisting staircase like Ralph's.

And she felt a sudden glow of pleasure that all this was virtually going to be hers. It was going to be such a perfect place to raise her child, the boy she was sure she was carrying, whom she had already decided to call Liam Dermot, a twist on her father's names.

'Mammie, can we see the horses *now*?' Cassie tugged at her hand, and Bridget looked down with a little shock.

Rosewall Cottage was a perfect place to raise *both* her children, she thought swiftly, knowing to her guilt and shame that for a moment she had seen nothing but the new child that she considered hers and hers alone. Because of her hatred for Thomas Finley, it continued to be incredibly easy to blot out the fact that he had impregnated her body to give the child life. Because she welcomed it so much, she had simply forgotten all about the angelic-faced four-year-old, Cassandra Mavreen . . .

*

230

Liam Dermot Finley came squalling into the world early on Christmas morning, giving his mother far less trouble than his sister had, a fact that endeared him even more to Bridget. The midwife, pleased that the birth hadn't been lengthy enough to spoil her own family festivities, handed the infant to his mother, smacked his buttocks, and said that he was a grand and healthy boy.

And Bridget looked down into the furious red face, and caught her breath in a moment of pure ecstasy. This child had such a look of her brother Michael about him, it was almost uncanny. She steadfastly believed that if Michael had been spared from the earthquake to become a man, he would have looked exactly like Austen Hamilton . . .

In Bridget's mind, still swimming from the exertions of childbirth, the three of them became one. This child, this beautiful, adored child, was both Michael and Austen. And everything dear that she had lost, was miraculously, wondrously restored to her. She hugged the child close and wept over him.

When she was tidied, Ralph and Alma brought Cassie upstairs to see her little brother. From downstairs, the smell of the Christmas goose roasting made Bridget's mouth water. She was incredibly hungry. She had just given birth, and she was physically exhausted, yet her spirit was revitalised and exhilarated. She was whole again, complete.

She smiled at the trio as they came towards the bed, fussing and smiling and longing to see the new arrival. Cassie reached out a tentative hand to stroke the dark downy hair on Liam's head.

'No, Cassie!' Unconsciously, Bridget's arms tightened around the shawl-wrapped bundle. 'Be careful. You musn't poke him. He's very tiny –'

'She only wants to see him, Bridget,' Ralph said reproachfully, seeing the crestfallen look on the girl's face. 'She's never had a brother before, have you, darling?'

Cassie looked mutinously at Bridget and the baby, seeing the completeness there. Unable to define it, but sensing it, knowing it.

'I don't like him,' she scowled. 'He won't be able to

231

play with me.'

'Well, of course he won't, not yet. He's just a baby,' Bridget snapped. 'You'll have to wait until he's older. You knew that.'

'Then I'll be older too, and he'll never catch up with me.' Cassie began to wail.

Alma gave her a consoling hug, looking over her head at Bridget.

'She's been around adults too much,' she said dryly. 'She's too clever by half, aren't you, poppet?'

Cassie glared up at this adult who was usually on her side, and who seemed to be criticising her. But it wasn't Alma's approval she wanted, anyway. Nor Ralph's. And certainly not this new thing, so very tiny, who was being held so lovingly in her own Mammie's arms. Held closer than Bridget ever held Cassie. Being stroked so softly, and kissed so gently in a way that Bridget never kissed Cassie. The pangs of jealousy were sharp and miserable in Cassie's childish heart. She didn't even recognise them for what they were. She only knew she wanted to hurt somebody because she was hurt, and she kicked out savagely at Alma's shin.

'Oh, you little vixen!' Alma gasped, rubbing her leg, while Ralph scolded her and told her she was being very naughty, and couldn't she see that she was upsetting her mother, and making her new brother cry?

'Don't care!' Cassie shouted. 'I wish Uncle Harry was here. I wish I could be with Smokey Sam and Bright Light and Hillside –'

'Cassie, for pity's sake, stop it.' Bridget was upset and alarmed. 'Come and sit on the bed, and say hello properly to Liam. Look, he's opening his eyes. I think he wants to meet his big sister.'

Cassie stopped bellowing and took a small step forward, standing on tip-toe. The baby was properly awake now, cross-eyed at the daylight, and turning his head a little to where Cassie stood. He gazed blindly, but for her it was enough. The temper changed to delight, and she held out her arms impatiently. After a second, Bridget put the baby into her daughter's embrace, still holding him herself, and Cassie planted a sloppy kiss on Liam's puckered mouth.

'He likes me,' she said joyously, 'He's going to be my real doll-baby from now on.'

Bridget smiled, but inside she was overcome with remorse. Cassie had shown real, searing jealousy, and Bridget couldn't be sure that this change of heart wasn't merely to try and please her mother. To win a share of her affection. Bridget knew to her shame that there had been little to spare for this child of Thomas Finley's. She wondered uneasily now if she had gone so far away from her daughter that there was no way back. The girl was not yet five years old. These were still formative years, and Bridget vowed to make things better between them when they went to live in Rosewall Cottage. Cassie was her father's daughter, and nothing could change that, but there was still a part of her that was Bridget's . . .

After a month, they moved into Rosewall Cottage, and if Bridget had been anxious about the interpretation the neighbouring community might put on her presence there, it was soon squashed by Mrs Green and the trainer, a stocky bull of a man not unlike Bridget's memories of her father.

'You let anybody say a bad word about you, Mrs Finley, and I'll soon put 'em in their place,' both stalwarts said keenly, and she believed them.

Harry came to see her settled in with the children, made the right noises over Liam, and went back to his home in Sussex again. The next time he came, he told her he'd take her dancing, before she got too old and domesticated to remember how to enjoy herself. Alma could be roped in to sit with the children, and they would go into Dublin to a night-spot.

'You don't have to do this, Harry. I'm perfectly happy. And I'm not looking for, for –'

'An affair?' He said, just as bluntly. 'Neither am I, so we'll put all that nonsense behind us. I merely want to take a beautiful woman dancing, which I enjoy, and can hardly do by myself.'

'And you promise there'll be no hanky-panky?' She said daringly. He laughed, leaned forward and kissed the tip of her nose like a Dutch Uncle.

'Not a breath of it,' he said lightly.

So over the next few years, whenever he came on his regular trips, they went dancing, and she wore the new-style frocks that were all the rage, with knee-length skirts that made her feel more young and frivolous than ever before. The young girls were being called 'Flappers', and even though Bridget was in her thirties now, her delicate features and her slim shape that suited the fashions so admirably, kept her young enough to be included. Ralph and Alma encouraged her to go out when Harry came to Ireland, clearly hoping that a romance was blossoming.

But she never thought of him in that way, and when he told her briefly that he'd once had a passionate love affair with a French girl during the war that had ended tragically when the Germans blew up her home, Bridget knew that she was safe with Harry. He wasn't interested in a romantic entanglement either. She even told him fervently how relieved she was to know that their feelings matched.

They became quite the classiest couple about town. Bridget began to wear make-up again, and kept her hair shingled. They danced the shimmy-shake and the charleston, and Harry bought a gramophone for the cottage and a selection of the new jazz records for Bridget to enjoy while he was away, or to practise their dance steps in the tiny sitting-room. She sang the latest songs in his ear while they danced. They went to the cinema, mesmerised by the flickering screen while Bridget sighed over Rudolph Valentino, and ached to look like Lillian Gish, which Harry assured her she already did. They laughed together over Charlie Chaplin and Buster Keaton until tears rolled down their faces. They were as close as two people could be while remaining friends and not letting any other emotion intrude.

By the time Liam was four years old and Cassie was eight, Bridget had given up pretending to herself that she loved her two children equally. Liam was the light of her life. His likeness to Michael/Austen had grown, not lessened. She saw Austen in every turn of the child's head, the squareness of his stature, the quick pleased smile, the clearness of his eyes. She

234

adored him. And Cassie knew, and grieved, and ached to feel part of that closeness that she knew she would never share, without ever knowing why.

Cassie was dark-haired, exquisitely pretty, quick and intelligent. She had learned to ride a horse, and all Harry's employees made a pet of her. She attended the village school and was streets ahead of the other pupils. She was ever eager to show Harry her latest prowess each time he was in Ireland.

He came home to Rosewall Cottage for the Christmas of Liam's fourth birthday, and they were all invited to the Bretts' for the entire day. It was cold and wintry, and Bridget snuggled into the fur of the coat Harry had given her, as she herded the children into Harry's car for the short journey.

She constantly protested at the amount of money he spent on gifts for her and the children, but he told her there was no one else to spend it on, and why shouldn't he get pleasure out of giving it to his family? He called them all his family, yet to outsiders it must seem a strange kind of relationship, with no obligations on either side.

After a splendid Christmas dinner, lulled with wine, the men smoking expensive cigars, the children playing happily with their toys in an upstairs room, Harry made the quiet announcement that was to change the direction of Bridget's life again.

'I'm glad we're all together this Christmas, because I have to tell you that I'm putting Rosewall Cottage and the stud on the market in the new year, the whole kit and caboodle of it to be sold as a job lot.'

The fact that he used the jokey slang language that was so unlike him, had the effect of telling them all that he was perfectly serious. And more than that. That he was apprehensive as to their reaction, as well he might be. None of them said anything for a minute, and the crackling of the fire in the frosty weather was the only sound in the room.

Bridget was the first one to find her voice.

'Harry, you can't mean it!' She said, aghast. 'You should have given me some warning, told me you were thinking about doing this –'

. . . about making her homeless . . .

He made an angry gesture. 'If I had discussed it with you, or told you what I was contemplating, you'd have had weeks of worrying –'

'And what do I have now?' She said shrilly, suddenly uncaring of the way Christmas Day was being spoiled. None of it was her doing. 'Don't you think you owe me something, instead of throwing me out in the street?'

'Don't be ridiculous, Bridget,' He said shortly. 'There's no question of that.'

'Why don't we sit down calmly and listen to Harry's explanation?' Ralph said mildly. 'It's not like him to be reckless, and he must have a good reason for this decision. I trust that you do, Harry, otherwise you've chosen a fine time to drop this bombshell, old boy!'

They were aware of the silence from upstairs, and then they heard the creeping footsteps of the children, hearing the grown-ups arguing. Harry called them down.

'Of course there's a reason, and Cassie and Liam may as well hear it too, since their future's involved as much as anyone's.'

Bridget stared at him, her face white. They were friends, and more than friends, and she owed him a hearing. The children ran to her, and unconsciously her arms went around them both, drawing them close.

She felt vulnerable and threatened, and inside her the desperate need to feel safe was very strong, in a way it hadn't been for years. Not since she had vowed to keep Kitty safe, after the earthquake.

Chapter 18

Harry looked at the expectant faces. Only Bridget's was angry. Only the one he loved the best . . .

'A man can't go on aimlessly for ever,' he said somewhat abruptly.

Why did she have to look at him that way, with the face of

an angel, and the temperament of a devil!

'Hardly aimless, old man,' Ralph said lightly, obviously trying to keep the atmosphere as calm as he could. 'A large estate like yours doesn't run itself, and you've got the horses here and your involvement in the races, and a few directorships –'

Harry smiled tightly in agreement. And all of it superficial. Nothing that couldn't do as well with somebody else at the helm. A title opened many doors, but not the one he'd begun to realise he coveted most.

'I accept all that, Ralph, but I'm not prepared to sit back and let life flow around me, any more than you are. A couple of years in the trenches takes away the ability to settle back to a soft life. For some, it emphasises the need to keep on fighting to keep their self-respect.'

'You're not looking for another war, are you, Harry? Alma teased, uncertain where this conversation was leading.

'No. I'm buying a newspaper,' he stated. 'And as controlling owner, I shall supervise every damn thing that goes into it. I shall print the truth about everything from politics to society scandals, and give the people what they want to know, and have a right to know. I've been thinking about it ever since the General Strike earlier in the year, and the plight of those poor devils, the miners.'

'Bravo,' Ralph said dryly. 'And with all this honesty you'll land yourself in a dozen libel suits in the first week of circulation.'

'I'm not that crazy,' Harry assured him. 'I've a good team of legal chaps behind me and some first-class reporters who aren't afraid of the truth. Between us, this is going to work.'

'It sounds – splendid,' Bridget muttered, knowing she must say something, but hardly knowing what to think. It was obviously no split-second decision. He must have been planning it for some time, and it was just as clear that he was stimulated by the whole idea. She had never seen him quite this alive.

'But why give up the cottage here, even if you feel you must sell the horses? Wouldn't you want the cottage as a place to come back to, to relax?' She ventured.

Cassie hadn't dared to interrupt this animated conversation, but now she moved away from her mother and threw herself onto Harry's lap.

'You're not going to sell Smokey Sam, are you, Uncle Harry?' She started to sob. 'I'll never see him!'

He stroked her dark hair. 'I hope you will, sweetheart. I'm coming to that. Although his racing days are over now, he'll be put out to grass at Ashworthy, my home in Sussex. I shan't sell Smokey Sam.'

He looked at Bridget, and her heart began to beat almost painfully as she saw something in his eyes that was usually hidden from her. If he was about to propose to her, then it was nothing short of emotional blackmail. Using Cassie's love for the horse to get her to agree . . .

Harry looked down at the child again. Liam stayed where he was, chewing his thumb and pressing into Bridget's skirt, warm and comforting.

'Running a newspaper isn't a part-time job, Bridget. And the horses were only ever a side-line. A rich man's amusement,' he censured himself, then turned to Cassie again. 'And since I know your mother will never agree to marry me, I shan't bother asking her.'

'I'll marry you, Uncle Harry,' Cassie said in a tremulous voice. She looked up at him devotedly. To Bridget it would have been comical were it not for the shock of seeing the unconscious coquetry in the child's eyes. Small girls had no idea of the power they wielded. Her daughter was not yet nine years old, and Harry Ashworth was forty-three. But in ten years' time, the difference wouldn't seem so great. Bridget shivered, hearing him laugh gently as he squeezed Cassie's waist the way he'd done a hundred times before.

'We'll have to wait until you're all grown up for that, my love! What you need first is a good school where you can work hard and learn all you can, because that clever little brain of yours is going to waste in Dundemanagh.'

'That's absolutely true,' Alma nodded at once.

'What kind of school?' Bridget said sharply, since they all seemed to be taking the initiative away from her, and it was her daughter they were discussing.

238

'I've made enquiries about an excellent Catholic boarding school where they specialise in languages and the arts. Cassie deserves her chance, Bridget, and I'm sure she'd do well there.'

'And it's in England, I suppose.'

There might have been only the two of them in the room now, their eyes clashing, Bridget's pride fighting with Harry's desire to do this for her, for her family, since he considered them his family too.

'Oh, Mammie, please say I can go!' Cassie's blue eyes were blazing with excitement at the thought of such an adventure now, her face glowing. She was such a beautiful child when she wasn't scowling, Bridget thought anew, struck by the perfect contours of Cassie's cheeks and the delicate, peach-like complexion. She was going to tear some man's heart to pieces when she was a woman . . . she dragged her thoughts back to the important issue of the moment. Cassie had already turned to Harry again.

'Will I sleep in a room with lots of other girls, and have pillow fights and secret midnight feasts – ?'

'I can see you've been reading too many books,' Ralph chipped in, laughing.

'Well, Bridget?' Harry asked quietly.

'How can I possibly decide just like that? You take my breath away with your preposterous suggestions. Manipulating people's lives with your money and your influence –' she found that she was clenching her hands, and her palms were damp. 'Do you really expect me to let Cassie go off to England alone? She's just a child –'

'Naturally, I wouldn't expect her to go without her mother,' he said calmly. 'What kind of a fool do you take me for?'

Oh, he wasn't a fool at all, Bridget thought bitterly. He knew very well what he was doing. Making it impossible for her to refuse, that's what! Even all the talk of marriage meant nothing, because their relationship didn't include sex and passion and the intimacy of living together.

She looked at Ralph and Alma, saying nothing right now, and giving her no help, and felt a twist of envy at their

239

closeness. She had deduced long ago that theirs wasn't a marriage of high passion. They shared a very real and gentle affection and for them it was enough. But Bridget Finley had once tasted the ecstasy of passionate love, and nothing else could ever come close to it, and nor did she want it to. She was angry at her own thoughts.

'Are we going to live with Uncle Harry, Mammie?' Liam wanted to know, taking his red and sodden thumb out of his mouth to speak in an uncertain voice.

'No, of course not, darling,' she said vigorously. 'And all this talk of good schooling for Cassie is fine and dandy, but I can't afford fancy schools and there's an end to it.'

'She can sit an examination and if she passes, the fees will be waived,' Harry said relentlessly. 'Her uniform must be provided, but you will allow me to buy that and you can pay me back, if your pride won't allow you to accept a gift from a friend.'

'With what?'

Now came the moment. Whatever else was happening here, she was still going to be left without a home, and without the steady allowance Harry paid her for caring for Rosewall Cottage. She always knew it was far too much for the job, but she had become used to the money. She couldn't move back with Ralph and Alma. it wouldn't be fair on them even if they offered, and besides, she had become her own mistress all these years at the cottage.

She could have wept with frustration. A fine Christmas this was turning out to be. A fine birthday for poor little Liam, who didn't understand what was happening. And for Cassie, who was snivelling now, seeing her own small dream slipping away from her before it ever became real.

'Do you still want to sing, Bridget?' Harry said.

She looked at him, startled and suspicious. What was he offering now? To buy her a theatre?

'Harry,' she said deliberately. 'I'm not a star-struck flapper of nineteen any more, with the sort of wide eyes and soft red lips that people pay to see. They can get all that on the picture-screens now. I'm thirty-four years old. I have two children. It's a bit late in the day for me to start treading the boards, wouldn't you say?'

'Bridget, don't belittle yourself. You're still a very beautiful woman,' Alma said generously.

'I'll say,' Ralph added.

'What I suggest is this,' Harry went on patiently. 'Just for once will you hear me out and not say anything until I've finished! I want Cassie to have her chance at the La Retraite school, and I'm sure she'll pass the examination with no trouble. You've never seen Ashworthy Hall, but it's a huge, rambling place, ridiculously big for one person. I'd like you to consider a small part of it as your own. Your own rooms, Bridget. You can do what you like there, entertain whom you like – even me, occasionally, with no strings attached. Liam can go to a good preparatory school as soon as you're settled in. And as for you –'   'Oh, yes! do please tell me what you have planned for me once you've disposed of my children.' Her voice was brittle, heavy with sarcasm, which he ignored.

'There's a very elegant little nightclub in the vicinity. They have a resident band, and there's dancing every night, and lately it's begun to attract the very highest *clientèle*. The odd Arab sheikh and French Count drop in for dinner, and a fair sprinkling of the British nobility and high society is always there. My newspaper is going to run a diary column on fashionable places to be seen in, and Strachey's will certainly be included.'

'And what has this to do with me?'

Harry smiled gently. 'Come on now, Bridget. You're not that dumb. And your mouth may remain pursed in that most unattractive way, but your eyes are already telling me that you're interested. As for being thirty-four years old, I'd say it's the very best age to be. You have none of the silly falseness of the vamp, and you have all the sensuality of a lovely woman. Absolutely right for late-evening romancing couples. You'd be a sensation as the regular singer.'

'My God, Bridget, you're not going to refuse, are you?' Alma almost squeaked. 'You *can't* refuse after Harry's gone to all this trouble.'

'I say, old man, this is hellish good of you,' Ralph said enthusiastically. 'Of course Bridget won't refuse!'

She caught her breath.

'Just why *have* you gone to all this trouble?' She said weakly.

'Will you marry me?' He demanded.

'No!'

'Then this is the next best thing. We'll be business associates. When you've made your fortune as a singer, you can pay me back, if you must. As far as I'm concerned, the pleasure I'll get out of seeing the three of you making something of your lives instead of stagnating, will be payment enough.'

'Mammie? Oh, Mammie, *please*.' Cassie was querulous, desperate.

'Are we going to live with Uncle Harry then?' Liam said plaintively, tired of all this arguing.

She gave in. Together, they were too much for her.

'Yes,' she said, and was immediately smothered by two small pairs of arms hugging her tight, and nearly deafened by screams of excitement. And thinking wryly that it took all this to make her daughter hug her so spontaneously.

When she could free herself from their embraces she went across to Harry, while their hosts busied themselves pouring glasses of wine to celebrate.

'I know I should thank you,' she said. 'I'm still not sure what's happening, but the children are wild with joy, and I want you to know that I do appreciate what you're doing for them.'

'I'm doing it for you.'

She looked at his dear kind face, put her arms around him and kissed his cheek. 'You're the best friend I ever had, Harry.'

His arms closed around her, pulling her into him. They had kissed before, friendly, uncomplicated kisses, but now his arms held her differently, and a *frisson* of fear showed in her eyes. Don't spoil it, they begged him, not now. No strings, he had said . . . His gaze was unfathomable.

'That's no way to kiss a friend,' he said, cursing the huskiness in his voice at finding her so unexpectedly in his arms. He placed his mouth on hers, holding her head so that she couldn't move, holding the kiss until she felt her heart begin to pound.

Vaguely, she heard the children clapping and cheering, and she broke away, flushed and awkward.

A month later, the children stayed with the Bretts while she took her first boat trip to England with Harry on a brief visit. The Irish Sea was rough, and she didn't enjoy the voyage, but she needed to inspect the schools, the nightclub, and most of all, her future home. Ashworthy Hall was the kind of solid old English house she'd never really believed existed. It was enormous, built in warm reddish stone, with great mullioned windows, and carved gargoyles supporting stone steps leading from the house to the seemingly endless gardens, woods and parklands.

'And you own all this?' She gulped. 'Thank God I never knew it before. I'd never have dared speak to you without bowing.'

He laughed easily. 'You'll get used to it, darling.'

She hesitated, then said, 'Harry, I wish you wouldn't do that. Call me darling, I mean. It might give people the wrong idea.'

'You mean they might think I'm installing my mistress in my stately home?'

She drew in her breath. 'Something like that. You must have thought of what people might say. You with your newspaper that's going to print the truth about politics and society scandals and the rest.' She quoted his own words.

'Don't worry about it. You'll be my lady of intrigue, that's all. Nothing scandalous about you will be printed in *Night News*, I promise you.'

But what about rival newspapers, if *Night News* became the success it was destined to be, with Lord Harry Ashworth at the helm! Bridget didn't dare to ask about that.

Inside, the house was elegant and filled with valuable antiques. The furnishings were costly, the carpets were thickly piled, the paintings adorning the walls were either Old Masters, or portraits of Harry's own ancestors, smiling benignly down on this Irish-American intruder who seemed so modern by comparison.

'Harry, it's all just beautiful,' she said at last. She had met the staff, and clearly her own position had been explained to them, and she never saw one curious glance.

'Come and see your own rooms,' he said. She realised how much he was enjoying this. She had often thought what a kind man he was, now she saw how much he relished acting the benefactor. Money was there to be used. It was so easy for those who had it to be lavish, but as she'd observed before, not all of them did. She was so lucky to have him as her friend.

Her own rooms were perfect. If she didn't like anything, she only had to say so, and it could be changed. He had put some new pieces of furniture in with the old, in a clever blend that seemed to suit Bridget's personality. She was overwhelmed at his thoughtfulness.

'Oh, Harry, I do love you,' she said in a catchy voice, clasping her hands and whirling round her own sitting-room with its vista of rolling Sussex Downs stretching away as far as the eye could see.

'I should think so,' he said practically, knowing that despite the words, and the fact that she would be living in such close proximity to him, she was as far out of his reach as ever. And in fact, he told her, he would be in London for much of the time. He had an apartment there, and until the newspaper really got going, he wanted to be on hand as much as possible.

'Now, how about some tea before we take a drive around the grounds?'

She giggled. It sounded so grand. Taking a ride around the grounds indeed. It was all far, far grander than the Pendletons' house on Nob Hill, though why she should have thought of it at that particular moment, when she was so happy, she couldn't say. But as always, the memory never failed to send a tremor through her veins.

'I don't really know why we were all so cheerful at Christmas, when we knew we were going to lose you, Bridget,' Alma said mournfully, when the time came for them to part, three months later. 'You are happy about all this, aren't you, darling?'

'How could I not be? And the children will have a wonderful chance –'

244

'Never mind the children. I'm asking *you*. Of course, Ralph and I always hoped that you and old Harry would make a go of it, but I suppose that's out.'

'I'm afraid so,' Bridget laughed. 'And don't worry about me. I'm going to be a singer!'

Even now, she couldn't believe it was all true. She had had an audition at Strachey's Nightclub and been hired on the spot. Cassie had passed the entrance exam to La Retraite, deep in the Sussex countryside, and would be starting right after Easter. Liam too, would be placed in his preparatory school at the same time.

Bridget tried not to think of that. She would have a lovely home and a exciting job where she would meet all kinds of people, but she was losing her children. She was losing Liam. It was foolish to mind so much, when it was all for their good, but she would miss Liam so badly. He was still her darling, her cherub, and he was so small to be going away from home.

This was the way society ladies behaved though, so she might as well get used to it, she thought, with an absurd little laugh to be putting herself in the same category.

'All right?' Harry asked her as they sped through the English countryside in his silent, smooth-running car. They were driven by a chauffeur now, and Bridget had to keep reminding herself that this man that she had known for so long, was important and rich and influential, and it could still take her by surprise.

'M'm,' she nodded in answer to his question. The children were agog, exclaiming at everything they saw through the window. Bridget felt Harry's hand clasp hers for a moment.

'It's not so different from Ireland, is it?'

She knew he was trying to reassure her. 'Not really,' she admitted. The fields were still green, the sky as slate-grey on this windy April day, the spring flowers still struggling to emerge from their winter sleep.

She was different, not the countryside. Bridget Finley, who had once been Bridget O'Connell, and had cherished dreams of Ireland for so long it had almost become an obsession. And now she had left it all behind, and her children would soon learn to speak with correct English accents and forget all

245

about their heritage . . . but Cassie was American, she reminded herself. It was only herself and Liam who were truly Irish . . .

It took a while to get accustomed to the new way of life. One of the first things for Bridget to do was to write to Mr Donaldson in New York, informing him of her new address for the annual reports of Cassie's investments to be forwarded. The lawyer had invested well, and the trust fund had already swelled considerably in the ten years since it had been set up. Cassie knew nothing of its existence, and it was only occasionally that Bridget wondered uneasily what Liam's reaction would be when he discovered it.

By the time a year had passed since leaving Rosewall Cottage, Bridget felt that her life was becoming ordered at last. She had her own place in the world. She was happy.

Cassie wrote to her once a week as the nuns insisted all the pupils at La Retraite did. Cassie now spoke of everything being 'simply spiffing', and of the high praise heaped on her at her quick grasp of French and German. Sister Thérèse had seen the potential in the child, and had suggested she might think of becoming a linguist. It was a word that cropped up so often in the letters, that Bridget knew her daughter was charmed by it.

Liam had also settled remarkably quickly into his preparatory school, where the teachers were gentle and kind to the children of well-to-do families, and had no reason to think that Liam Finley deserved any different treatment to the rest of the young children in their care.

Harry's *Night News* had got off to a slow start, but had gathered momentum at the end of 1927 with an exclusive and undeniable story of scandal about a member of parliament and a music-hall artiste. That, coupled with the hard-hitting political pages and the society diary that carried news stories about royalty as well as all the scatty goings-on at Ascot and Henley, and the reported twosomes seen at fashionable night-spots assured the newspaper of continuing success.

'I hardly see you these days,' Bridget complained one evening as she was getting ready to go to Strachey's, and Harry had knocked on her door as he always did before being allowed admittance. He sprawled easily on the velvet sofa in Bridget's sitting-room and drank his fill of her.

She was like a beautiful butterfly emerging from the chrysalis after a long and painful metamorphosis, he thought. She was even more beautiful now than when he had first seen her. She was assured, more self-confident, a queen among women as far as Harry was concerned, and he loved her more deeply than ever.

She turned to him now, after checking that her make-up was perfect, her glossy black hair sleekly in its feathered cap, before driving herself in the little car he had put at her disposal, to the nightclub ten miles away.

Harry grinned. 'That's the price you pay for success, my dear.'

'But you don't need to work so hard. For pity's sake, Harry, you own all this. You must be worth millions. There's no need for you to drive yourself so hard.' She knew him well enough now to be as frank as she liked. 'And when did you last come to hear me sing?'

He laughed out loud now. 'That's the real reason you're so piqued, isn't it? You think I'm neglecting you.'

'Well so you are. We hardly spend any time together, and I – I miss you.'

He drew in his breath as her voice softened. But he had long ago resigned himself to the fact that she missed his company as a friend, a companion, no more.

'I promised to come with you for Cassie's Speech Day, didn't I?'

'Oh, Cassie! It's always Cassie! You never miss one of her school occasions, do you!' She said in irritation.

'Would you want me to? All the other girls' parents turn up, and I'm the only apology for a father she's got. Not that any of them look at me when Cassie's beautiful mother is around, of course. Nor even at Cassie, however well she's done.'

'That's not true.' But they both knew that it was, and Bridget didn't know whether to be flattered on her own account, or worried on Cassie's. Once recently, the girl had flounced off because the French tutor on whom she had a crush, had spent more time chatting to Bridget about her singing than discussing Cassie's recent brilliant report.

He saw the frown on her face and spoke lightly.

'It's not always easy for a child to live in the shadow of a star, Bridget, but Cassie will find her own way in the world, I'm sure of it.'

'Liam's all right though, isn't he?' She said defensively, since he still made it sound all Bridget's fault. 'He doesn't go all temperamental on me when I visit his school.'

'Ah, but Liam's Liam, and Cassie's Cassie.'

'What a ridiculous thing to say,' she began crossly, and then gasped as the grandfather clock in the corner struck the half-hour. 'I must go or I'll be late, and we've some very important people coming in tonight, Harry. I'm surprised your spies haven't been out. The elderly Lord Winstanley and his new Portuguese bride. They say she dances divinely.'

'Heaven help the old boy, then, for she'll probably wear him out in the first month,' Harry chuckled.

'Oh, our paid lounge lizards will keep the lady happy. We've a new one, did I tell you? A Spanish chap called Pablo, dark and sultry and a wow with all the old tiara-biddies,' she said irreverently.

'Mind he doesn't set his cap at you, then.'

'A fat chance he'd have. I'm not being caught by anyone, least of all a lounge lizard. They're all suspect!'

She laughed, blowing him a kiss as she went out, her little velvet cape slung over the shoulders of her fluted white frock, leaving him to turn out the lights and shut the doors. She loved it when they had these little exchanges of light repartee. They were gay and amusing, and she felt as much of a society hostess as the next one.

As for the lounge lizards – the professional dancers hired by nightclubs and hotels to keep their elderly guests happy – she wouldn't touch them with the proverbial barge-pole. Most of the ones she'd met were gigolos, and some were definitely on the queer side. But in the bright and hectic world of dancing and nightclubbing and jazz, anything went these days . . .

As always, Bridget felt a glow of excitement as she drove off in the little car and eventually parked it in her special place at the rear of the brilliantly lit nightclub. Harry had taught her to drive, giving her another new and delightful freedom. Her life was serenely pleasant now, she thought, and she no longer felt guilty at accepting things from Harry. She knew she repaid him in plenty with her own companionship and that of the children. He simply liked having them around. They filled his life as much as he filled theirs, and it was a perfect, uncomplicated and platonic arrangement on both sides.

She was well known at Strachey's now. People came there especially to hear her sing. She had developed a new and intimate way of singing in the dimly lit room, looking at each person for long moments while she sang the words of love or disillusionment, as if she sang for them alone. The adrenalin flowed with every reaction from her audience, and sometimes she wondered if they ever guessed that her own heart was quite stony with regard to all the sentiments that brought tears to many eyes.

> '. . . let us not forget tomorrow,
> while we dream of yesterday . . .
> for maybe just around the corner,
> is the one for whom we pray . . .'

The lights were soft and rose-coloured, the amber spotlight playing on her. She finished the new song to rapturous applause, and smiled in her own practised way. She acknowledged the accompaniment of the band and turned slowly all around the room to accept the adulation, until she looked directly at someone who was vaguely familiar. He was a smartly dressed man with an unmistakable military air who sat with his face wreathed in cigarette smoke. Her memory caught up, and then the man's appearance sent the colour from Bridget's face, causing her to summon up all her stage presence to make her exit gracefully.

Chapter 19

As she expected, a note was delivered to her small dressing-room a few minutes later. She told the boy it was all right, and composed herself before greeting the man she hadn't seen for eleven years.

'Charles Keating! I can't believe it's really you!'

She held out her hands and he took them both in his own. The last time she had seen him was when he had married her friend, Mary-Jo, and Bridget had needed all her strength to go to that wedding, so soon after Austen Hamilton's death.

'I wasn't sure it was you, either.' He said, in the clipped American accent she knew so well. 'I saw the posters advertising Strachey's with their lovely songstress called Bridget, and wondered if it could possibly be the same girl. And here you are! And just as lovely!'

There was a small silence between them as each sized up the other. He'd changed. Become harder, his eyes more hooded than she remembered them. He wore a neat little moustache now that gave him a slightly more sinister air than of old. He had almost filmstar good looks, but they were those of the wicked villain rather than the hero on a white charger. And she had changed too.

'But hardly the same girl any more,' she protested laughingly. 'I've been a widow for more than six years, Charles, and I have two children.'

'Good God, is that so? I'm sorry, though Mary-Jo always said you'd never get married again, after – oh well, it's all water under the bridge now. She'll be mighty tickled to hear that we've met, though.'

'How is she? Oh, I always regretted that we lost touch. You

had a child, didn't you?'

'We have four now,' he said with puffed-up pride. 'We have Charles junior and Josephine-Ann, Eleanor-May and little Eva. And Mary-Jo's fine, except that she's run to fat a little.'

He ran the names together like a music-hall turn. Bridget swallowed a smile, though she found it hard to imagine Mary-Jo running to fat, and didn't care for the description.

'So now you're singing for your supper, Bridget. I must say, you're easy on the eye. I guess you attract plenty of followers. And what do you do with the children at night? Hire a baby-minder?'

She laughed then. Americans were always so direct. If they wanted to know something, they asked. No wonder the trait had rubbed off on herself.

'The children are away at school, and I was never interested in followers! But there's so much I want to ask you, and it keeps going out of my head! How are Mary-Jo's parents, and do you ever see any of the other boys, and – oh, this is ridiculous. You haven't told me yet what you're doing here. Or if Mary-Jo's here with you – but of course not, or she'd have been at Strachey's with you, wouldn't she?'

The words ran away with her. She was startled and confused at seeing someone from her past. All those years ago . . . the first time she had seen Charles Keating was at the Carsons' garden party. It was also the first time she had seen Austen Hamilton . . . that fact alone would draw her to this man, even if she had never been particularly charmed with him at the time.

Nor now, if the truth were told, and the single men who came to Strachey's were generally after one of two things, neither of them pleasant. They sought out the rich un-attached elderly women with money to spend on young men who would oblige . . . or they sought other young men for a different kind of sport. She pushed such unworthy thoughts away, because clearly none of that applied to Charles Keating! He had seen her name and wondered if she could possibly be his wife's old friend.

'I'm over here on business. My family's into freight

251

movement now,' he said, using an impressive-sounding phrase that told her nothing. 'I'm staying in town, but I've hired a car and motored down here for the evening. Being on your own in a strange country can be pretty boring.'

She knew she should show some hospitality to Mary-Jo's husband. She had one more song to sing that evening and it would still be daylight for a good while. It was the end of July, and the summer evenings were long and warm and glorious.

'Would you like to see where I live? We could have a good gossip and bore each other with talk about our children as well as the old days. It would only take you an hour to drive back to London from my home.'

'I accept!' He said at once, and she hid a smile. She was hugely anticipating the moment when she would lead him into the imposing grandeur of Ashworthy Hall. She had always felt that Charles Keating slightly patronised the little Irish friend of Mary-Jo Carson, bank manager's daughter. Let him patronise her now!

'And perhaps you'd like to come to lunch on Sunday. The children will be home for the weekend, and you could meet them.'

'Fine.' But his smile wasn't quite as wide, and for all that he had four of his own, Bridget sensed that Charles was more at home flattering women than playing with children. But suddenly she wanted to show hers off. She wanted him to report back to Mary-Jo that Cassie and Liam Finley had grown into a real little English lady and gentleman with their cute plummy accents and stiff manners.

With a shock, Bridget realised how true that was. For a few minutes, she seemed to stand back and see her children through a stranger's eyes. Cassie in particular, was growing into a real snob, and Bridget wondered just how she'd take to this easy-talking American. But first, there was this evening to get through, and once her duty at Strachey's was done, she slid behind the wheel of her car and told Charles to follow her.

His awe at the sight of Ashworthy Hall was something she wished Harry could see, Bridget thought with an inward chuckle. She remembered that Charles Keating had been rarely lost for words, but he was now. When they got out of the cars, he leaned against his hired vehicle and gaped at the great building in front of him.

'Dear God in heaven,' he said irreverently. 'You aren't telling me you own this pile of stones?'

Bridget laughed, enjoying herself immensely. Americans! Forgetting that for years she had considered herself Irish American herself, she felt a swell of pride at this beautiful piece of English heritage set in its own land.

'Hardly! I have rooms here,' she told him. 'The estate belongs to Lord Harry Ashworth.'

His eyes became mildly speculative. 'Is that so? I seem to have heard the name. Doesn't he own newspapers or something?'

'One newspaper,' she corrected, as they walked to the west wing of the house. 'It's called *Night News*.'

'That's the one. He's a hard-hitting guy, by all accounts.'

'He's truthful. And fair.' Bridget said briefly.

'And you're in love with him, right?'

'Wrong. We're very good friends.'

He pretended to back away with a grin. 'OK. I just wanted to get the position clear, that's all.'

It shouldn't matter to him, Bridget thought. He was married to Mary-Jo, her friend, and that was the only reason she had invited him here. She pushed down the small feeling of unease that she was here alone with this man who was a virtual stranger to her after all. Alone, except for a small army of servants who would come running in a minute if she touched a bell. She relaxed, and opened her own front door.

'I don't keep any drink in my rooms,' she apologised. 'But tell me what you'd like, and one of the servants will bring it. Then I'll ask someone to open up the main rooms and give you a quick tour of Ashworthy Hall, if you like, before you return to London.'

That made another position clear, she thought. She wasn't a stupid woman alone in a great mausoleum of a house, nor had she invited him here for anything other than renewing an old acquaintanceship.

'Coffee would be fine,' he said. 'I've had my fill of brandy at Strachey's, and I do have to drive back.'

She relaxed still more, and made the coffee while he browsed around, examining everything, still staggered at her rise in the world, and having a job not to show it.

And whatever she said, he was pretty sure there was more than friendship between her and his Lordship. It was obvious. He'd always thought Bridget a cold fish, but he was seeing her very differently now. He'd seen the way she ogled the guys at the nightclub when she sang in that sexy, husky voice. And before he went back stateside in a week's time, Charles Keating meant to get himself a little bit of the goodies, but for now he'd play it coolly and correctly.

Playing the fish before getting the bite, he thought inelegantly.

Bridget was glad when he finally left. Not that he wasn't good company, but she was tired. She always was, after her evenings at Strachey's. She sang there four evenings a week, and was paid an exorbitant amount of money for her brief appearances. It enabled her to buy lovely clothes for herself and the children, and to feel really independent for the first time in her life. She had wanted to pay Harry some rent for her rooms, now she could easily afford it, but he wouldn't hear of it. She was sorry he hadn't been home tonight. He would have enjoyed meeting Charles Keating. At the weekend, perhaps. She would invite Harry to lunch on Sunday as well. That would really give Charles something to brag about when he went back home.

But first there was Cassie's Speech Day on Friday, and then the children would be home for the holidays. She looked forward to Cassie's Speech Day, knowing the girl was to do something special that even Bridget hadn't been told about. It was all a great secret, Cassie had said importantly in her last letter, in which she now addressed Bridget as 'Mother'. Cassie always came top in everything, and had now begun talking about going to finishing school in Switzerland when she finished at La Retraite. That time was years away yet, but Cassie knew just what she wanted, and was not above coaxing Harry into it, knowing he would persuade Bridget. Cassie invariably got what she wanted where Harry was concerned.

He indulged her far too much, Bridget thought with some irritation.

They decided to pick up Liam from his prep school on Friday morning and drive straight on to La Retraite. Cassie's face when they arrived was less than pleased. She was tall and gangly for nine years old, and every time she saw her, Bridget felt a little shock at how fast she was growing. She was still a child, but with the poise of someone far beyond her years who knew she was more attractive and intelligent than those around her.

'What did you have to bring him for?' She snapped when she saw the four-year-old Liam. 'You know how he wriggles about, and I have to –'

She clapped her hand to her mouth, nearly giving the secret away. It was beastly of them to bring Liam along when this was her day, and especially when she felt less than perfect after hearing she had come second in one of her exams. She had never come second before, and it was very important to Cassie to be first in everything.

The one thing in which she knew she could never succeed was her mother's affections, so she compensated by striving to be first in everything else. She wasn't really as brilliant as everyone accepted. It was just that she worked harder.

The speeches were made out of doors, since the weather was so fine. Rows and rows of chairs had been placed in front of the central dais, and a few whispers ran round the other parents as the slim figure of Bridget Finley appeared with her small son and her handsome escort.

La Retraite was a school for the daughters of the wealthy, both British and foreign, and once the usual business of the day had been conducted and Cassie held a clutch of end-of-term certificates in her hand, Sister Thérèse held up her hand for silence.

'We pride ourselves on being a cosmopolitan school at La Retraite,' she said in her soft voice with little trace of Irish in it. 'We encourage our girls to be good decent citizens with the very best of education as their strength. Each girl is given the same chance, but because of their own ideals and aspirations, one girl often stands out above the rest, and this year is no exception. Our star pupil of 1927 is undoubtedly Cassandra Mavreen Finley –'

She had to pause while the applause rang out, and Bridget saw her daughter's face go pink at the praise. For the first time, Bridget realised how much Cassie needed that praise, as badly as a desert thirsty for rain.

'We have many pupils from countries other than our own, and I'm very pleased to see some of those parents here today,' Sister Thérèse went on. 'And because Cassandra's brilliance lies in her linguistic ability, I call upon her now to say the final few words for this school year in English, French and German.'

This then, was the surprise. Cassie stood, tall and composed, and recited the few well-rehearsed sentences in the three languages, as effortlessly and fluently as if she had been born to it. Bridget felt her throat constrict at this daughter of hers, so unloved, yet capable of holding this audience in the same way Bridget held her own. The similarity struck her at once. Today, Cassie too, was something of a star.

And she wasn't totally unloved, Bridget thought quickly. Harry adored her. Liam was boisterously affectionate when Cassie allowed him to be. Ralph and Alma wrote regularly to her at school, and she answered their letters with enjoyment. The nuns were obviously fond of her, and she didn't lack friends at school, for all her cleverness.

It was only Bridget who persistently found it hard to show any feelings towards this child of Thomas Finley.

Guiltily, she made up for the knowledge by hugging her daughter when she finally reached them after all the formalities, and Cassie was flushed with pleasure at all the congratulations.

To her surprise, Cassie moved out of her arms after a moment and glared at her.

'You never kiss me, do you, Mother?' She said in an odd little voice, and turned her back on her.

Bridget saw Harry scoop her up in his arms, and plant a kiss on Cassie's cheek. She couldn't tell if he had overheard or not. Then Liam clamoured for a hug, and Cassie graciously permitted it for once, grinning down at him, and making a great fuss of him as several of her admiring friends came near.

I've lost her, Bridget thought. I've really lost her, and it's all my own fault, and now I have no idea how I can ever get her back. Or if I really want her back . . . but the pangs she felt were almost as sharp as birth pangs, and she couldn't make any sense of them.

And then some parents claimed her attention. They had heard Bridget sing at Strachey's and had brought their dinner menu especially for her to sign it if she would. Bridget switched on her dazzling professional smile, and the moment of introspection was gone.

Charles Keating arrived sharp on time for Sunday lunch at Ashworthy Hall. Harry was quite ready to meet this old acquaintance of Bridget's, and Cassie insisted on wearing her newest frock. Liam paraded about like a little swell because he was going to meet an American, and Cassie had told him with her superior knowledge that he'd have to listen carefully all the time, because they spoke so funnily.

'You're in the freight business, I understand?' Harry said to Charles, when they were all seated around Bridget's table.

'That's right, Lord Ashworth. We mainly ship furniture, but there's a growing market in automobiles, and that's what I'm here to investigate.'

'That's very interesting.'

They made genial small talk, but to Bridget's surprise it was clear to her that Harry didn't like this man. The first indication was that he made no move to put Charles at his ease by using first names. Normally, there was no side on Harry, and a friend of Bridget's was usually a friend of his . . .

The children played up too. Cassie plagued the life out of Liam, who howled that she had pinched him beneath the table, and Bridget was annoyed that the picture of quiet English elegance here should be spoiled by these two irritating spoiled brats.

'Please don't worry on my account,' Charles laughed. 'My own four aren't exactly angels.'

'But at the table one does expect a certain amount of restraint,' Harry said.

He rarely censured the behaviour of the children so blatantly, and then Bridget saw that he was really reproving Charles for his free and easy attitude.

Personally, Bridget was delighted when Charles played so happily with the children on the lawn after the meal, getting down on all fours and letting Liam climb all over him, and making Cassie unbend enough to screech to be allowed to do the same. Bridget considered it a successful visit. Harry did not.

'Why didn't you like him?' She demanded to know later that same day when the children had gone to bed and they were alone in her sitting-room. The long French windows were open, the air still lingeringly warm, and the scents of summer drifted into the room.

Harry stretched out his long legs, comfortable on the sofa, and let his cigar smoke spiral into the air.

'Who says I didn't like him?'

'I say it. Oh, come on, Harry, I know you too well. The minute you saw him you were antagonistic towards him. If I didn't know you better, I'd have said you were – well, jealous!'

He looked across at her, elegant and successful, the years making her more beautiful and unaccessible. She oozed a peculiar mixture of sensuality and frigidity. It was a mixture that intrigued everyone who met her, the more so since she was entirely unconscious of it.

'Is that such an impossibility?'

'Of course it is. Why should you be jealous of an old acquaintance whom I shall probably never see again after this visit?'

'Why indeed?' He said thoughtfully. Bridget exclaimed in annoyance.

'What kind of an answer is that? I hate it when you answer my question with another one,' she said crossly.

'Shall I tell you exactly what I thought of your Mr Charles Keating?'

'Oh, I do wish you would, and then we can end this conversation and go to bed.'

'Is that an invitation?' He grinned.

258

'Harry, please be serious.'

And who said I wasn't . . . Harry stopped himself from teasing her further as he saw the impatience in her eyes.

'I thought your Mr Keating fitted one of your favourite descriptions perfectly,' he said. 'He seemed the archetypal lounge lizard.'

Bridget burst out laughing.

'Now you're being ridiculous. Charles Keating was at West Point with – with – my best friend's brother. He's an ex-military man, and he and Mary-Jo are blissfully happy. For pity's sake, they've got four children!'

'The two things don't necessarily go together,' Harry said dryly. 'You should know that.'

She felt her face go hot. 'That wasn't fair.'

'The truth is frequently unfair, my darling, but you can't spend your life avoiding it.'

She stood up, and he got the full force of those spectacularly blue eyes, and saw instantly how brittle she was beneath the fragile veneer of sophistication. He had felt certain for a long time that there was something in her past that he was never destined to know. Something she could never trust him, or any man, to know.

'It doesn't mean I have to discuss it, either. I'm tired, Harry. I'd like to end this conversation now.'

'Of course. I'll see you tomorrow, my dear.'

He got up at once and made no attempt to touch her. Normally he kissed her good-night, but she had forfeited any right to such closeness, however platonic. She felt very alone when he had gone, annoyed with herself and with him, and with Charles Keating for stirring old memories that were best left hidden.

Harry Ashworth had cursed himself a thousand times for his devotion to a woman who was never going to feel more for him than a dear friend. If she ever guessed of his true feelings towards her, he had no doubt at all that she would take flight.

He himself had given her the means of independence and self-respect, and if she chose to, she could leave Ashworthy Hall tomorrow and make a new life for herself and her children without him.

If he had any sense he would find himself a good wife who would give him heirs to this vast estate, and forget all about Bridget Finley. But he knew he couldn't do that. Since the first day he had met her, leaning against the wall of Ralph Brett's cottage with the slight mound of her pregnancy giving her that small air of vulnerability, he had loved her.

And he would go on loving her, even though there was no possibility of sexual fulfilment in the relationship, and sometimes the torment of his desire was hard to bear. But if he had nothing else, he had strength of character, and he'd go on loving her and respecting her if he had to remain celibate for the rest of his days, Harry thought angrily, as bloody well celibate as a priest.

It wasn't natural to a healthy, normal man . . . but he considered it more natural than the way that slimy lecher Keating looked at her, and if Bridget couldn't see it, then it was only because of her basic innocence about men. He'd tried to warn her, but she simply didn't hear him.

Harry hoped to God the man wouldn't come near them again. He remembered that Bridget had asked him to tell Mary-Jo to write to her when he went back to America, which indicated that Bridget didn't expect to see him again, and Harry fervently hoped that that would be the end of it.

Charles Keating had other ideas. Bridget was surprised to see him at Strachey's the next time she was there. And the time after that too. Each evening he invited her to sit with him and take a drink when she had ended her performance, and she could hardly refuse. But no matter how he tried, he couldn't get past that shell of hers, and would have to try more devious methods of getting her alone.

By then, Bridget had realised he was a past master at innuendo, and was glad that he was going back home in a few days' time. He walked to her car with her on his final evening, and swung the starting handle for her. It was all to no avail. The car simply wouldn't start, and Bridget felt like kicking it in frustration. It was getting dark and she was ready for home.

'You may just be out of gas,' Charles said.

'I can't be. I always make sure there's plenty for the journey here and back.'

'Well, this little beauty's going nowhere tonight,' Charles said practically. 'Come on, leave it here and I'll run you home.'

She had no choice, and it was good of him to bother. She found out how good when he had driven for some distance, talking amiably all the way, and she realised they were nowhere near Ashworthy Hall.

'You've taken the wrong road,' she said, still not concerned. 'You should have turned back there instead of coming through these woods –'

She knew her mistake as soon as the car slowed down and he stopped the engine. Her heart began to thud with fear. She could see his leering smile in the half-light.

'Charles, don't be silly. Take me home.'

'All in good time, honey. First of all, how about giving me a bit of what you've been promising all those guys in the nightclub?'

'What are you talking about?'

'You know very well. All those come-on stares and the slinky dresses and that sexy way of singing. Don't tell me you don't know you're getting every one of 'em hot for you! As for me, baby, I'm randier'n hell right now, seeing that ice-queen performance and knowing what's underneath.'

She felt sick. His arm was around her shoulders, his breath on her face was sour with the smell of brandy.

'You're wrong!' Her voice was shrill and ragged with fear. 'I don't encourage anybody –'

'Oh no? I ain't forgotten about you and Austen Hamilton, babe! He got his all right, didn't he? And don't try telling me his Lordship ain't getting his neither.'

His manners coarsened, his breathing quickened as she struggled against him. His hand was on her leg, hot and furious as he tried to drag her skirt away. She screamed, but there was nobody around to hear. It was all going to happen to her, just as it had happened to Kitty all those years ago . . .

The thought of Kitty, dying in her own blood after the butchery of the abortionist, seemed to give Bridget reserves of

261

strength she didn't know she had. She fought him with her fists and bit his face, but it only goaded him on.

'That's it, honey,' he crowed. 'I like bit of a fight. Mary-Jo's become too soft and willing. It's like lying on top of a feather mattress –'

'You *bastard*!'

Bridget wrenched herself away from him. She swung her arm like a piston and shot it, full-fisted, straight into Charles Keating's groin. He let out a great howl of pain, let go of her and sat doubled over, clutching himself, gasping and sobbing.

'You lousy whoring bitch! I'll make you pay for that. If you've ruined me, I'll –'

She didn't stop to hear his threats. She leapt out of the car and fled, the breath tearing and stabbing in her chest, through brambles that snatched at her legs, stumbling over tree stumps and stepping on things that shifted and moved beneath her feet, terrified and distraught. It seemed an eternity before she reached the main road again, and every second she expected to hear Charles's car behind her.

It never came, and she set out to walk and run and stagger the rest of the remaining four miles back to Ashworthy Hall. When she reached it, she crawled into her own part of the house, shamed beyond reason. How could she have been so asinine as to let that animal near her?

The children were in bed asleep, the maid in charge of them lolling in a chair outside their doors. Bridget called out to her that she could go, then locked herself in the bathroom. Gently, she bathed her slashed and tender feet, and applied salve to the cuts and bruises on her face and body.

She shook violently every time she thought of Charles Keating touching her, and guessed now that he must have let the petrol out of her car in order to get her into his. And she had been imbecilic enough to fall for it. She had never despised herself more.

As she went to leave the bathroom, she caught sight of herself in the mirror, at the dishevelled clown's appearance, so different from the fashionable and successful Bridget Finley, songstress. Her face was streaked with make-up and blood and tears. Her lovely, expensive dress was stained and in ribbons. She could hardly believe that she, who had always wanted above all to feel safe, had let this happen to her. She looked down mutely at her poor stinging hands, sank down on the floor and wept.

Chapter 20

'Uncle Harry, Mother's ill,' Cassie announced.

He looked up from his breakfast sharply. In all the time he had known Bridget, she had never had more than a cold. She was extraordinarily healthy. He looked at Cassie's placid, uncaring face, and asked irritably what she meant.

'She's staying in bed, and she won't come out of the bedroom, and her door's locked. She won't even let Liam go in, and he's crying like the baby he is, and won't eat his breakfast. Agnes keeps scolding him, and telling him Cook will be cross because it's all a terrible waste of food, but he still won't eat it. He's sitting at the dining-table like a sphinx with his arms folded and his mouth all screwed up.'

She paused for breath, pleased that she'd managed to air her bit of knowledge at the same time. They had just done Ancient Egypt at La Retraite.

'I'd better come and see what's wrong,' Harry said.

'She won't let you in,' Cassie said importantly. 'Do you think she's going into a decline?'

'Cassie, shut up,' he said pleasantly. 'You and Liam can go and see Smokey Sam this morning. Tell Barnes I said it was all right, and you can stay away for one hour.'

'You want to get us out of the way, don't you? It's all right, really it is. I understand. If Mother's going to die, it would be awful for us to be around and witness it.'

'You're becoming a pain in a certain place that a gentleman doesn't usually mention in front of a lady,' Harry's eyes glinted. 'Your mother's certainly not going to die. What a lot of rot you talk.'

'I know,' Cassie said cheerfully. 'It's the only way I can get people to listen to me sometimes. the people that matter, that is. *C'est la vie, mon oncle!'*

He stared after her as she swung away from him, yelling to Liam that they needn't bother about breakfast and could go and see Smokey Sam. She was getting impossibly precocious, Harry thought. Yet he had the uneasy feeling that those remarks were more revealing than many that she made. He knew he should register them. But then he forgot about Cassie as he went into Bridget's rooms in the west wing, where Agnes was clearing away the breakfast things in a gigantic huff.

'Left every bit of this good nourishing food, the little 'un did, Sir. I told 'im there's people starving in India wot 'ud kill for 'is chances.' the maid said, flushed with outrage. 'And the little madam was ranting on at him summat cruel, with the missus none too well, neither. It's a cryin' shame. Real naughty little beggars they can be at times, begging your pardon, Sir.'

'All right.' Harry broke into the tirade. 'Leave all that for now, Agnes, and see to it later, while I try to find out what's wrong with Mrs Finley.'

'Yes, Sir.' Agnes bobbed, reporting to the kitchen staff that it didn't seem quite proper for a gentleman to go into a lady's bedroom when she wouldn't even let in her maid and children, whether he was a Lord or not.

'Bridget, will you open that door?' Harry said for the third time. 'I refuse to go away, and I do have duplicate keys to all the rooms, but I'd much prefer it if you opened it yourself.'

After a lot of shuffling inside, he heard the key turn on the other side and then her voice telling him to wait a minute. When she said he could come in, she was back in bed, the bedcovers pulled up to her face, the curtains at the windows still closed.

'It's like a dungeon in here,' he said at once, and strode to the windows to pull back the curtains and let some daylight into the room.

He saw her huddle down still more. He began to lose his patience. Clearly she was capable of walking and talking, and this wasn't Bridget's style at all.

264

'I suppose you know your son won't eat and your daughter thinks you're dying?' he said matter-of-factly, hoping to draw a smile out of her. Instead, he heard something that was like a sob. After a few seconds, she threw back the covers so that he could see her face and neck and the long line of her throat.

'Good God, what's happened to you?' He said, appalled. 'You look as if you've been savaged by an animal.'

She began to laugh, quietly and terribly, and her voice was thick and slow and choked.

'So I have, my dear kind Harry. So I have, only this one had two legs, not four.'

He didn't understand for a minute, and then, instinctively, he knew.

'Was it that bastard, Keating?' He said harshly, using her own word for the man. She nodded painfully as the paroxysm ended. 'Oh Christ, Bridget, I tried to warn you. Did he – ?'

'*No*. I got away from him. My car's still at Strachey's. Out of petrol. He said he'd bring me home. Instead, he, he –'

She felt his arms close around her, warm and comforting. She seemed only able to speak in short sentences, as if Charles had taken her breath as well as her self-respect. And with it the last remnants of her friendship with Mary-Jo. She guessed that he wouldn't tell her of their meeting now. It was one more sad and bitter thing to remember him by.

She sobbed relentlessly in Harry's arms. The tears stung her cuts, and through it all he never said a word, just sat and held her as if she were a child. For wild moments she longed to tell him everything. All of it, about her parents and Michael and Kitty, about Austen and the baby that died, and the hell of her marriage to Thomas Finley and the reason why she couldn't love Cassie. And cowardly, she shrank away from the telling, and remained just where she was, because the feeling of being safe was too fragile and too precious to lose.

At last he spoke against her shaking body.

'I've really no objection to sitting here all day with you in my arms, Bridget, but if you're not going to stop crying, then I'll have to go and get another shirt,' he said calmly. 'And since you've come out of it all relatively unscathed, why don't we have some breakfast together? I'd hardly started mine when Cassie came in like a whirlwind.'

He bent the truth a little. Cassie had been carelessly unconcerned, and sent by Agnes to tell him of Liam's tantrum. And Bridget knew her too well.

'She wouldn't care,' she muttered. 'But I suppose I should eat something.'

'Good.' Harry stood up. 'I'll get two trays sent in here, and we'll say you had an accident falling into some brambles and you're staying in bed for a couple of days. I'll see to your car, and let Strachey's know you won't be back for a while. Right?'

She nodded, the weak tears starting to her eyes. He was so good to her. Better than she deserved. The best friend in the world.

'And we'll forget all about Mister Charles Keating,' he said. 'From now on, he never existed.'

A week later, they discovered the man's method of revenge. Bridget's cuts had mostly healed by then, and she remembered thankfully that Charles would be leaving for America that day. She slit open the letters by her plate. Several of them were the usual fan letters, one was an invitation to open a *fête*, and the last . . .

She stared at the newspaper cutting that they called a *rough*, date-stamped for the coming evening's edition. It was enclosed without any message. For a few seconds she couldn't take in the words. The cutting didn't come from *Night News*, but from a rival paper that dealt mainly in salacious gossip.

Someone had given them a choice piece of garbage. Someone who didn't care if his own name was bandied about, because he'd be somewhere in mid-Atlantic by the time this hit the news-stands that evening. Not that Charles had named anyone. It wasn't this muckraking rag's policy to do so, but the implication was there for all to see. She read it dumbly.

'A certain member of the aristocracy had better keep a closer watch on the little love-nest at his stately home. His lady-love has been singing in the ears of a dashing American ex-West Point officer lately, while poor Lord whatsit sits at home and twiddles his thumbs doing the baby-minding. But with her background, who can wonder? She's Anybody's

Baby, as the song says. Can this refer to our little songstress's misty past in upstate New York with a certain Lieutenant Hamilton? Our noble scribbling Lord might like to know that she has a fancy for the uniform. Bring out the ermine robes!'

Bridget felt the room swim, and found it hard to breathe when she got to the end of the paragraph, which also revealed just how bigoted and vindictive Charles Keating really was.

The reference to Austen was painful and despicable, but that wasn't her main concern. The information was included in a column avidly read by the scandal-mongers. It wouldn't take them long to put two and two together, with the vague allusion to journalism. Harry's name would be dragged in the mud because of her, and she just couldn't bear that.

He'd gone to London early that day, unaware of the storm that was about to burst. She had all day to worry on her own. She couldn't think properly. Her mind seemed to be like scrambled eggs. In the end, she took the children for a picnic to stop them squabbling, but her thoughts were miles away from them, until Cassie said crossly that she'd asked her a hundred times if she could have a pony.

'No, you can't and don't exaggerate,' she snapped.

Cassie's mouth became mutinous.

'You never let me do anything I want. Liam can do anything. You like him better than me. It's not fair.'

'Don't be ridiculous, Cassie.'

The day had begun appallingly, and it wasn't improving. Bridget's upset had been quickly transferred to the children. They didn't understand it, but it made them both irritable and quarrelsome.

'I want to go home,' Liam began to snivel.

'I think that's the best idea.' Bridget vigorously packed up the picnic fare as large spots of rain started to dampen her skirt.

'You *see*?' Cassie said theatrically. 'Liam wants to go home, so we go home.'

Bridget sat back on her heels on the grass.

'No, Cassie. *I* want to go home. It's raining and I've had enough of your dramatics.'

The girl grumbled all the way back in the car. She wished

she was back at school. She wished she still lived at Rosewall Cottage. She wished she could see Ralph and Alma, who never got cross with her and didn't make such a pet of snitchy little Liam. She wished Uncle Charles hadn't had to go back to America. She wished Uncle Harry was home more often. When they reached the house, Bridget pulled the car-brake on with such a jerk it threw them all forward, and Cassie howled with indignation as Bridget twisted round to glare at her.

'Oh, honey, I wish you were somewhere else too,' she raged. 'B*elieve* me, I do!'

'Why did you call me by that silly name? When Uncle Charles called me that he made it sound nice. It sounds stupid when you say it. *You're* not American!'

It was on the tip of Bridget's tongue to retort that Cassie was, though, and maybe she'd met a kindred soul in Charles Keating, and some of his brashness had rubbed off on her. Bridget bit her tongue hard, knowing this wasn't the moment to tell Cassie anything, even though she knew that very soon she must explain her daughter's background to her. She was growing up fast, and it was her right to know. But not now.

This was hardly the time to tell this little whirling dervish that her father had been a swine and her mother had loved someone else . . . not that she would say any of that, of course. Thomas Finley would have to be a little white-washed for Cassie's ears.

She felt Liam's chubby little arms reaching around her neck, and smelled the still-babyish scent of his four-year-old body.

'I love you, Mammie.'

'I know you do, darling.' Bridget said, sensing his bewilderment at this fracas between her and his sister, and wanting to put things right for him.

Cassie gave an exclamation that sounded remarkably like an oath. She wrenched open the car door and started running towards the west wing.

'You see? He's Mother's little pet as usual. It's always him. I don't count at all.'

'Cassie, wait –'

But it was too late. The damage was done, however unintentionally. Cassie was beginning to be really disturbed, and it didn't seem as if Bridget could do a thing to stop it. Except love her – the one guilty, shameful thing it was so hard for Bridget to do.

And there was still this other thing hanging over her head – this damnable newspaper cutting that had to be faced. Her head throbbed as if steam hammers were at work in it for the rest of the day until Harry came home. During the afternoon she telephoned his newspaper office. She couldn't possibly tell him over the 'phone, but she could ask him to get home as early as possible, and warn him that there was something unpleasant in the rival paper that evening. But the voice at the end of the line said that Lord Ashworth was in conference and couldn't be disturbed, and was there any message?

'No. No message,' Bridget said, and hung up.

She heard his car arrive home around eight o'clock, later than usual. He generally picked up a selection of newspapers to see what the opposition was covering, but never read them until he'd had his evening meal. Bridget couldn't wait for that. The children had gone to bed early, and Bridget felt ill, knowing what she had to tell him. He looked up in surprise from pouring himself a drink in his drawing-room.

'Bridget, this is an unexpected surprise. Come and join me.'

'I don't want a drink. Though you may need more than one when you've seen this.'

She was nervous, upset, wild with anger. He registered all three emotions, and with a small frown he took the piece of newspaper she held out to him between finger and thumb as if on the end of sugar tongs. He scanned it quickly, used to reading at speed.

'How much of it is true?' He said gently, seeing her white face. It wasn't the reaction she had expected.

'True! Do you need to ask me that, after the state I was in after he attacked me –'

'But the rest, Bridget. This Lieutenant Hamilton –'

He saw her flinch, and then she gave in.

'Yes, there was a Lieutenant Hamilton,' she said wearily. 'And yes, I was in love with him and hoped to marry him one

269

day. Only the Mexes had something to say about that – Mexicans – I'm sorry, I was forgetting you wouldn't understand our colonial slang.' She took refuge in sarcasm.

He walked swiftly to where she stood, as brittle as glass, and put his arms on her shoulders.

'My love, you don't have to explain anything to me. So you once loved a man who wasn't your husband. Whether it was before or after you married him is no concern of mine, nor anyone else's. It changes nothing as far as I'm concerned.'

'But that piece of filth changes everything.' Her lovely eyes filled with tears now. 'Oh, Harry, you've said nothing about how you feel about it. About what it's going to do to your reputation. Oh, I can't bear what it's going to do to you.'

To her bewilderment, he gave a wry smile.

'It will sell newspapers, my darling, and that's the hard and painful truth of it. It will sell theirs, and it will sell ours – for perhaps a week, which is about the time it will take for the excitement to die down.'

Bridget felt as though her legs wouldn't hold her up any longer. She sat down heavily on an easy chair, staring up at him. All day long she had been in a state of panic over this, and he was taking it so calmly. So bloody ludicrously calmly that she could have hit him. She saw at once that he was bigger than this fuss in a typesetting machine. He had far more power in his own little empire than a snide would-be lover who'd left his calling card in the most dishonourable way. She felt utterly stupid.

'What will you do about it?' She said tightly. 'I thought you'd be calling lawyers – a court case –'

'And give it far more importance than it deserves? Everybody knows this rag goes in for sensationalism. What it can't verify, it invents, and for us to go to court for damages or even to print a counter-attack will only give the thing credence. To ignore it will put it in its rightful place – the rubbish bin. I promise you this is the best way, Bridget, so darling, please don't look so stricken. We're living in a different world from the genteel days before the war. I'm afraid that the wretched cliché that no publicity is bad publicity is becoming truer these days, and even Strachey's will find its *clientèle* widening. People will be more intrigued than ever by the beautiful songstress with a secret past.'

Harry said it teasingly, hoping to make her see things in perspective. It would all blow over, and as for his reputation, he had nothing to fear from this muck-raking rag. He hadn't been specifically named, and neither had she. He had money and power and position, and more than that. He was well-liked, in the city and in private life, and he was confident on that score. But not so Bridget Finley. She leapt to her feet, scarlet now, where earlier she had been so ashen.

'Surely you don't think I'm going back there after this, do you?'

'The worst thing you can do is to leave,' he said, steely now as he saw the determination in her face. 'Do you want people to believe the story? To start saying that you're running away?'

'I *am* running away. From Strachey's, from you, from here. I can't stay here either, Harry. You must see that. You must, please –' she felt the hot tears running down her cheeks, knowing all along that this must be the result. Trying all day not to admit it, but knowing it all the same.

'No. I'm not letting you go. This is your home –'

'It's your home, Harry, not mine. I was only ever here on borrowed time. We always knew that. It's time for me to make a life of my own.'

She hardly knew what she was saying. She only knew this was what had to be. He saw her weakness and her strength, and spoke harshly.

'And if you leave, where will you go? Back to Ireland? Crawling back to Ralph and Alma with the children, and allowing them to become cabbages in some backwater instead of moving towards the brilliant careers ahead of them? Cassie with her languages that could take her anywhere she chose to go. And Liam – I had high hopes of Liam coming into the business with me eventually. Liam Dermot Finley, the cracking newspaper reporter –'

'Don't,' Bridget said thickly. 'Stop it, Harry. Don't blackmail me into this.'

Thomas Finley had blackmailed her into marrying him. It

271

had got her nothing but heartache and pain – and Cassie.

'Is it to be Ireland then?' Harry went on relentlessly. 'That was the great dream, wasn't it?'

It was, once. For years it had been the dream of her life. And she had realised that dream, and then, again because of this man's tempting blackmail, she had come here, to England. And the green rolling countryside of Sussex wasn't so very different from Ireland after all. And she saw clearly now, that it wasn't the place that mattered. It was the feeling of being home. It was being safe. And it was the children's future. She couldn't take that away from them. She controlled a sob with an effort.

'No, I shan't go back to Ireland. I'll find a small house somewhere so that the children can continue their schooling. I wouldn't take that away from them –'

'You'll still let me see them, I suppose? I mean, I know I have no paternal rights to them, but I do have an interest in them, and I do love them, Bridget.' He was sarcastic now, losing her.

'Oh God, Harry, I know you do, and of course I wouldn't want to cut you out of their lives. Nor mine!' She bit her lips, feeling them shake. 'But please don't try and stop me. I can afford to buy a modest house, and it's what I want to do.'

'I'll agree to it if you let me find the house and see to the legalities,' he said shortly. 'You know nothing of house purchase, and you'll land yourself with a heap of falling masonry if you're not careful. Agreed?'

She didn't have to agree with anything he said. He didn't have to take charge of her affairs! But, hardly knowing how it was happening, she found herself nodding, seeing the sense in his words. And somewhere among all the muddle of her thoughts, there was still the question of what she was going to do with her life. She would want a house with a garden, and she would learn to sew, and bake . . . and then? It sounded very bleak and vegetative after being a minor star at Strachey's Nightclub. That was all she had ever been, she reminded herself. A very minor star . . . But she should have remembered that Lord Harry Ashworth had influence and connections, and the quickness of mind that was already

272

moving way ahead of her own garbled intentions.

He took her to see the house after the children had gone back to school, in September. As he had surmised, the newspaper story had died a very quick death, but Bridget's nerves were still too fragile for her to change any of her plans. Her backbone was still strong though, and she wouldn't change her mind again. She wanted a quiet life from now on.

'Harry, this is impossible.'

She looked at the lovely little cottage in exasperated annoyance. A cottage, yes, but in such a select area of Sussex countryside with neighbouring cottages of the same rambling rose effect, thatched and expensive, that it was clearly beyond her means. The Downs were at their loveliest. A small stream meandered at the foot of the scattered cottages, a lazy blue in the September sunshine.

'It's yours,' he stated. 'A gift. I refuse to listen to any arguments, so don't start any. Do you want Cassie to be ashamed of her home when she starts growing into a young lady? Do you want Liam to be so far from London that he can't get into town when he starts work on *Night News*?'

Bridget began to laugh, wondering if Harry had gone completely mad. 'The child's not five years old yet –'

'The one thing you can rely on children to do is to grow older, darling. Or maybe you hadn't noticed. And I know very well that you could make payments on this place, but you'd be left with very little capital. Instead, I suggest you put your savings into an account that earns you good interest and you'll be sitting pretty, until you decide to start work again. Knowing you as I do, you won't want to stagnate here for ever.'

She looked at him suspiciously. He took her breath away, but the charm of the cottage was such that right now she felt she could very well stagnate here for ever. If it wasn't all so impossible . . .

'I told you I'm never going back to Strachey's. I couldn't, Harry.'

'Of course not.' He said it so readily she was even more suspicious. 'It was just a thought. Do you want to see inside the place?'

273

It was called Magnolia Cottage, because of the huge magnolia tree in the front garden, its delicate waxy blossoms still lingering on the branches in the warmth of the sheltered Sussex countryside. Some petals had already fallen, making a soft pinky-white carpet over the lawns and flower borders. It was homely, welcoming. Inside, the new furniture was almost a replica of Bridget's rooms at Ashworthy Hall, scaled down to fit the smaller rooms. She drew in her breath at his thoughtfulness.

'I don't deserve you,' she said at last.

'No, you don't. You deserve a man in your life who can give you more than sticks and stones. I only regret that I'm not the one.'

He spoke without emotion, and she looked at him helplessly. 'Harry, it's not your fault. You know that I love you dearly, but – marriage is not for me.'

'I know. Now then, I'll leave you here for an hour to browse around on your own, and then tell me if the cottage fits. Make some tea, put your feet up and pretend you're already at home. I've brought you some journals to read. When I come back, you can let me know when we're going to tell the children about their new home.'

He considered it already a *fait accompli*, and his last little comment about telling the children sent a small shiver down her spine. Neither knew anything of the change of plans yet. They were both back at school, and Bridget had said nothing to them before they went.

She gave up worrying about them, and did as Harry said. The kitchen was adorable, small enough to be called compact, but large enough so that she didn't feel cramped. All the rooms were more than adequate. Everything was provided for making tea. Harry was nothing if not efficient. She made a pot and let it brew while she examined cupboards and drawers, and all the time she was slipping more and more into the idea of living here, being part of the place, already falling in love with it.

Fleetingly, she imagined the children's reactions . . .

'Mother, it's so small! It's terrible! How could I possibly ask any of my friends to come here?'

'It's ever so lovely, Mammie. Can I grow fings in the garden? Can I have a tree-house? Can I catch some fish in the stream?'

'Liam, you're such a little squirt. How can you like it here after Ashworthy Hall? It's such a come-down!'

Bridget knew that none of it mattered. Magnolia Cottage fitted her, and she fitted it. Like a favourite garment, she was already comfortable and easy in it. She took her tea into the sitting-room and settled down on one of the chairs with its view of the green meadows beyond. She reached for the journals Harry had brought and opened them idly. They were all stage journals. She never knew such things existed. She began to sit up straighter.

Harry had circled various items in the journals. Advertisements for chorus-line singers in amateur shows; for young women to be trained as dansettes in end-of-the-pier reviews; a singer required for a West End nightclub, 'only professionals need apply'; a comedian was needed, 'no saucy jokes required'; a band sought a singing duo to work Saturday nights at a suburban Locarno dance-hall; a picture-palace advertised for an organist to entertain clients between shows; someone wanted a pianist capable of conducting sing-songs at an old people's home; several troupes of actors needed good singers and extras.

And so it went on. And by the end of it, Bridget was laughing and crying, because beneath all Harry's circled items he had added his own comments. 'Not your style, this one.' 'I'd say you're more of a tragedienne.' 'Didn't you tell me you could play the piano?' 'I can't see you high-kicking at the end of a pier. Right off the end, would be more like it, knowing you.'

She heard the tap at the door and ran to answer it, sure it would be him. She felt ridiculously light-hearted. The adverts were all so much nonsense, and Harry had obviously circled them to make her laugh. Well, he'd succeeded, and she felt good for the first time in weeks. She flung open the front door, all smiles.

'Wotcher.' The youngish woman with the unnaturally flaming red hair said, smiling back. 'We heard you was moving in, and were so pleased to know another theatrical was coming among us. The name's Marlene – Marlene de Wolfe. I'm a magician's assistant. Me and my husband are doing a reg'lar turn at the Corbonna Restaurant ev'ry Saturday night at present. We run the de Wolfe Follies, in case you didn't know, and why should ya, fer Gawd's sake! I'll give you and yours a coupla free tickets if you fancy it, and you can tell me if you can spot my Norman's sleight-of-'and, being a professional yourself, like.'

She took a great gulping breath after this bizarre spiel. She beamed at Bridget, who had a job not to double up with laughter at the sight of this impossibly blowsy, over made-up, voluble and instantly likeable woman, coming so soon on the heels of the adverts Bridget had just been reading. Through hysterical tears, she managed to choke out an invitation to come in and have a cup of tea, which Marlene accepted with alacrity.

Chapter 21

Six months later, Bridget saw that it had all been inevitable. She slipped into her new way of life quite effortlessly, and as Harry had predicted, the excitement about the slanderous newspaper paragraph was no more than a six-day wonder. She needn't have moved out of Ashworthy Hall after all . . . but she still thought it was for the best. She had her independence at last. She had new friends too. Marlene and Norman were cockneys, as open and honest as a fresh mountain stream, and the way Marlene and Lord Harry Ashworth got along was nothing short of hilarious.

''E's the most normal Lordship I ever seen,' Marlene frequently declared, as if she knew dozens.

By then, Bridget was firmly included in the de Wolfe Follies, though she hadn't yet agreed to sing at any of the various engagements they had, other than every Saturday night for the season at the Corbonna Restaurant. The affair with Charles Keating still hurt, making her apprehensive of singing in front of an audience in case every look should be misinterpreted.

Whereas before, she had made her songs intimately personal, she had now developed a more remote and aloof attitude, that nonetheless had the audience shouting for more. She certainly qualified for the ice-queen label now, she sometimes thought ruefully, but it seemed to be a perfect foil for the rowdiness of some of the other acts in the troupe.

The whole tempo of the Follies was hectic and fun, and Norman said cheerfully that Bridget gave them an extra bit of class, and billed her as the Sussex Songstress. It made her squirm a little, but gave her a kind of anonymity to hide behind, which suited her admirably.

The children had reacted exactly as Bridget had thought, but none of it mattered. Cassie found fault with everything at the cottage, thought Marlene was terribly common, and said that Norman's thin black moustache looked as if it had been pencilled on with the same hair-dye he used on his hair. Liam loved the cottage, the garden, Marlene and Norman, the other theatrical folk who were often around in the holidays, and especially Norman's clever magic tricks.

The children were home now for the Christmas holidays, and to the delight of the de Wolfe Follies, the whole lot of them had been invited to Ashworthy Hall for a huge Christmas party given by Lord Ashworth. He was having his newspaper people down, and the Follies were going to perform for them and his staff, and the few toffs he was inviting, but then they were going to join the eats and the fun. It would be Liam's fifth birthday as well, so it would be extra-special for him too.

'He's a little love, that boy o' yours,' Marlene said affectionately, when Liam went bellowing after Cassie to tell her there were toffee apples in the kitchen, a gift from Marlene. 'And I'd say you've got a bit of a problem on your hands with the other one, ducks.'

'She'll grow out of it,' Bridget said, in hope more than certainty. She saw Marlene frown slightly.

'Y'know, I been puzzling over the way you talk, Bridget.

Sometimes it's posh, like 'is Lordship, and sometimes it sounds a bit – well, American with a dash of Irish or Welsh or summat. It's ever so nice, mind,' she added hastily, 'and tell me to mind me own business if you want. I know I'm a nosy bitch.'

Bridget laughed. 'You're very clever. I'm Irish, but I lived in America until five years ago. I once went to a kind of finishing school which tidied up my accent a lot, and I went to the Connecticut Academy of Music for a while to have my voice trained, but I wasn't there long enough to learn all that much. I married of course, and after my husband died I decided to go back to Ireland, and Liam was born there.'

There. It wasn't so difficult to say if you didn't think about it too much . . .

'You mean your 'ubby died before he was born? Oh, you poor thing,' Marlene was all sympathy.

Bridget was kneeling down, trying to coax the wood fire into life. The December days were cold, and suddenly she didn't want to continue this conversation. She turned, meaning to ask Marlene what she would wear for Harry's party, which was guaranteed to send Marlene off into a world of fantasy and colour.

Cassie was standing in the doorway, her eyes deep and intense, her whole body still.

'Where was I born then? Was it in America, Mother?'

Marlene looked at the two of them, and sensing a confrontation, got to her feet quickly.

'I'll see ya tomorrer, Bridget –'

'*Was* I, Mother?'

Neither of them saw Marlene go. It was stupid, but Bridget's heart seemed to thrash about in her chest. It was only a simple question, for God's sake. There was no big drama in answering it.

'Yes, you were, love –'

'Why didn't you tell me? Why did you keep it from me all this time? I'm not – I'm not a bastard, am I?'

Bridget nearly laughed out loud for a second, at the same time knowing she should censure Cassie for the word she used so boldly. Heaven knew where she'd heard it . . . but all that went out of her head as she saw the stark misery in Cassie's face, and realised how unsure she was of herself. Confident Cassie, who was still not ten years old, after all. Bridget stood up and reached out her hand to her daughter.

'Come here, love –'

'Tell me first!'

Bridget felt her usual impatience rising up, and did her best to control it.

'No, Cassie, you are not a bastard,' she said shortly. 'I was married to your father for three years before you were born –'

'But I'm an *American*!' From the way she said it, Bridget wasn't sure whether Cassie considered herself to be privileged or an alien being.

'Yes, you are, and that's all there is to it.'

'No, it's not. Where was I born? Why haven't you ever told me anything about my father? You never talk about him. I think I can remember being on a big ship with a man who spoke in a funny way. Was that him?'

'No, that was Monsieur Alphonse, my singing tutor, and he was French. Your father died, Cassie, which is why we went to Ireland, hoping to find some of my family.' She bent the truth a little. 'You were too young at the time to remember it. My family were all dead by then, though, and Ralph and Alma became our good friends –'

She kept her voice even, trying to make it all sound natural, making it seem a sensible thing to do, but Cassie's eyes were still burning with frustration.

'So who was my father? Was he big and fat?' She was furiously trying to remember now. 'Did he laugh a lot and play with me in a big house?'

'That's right.'

'How did he die?'

'He was in a fight, darling. It was an accident.'

She wished the questions would stop. She didn't want to remember Thomas Finley. Not the hatred of him, or the shameful thankfulness at his death. Nor the fury at the pittance he had left her. She wondered if she should tell this child about the trust fund set up for her when she was twenty-five, and decided against it. Cassie gave herself enough airs already. Her next words confirmed it.

'Well, I think you should have told me. I shall tell all the girls at school that I'm an American. Did Uncle Charles know?' She demanded.

Bridget nodded.

'I shall write and ask him to tell me about America. Do you have his address?'

'No, I do not,' Bridget said flatly. 'And even if I did, you would not write to Charles Keating, Cassie. He's not a good man.'

Cassie stared at her. 'Why not?'

Bridget knew she was floundering. What had possessed her to say such a thing? The child wasn't old enough to understand a man's evil intent.

'Just accept it, Cassie. He's gone, and we'll never see him again.'

She glared at her mother. 'Well, I shall go to America one day and see it for myself. You can't stop me. I belong there. I shall be – a – a filmstar or something!'

She swept out, and Bridget didn't know whether to laugh or cry at the absurdity. It should never have happened like this. She should have had something prepared to tell Cassie calmly, not have to blurt it all out like that. And making such a bloody mess of it.

Christmas Day was cold, with patchy snow everywhere. They all wrapped up warm, and bundled into Bridget's car, and even Cassie forgot her resentment with her mother and was as excited as any other child. Presents had been heaped on her bed as well as Liam's and now she wore a new party frock and was going to meet some toffs. At least there was that consolation. Harry had said there would be important people at the party, as well as those awful theatrical people. He didn't call them that, of course, but it was the way Cassie thought of them.

Ashworthy Hall was decked out with great bunches of holly and mistletoe, with an enormous Christmas tree in one corner of the drawing-room. There was a lot of kissing and hugging, and Harry caught Bridget beneath the mistletoe and held her very tight, to the cheers of the Follies folk. She moved away from him, breathless, and busied herself with Liam, protesting laughingly that Harry might have waited until she took the child's coat and gloves off!

'Why? You'd have been captured by an admiring crowd then, and I might never see you again in a place this size.'

'What rot you talk sometimes,' she smiled up at him, her friend, who didn't seem in the least like a Lord. She agreed with Marlene in that.

She glanced across at the de Wolfes, silent for once as they looked about them at this lovely old mansion and its awe-inspiring rooms.

'She'll be "My-Gawding" all afternoon,' Bridget whispered to Harry, who squeezed her shoulder and laughed with her, and drew her into the warm and friendly atmosphere of his home. They didn't make the children wait a second for their presents, and it touched Bridget to see there were gifts for everyone else too.

'He's a real duck, ain't he?' Marlene said in a stage whisper to Bridget, noisily opening her package and squealing with pleasure at the silk scarf inside.

It was just the thing for swanning about the stage in, she declared to Harry, planting a kiss on the side of his face, Lord or no Lord.

The children loved their gifts, and Cassie smothered the usual feeling of disappointment that Liam had two to her one. It was his birthday, and it was only right, but it always seemed unfair that it should be on Christmas Day, when everybody should be equal.

She didn't bother talking to the newspaper men, who mostly clustered together and talked of things she didn't understand. She easily ignored the Follies troupe. Instead, she became the centre of attention of the quartet of people who had arrived in a huge limousine.

'I'm going to be a linguist,' she said importantly.

'Is that so?' The gent with the twirling moustache grinned. '*Parlez-vous Français?*'

'*Naturellement, Monsieur,*' Cassie replied fluently. '*J'attend*

281

l'école où le Français est le premier sujet, et l'Allemand le deuxième. Sprechen sie Deutsch?'

'She's cleverer than you, Vernon,' the woman beside him laughed. 'The child's something of a genius already!'

Cassie looked at her. She was elegant and smart, her hair shingled in the latest style. She wore a flowing chiffon gown with strings of glittering beads that clanked as she walked, and a headband with a feather in it. She wasn't pretty, but she was striking in a horsy and aristocratic way, and she had clung on to Harry's arm for a while with an air of possession. Her name was Lady Fiona Torrington, known as Fee. All that, and her unmistakable chic, was enough to make Cassie sick. Without realising it, she glared at the pair of them.

'What nonsense,' she snapped. 'I'm not a genius, which is defined in the dictionary as someone with a high power of mind, whatever that is. I just have a brain that absorbs language and accents easily. I could imitate anyone here if I chose.'

Far from annoying the lady and her companions, the dictionary quote and subsequent statement from this pre-cocious little madam only made them laugh louder.

'Go on then,' the one called Vernon challenged. 'I dare anyone to imitate Lady Fee's voice.'

The lady screamed with excitement. For a Lady she was as common in a different way as Marlene, Cassie thought irritably. And then there was one of those moments that sometimes invaded any gathering. One minute there was a babble of noise, and in the next, it seemed as if there was a tiny lull in everyone's conversation, as if they all drew breath at the same time. And into this lull came Lady Fiona Torrington's ringing tones, through Cassie Finley's mouth.

'I don't find it at all difficult to talk with a pound of plums in my mouth. With all these teeth, it would be hard to speak any other way.'

There was a scandalised silence for an instant, and Bridget's face went brilliant red as she realised what had happened. Cassie too, knew she had gone too far as she saw the frown on Harry's face. The last person she wanted to annoy was Harry, her hero . . . and then she heard Lady

282

Fee's screeching laughter.

'That was simply spiffing, my dear. You should be on the stage, shouldn't she, Vern? When are they going to engage you to replace your mother as the star turn in these Follies, little girl?'

The conversation flowed again, and both Cassie and her mother were united for once, mortified in different ways. Cassie knew she had done wrong, letting her caustic tongue run away from her. She was humiliated at being called a little girl, and especially by this woman to whom Harry Ashworth was now smiling so affectionately, and sending searing shafts of jealousy through Cassie's young heart.

Bridget saw it too, and was struck by similar, quite unexpected feelings. It shouldn't matter to her if Harry was enamoured of a dozen women. She had no right to be jealous, and he really should be married and have a family of his own . . . even as the thoughts went through her mind, she knew she didn't want that to happen. Harry was hers . . . and just as instantly, she knew that he was not. Not unless she agreed to marry him, and after all this time there wasn't even any guarantee to think he still wanted her . . .

She turned angrily to her daughter, ridding herself of turbulent thoughts in a sharp rebuke for Cassie's rudeness.

'How could you show us all up like that!'

'I didn't mean anything,' Cassie said sullenly. 'And the man asked me to do it –'

'There was still no need to be insulting. You hurt people, Cassie. You do it all the time.'

Bridget turned away as Marlene touched her arm and said they were going to begin their performance. Cassie watched her mother mutely, wishing she could run and hug her and beg her forgiveness. Loving her, with a strange and unfulfilled love that more often ended in bitter words and resentment against Bridget and the whole world.

She sat through the whole Follies performance without seeing or hearing a single thing, wrapped up in her own misery. She was dimly aware of Liam's shining, excited face at Norman de Wolfe's mysterious magic tricks; she vaguely heard the applause for the jugglers, and then the silence while her mother sang in a lilting, plaintive voice about a lost love; and the jollifications when the Follies pianist lightened up the proceedings with a few jigs on Harry's piano. And then Bridget leading the Christmas Carols, and finally the 'Happy Birthday' to Liam. And all of it flowing over her, meaning nothing, only that no one understood her, or wanted her, or cared if she was there or not . . .

'Well, little lady, that was quite a performance you gave us earlier,' the genial Vernon Lacey said beside her. 'Are you going to give us some more?'

'*No*,' Cassie said vehemently. 'Please don't ask me. I don't want to. I don't – I don't –'

To her horror, she felt tears welling up in her eyes, and any minute now they were going to burst out and disgrace her. She glared fiercely at Vernon Lacey in order to keep the tears at bay, and then Harry was there too, and saying that it was all right, and nobody was going to force her to do anything. She looked up at him with adoration.

'Aren't you setting out for a theatrical career then?' Vernon grinned.

Cassie tilted her chin. She looked so much like Bridget then that Harry was startled for a second.

'Not unless I can be a filmstar in America,' she said, with a piquant adult aplomb, remembering the absurd remark she'd once made. 'But I don't expect I shall bother. I expect I'll marry Uncle Harry instead.'

The men roared with laughter and moved away, leaving Cassie wondering what she had said that was so funny and so unlikely. Harry wasn't so much older than herself. She glibly overlooked thirty-four years. Lots of women married older men. Her mother had. She seemed to remember the corrugated face of her father with new clarity. What she didn't remember, because she didn't know, was the reason for and the unhappiness of that marriage.

And anyway, it was still just a game. It was all a delightful make-believe, the dream of marrying a rich and handsome Lord with a vast estate. It would be nothing short of a fairy-tale ending, to a child with a more romantic heart than anyone suspected beneath the prickly veneer.

The Convent School of La Retraite didn't concern its pupils with politics or world affairs in any great measure until they were approaching puberty. That was time enough for their girls to learn the facts of life, about themselves, and about a wider world. From the day the girls entered La Retraite the nuns dealt with religious instruction expertly and relentlessly, so that many of their listeners, Cassie Finley included, were bored by the whole thing long before they left school.

Teaching them about sex was a different matter. The nuns were innocent about procreation other than what was given in text-book information, and explained to every new riveted class of eleven and twelve-year-olds what they themselves never knew, and failed utterly in imparting the joy and love and emotions involved in sexual relationships.

'Well, I'm never going to do *that*,' declared Cassie Finley's closest friend vigorously.

Cassie looked at her as they sprawled on the grass in the quadrangle, that late September afternoon in 1929, after this illuminating lesson. Evelyn Oakes-Johnson was a month older than Cassie, and despite the fact that they often argued like mad, and enjoyed it, the two of them usually had very similar opinions. This time, Cassie wasn't so sure, and the references to the mating habits of rabbits and farm animals, finally applied to humans by the scarlet-faced Sister Thérèse had intrigued her considerably.

'It must be all right, or there wouldn't be so many babies born, would there?' She said, reasoning that after all, her favourite nun had assured the class this was the only way mammals reproduced. 'People must like it – I suppose.'

'Well, I certainly don't want to think of my parents doing it,' Evelyn was still scandalised. 'Do you?'

'My father's dead, so it would be hard for me to think of it,' Cassie said shortly. All the same, she understood what Evelyn meant. To think of one's parents actually doing *that*, as Sister Thérèse had described . . . Yes, it was all pretty disgusting . . .

'Anyway, do you want a man putting his thing inside you?' Evelyn persisted.

Each of them felt a darting thrill that neither admitted to the other, at actually discussing such a topic.

285

Cassie considered. 'It might depend on the man –'

The image of Lord Harry Ashworth flitted through her mind and out again, because she didn't want to think of these new revelations with regard to Harry. She always put him above ordinary men, and despite her sudden interest in sexual matters, she had to agree with Evelyn that it was all so – so base. Evelyn plunged on.

'Oh Cassie, it would be terrible. You'd have to let him see you without your knickers. You'd have to see him naked too.' Her voice became hushed at the thought.

'No, you wouldn't. You could do it in the dark.'

Evelyn got cross now. 'Why do you always have to have an answer?'

Cassie scrambled to her feet. 'Don't bother asking me questions if you don't want any answers! I'm going for a walk. I want to think, and I can't do it with you being so daft and scaredy.'

'I'm not scaredy –'

She followed at a distance, knowing Cassie's steely look. She wished she was like Cassie, tall and thin and dark and rather mysterious-looking, instead of being spotty and square-shaped and mousy-haired. Evelyn tended to think in hyphenated terms, on account of her surname. Eventually Cassie stopped walking and turned round, and Evelyn knew she was forgiven and it was time to catch up. Cassie was actually smiling.

'I don't know why we're getting so hot and bothered,' she said. 'We needn't get married for years and years, and not at all if we don't want to.'

'Of course,' Evelyn said, relieved at only just realising they had a choice. 'We could be career women. You could, anyway, with your brains. I could just be a society hostess, flower arranging, or something like that –'

Cassie went on relentlessly. 'And even then, we can tell our husbands we don't want to do *it* at all, unless we want children. That's all it's for, isn't it?'

'Oh, yes!' Evelyn beamed ecstatically, able to defer the thought of Sister Thérèse's delicately worded connection with a man for ever, if need be. 'You really are a clever-clogs, Cassie.'

'I know,' Cassie said with false modesty, and they doubled up laughing.

Sexual Instruction took up most of the thinking and whispering of the La Retraite middle-school girls for the next month, and then something more important happened that was considered required teaching in Current Affairs. One that interested Cassie Finley, if only because it was taking place on the other side of the Atlantic, to which she now grandly referred as 'home' to anyone who would listen to the tragic tale of her father's demise.

But now, something called the Wall Street Crash became the new topic of class instruction, and even the nuns, who were supposedly not too interested in worldly things, were saying that what affected a powerful country like America eventually affected the rest of the world.

The girls didn't understand it very well. They only knew that in some street in New York there was a lot of panic going on, and Cassie imagined men rushing back and forth, wringing their hands and crying because things called stocks and shares had fallen dramatically, and mass unemployment was just around the corner. Words like Depression and Slump now formed part of Sister Thérèse's vocabulary, replacing those wicked-sounding and therefore exciting part-of-the-body names that the girls had scribbled in their exercise books for the past few weeks, just to see what they looked like written down, and just as quickly scrawled out again with trembling fingers and palpitating hearts.

The Wall Street Crash sounded to them at first like a vaudeville act. They couldn't equate it with something terrible that was happening now in faraway New York. Not when they looked out of their classroom windows at a sleepy Sussex countryside where nobody ever rushed. To the La Retraite girls it was just another boring Current Affairs lesson they were obliged to sit through, except that it interested Cassie Finley more than most, because her roots were in America, she reminded Evelyn Oakes-Johnson importantly.

'You're becoming a real bore about your old American roots, Cass,' Evelyn snapped, out of patience with her again. 'You don't talk like an American, and we've only got your

287

word for it, anyway –'

'That's because I went to live in Ireland when I was three, you ninny, and anyway, my mother has a beautiful accent, and everybody knows that children learn to talk like their mothers.'

She never noticed that it was the first time she had ever aknowledged Bridget in that way. She was so annoyed with her friend Evelyn that she didn't care what she said.

'Is your mother still a music-hall singer?' Evelyn's tone was insulting now, smarting at Cassie's superiority.

'You know very well she never sang in the music-halls. She trained at the Connecticut Academy of Music,' Cassie said haughtily. 'And it doesn't really matter where you apply your talent. It's having some, that counts.'

This remark was a masterly triumph, and the latest clash in a friendship that sometimes teetered on the edge of hatred, but was still strong because it had grown from a tender plant. Two little girls growing closer together at boarding school than most sisters. That day they parted company again, but each knew in her heart that nothing so petty was really going to separate them.

Lord Harry Ashworth knew far more about the Wall Street Crash, its implications, and its likely repercussions on the rest of the world. *Night News* had its own news service across the Atlantic, and the telephone lines were red-hot with speculation and dire certainties. Every newspaper blazoned the same news in varying degrees of scaremongering. On October 24th, the day they called Black Thursday, thirteen million shares changed hands in a single day. On October 29th, sixteen million followed.

Amid similar stories, within nine days 40,000 million dollars were lost in the value of American securities. Banks failed, and major businesses went bankrupt. 'Disaster' was the word on everyone's lips. The stock-market virtually collapsed, America stopped all lending to Europe, and existing loans were recalled immediately.

To Europe, still recovering economically from a war that had ended eleven years previously, this heralded massive reorganisation and the prospect of lowering standards of living across all strata of society in order for governments to repay national debts.

'But what does it mean to *us*, Harry?' Bridget said agitatedly.

She and Marlene and Norman were in town that morning to buy new stage-dresses. Marlene and Norman were now having lunch with their theatrical agent, and Bridget had taken a cab and gone on impulse to the newspaper offices.

It was the first time she had been there. It was a bewildering new world where typewriters rattled continuously; young boys rushed around with bits of paper in their hands and yelled out information; older men smelled of cigarettes and stale sweat and printer's ink and bellowed at everyone else; total chaos seemed to fill the entire place, and when Harry closed the door of his tiny office against the din outside, he ran his fingers through his hair, making it more dishevelled than ever.

There were definite grey streaks in it, Bridget thought with a little shock. Harry was no longer as young and dashing as when they had first met. He looked quite harassed today, and she knew at once that she should never have come. Before he could even answer her question, she put her fingers on the door handle again.

'I'm sorry. I can see you're terribly busy. I'll telephone you at home, shall I?' She had just had an instrument installed at Magnolia Cottage, and it was her new pride and joy.

'Don't be silly. Sit down now you're here. I've had some food sent in for a working lunch, so you might as well share it, as long as you don't expect the Ritz.'

She sat down abruptly. It certainly wasn't the Ritz. It wasn't Harry's normal environment, at least, not the one she was used to. She had known Harry at Rosewall Cottage in Ireland, the country squire with his string of horses; at Ashworthy Hall, where he was the undoubted Lord; at her own cottage, where his presence warmed and enriched the place. Here, although she had already seen that his staff deferred to him, he was still endearingly – Harry.

She took a hunk of bread and a piece of cheese to go with it, realising she was hungry, and repeated her question. He answered with brutal frankness.

'What it means, my dear, is that there'll probably be food shortages and bread lines, and useless petitions to the government to do something, and people will be scratching for coal, and shipyards could close. And the countries affected could take years to recover.'

Bridget put down her make-shift lunch, as if it shamed her to eat when food shortages seemed imminent.

'And what of ordinary people here who might be holding stocks and shares in America?'

She had never told anyone about Cassie's inheritance. The child herself didn't know, and since the trust fund had been set up by Thomas Finley, the less Bridget had to do with it the better. But it *was* Cassie's money, and if she lost it all . . .

Harry looked at her sharply. 'You're not telling me you've ever dabbled in the stock market, are you?'

His meaning was clear. While she had never thrown herself on him for money, she had never let on that she was wealthy. She gave a short laugh.

'No, dear Harry. I haven't been keeping things from you. It's not my money. It's Cassie's trust fund, left to her by her father. She knows nothing about it, and doesn't get it until she's twenty-five. It's all invested –'

'Then you'd better get on the phone pretty damn quickly to your lawyer or whoever's handling the funds. I'd help if I could, Bridget, but it's all hell around here at present, as you can see. Phone from here if you like, but do it fast.'

The urgency in his tone alarmed her. She wanted to ask him to at least get the number for her, but four of his staff appeared in his office at once, claiming his attention. He cursed beneath his breath at the latest information they gabbled excitedly, and then he was gone, slamming the office door behind him.

Bridget felt completely disorientated. She forced herself to think straight, remembering that she had the New York lawyer's phone number written in her diary. She had never used it before.

She searched for the diary in her bag, found the number,

and stared at the unfamiliar telephone on its black cradle. She picked it up and spoke quickly to the operator, asking for the New York number before she panicked completely.

It seemed to take forever before she finally heard the thin and disembodied voice all those thousands of miles away. Her heart was thumping very hard as she gave her name, but thankfully, the twang at the other end was undoubtedly the voice of Donaldson, the Finley lawyer.

Chapter 22

It was almost blasphemous, Bridget remarked to Marlene some months later when a new decade had begun, how world events only came into sharp focus when they affected you personally. It was terrible to think like that . . .

'Everybody does, though, ducks,' Marlene said comfortably. 'If ya don't think of number one, nobody else is going ter bother about ya. And don't worry. It'll be a long while yet before the old Follies give up the ghost. No matter how lean times are, there's always toffs who wanter be entertained.'

Bridget blinked. It wasn't the future of the de Wolfe Follies she'd been thinking about. She was still anxiously awaiting news from Donaldson in New York. The first information had been varied. Cassie's trust fund had been spread wide, and while certain businesses had collapsed completely, others had wavered, and one had even benefited a little. Donaldson had advised Bridget to sit tight and do nothing, unless she wanted to pull out the entire amount remaining, until things steadied themselves.

'If you think we should hold on, I'll be guided by you,' Bridget had said, not understanding too much of the quick-fire nasal information he'd thrown at her that day in Harry's office.

'I do think so, Mrs Finley,' he'd said urgently. 'The accountant thinks the same, but I'll send you weekly reports for the time being, if you wish, so you can see exactly what's

291

happening. But please call me again whenever you feel the need.'

'Thank you,' she said, sensing that this was his way of ending the conversation. Just as well, since Harry's newspaper would be paying for it. She'd put the receiver down very quickly.

'Bridget? Is something on yer mind lately? Ya don't look yerself.'

She came to with a start, hearing Marlene's concerned voice. They were sitting in Bridget's cottage, cosy with hot tea and scones, and warmed by a roaring fire. It was mid-February, windy and cold, the winter snow still thinly blanketing the fields.

'I'm fine. Just that these newspaper reports are so depressing. So many people losing jobs and no chance of finding anything else. How long can it go on, I wonder?'

'Don't ask me, but I always say if there's nothing ya can do about it, there's no sense in worrying over it.'

For once, her chirpy words didn't bring a smile to Bridget's face. Marlene looked at her knowingly.

'You know what you want, doncha? You want a good man ter take care of ya, Bridget. Tain't normal, a good-looker like you, with no man to take care of her.'

'I can take care of myself,' Bridget said, not minding such candid advice from this outgoing woman. 'I don't need a man in my life –'

'That's daft talk. Every woman needs a man. It's yooman nature. Where'd we all be without men, I'd like ter know? You ask old Adam and Eve about that. She knew what she wanted all right, didn't she?'

Bridget started to laugh and Marlene pressed on.

'And your Cassie's got an eye for the men an' all. You'll 'ave to tell her summat about the birds and the bees soon, I reckon.'

'Now you're the daft one! Cassie's only twelve years old, for pity's sake –'

'That's old enough to give a man the glad eye, even if she don't know what she's doing,' Marlene persisted. 'Ain't ya ever noticed the way she ogles Lord Harry as if

292

he's some sort o' Greek God?'

'Oh, that. He once told her he'd marry her when she grew up, the way Dutch Uncles say things.'

She bit her lip, wishing she'd never used that phrase. The prize fighter who'd raped her sister Kitty all those years ago had been Dutch, and she didn't even want to be reminded of that horrific time . . .

'You see?' Marlene said, not understanding her pause. 'Makes ya think, don't it? Kids grow up fast these days, even in a Convent, and your Cassie's got her eye on me Lord, I'm telling ya."

'And I'm telling you she's too sensible to take such a thing seriously. Anyway, I don't need to tell her about the birds and the bees. I mentioned it in the last holidays, when she started getting the curse, and she told me airily she knew all about it already, and that they'd "done sex" last term.'

'My Gawd, Bridget –!'

'I don't mean literally! I mean they'd had a lesson about it. It's part of the curriculum.' Bridget tried not to smile at Marlene's thunderstruck face.

'Ya mean those tight-arsed nuns told a bunch of kids what to do in the dark?' She said irreverently. 'Sorry, ducks. I was forgetting you used ter be a Catholic, but I meanter say!'

'I still am,' Bridget said.

Marlene was ready to argue. 'Ah yes, but not the kind that really counts, are ya? I mean, ya don't go ter church reg'lar and light candles and say confession and all that twaddle, do ya?'

'No,' Bridget said, and for some reason a great wave of sadness ran through her. Once, she had believed implicitly. Once, she had clung to the church as a great mother figure, always there, always reliable. Once, she had confessed her sins, large and small. Now, she simply pushed them out of sight. If God meant to punish her for them, He'd do it without the aid of a priestly intermediary. She gave a wry smile. If she could even think like that, in a way that she'd once heard Thomas Finley brag, then perhaps the faith was still there. It hadn't gone completely after all.

'Anyway,' Marlene went on. 'What about you and Lord Harry?'

'What about us?' Bridget smiled.

Marlene sighed. 'You'd make such a perfect pair. Me and Norman are always saying as much. I'll tell you summat, Bridget. If I wasn't already hitched, he could have the knickers orf of me quicker'n winking.'

Bridget laughed until she had a stitch in her side.

'If you don't stop this wicked theatrical talk, I'll stop inviting you here,' she gasped at last, wiping her eyes. But they both knew she wouldn't. They were far too fond of one another for that. They had already shared a lot since knowing each other, and Marlene's words regarding the Follies were oddly prophetic. No matter what the world situation, people always needed entertainers.

In the next couple of years the Follies proved that laughter was indeed good medicine, and in between the nonsense acts, Bridget's songs could bring happy tears as well as sad ones. But for her, all the laughter threatened to disappear when Harry Ashworth came calling at Magnolia Cottage one late April morning in 1932.

'I wanted you to be the first to know,' he said evenly.

She looked at him dumbly. What was she expected to say? All the usual clichés flooded her mind. The best of luck . . . I hope you and Fee will be very happy . . . and that all your troubles will be little ones . . . she caught her breath on a sob, knowing she had lost him. And he was hers. He had always been hers . . . she forced back the lump in her throat.

'When?' she whispered.

'At the beginning of September,' Harry said briefly. 'We don't see any point in waiting, and neither of us believes in long engagements. Besides that, I'm forty-nine. If I'm ever going to get an heir for Ashworthy Hall, I'd better get on with it.'

The small joke fell into the silence between them. He was forty-nine years old . . . and Bridget herself was forty. She had looked into the bathroom mirror that very morning, and seen the sheen of silver in her own dark hair, the little lines running from the corners of her eyes, and the indented furrows in her forehead, and known that her face was no longer young. It hadn't mattered then.

She felt Harry seize her hands in his.

'Bridget, Fee and I have known each other for a long time,' he said gently. 'This isn't a marriage of high passion –'

She snatched her hands away. 'I don't think you should be saying these things to me –'

'But I want to say them. If you had ever shown the slightest interest in me as a man, do you think I'd ever have asked another woman to be my wife? Do you think I could have looked at anyone else, if you had wanted me?' He sounded oddly angry now, and she couldn't look at him.

'It's all right, Harry. I do understand,' she said in a muffled voice.

'No, you don't. I need a son,' he said brutally. 'It's a bloody putrid reason for marrying, but it's not as if I dislike Fee. I'm very fond of her, and she of me, and we both know where we stand. She'll be gaining security, and I shall have a child to inherit Ashworthy Hall. In my position, it's important, and I've overlooked the fact for far too long.'

'Yes.'

'And it's not going to make any difference to you and me.'

Bridget looked into his eyes very slowly, and his heart stopped for a second. It was as though he glimpsed the memory of all the years of pain and mistrust he still didn't understand. Something long ago in this woman's past had scarred her deeply, and she had never been able to trust him enough to tell him of it.

'It will make all the difference in the world, Harry,' she said huskily. 'You'll still be my dearest friend, but I won't be yours. That must be Fee. Promise me that you'll give her all that she deserves as your wife.'

She couldn't say any more, or she was sure she would break down and beg him not to do this. She burned to hear him say that it was all a mistake, and that he was going to marry her, Bridget Finley, and not Lady Fiona Torrington with the terrible plummy voice and great horsy teeth . . .

And dear God, how was she going to tell Cassie?

The mixture of emotions racing away with her, cleared in her mind in an instant. She had vowed never to marry again, so how could she be so hypocritical as to begrudge Harry this chance of happiness? Many good marriages had been made from such precarious beginnings. As he didn't answer, she cleared her throat, forcing a smile to her lips.

'You know you're going to break my daughter's heart, don't you?'

'That's something we have to discuss, too.'' He sounded fractionally relieved, moving slightly away from the intimacy of their own relationship.

'She has this crazy notion that you're only waiting for her to grow up and you'll marry her,' Bridget went on lightly.

'That's only a childhood fantasy, surely. I was someone for her to attach herself to, having no father of her own –'

Bridget gave a brittle laugh. 'Darling Harry, I assure you that Cassie never sees you as a father-figure. I'll have to be very careful how I tell her. A letter might be best. She'll assume I'm being cowardly, of course, but it's better for her to find out at school, with her friends all around her. Don't you think so?'

Harry looked at her uneasily. He knew of Cassie's passion and assumed it to be a schoolgirl thing. He hadn't expected Bridget to take it so seriously. He didn't sense, either, that this new project, saving Cassie from being too hurt, was Bridget's instantly discovered way of keeping her own feelings at bay. Of letting the treacherous thought creep back into her mind that she hadn't thought of for years. *Everything she loved was taken away from her* . . .

'I'll leave it to you, my dear,' he said at last, since women's ways were still a mystery to him, and Bridget must know her own daughter best. 'And what of Liam?'

Her eyes lit up. 'Liam won't be any problem,' she said confidently. He never was. He was nine years old now, and growing more like her brother Michael in looks every day. It was uncanny, and a private joy, because no one knew of it but Bridget herself.

'Anyway, there's an extra bit of news you can tell them, and especially Cassie,' Harry added. 'Fee's mad on horses, and we intend to start up a breeding stable again. I know it upset Cassie a lot when we had to have poor old Smokey Sam put down, but you can tell her she can come and ride whenever she wants. Fee will enjoy her company.'

Oh dear sweet Harry, do you really think so?

'I'll tell her,' Bridget said, poker-faced.

There was a sudden awkwardness between them that had never existed before. They had said everything pertinent to the marriage, and now there was nothing left, until they both spoke at once, putting things on a wider scale.

'Will you ask Ralph and Alma to come for the wedding? I'd love it if they stayed here for a few days –'

'We'll invite Marlene and Norman, but not the entire Follies troupe. You do understand that, don't you –'

'Yes. Of course.'

'It'll be a small wedding. I'm writing to Ralph and Alma tonight, and I hope they'll come. Fee wants a white dress and all that, but we're not hiring Westminster Abbey or anything ridiculous.'

He tried to make her smile, but her thoughts wouldn't get beyond the white dress. Fee would be entitled to it, presumably. Untouched by human hand, or anything else, most likely. Bridget got a brief mental image of Lady Fiona, spread-eagled on Harry's bed, and Harry . . . doing it for the good of Ashworthy Hall, to ensure an heir . . . it was sad and terrible, and so much less than this wonderful man deserved.

'I do wish you all the luck in the world. You know that, don't you?' She finally managed unsteadily.

He held her close, feeling the fragility and the strength in her. He kissed her mouth very slowly, and then he let her go. Somehow it was symbolic.

'And you'll write to the children right away?' He said brusquely. 'We wondered if Cassie would like to be a flower-girl, and Liam a page-boy. What do you think?'

'I'll suggest it.'

She couldn't go further than that. And when he'd gone she sat down carefully on her sofa, as if she was a very old woman whose bones would break if she moved too fast. All these years she had been saying that Harry should be married. Saying it complacently, selfishly, because deep down she never thought it would happen. She expected that they would go on together, towards old age, the world's greatest lovers who never physically loved, the perfect couple who never married, their relationship pure and unsullied and intact. And now there was Fee. Ten years younger than Harry, and still able to give him a child, or children . . . giving him love . . .

Her face crumpled suddenly, and she wept as if there was an ocean of tears inside her bursting to be let out. Marlene found her there, and heard the garbled words that told their own tale of frustration.

'Well, it's your own fault, ducks.' There was little hiding Marlene's disappointment. 'You let him go, and there's no one to blame but yerself.'

'I know that!' Bridget said angrily. 'I'm not blaming anybody. It's just – just a shock, that's all. I didn't even know he was seeing her.'

She knew little of what Harry did these days, she realised. They didn't live in each other's pockets, and it was obvious he'd decided to make a life of his own without her. It was only right. And it was hell.

She wrote to the children that night, wording it as best she could. Whatever she said, it still sounded flat and final. Harry was marrying Fee, and there wasn't a damn thing any of them could do about it.

Cassie opened the letter from her mother. They wrote spasmodically, but she had only seen her mother two weeks ago on her birthday, and hadn't expected a letter so soon. She took out the few pages, and her face went white as she read the words.

'What's up?' Evelyn said. The two of them were lying on their backs in the spring sunlight, knowing the nuns would scold them if they caught them, because the grass was still damp and they'd probably end up with rheumatism when they were ninety. Cassie bolted upright, giving a gasping cry, and Evelyn squinted at her curiously.

'No. Oh *no*. He can't – he just can't!' She said in a shrill, agonised voice.

'Not your man?' Evelyn said, with unusual perception. 'What's he done?'

Cassie fought to say the words. 'My mother says he's

getting married. To that awful horsy woman I told you about ages ago.'

She couldn't seem to breathe properly. Those few words on paper had had the effect of knocking all the stuffing out of her. She was like a rag doll.

'Well, honestly, Cass, you didn't really expect him to marry you, did you? That was all kids' talk, and besides, he's old. He's nearly fifty, isn't he? You wouldn't want to marry an old man. Ugh. Imagine it. Gropey fingers and wrinkled you-know-what! I bet it's like a prune –'

Cassie found her breath. 'Shut *up*! I don't want to talk about it. I'm going – I don't know where – I want to get away – I just want to be left alone –'

She scrambled up, and to her fury, Evelyn grabbed her arm, hurting it, pulling her down on the grass again.

'You're not going anywhere. You always run away from things you don't like, instead of facing them. Your fantasy about Lord Harry was stupid, anyway, and it was obvious he'd end up marrying somebody older than you. And who wants to think about marriage yet? I'm going to have some fun first, and so should you. Now we've got Harry out of our hair, perhaps we can both enjoy ourselves, and find some younger ones who are more virile and won't fall asleep before they get to stage one,' she said meaningly in their own brand of easy-speak. 'I always thought you were wasting your time on this one, anyway. He was more suited to your mother than you, and I don't care if you do think I'm nagging. You had it coming a long time ago, if you want my opinion.'

Cassie's eyes flashed angrily. 'Well I don't! And if this is how my best friend behaves when my heart is breaking, I shall find myself another one. Besides, I shall never marry now,' she said dramatically, and to her rage, Evelyn burst out laughing.

'Oh Cass, you are a scream. What play did that line come from?'

They glared at one another for a few seconds, and then, unwillingly, knowing the truth of it, Cassie felt her mouth shape into a half-smile. She had accepted long ago that Evelyn was more level-headed than herself. Cassie was the one who blew up into instant rages, who stormed through life

in true theatrical guise, who needed Evelyn to calm her down
. . . Already the shock news in her mother's letter was
beginning to be a reality, and so much of what Evelyn said
was true. And she was only fourteen, after all. Easily hurt,
easily mended, as long as there was something else to take the
place of the pain. She skimmed through the rest of the letter
from Bridget.

'Well, I'm not doing that for a start,' she scowled. 'I'm not
being a flower-girl like some soppy infant. Liam can be a
page-boy if he likes, togged up in velvet like Little Lord
Fauntleroy, but you won't catch me –'

'I bet they'd buy you a gorgeous frock though. You'd have
to have one of those long frilly ones, and you'd get an
expensive present. The bridegroom always gives the atten-
dants presents. What would you like most, Cass?'

'A horse,' she said promptly, which set Evelyn off again.
But that wasn't so funny. Cassie had read on to the end of the
letter by now, and there was one bit of cheerful news to catch
her attention in this whole miserable business. Harry was
starting up breeding stables again.

She smothered the thought of the ethereal white wedding of
her dreams and turned her thoughts to more practical
matters. If only he would buy her a horse, she'd agree to being
a flower-girl at this farce of a wedding. He couldn't be
marrying for love, anyway. Her thoughts went off at their
usual tangent.

He couldn't actually *love* Lady Fiona Torrington . . . it had
to be one of those aristocratic marriages of convenience, and
they weren't real marriages at all. With the ease of
adolescence, Cassie twisted everything to make it more
palatable to herself, and finally shook off Evelyn's restraining
hand on her arm.

'All right. I'm not going anywhere,' she said coolly. 'But I
think I'll write to Harry to congratulate him, and just
mention about the horse, and see what comes up. Good idea?'

'Spiffing,' Evelyn said, chortling and triumphant, because
if Cassie had been in a satanic mood for the rest of the term, it
would have been hell on the rest of them too. She couldn't
resist one last question though.

300

'But Cassie, you haven't stopped loving him, have you?'

'Of course I have, in *that* way. If he doesn't want me, then I simply won't want *him*.'

Hadn't she been practising something similar all her life in regard to her mother . . .?

The wedding breakfast was held at Ashworthy Hall, where the happy couple would make their future home. After the brief ceremony through which Bridget sat as if carved from stone, the entire party drove back to the Hall for the feasting. Ralph and Alma were staying with Bridget at Magnolia Cottage for three days, just before the children went back to school after the holidays.

'Though I can't call them children any more!' Alma had said in amazement. 'Liam's such a sturdy boy, and as for Cassie – well, she's so grown up and a real young lady now.'

Hearing her, Cassie almost purred with pleasure. She liked the Bretts far more than the de Wolfes, though she admitted that Marlene was what they called the salt of the earth. If only she wasn't so common . . .

Bridget smiled at both her children, seeing them through her friends' eyes. Yes, Cassie was growing up fast. She had lost her gawkiness, and was filling out with gentle curves in all the right places. Cassie was nearly a woman. And she had taken Harry's marriage surprisingly well, apart from a few tantrums about the colour of her dress, and the arguments about wanting shoes with heels to make her look taller.

Liam too had argued about his velvet suit and been allowed to wear a miniature morning suit . . . her sweet baby . . . Bridget revised the thought. She shouldn't baby him, because he was no longer a baby, and there was nothing sissyish about him. For all that she had favoured him so blatantly, he was a normal, likeable little boy. The image of her brother Michael . . . the image of Austen . . .

Since Harry's wedding announcement, Bridget had clung to the memory of Austen Hamilton almost fervently. His memory was the one good thing in her life. The one thing nobody could take away from her. Yet desperately, she knew that the memory was fading. She couldn't hold it, nor see his face so distinctly. Even when she looked at Liam and tried to assure herself that these feelings still remained, she knew that the images of Michael and Austen were more in her own head than in her son's face. It was hard to accept, and harder still to let images go.

And now she had to let Harry go. Now, when everyone was congratulating him and Fee, and the two of them looked so happy in their wedding attire. Fee in her bridal white, that somehow even lessened the effect of the huge teeth. And Harry, in his own morning suit, so correct and stiff, and not Bridget's Harry at all.

Nor Cassie's . . . just how had that little minx wormed a horse out of him, Bridget wondered? And because he was so fair, Liam had got a pony as well, kept at the stables, for them to use whenever they wanted. It was so good of him, so dear and good of him . . .

Long after the happy couple had gone away on a honeymoon to Switzerland, and the children had gone to bed at Magnolia Cottage, Bridget sat comfortably with Ralph and Alma. Their friendship hadn't diminished in the least for the years of parting. They didn't communicate often, but it was one of those friendships that could be put down and picked up again like a favourite novel, losing nothing of its enjoyment.

'You know, we always hoped that you and Harry would make a go of it,' Alma said. 'I can't help feeling sorry that you didn't, Bridget.'

'We still have our friendship, and that's important,' she said.

Ralph agreed wholeheartedly. 'Friendship sometimes lasts longer than love.'

He was always logical and honest. Bridget saw them exchange affectionate glances, and remembered that theirs too hadn't been a marriage of high passion, but its roots were deep and strong for all that. Harry and Fee's could well weather many storms on the same basis.

'I'll make some tea, or cocoa, whichever you prefer,' she said quickly, not wanting to think of them together in any way. And well aware that for all her bravado that day, Cassie had come out of the bathroom earlier with red eyes, and was probably sobbing into her pillow right now. The thought of the beautiful grey mare she was going to ride tomorrow wasn't going to compensate for tonight. Not tonight . . .

The photographs Harry and Fee produced in due course after their honeymoon only confirmed Cassie's determination to go to finishing school in Switzerland. Bridget and the children were invited to Sunday tea, and Fee was now very much the Lady of Ashworthy Hall. The Swiss school was something Cassie had wanted for a long time, and Evelyn's parents were perfectly agreeable to letting Evelyn go.

'You must let me go, Mother!' Cassie said passionately. 'I'll die if you don't.'

'No, you won't –' Bridget said, irritated by this little drama, especially in front of Harry and Fee.

'Oh, she must go if she wants it so much, Bridget,' Fee smiled graciously, showing her teeth and gums. How could Harry kiss that mouth and not be stabbed every time, Bridget thought irreverently . . .

'Of course she'll go. A long time ago I undertook the children's education, and Cassie will perfect her languages in Switzerland better than anywhere else.'

'Oh, thank you, Harry!' Cassie leapt up and threw her arms around him, planting a noisy kiss on his cheek, regardless of Fee or her mother.

Bridget noted that she'd left off the Uncle when she addressed him now. Cassie was annoying her more than usual today. Everything about the girl annoyed her, from the touches of make-up she had begged to use, to the awareness of herself as she preened in front of the mirror, her curving shape in the new skirt and blouse, nipped in at the waist with a belt and shiny buckle, to the sudden adultness of her. Cassie grew by leaps and bounds, and made Bridget conscious of her own ageing. She was forty, and sometimes it felt like a hundred.

'I can't let you do this, Harry,' she heard herself say sharply. 'It costs far too much, and since it's beyond my means, it's out of the question.'

'Mother, how could you!' Cassie said, humiliated. 'It's not

fair. You know how much I want this –'

'And you know very well we can't always have what we want in this life –'

'You always say that!' Cassie howled.

Wasn't it true? Hadn't Bridget wanted Austen Hamilton more than life? Hadn't she wanted his child, the precious child that died?

'Cassie, let's go and see the horses,' Fee said brightly. 'You too, Liam. Let's leave these two to sort things out between them.'

Cassie looked suspiciously at this unexpected ally. But she went, and so did Liam, and Harry took Bridget's rigid hands in his own.

'Oh Bridget, why must you always fight me?' He said in a sorrowful voice.

'I don't. I just know it isn't right for you to go on paying for my children's education. It makes me feel like a – a –'

'Kept woman?' He finished for her. 'That's one thing you'll never be, my darling. I doubt that any man could hold you, let alone keep you. Fee and I have already discussed my interest in Cassie and Liam, and my plans for them. She knows that I look on them as my pseudo godchildren, so don't deny them their chances because of your own stupid pride, Bridget.'

What affected her most in all of that was that Harry and Fee had discussed her children. Harry and Fee were now a unit who consulted over everything. It was right. It was natural. And it hurt. And yes, she still had her pride.

'If Cassie goes to Switzerland, I'll pay for it myself,' she said defiantly, and they both knew it was a submission. Harry smiled gently.

'No, you won't, darling. Once you see the size of the fees from those schools, I assure you you won't. But Cassie will still go. Won't she?'

She knew he was right. And in that other way too. She couldn't give in without a fight.

'Yes. And I still have two years to work like mad to save the money to send her."

Chapter 23

Switzerland was exactly like Cassie and Evelyn had always imagined it to be. Stepping out of the stuffy, smelly train at Gstaad was like being transported straight into fairyland, Cassie declared dreamily. At sixteen, she was even more romantic than at fourteen, though it was a trait in her character that only Evelyn really knew. After the long journey across France, they alighted stiffly from the carriage with all their baggage and stood on the wooden platform, breathing in clear air that smelt quite unlike anything they had known before. It was clean and pure and wonderful.

'Are you the young ladies for Miss Poole's?'

A man's voice spoke beside them, and they whirled round to see a stocky fellow who didn't look or sound in the least French. They identified his accent as north of England. Yorkshire, Evelyn whispered in Cassie's ear.

'You're English!' Cassie stated, disappointed. The man grinned.

'Sorry, love. You'll meet all sorts at Miss Poole's. Is this stuff all yours?'

'Yes, but –'

'It's all right. I'm not abducting you. Garth's the name, and I'm the porter. Follow me.' He spoke in short quick sentences that instantly made them want to mimic him.

They had no option but to follow since he was stacking their baggage into some trolley affair. A large van stood outside, with the impressive name of Miss Poole's Academy for Young Ladies imprinted in gold on the side. It was all right then. They sighed with relief, though it would probably have been tremendous fun to have been really abducted and whisked off

305

through the night to some Swiss hideaway, Cassie confided later, when they had been allocated their room at the imposing Academy.

'No, it would not. Besides, it's not the middle of the night, and this is far more comfortable – I think.' Evelyn said, bouncing on her bed and wincing at it. The two other girls who were to share their room appeared, curious to see the new arrivals, and grinned at Evelyn's face.

'It gets better. We've been here three days, and you soon ignore the bed boards. They don't believe in soft beds here, except for these divine quilt things. Soft beds are bad for your spine, according to Matron. I'm Janine Harker, by the way, from Michigan, and this is Katriona Macnab, and guess where she comes from!'

They all laughed, as the American girl easily broke the ice between them. An American girl, what fun! Cassie quickly told her she too was American by birth, but since she didn't know much else about her background, the piece of information soon fizzled out. And anyway, it really didn't matter. There was too much to see and do, and the whole world suddenly became a magic vista. Freed from the restrictions of La Retraite, where they were treated like children, Miss Poole's girls were very much the Young Ladies, trusted to come and go as they pleased, providing they gave sufficient attention to lessons and decorum and behaved themselves at all times.

And Gstaad itself was magical. Surrounded by snow-capped mountains and pine-clad forests, it emitted that wonderful freshness the girls had experienced the minute they stepped down from the train. Garth had driven at a fair rate from the station to the outskirts of the town, where the Academy was situated, and Cassie and Evelyn had constantly exclaimed at the picturesque brown chalets with their slatted shutters and overhanging eaves and wooden verandahs.

'If they didn't have overhanging eaves, they'd be snowed-in come November. You just wait till the snow comes, then you'll know what cold is,' Garth said with typical Yorkshire dourness.

It hadn't worried them. Everything enchanted them. And

snow meant skiing, one of the Academy's activities that turned out perfectly cultured and educated and finished specimens of womanhood, skilled in all the social graces.

Cassie sent up a silent prayer of thanks to Lord Harry Ashworth and Fee, to whom she'd become coolly attached, if only because of their mutual interest in horses. She guiltily thanked her mother too, because she knew damn well Bridget had taken on far more singing engagements than she'd wanted in the last two years, simply to kit Cassie out with everything she needed and make her a generous monthly allowance, so that Harry wasn't doing all the paying.

A lot had happened in the last two years, Cassie thought fleetingly. Norman de Wolfe had dropped dead during a show, and everyone had thought it was part of his magic act, and the audience in the small theatre where the Follies were performing had disintegrated in pandemonium when they discovered the truth. Marlene had disbanded the Follies at once, unable to go on without her Norm. The rest of them had found theatre work elsewhere, and after much dithering and doubt, Bridget Finley had been persuaded to take up the new-fangled career of recording her voice onto gramophone records.

Bridget found that it suited her admirably. She didn't have to perform in front of an audience, which was becoming more of an ordeal than an excitement now. She was conscious of her age, the lines in her face, her slightly spreading waistline, and the fact that in the mad and hectic thirties, everyone searched for things new and exciting. And that meant new faces and talents, and the glamorous movie stars of Hollywood were what the public were frantic to see. The talkies had arrived, and people flocked to the picture palaces instead of the theatres.

The new arrangement suited Cassie too. It was far more prestigious to have a mother whose voice was heard by mechanical means, than one whose listeners could ogle and whistle and stomp and clap, and make whatever rude remarks they chose.

She was cheerfully aware that she was still a snob, and would probably always be one. But here at Miss Poole's, which she soon discovered was known as Pooley's by the locals in Gstaad, in the company of girls from different countries and backgrounds, but who all thought as she did, none of it mattered. Cassie had found her niche at last.

'The classes aren't all that intense,' she wrote dutifully to Fee, after an enthusiastic letter from Harry's wife telling her about the new foal who had just arrived that day. 'We're expected to do our quota, of course, but everyone puts into classes as much as they want to take out. Don't tell Mother I said that, though! Anyway, I'm so keen on the language classes that it's no trouble to me, and I quite enjoy the other things too.

'Social activities are taken very seriously. Now that the skiing season is here, it's fantastic, and the town is transformed from a pretty little place to something out of a child's picture-book. You didn't see it in Winter, did you? It's incredibly beautiful in the snow. On Saturday nights we have dances here, to which young men of 'good character' are invited. It's a scream, really, because they all look the same in their Saturday best, good or bad!

'We're taught to ski and to dance and to ride, and especially the art of conversation. By the time I come back to England, I shall be able to skid down a Sussex hillside, dance the polka and ride my lovely mare like an expert – and do it all while telling you everything in ten minutes flat!'

She paused in her letter-writing. Going back to England sounded terribly tame. She was to stay at the Academy for two years until she was eighteen years old. Then, most of the English girls contemplated a London Season, when they would presumably meet a suitable beau, and marriage and children would follow in that order.

Cassie gave a sudden shiver. It all sounded so regimented. Like something on a factory conveyor belt. Toss in a gauche *ingénue* at one end, and come out with a sophisticated swan at the other. Marriage-bait.

She knew that was what some of the Swiss boys about town called the Pooley girls. She and Evelyn overheard two of them at the latest Saturday night dance, and daringly, they challenged them.

'We don't all intend getting married straight from school,' Cassie said in her most superior voice. 'Some of us prefer careers to men.'

The two boys looked at her and Evelyn, and then at each other.

'Pardon, Mam'selle,' the dark-haired one said. 'We meant no offence. It was meant as a compliment. And for two such lovely ladies to prefer careers to wedded bliss would be a tragedy indeed.'

Cassie felt her mouth twitch. It was an outrageous cover up for a faux pas that would certainly incense Miss Poole, and she could tell by Evelyn's irregular breathing beside her, that her friend wasn't in the least put out by the sudden attentions of these two.

'May we have the honour of this dance, perhaps?' The boy went on persuasively. 'My name is Henri and my friend is Denis. We've just arrived in Gstaad for the skiing instruction. With luck, you may be in our party.'

Cassie decided this was too good a chance to miss. All the girls were panting after the ski instructors, many from different areas, now taking up residence in the town. For her and Evelyn to have found two of their very own before the classes even began would be an undoubted feather in their caps. And these two were very personable. Decked out in the bright woolly caps and sweaters, tanned by the winter sun, and obviously favouring the two ex-La Retraite girls, Cassie and Evelyn would be high on the élite list among their classmates.

'Yes, we'll dance with you,' she was gracious, speaking for them both.

'Then may we put your names on our list of pupils?' Henri's Gallic features were alight now with the prospect of holding this tall, sparkling girl in his arms so unexpectedly.

'It all depends if we move well together on the dance-floor,' Cassie said archly, and after half an hour decided that they moved together very well indeed. Close-coupled, she already felt as if she knew every sinew of Henri's body, and when they went back in their room that night, she and Evelyn and the other girls compared notes.

'Take care, Cass,' warned Janine. 'Some of these over-nighters just come in to make a killing with an heiress!'

'Well, that lets me out,' Cassie grinned. 'I'm not an heiress!'

'They wouldn't believe that if you told them.' It was clear from Katriona's tone that the other girls didn't believe her either. 'They see money signs in all our eyes. To them, we've all got rich daddies with great inheritances waiting for us. They try anything to make us fall for them. My sister was here a few years ago, and she told me.'

'Anything?' Evelyn echoed.

Katriona went pink. 'Mairi said one of the girls in her class got pregnant and was expelled. And the boy was nothing but a gardener, even though he looked as rich as anyone. She was completely taken in by him.'

They all looked at one another. The thought of it was terribly wicked, and wickedly exciting.

'Well, don't worry about Evelyn and me. We learned all we need to know from the nuns.'

'From *nuns*?' Squealed Janine, and the four of them spent the next hour in ecstasies of laughter as Cassie and Evelyn remembered and exaggerated all that the nuns had told them about the virtue of virginity and the mechanics of sex.

'Don't let Matron catch you talking about such things,' Janine said eventually, wiping her eyes. 'Pooley's girls are expected to be beyond reproach and to uphold the honour of the school, don't y'know!'

They went off into peals of laughter again. But Cassie had her own rules, anyway. She wasn't allowing herself to be deflowered unless it was for love, and *then* he'd have to be mighty persuasive, and it wasn't going to happen until after the wedding, in a huge four-poster bed with a blazing fire crackling in the hearth, and on a night filled with stars, and soft music playing somewhere in the distance . . .

'Cass, are you all right?' Evelyn's face came into focus, and she said crossly that of course she was, and she was going to do some work if she could get a little peace around here.

But the turbulent feelings inside her body wouldn't settle down, and they were the most frightening and extraordinary and almost mystical feelings she had ever known. Like the feel of a small breeze over shimmering silk, they had begun at her toes and worked their way up her limbs to her thighs and spread out to every part of her, driving her into a state approaching ecstasy.

She didn't understand them, and she didn't want them, because for those few isolated seconds in her life, she hadn't been in control of herself. And above all, Cassie needed to be in control of herself.

She wrote dutifully to her mother as well as occasional letters to Fee and Harry, and the odd one to Liam, since she always got exuberant ones back from him, extolling the virtues of his new school which was full of boys with names like Clarence and Roderick, and the occasional Spooky-boo, which brought the whole thing down to earth. Liam was enjoying himself tremendously with his little chums, and it was only when he sent her a smudgy photograph of himself outside his impressive new school building, that she saw how tall and broad he was becoming.

'Good God, my little brother's growing up at last,' she said involuntarily, and Evelyn asked to see it.

'He's going to be a corker in a few years' time. Cass. He'll have all the girls falling for him.'

Cassie felt an odd tug of love for the brother she'd never really bothered with, simply because he was her mother's favourite, and therefore had enough love without needing hers. And because she still felt that division between them sharply. She knew her mother didn't love her, and she had never been able to bridge the gulf between them that was none of her making. She didn't understand it, and she covered up her loss by being bright and brittle and witty, and popular with everyone around her for being such fun, but the resentment still rankled beneath the surface. For all her popularity, there was still one person whose face she longed to see light up with love when she walked into a room.

'He's not bad, is he?' She said now, with an older sister's indulgence over a brother's photograph. 'He's still mad on this idea of being a journalist on Harry's paper. I thought he'd have changed his mind as he got older, but apparently not. And Harry encourages him, of course.'

Evelyn glanced at her friend.

'How do you feel about him now, Cass? Tell me to mind my own business, if you like –'

'Mind your own business,' Cassie replied at once, then smiled ruefully. 'No, it's all right. I guess the great love of my life wasn't so great after all. What a sell, isn't it? You're given these great explosive emotions and you concentrate them all on the one person who fills your life, and then you find out it's not the real thing at all. I think God played us a dirty trick.'

'So you really don't mind that he's married to this Fee then?'

'No.' Cassie shrugged. 'Not that she's doing her bit, mind. I know Harry wanted a son, and so far nothing's happened.'

'Perhaps they don't do it,' Evelyn suggested.

At sixteen their sex education was still limited to the nuns' instruction and lights-out discussions, and they were still naive enough to think that sexual intercourse only happened for the purpose of producing children and not for mutual enjoyment.

'Well, they'd better hurry up, or Fee will be past it,' Cassie grinned. 'Harry too. I wonder when a man's thing stops working. Do you think it keeps popping up and down until he dies?'

'Poor things,' Evelyn said. 'It must be an awful problem keeping it inside their trousers. They probably don't always know when it's going to happen. Like in the middle of dinner, or in church.'

They convulsed again. Sex was lewd and funny, and discussing it in those terms was the only way they could each hide from the other the fact that it was a bit frightening too.

Skiing was the best activity of all. To be a good skier was the goal of every girl at Pooley's. Cassie and Evelyn had bruised knees and aching muscles and were privately petrified of even the gentlest nursery slopes at first, but they persevered grimly. And they had the delicious help of Henri and Denis, who called them their extra-special pupils.

Hearts pounding after the soaring ride to the top of the

mountain on the ski lift, they would crouch, knees together –
glad that their goggles and scarves hid their terrified faces,
their expensive ski outfits doing nothing for their self-
confidence – and await the moment when their number was
called.

Then they would head off, feeling as though they surged off
into space, slithering and sliding down the seemingly endless
mountain, usually to fall in a heap at the bottom, a jumble of
arms and legs, laughing and spluttering in relief, snow
scattered all around them, with the encouragement of their
tutors ringing in their ears, and all heading off to the nearest
hostel for a hot drink.

'Skiing is wonderful fun,' Cassie wrote to her mother a year
later. 'The divine ski instructors we met last winter have
returned this year. They're impressed with our progress, but
we're not all that proficient yet, and after a year without
being on skis, we have to start all over again. We do try to keep
our feet on the glassy slopes, though, and we'll get there in the
end.'

Bridget folded up Cassie's letter with a small smile. How
many times had she heard her daughter utter those words? No
matter what the task, Cassie was always determined to get
there in the end. She had a very stubborn streak inside her
that would never admit defeat in anything. Bridget frankly
admired the way she had picked herself up after Harry's
wedding, and was thankful that the adolescent crush hadn't
been as serious as she'd thought.

But now she had something else to tell Cassie, that would
undoubtedly upset her. She tried hard to find the right words
in a letter, and in the end she telephoned the news, giving the
bare details to Miss Poole to relate to Cassie. When she got
back to her room, she leaned against the door, unable to tell
Evelyn for a few minutes.

'Fee's dead,' she said brutally, before Evelyn could even
ask. 'She had a riding accident. The doctor said she was two
months pregnant. She hadn't even told Harry yet. It was to
be a surprise for his birthday. He's lost them both, and oh
God, I feel sick. It's just too awful.'

She ran out of the bedroom, and clattered down the wooden stairs of their quarters, and out into the snow without bothering to put on outdoor clothing. The wind struck her at once. It was freezing. People glanced her way. Crazy English girl, their glances said. They always referred to her as an English girl. Haphazard, inconsequential thoughts spun through Cassie's head. She stood uncertainly. She didn't know what she wanted, or where she was going. She had no idea why this news should be affecting her so much, or why Fee's death should make her searingly aware of other losses. Her father. Her real identity, if it came to that. Her mother's love . . . oh yes, her mother's love . . . but that wasn't a loss. That was something she had never had.

She ached for Harry, losing Fee and the baby at one blow. She recognised even through this mist, that what she felt now for Harry wasn't the love of a woman for a man, but for a favourite uncle. Recognised it and accepted it uncomplainingly. She ached for Fee, funny, horsy Fee, with those huge teeth and the plummy talk. She longed to be home, wherever home was . . .

She heard a metallic sound grinding over the snow, and a small car drew alongside her, its wheels still spinning slightly, despite the chains. Henri jumped out.

'Are you mad, *chérie*, standing out here like this? It's time for your lesson, but you look as if you need a hot drink instead.'

Cassie looked at him, her eyes suddenly spilling over. 'Yes, a drink. Do you have any, Henri? Something to make me forget the things I don't want to remember.'

He stared at her. This wasn't the Cassie he knew. It wasn't the bright, sharp girl who got everybody laughing. This was someone suffering, for whatever reason he couldn't guess. But he was not a young man to miss an opportunity like this.

'Jump in, and I'll tuck a rug around you before you freeze,' he said quickly. 'I'll take you somewhere, Cassie. I'll get you warm.'

She got in trustingly. All she wanted was to be taken care of. To drink something hot and stinging that would make her forget. He drove as fast as he dared, blessing his luck, and helped her out of his car in a narrow street, where the cobblestones were thick with snow, and the windows on opposite sides almost touched each other.

'It's not as grand as Pooley's,' he grinned. 'But we'll be cosy in my room, *chérie*, and then we find ways to make each other warm, non?'

She allowed him to lead her. A lamb to the slaughter, Henri thought gleefully, finding piquancy in the English idiom. And he had a bottle of cognac in his room with which to lull his cool English rose before he taught her the art of seduction . . .

Half an hour later, Cassie was drowsy with the spirit. Her head swam whenever she moved it, and Henri was getting far more intense than she liked. She had agreed to sit on his bed in the corner because there was only one chair, so it seemed reasonable to be comfortable. He had prodded the miserable fire into life, and now with the cognac inside her, she was feeling decidedly hot. Henri had removed his jacket and was cuddling up beside her in a way she didn't altogether like. It was all right on the dance-floor where it was accepted behaviour. It was exciting on the ski-slopes when your very own instructor put his arms around you and you could preen in front of the other pupils. It was different here, alone in a rooming-house with a young man whose breath smelt faintly of garlic and whose arms suddenly resembled the tentacles of an octopus.

'Henri, don't be silly,' Cassie said, aware that her words were slightly slurred, and pushing away the clutching hands that were quite clammy, she thought in disgust.

He whispered in her ear, his voice hoarser than usual. 'We could do wonderful things together, Cassie. I could teach you the art of love, in which the French excel so madly.'

'I don't want to learn the art of love,' she said crossly, but still not too perturbed, because it all seemed so ridiculous to be silently fighting on this narrow bed. He'd told her quite earnestly not to make too much noise, because the walls were thin and there were other occupants in surrounding rooms.

She felt his fingers crawling over her breasts, squeezing

them, knowing them. Cassie knocked his hands away.

'Stop it,' she snapped. 'I don't like it.'

'Ah yes. I forget that you English girls like to play hard-to-get. But we have plenty of time –' Henri was still smiling, still not believing that she could really be refusing him.

'I'm not English. I'm American,' Cassie summoned up her haughtiest voice, enraged to hear the sibilance in the word English.

'Well then! American girls like it, so I've heard.'

'You mean you don't know? The great lover doesn't know?' She crowed, shoving down the hand that kept wandering to her leg as it tried to thrust itself up her skirt.

'The great lover means to find out,' Henri sounded more menacing and a shade uncertain at the same time 'Don't go all virginal on me, Cassie. I don't like it, and besides, it dampens my ardour to have a weeping female in my bed.'

He laughed self-consciously at his own confession, confidently thinking she would give in at once and help him with the seduction. Even hoping that she might take on a more active role, since Cassie Finley was so bright and alluring and not above giving the boys the glad eyes, as they said in England. He heard her give a brittle, answering laugh, and with an almighty shove, she pushed him off the bed and on to the floor.

'Why not? A virgin is what I am, stupid, and that's what I mean to stay! It'll take a better man than you to get into my knickers!'

The old jokes she and Evelyn had invented at La Retraite came to her aid even while she stood there, tears brimming, humiliated and furious with herself for getting into this situation in the first place. As if iced water had been thrown in her face, the effect of the cognac was leaving her, and she looked down at the pathetic Henri, struggling to get to his feet and telling her to keep her voice down, the bulge in his pants undoubtedly dwindling . . .

She saw him for what he was. A young *roué* who would probably never have what it took to be an old one. She doubted if he'd ever lain with a girl in his life. She might have spared him a little pity if she wasn't so disgusted with him and herself too.

'If you don't take me out of here this minute and drive me straight back to Pooley's where no one can see me going in without a coat, I shall shout and scream and tell everybody I've been raped,' she said quietly and calmly.

His jaw sagged, seeing that she meant it. She was a firecracker, and the quicker he got rid of her the better. He threw her the rug from his car without a word and shrugged into his jacket. They drove back to Pooley's in complete silence, and he jerked the car to a stop outside Cassie's quarters.

'I'm going home for a week,' she announced, the words forming before she really thought them out, but knowing they were inevitable. 'When I come back, we'll resume our skiing lessons. I see no reason for me to lose my excellent instructor, do you?'

He looked at her for a long minute.

'No,' he said at last.

She swept inside the Academy, head held high, for the first time knowing the power of a woman.

'Cassie!' Bridget exclaimed, opening the door of Magnolia Cottage to her daughter. 'What are you doing here?'

Not a word of welcome, not a kiss or a hug. At any other time, Cassie would have accepted that it was perfectly reasonable to expect her mother to behave like that at her unexpected appearance, but she wasn't feeling reasonable.

'There's a funeral in the family, isn't there? Miss Poole let me go at once. I have to be back next week.'

'Oh, Cassie,' Bridget said helplessly. She hardly knew this daughter any more. She had gone away an eager sixteen-year-old, giggling with that friend of hers, and a year later she was a sophisticated young woman with huge remote eyes the colour of the sky. Cassie pushed past her mother, dumping her suitcase on the floor. She looked around. The place was just the same, essentially Bridget. And then it seemed as if a hurricane burst into the place as Liam hurtled down the stairs.

'Oh, Cass, I'm glad you've come! I wanted you to be here. They said I couldn't go to the funeral, but I wanted to, and now you're here, they'll let me go. They will, if you say so.

317

You can make them do anything.'

He held her tight, and involuntarily, Cassie's arms went round him. Her little brother, who wasn't so little any more, and to whom she'd never felt particularly close, was holding her and needing her, and the feeling was spectacular and extraordinary.

To be held and needed and wanted . . . even by this little brat . . . her usual breezy manner came to her aid as she shook him off.

'Of course you'll go. Fee was a friend to us both. We'll go together, and nobody will stop us saying good-bye to her. They'll have to fight me first!'

She looked into Liam's face, almost level with hers now, and was shocked at the grown-up expression she saw there. He was fighting too, she realised, to keep back the tears. It was his first real brush with death, and however much it hurt, he needed to do this. To say good-bye to Fee as they put her into the earth. She challenged her mother with a look that dared her to argue.

Bridget moved forward, taking Liam away from Cassie so effortlessly she never knew how it happened. One minute the boy was hugging her, the next he was being shepherded towards the kitchen by his mother. The door stayed open, but they shut her out all the same.

'We'll all have some hot tea and scones,' the usual panacea, 'and then we'll talk.'

Cassie stared after them in sudden acute misery. They didn't need her. And although her mother's words had included her, and were presumably meant to welcome her home after her long journey, she felt rejected as always. Rejected and unloved.

She wondered briefly about shocking her mother with the tale of the farcical interlude with Henri, wrestling on his bed in a Swiss rooming-house. Just to see her reaction, to see if she'd care. And if she'd been a normal kind of mother, to explain to her that Cassie could never have done *it* with Henri, because she didn't love him, and doing *it* without love would be meaningless and horrible.

But she knew she'd never tell. What would be the use?

318

Bridget didn't understand about love, anyway. Only as far as Liam was concerned.

Chapter 24

On the 20th of January, 1936, King George V died, and his eldest son, Edward Prince of Wales, became King Edward VIII. The British girls at Miss Poole's Academy in Gstaad all wore black arm-bands as a badge of respect, and those well-versed in current and political affairs and the Effects of the Monarchy classes, speculated avidly on the new king's policies and personal life-style. George V had been a well-known traditionalist, opposed to change, and the remark most bandied about among the racier set at Pooley's was that the new king was modern to his eyeballs.

'He's terribly handsome, too,' Evelyn Oakes-Johnson sighed. 'No wonder the ladies are so wild about him.'

'Wouldn't you be, with the prospect of becoming Queen of England?' Janine Harker said cynically. 'But I grant you he's a wonderful dancer. Everyone wants to dance with the Prince of Wales at house-parties. They wrote that song about it, didn't they?'

'He's not just a prince any more, and he'll be too busy for dancing much right now, with Prime Minister Baldwin breathing down his neck. Or so Harry's newspaper says,' corrected Cassie Finley.

She had *Night News* sent to her every day. It was always some days late arriving in Switzerland, but it kept her abreast of what was happening in England, and it pleased her to remind the other girls of her vested interest in this particular paper. She read the French and German papers too, supplied by the Academy for the Current Affairs class, and had a fair assessment of the European situation.

In the early months of that year, Britain was torn between gossip news of the new king's whispered amorous adventures, couched in discreet terms because of his rank, but nonetheless obvious, and the growing anxiety over Germany, arming itself under their aggressive leader, Adolf Hitler. And for what, if not war?

'Harry says there'll be another war. He says it seems inevitable,' Cassie observed positively to Evelyn as they took an exhilarating walk through the forest alongside the Academy one Sunday morning in early June.

Gstaad was at its loveliest then. The winter snows had melted apart from on the mountain-tops, where it remained like glittering frosting on a cake in the early summer sunlight. The wild flowers had begun to blossom in the meadows, and the pale-coloured, doe-eyed cows were being taken up to their winter pastures again, the sound of their cow-bells tinkling with every movement.

'Well, I don't,' Evelyn stoically refused to contemplate anything as awful as a war disturbing this peace.

Cassie stopped walking so abruptly that Evelyn nearly fell over her. She put her hands on her hips and looked at her friend in exasperation. There were few other walkers about on this track, and all around them the silence was magnificent. The scent of the pines was heady and strong, and Cassie glared at Evelyn.

'You're such an ostrich, Evelyn. Sometimes you just put your head in the sand and refuse to see what's going on all around you.'

'I do not,' she said crossly. 'I just don't see any point in anticipating trouble, that's all.'

'A fat lot of good that would have been in 1914 if we hadn't been prepared for war. It's the same now. The Germans – at least, the Nazis – have become fanatical for power under Hitler, and Harry says –'

'Oh, I'm sick of hearing what Harry says!' Evelyn stamped her foot childishly, scattering leaves and dirt. 'He's not God, and just because he prints a newspaper, it doesn't mean you can believe every word that's printed!'

'Yes, you can. At least in Harry's paper you can.'

They glowered at one another, until Cassie gave a sheepish grin.

'Anyway, I don't know what we're arguing about. If a war

does come, you and I aren't going to stop it, are we?'

'I still think you're wrong about the Germans. They're holding the Olympic Games in Berlin in August, for God's sake. That does't sound like a nation on the brink of a war, does it?'

Cassie shrugged her shoulders. 'Not until after August, anyway,' she said, half-seriously, but Evelyn took her all the way.

'Well, I just hope it holds out until after September. We'll be safely back in England then, and the Germans would never get that far.'

'Perhaps they would. Imagine how awful it would be to hear jackboots marching through the English countryside! Oh, I'm just teasing, you idiot,' she said hastily, seeing the round-eyed alarm on Evelyn's face. 'Anyway, I may not go back to England after we come out. What have I got to go back there for?'

They began walking again, and Evelyn resumed her irritation. It was safer than discussing the frightening prospect of war.

'Now you're talking nonsense. You've got your mother and brother, and Harry –'

'My mother doesn't want me. Adolescent boys don't bother with their sisters. And Harry has his own life. We're not part of it any longer, not in the way we once were.'

Evelyn glanced at her. She so rarely spoke about her feelings for Harry Ashworth any more. Ever since his wife died, and Cassie had said briefly that he'd seemed pretty cut up at the funeral, but was burying himself in his work to get over it, Harry was only mentioned in terms of chief adviser and mentor.

'What do you intend to do, then? Stay here and marry a ski instructor?' Evelyn grinned. Few of the girls stayed on. Finishing school was no more than a social interlude in their real lives.

'No. I shall go to Paris,' Cassie said calmly.

But she couldn't keep up the cool façade when her heart was thudding at the very thought, and her eyes suddenly blazed with excitement.

'I wasn't going to say anything to anybody yet, but now we've got this far, you may as well know the rest. I saw an advertisement in a Paris newspaper. A firm of high-class textbook publishers are looking for a linguist to translate books from English into French and German, and vice versa, and I've written to apply for it. The post begins in October.'

She couldn't have shocked Evelyn more if she'd said she was going to be an African belly-dancer.

'You've already done all that without even telling me?' she raged, clearly affronted.

Cassie slid her hand through Evelyn's arm, wanting her to understand.

'Oh, Evelyn, don't be angry. I wasn't shutting you out. It was just that when I saw the advert, it seemed like the answer to a dream, and I thought if I told anybody at all, it might not come true. It's been hell keeping it to myself, but I got all silly and superstitious about it. Of course I was going to tell you when I got an answer.'

'So you haven't heard yet? It might not happen at all.' Evelyn was slightly mollified.

Cassie withdrew her arm. 'No,' she said, deflated. 'It might not happen at all. And with my usual luck, it probably won't. But I had to seize the chance when it came, don't you see?'

'Of course I do, darling. And I see no reason why you shouldn't get it. You're wrong about your luck too. You may have had some setbacks, but you usually get what you want. You came here, didn't you? And you got your horse from Lord Harry when he got married, and your broken heart soon mended! You're a brilliant linguist, and you'd do a wonderful job on dry old textbooks – if that's what you want.' She paused for a breath.

Cassie laughed, her good humour restored at the ambiguous compliments.

'It's what I want, Evelyn. So now we'll both be watching out for a letter from Paris, won't we?'

It came a week later, in a long impressive envelope with an embossed seal on the back. Cassie could hardly open it, because her fingers shook so much.

'They want me to go for an interview,' she gasped, as if such a thing had never occurred to her. 'They think I'm rather young, but my qualifications are sound, providing I have good grades in the final exams here. They'll require me to do a test while I'm there, but if they find I'm suitable, the post is mine from October 14th.'

She looked at Evelyn, eyes as round as saucers, sparkling and blue. She grabbed Evelyn's hands, letting the letter flutter to the ground.

'Oh, Evelyn, I'm going to live in *Paris*.'

'You haven't passed the test yet,' Evelyn laughed.

But she would. They both knew she would. When Cassandra Mavreen Finley set her mind to something, she accomplished it.

And it was a fait accompli before she wrote to her mother to tell her that after she came out from the Academy, she would be coming home for six weeks, and then taking up the new post in the *Rue de la Corse* in Paris. Harry tried yet again to calm Bridget's fears.

'She'll be fine, Bridget. She's self-assured and intelligent and languages were always destined to be her forte. And working for a publisher is rather nice. It's allied to my own trade in a way.'

'But *Paris* -' Bridget heard nothing but what she wanted to hear. 'And she's only eighteen, Harry -'

'Eighteen is pretty old these days,' he said dryly. 'What were you doing at eighteen? Didn't you think you knew it all?'

'Perhaps. But I didn't.' She didn't want to think of herself at eighteen. The years between the earthquake and setting foot on the ship bound for Ireland were still a tightly closed chapter in her life. No one knew the whole truth about them but herself . . .

'Cassie has to make her own mistakes, Bridget. You can't live her life for her,' Harry said.

Bridget reacted to his kindness scratchily.

'I know that. I'm just trying to ensure that she doesn't do anything foolish. Living on her own in Paris at eighteen -'

'Is not necessarily the road to ruin and damnation, my dear. Didn't you once tell me your old music tutor lived there?

Perhaps he'd act as unpaid chaperone for Cassie, if you're so worried, though I must say all this motherly concern is a bit late in the day, Bridget.'

She felt the hot colour sweep into her cheeks. Never once had Harry censured her for her obvious favouritism towards Liam. In all their years of friendship, he had indulged her whims, cared for her children equally, been there with a shoulder for her to cry on, the few times it had been necessary. Harry had been gentle and kind . . . but since Fee died, he had shown the other side of him. The hard, newspaperman side that was usually reserved for business and had rarely intruded into private life. Since Fee died, Harry was definitely more cynical than of old.

Bridget didn't know, because he would never tell her, that in some totally illogical way, he blamed her for his misfortune. Because of it, there was a constraint between them that neither could quite overcome, despite their friendship being the same as ever, outwardly.

He had always loved Bridget, and still did, but when she steadfastly refused to marry him, he saw Ashworthy Hall bequeathed to the nation instead of future Ashworths, and had chosen Lady Fiona Torrington quite deliberately to be his wife.

Fee wasn't a highly-sexed woman. She wouldn't expect high passion, nor frequent love-making. She adored her horses, and she came from good breeding stock herself. She would provide a son, perhaps more. That Fee hadn't been instantly productive was the first blow for Harry. The second, and worst, the irony of the riding accident, doing what Fee loved best while she was carrying his first child, decided him against any thought of another marriage. His selfishness had killed a fine woman, but if the one he wanted most of all had been his wife, none of it would have happened . . .

'You're not listening to me,' Bridget said. 'Of course I care about Cassie. She's my daughter –'

'You care about her as you would any stray dog who needed food and warmth,' Harry told her bluntly. 'You give her that sort of care, but you never gave her love, Bridget.'

'I refuse to discuss my motives if you're going to be so

annoying all the time. All I'm saying is that I'm concerned about what happens to Cassie in Paris. Is that so unnatural?'

'Not at all,' Harry said mildly. 'Except when it comes from you.'

He knew he was antagonising her and couldn't seem to stop himself. He didn't know why he did it. Perhaps to break down the mask that hid the real woman he never saw. The flesh and blood, warm and loving woman he wanted her to be. He saw her square her shoulders and tighten her lips, and knew she wouldn't be goaded any more.

'I have to be at the recording studios tomorrow morning at ten o'clock,' she indicated that the subject was at an end by simply switching the conversation. 'My car seems to be acting strangely, and I wondered if you'd drive me into town.'

'Of course. I'll be here at nine. By the way, have you heard from Liam lately?'

Instead of her usual smile, he saw her frown, but he'd been expecting that too.

'Yes, I have. What's all this about not going to university and going to work for your paper as soon as he leaves school?'

Harry laughed. 'I thought you'd prickle at that. I took a bet with myself.'

'Then you won,' she said grimly. 'Harry, I had such plans for him –'

'Be realistic, Bridget. You have one brilliant child, and the other one is average. I would pay for him to enter university if you really wanted it, but he'd be out of his depth. He's no academic, my dear, but he has a keen and enquiring brain, and I'd say he's a newspaperman to his fingertips. Let him be what he wants to be.'

'If that's true, it's only what you've instilled in him. And I don't agree that Liam's only average –'

'My dear Bridget, it's far better to have one average, happy child, than a dozen borderline geniuses. Liam has the personality to take him anywhere he wants to go in my line of business. There will always be a need for journalists, not only in newspapers, but in other mediums too. Wireless journalism, for instance, and even television. Have you thought of that? We live in an exciting age. It won't be long now before the whole world is wide open to us through television – providing the Nazis don't blow us all to bits before it happens.'

Bridget's grudging acceptance of all that he said was caught by his last muttered comment.

'You think it will happen, don't you, Harry? You're convinced that there will be another war.'

He shrugged, his craggy face in repose looking older and more lined. His hair was almost white in places, Bridget noticed with a little shock.

'I pray not, but yes, I do think so. Hitler's already secured military occupation of the Rhineland and gained Mussolini as an ally. For anyone who's bothered to analyse his rise to power, it's been steady and relentless since 1933, when Hindenburg appointed him Chancellor of Germany. Our politicians would do well not to ignore the potential threat of one man so desirous of power. It's like waiting for a serpent to strike. God knows when it will happen, but I feel certain that it must.'

'God, and Adolf Hitler,' she said slowly. 'Which would seem to be a contradiction in terms.'

The Spanish Civil War began in July, and European agitators made dire predictions that eventually Germany would intervene and put a strain on international relations. But Britain's attention became taken up by more dramatic domestic matters before the end of the year, when the new king, Edward VIII, declared his intention of marrying the American *divorcée*, Mrs Wallis Simpson. A situation which threw the government and the whole country into turmoil. Some people were openly indignant that the king couldn't be allowed to marry whom he liked. Others were just as dogmatic that it was morally wrong for the nominal head of the Church of England to marry a divorced woman. There was much talk of a morganatic marriage, which would deny the king's wife the status of queen while allowing the marriage to take place, but the Dominion governments were opposed to that, and the government, under Mr Baldwin's direction, was swayed. The marriage was impossible, the king was adamant in his wishes, and therefore abdicated in December, in favour of his brother. The ex-king was now given the title of the Duke of Windsor, and he and Mrs Simpson left for France and exile.

'It's all terribly sad,' Cassie Finley said in April of the following year, just after her nineteenth birthday. She pored as usual over the latest newspaper headlines that never seemed to let up, during the morning break for coffee and pastries.

'What is, *chérie*?' One of her employers, Monsieur Macon, pushed his pince-nez farther up his thin nose and smiled indulgently. Madamoiselle Finley had brought a breath of spring into the dusty publishing house of Macon and Girard, when she'd come to work for them six months ago, and the two elderly Frenchmen had never stopped congratulating themselves on their astuteness in employing her.

'Why, all this about the poor Duke of Windsor and Wallis Simpson, of course. Won't they ever leave them in peace?'

Since Cassie still regarded herself as an American, she thought of Wallis Simpson as her countrywoman and spoke of her in intimate terms, as did all the Americans in Europe, with that peculiar disregard for monarchy that came from having none of their own.

'I think you are very much the romantic, Cassandra,' Monsieur Girard added his voice to the brief break in the working day, while the whispering underlings had their own thoughts about this beautiful dark-haired girl who seemed to have few menfriends, but who professed to be such an authority about this royal *affaire de coeur*.

'I just think it's a crying shame, that's all. It's obvious they are very much in love, and nobody tells ordinary people who they can or cannot marry, do they?' She went on doggedly.

'You may think twice about such a remark in time to come,' one of the spinsterish subeditors said coyly.

'Why do you say that, Françoise?'

The woman lifted her shoulders expressively. 'It was something my father said. If there was a war, then all the Germans working in Paris would be sent home. We'd be fighting with our friends.'

She saw the tinge of colour on Cassie's cheeks, and drew her own inaccurate conclusions about the young man living next door to Cassie in the tall narrow building where she rented a room in the old quarter of the city. He was a German, twenty-two years old and a student teacher of mathematics at an élite men's college.

He was large and blond and beautiful and coolly clever, and Cassie knew that plenty of girls were attracted to him. She had known him for two months now, and felt cheerfully that although it would be quite easy to fall in love with him, she probably wasn't going to do so if she hadn't done so yet. Being neighbours, they enjoyed a pleasant relationship where it was fun to flirt and engage in *double entendres* that were harmless and exciting, and never ruffled the surface of their lives.

And she didn't want to think of any reason for having to stop calling Stefan her friend. She brushed back the lock of dark hair that constantly fell across her forehead with a defiant gesture.

'There won't be any old war,' she said scornfully. 'People have been saying that for ages now, and nothing ever happens. Besides, it would take more than a war to make me fight with Stefan!'

She heard Monsieur Girard give a low chuckle.

'*C'est l'amour!*' He rolled his eyes in a teasing, all-embracing gesture, and Cassie gave up and got back to her desk, ignoring them all.

She was still saying the same thing months later. Nothing was happening, and it was all just talk, and she for one wasn't going to waste time on thoughts of war. Nor even on the tragedy of a thwarted royal love affair that had resulted in an American *divorcée* being created Duchess of Windsor, and yet another king on the British throne, the new George VI with his pretty queen and two little daughters. Nor on the fact that poor Mr Baldwin had felt obliged to resign as Prime Minister in May, and now there was a new man, Neville Chamberlain, that Harry didn't think too much of, if you read between the lines in his newspaper. She wasn't going to think about any of that.

She was going to concentrate instead on the tricky passage in the book she was translating for the rest of that hot sticky day in mid-June. And then tonight, she had invited Stefan to meet her mother's delightful old singing tutor, Monsieur Alphonse, who had greeted Cassie when she'd finally gone tentatively to his home at her mother's insistence, as if she was a long-lost relative.

Stefan had an old open-topped bone-shaker of a car, that he told Cassie merely added to his image of a poor but hardworking student teacher. That night she clambered in carefully as usual, being bounced about as he cranked the engine to get it started, and then feeling as if every bone in her body was being ground to jelly as the car jerked uneasily up the cobbled street and out of the city towards the suburbs where Monsieur Alphonse lived modestly.

'I swear I'll never be the same again after travelling in this old wreck,' she gasped, holding onto her hat with one white-gloved hand, and clinging onto the side of the car with the other.

Stefan laughed, his handsome chiselled features alight with the feeling of adventure this old car always gave him, and enjoying the company of this buoyant English girl as always. *American*, he amended, remembering how she always corrected him, though anyone could be forgiven for thinking her English, since she spoke it with such perfect diction.

'Don't worry, Cassie! We shall get there all in one piece, I promise you.'

'More likely in a million tiny pieces,' she shouted above the noise, wincing as they took off over a large rut in the road and settled down again with a gigantic rattle. 'How does this thing stay on the road, for God's sake?'

'With a wish and a prayer,' he bellowed back. His blond hair ruffled in the breeze over his collar, the bright university scarf flying out behind him. He was terribly proud of that scarf, Cassie thought affectionately. He rarely left if off, even in the heat of summer.

It took nearly an hour to reach Monsieur Alphonse's home, and then she had to wait impatiently while the two men prodded and inspected and discussed the merits of the engine and bodywork. Were all men so obsessed with machines, she thought in exasperation? As if realising her impatience, Alphonse turned to her with a charming smile.

'Forgive us, my dear, for neglecting you. Come inside, please, and we'll have some wine and cheese. You did say, you would have eaten before you arrived?'

'Oh yes,' Cassie said hastily, having already decided not to put the old man to any extra expense. 'But some wine would be heavenly. It's so hot this evening.'

The wine was chilled and delicious. They drank it in the small courtyard of the house, where a vine trailed magnificently over a pergola and provided shade from the fiercest rays of the sun during the day. The wine lulled Cassie pleasantly, and she let the men do much of the talking, until a word or two made her sit up sharply, staring at Stefan.

'You're engaged to be married?' she said stupidly.

'Why yes,' he smiled in that cool way of his. 'I must have told you, Cassie.'

'Perhaps you did, though I don't remember it.' She knew that he certainly had not, and she was distinctly ruffled by the news. Not that she thought of Stefan romantically, but he might have told her. It was a bit much for him to have kept it all to himself. She saw him pull a wallet out of his jacket pocket, and show a photograph to Alphonse.

'This is Helga, with me and my parents just after my graduation.' The pride in his voice was unmistakable, and Cassie took the photograph silently after Alphonse had made his expected comments.

Helga was pretty, and as blond as Stefan. His parents were remarkably ugly to have produced such a splendid son, Cassie couldn't help thinking. His father had the peculiar bullet-shaped head beloved of cartoonists portraying Germans, and his mother was huge and buxom, a typical German *hausfrau*.

'Very nice,' she said, handing the photograph back. Stefan replaced it, without noticing the touch of sarcasm in her voice. Why had she never realised how insensitive he could be, Cassie wondered?

'When do you plan to be married?' Alphonse enquired,

thinking suddenly how much Bridget's daughter resembled her at that moment, sitting so straight and arrogant, all her feelings momentarily composed behind that beautiful calm face. Who knew what turbulence such a mask of beauty hid? In his experience, Bridget had rarely let it out, though he suspected that in that way, Cassie differed. He guessed that no matter what the problem, her feelings had to come spilling out before too long.

'Not for two or three years,' Stefan answered him. 'Helga is going to college in Munich, and I want to prove myself here first. But we will eventually live in Germany, of course.'

'Of course,' Cassie said.

When they were driving back to their lodgings, she let out her breath explosively. It was no good. She had kept control of herself for too long in the cause of good manners, and now she had to let fly.

'I do think you might have told me before,' she stormed. 'You knew very well you hadn't told me you had a *fiancée* in Germany!'

Stefan glanced across at her flushed face in the dusky late evening, and in comparison with hers, his voice was remote and several degrees cooler than usual.

'Sometimes it's better to let these things be known in company. It keeps them in perspective, and it's less personal. My private life is my own, and I choose for it to remain that way, if you understand me.'

'No I don't. I don't understand you at all! I thought we were friends, and the friends I know confide in one another. I suppose you'll tell me next you're a member of the Nazi party!'

She almost felt the temperature of the car descend now, as he coldly evaded a direct answer. 'We have spent many pleasant hours in each other's company, Cassie, but there are some topics I prefer not to discuss. I'm a German, and that is enough for you to know. I do not ask you about your politics or religion, nor expect you to ask about mine. We're of different races, and our ways are different, and I apologise if I've offended you in the matter of my *fiancée* or in any other way. It was not my intention.'

331

She stared straight ahead as the car lurched on through the night. In those few ultra-polite sentences she saw the truth of what he said. Yes, they were different. She was emotional, open as Americans were. Honest, as the British were, or believed themselves to be. While Stefan – he had the coldness and single-mindedness of his race. He was able to dissect the pieces of himself he wanted to show the world, and keep the rest hidden beneath the surface, like the nine-tenths of an iceberg that was the most dangerous and menacing.

She shivered, pulling her light evening cape around her shoulders, because her thoughts sounded oddly prophetic inside her own head. And because her description of Stefan seemed ominously like the way the German *Fuehrer*, Adolf Hitler, was being described by those who hated him.

Cassie hated him too in those moments, if only because his unwanted image had somehow spoiled the easy friendship she had enjoyed with Stefan. There was no romance between them, just camaraderie, and there was no reason for anything to be changed, just because Stefan had a *fiancée* in Munich, and had shown her a kind of ruthlessness Cassie had never even suspected. Nothing had changed . . . but even as she thought it, it was with a kind of desperation.

Chapter 25

Their relationship definitely cooled after the episode with Monsieur Alphonse. They chatted on the stairs of the old rooming-house, they borrowed cups of sugar, they laughed over absurd cartoons in magazines, and occasionally they went for a drive in Stefan's car. But the friendship was now all superficial, and there was a new guardedness about each of them. Cassie was just thankful she hadn't actually fallen in love with Stefan.

To let out steam, she wrote somewhat heatedly to Harry Ashworth that she would never have forgiven herself if she'd fallen hook line and sinker for a Nazi. And chewed her pen for a long while afterwards, realising how that simple sentence stated the facts that everyone cocooned at Pooley's had been loath to recognise. The Nazis were a threat.

She wrote regularly to Evelyn, now at her family home in England, and apparently having 'a simply spiffing time' doing absolutely nothing but riding and cycling and going to tennis parties. Evelyn had been born rich, and didn't see why Cassie thought there was anything so marvellous about working for a living.

'I can hardly believe you've been working on those dry old textbooks for nearly a year,' Evelyn wrote at the beginning of September. 'You should be doing something far more glamorous. Whatever happened to the filmstar idea?'

Cassie grinned at that. Such childish ambitions! When you were little, you thought you could be anything you wanted. It was only later that you realised how impossible it all was . . . At the grand old age of twenty, she was thinking like a staid matron, she thought ruefully.

But she was happy. She felt a sudden burst of surprise to realise it so positively. She was really happy, working for the two old gentlemen in the publishing house of Macon and Girard. She was *blissfully* happy living in a room in the old quarter of Paris, simply because it sounded chic and bohemian at the same time, and by now she was tanned with a healthy Parisienne look from the hot summers. She had friends of both sexes, and she didn't miss having a special man in her life one bit.

She read to the end of Evelyn's letter between mouthfuls of crunchy breakfast toast, dipping it in her dish of coffee in the French manner.

'Darling, what's happening over there? Is everything as calm as it seems? Is the delectable Stefan still living next door? He was due to go back to Germany sometime, wasn't he? Did you know they're talking about issuing gas-masks to everybody at the end of the month? There was a piece about them in a magazine recently. Horrid, ghastly-looking things, all rubber and smelly, and just about impossible to breathe through I'd say. I shall refuse to wear one. I'd rather be gassed. Ye Gods, what am I saying!

'But joking apart, it does look serious, wouldn't you say? Otherwise, why make the bloody things in the first place? And there's that public air-raid shelter beneath Caxton Hall all ready and waiting. It would be like being buried alive to be herded in there with all sorts of people you didn't know. Very unsavoury, to say the least.

'Daddy says it looks bad, Cass, and I'm not sure you should be staying on in Paris. I know Hitler's an Austrian, but was that any excuse for his troops to go marching through Austria in March? In the night too, disgusting wretch. And that makes him too close to France for comfort. Mummy and I were going to visit Vienna this summer, but we changed our minds. I don't want to risk seeing the beastly little man, or his Nazis.

'Do take care, darling. And just to prove I'm not as yellow as I sound, I plan to come to Paris for a few days in October. I do so want to see you again, and we could live the high old life, couldn't we? I'll stay at an hotel, unless there's room for me in your place. A sofa will do. Write quickly and let me know.

'By the way, I bought one of your mother's gramophone records the other day. She seemed in splendid voice, though I think I heard somewhere that she's giving up the singing lark. I say – that was good, wasn't it? The Singing Lark! Anyway, love and kisses, Evelyn.'

Evelyn's letters always left Cassie feeling exhausted. They were newsy and frantic, flitting from one topic to the next, which probably reflected the way she lived her life now, Cassie thought. Flitting from one party to the next . . . for the moment she ignored the little warnings about the preparations for a war that always made her stomach lurch unpleasantly, and concentrated on the two other main points.

Evelyn was coming to Paris, which excited Cassie enormously, and already her fertile mind was planning where they would go and what they would see. And of course Evelyn would stay with her. She would borrow a second bed from the owner and shove the furniture around to squeeze it in to one side, and they would have enormous fun, and it would be just as though they were back at Pooley's, sharing all their secrets after lights-out.

But then the other part of the letter. Her mother was giving up singing? Cassie couldn't think where Evelyn had heard that. Her mother had sung for as long as Cassie could remember. There was a vague memory of Bridget singing on board a ship bound for Ireland, a rapt audience listening to every word, and the three-year-old Cassie, annoyed and frustrated because her mother belonged to all of them, and not to her . . .

Bridget had never belonged to her, she thought briskly now, folding up Evelyn's letter. She gathered up her breakfast things in one swoop, in the checked cloth, and dumped it on the tiny draining-board behind the kitchenette curtain to attend to later. Bridget had always belonged to the world, and to Liam. She must find out what was happening, though. If Evelyn's words *were* true, then her mother must be ill, and she'd better know what was wrong.

'Would you mind terribly if I used the telephone to call my mother this evening?' She asked Monsieur Girard.

'Of course not, *chérie*. You know it's at your disposal at any time, and no nonsense about paying for it please. Talk as long as you wish.'

He was a dear, she thought swiftly, and when everyone had left the building she got through to the operator and asked for the number of Magnolia Cottage. To her annoyance, she found that her hands were shaking slightly. Whatever was wrong, she could cope with the news. She was Cassandra Mavreen Finley, *manager-extraordinaire* . . .

'Mother?' She bellowed, when she eventually heard the faint voice at the other end of the line.

'Good heavens, Cassie, what's wrong?' Bridget said at once.

'Nothing's wrong with me. Everything's fine. How are you?' The crackling on the line didn't make the conversation any easier, and she knew she sounded loud and ridiculously overbright.

'I'm perfectly well, but I'm sure you didn't call me all the way from Paris just to ask me that.'

'Yes, I did! Evelyn says you're giving up singing and I can't think why, unless you're ill.'

335

The words rushed out, the import of them making her nervous, especially when she heard Bridget's musical laugh at the other end.

'Oh dear, that friend of yours! She'd make a good gossip journalist for Harry's paper.'

'But is it true?' Cassie persisted crossly, feeling all kinds of a fool now. Good God, she'd taken the trouble to call her mother all this distance, and Bridget was treating her like a silly little girl, scared over nothing.

'Well, I've decided not to make any more gramophone records. I don't find it at all stimulating to sit in a studio with headphones clamped over my ears and see people making frantic gestures to me through glass panels. It suited me for a time, but now it doesn't. It's nothing more sinister than that, darling.'

'Oh. I see.'

'And don't worry. I shan't embarrass you by becoming a variety singer, either.'

The teasing was still there, edged with something else, and in the small awkward pause, Cassie digested the fact that Bridget had obviously known all along how much her daughter hated having a celebrity for a mother.

'I was just worried that there was something wrong,' she said lamely. 'I'm surprised too. I know how you love to sing.'

'That's the most generous thing you've ever said to me, Cassie,' Bridget said without expression. 'Anyway, perhaps I'll just sing for my grandchildren one day.'

Cassie laughed loudly at that. 'You'll have to rely on Liam for that, then. I'm going to be a career-girl, like my mother. Well, as long as you're all right. I must go. This call is on the firm, and it must be costing them a fortune.'

'All right. Oh, Cassie – you will be coming home for Christmas, won't you? Harry wants us all to have a family party at the Hall. It's a shame Marlene won't be there. She's gone to live with her sister in Devon, but Ralph and Alma are coming over. She's having a baby, did I tell you? After all this time.'

'How lovely. Yes, I'll be there. Good-bye.'

She hung up quickly, hardly knowing why this news

unsettled her so. She calculated quickly. Alma must be in her mid-forties, the same as Bridget. She must be crazy to risk such a thing at her age. And all this talk about Bridget singing to grandchildren! She had a sudden vision of her mother leaning over the baby Liam, crooning to him with love in her eyes softening her lovely face. Such love as had never been spared for her. She dashed away the brittle, angry tears, turned out the lights in the office and clattered down the stairs to the street outside.

Cassie arranged to take a few days' holiday when her friend came to stay. Evelyn loved everything about Paris. It was incredible to think she had never been there before, when she and her parents had seen most of the other capitals of Europe. Paris had always been somewhere Evelyn meant to visit one day, and never had, until now.

She loved the meandering River Seine and the Eiffel Tower, the vendors with their hot roasted chestnuts, the flea markets, the Louvre Museum and the elegant shops along the Champs-Elysées. She loved the left bank and the artists, and the beautiful church of Sacré Coeur, sitting like a wedding-cake on top of the hilly slopes of Montmartre. She loved the contrast of the dour cathedral of Notre-Dame, and especially she loved Cassie's room.

They flopped down exhausted, after a tour of the city in which Evelyn wanted to see everything at once.

'You ain't seen nothin' yet,' Cassie groaned in the style of the movie gangsters as she flexed her aching feet.

'I know. Tomorrow I want to visit Versailles. Did you persuade Stefan to take us in his car, like you suggested?'

Cassie nodded. Evelyn was quite tolerant of the German boy, despite his 'obvious disadvantages,' she said airily. She wouldn't go farther than that.

'What disadvantages?' Cassie asked.

'His German-ness, of course, but since he can't help that, and we're not actually at war with them yet, I suppose it's all right for us to fraternise with him.'

Stefan had agreed to the request politely. He didn't care for Cassie's English friend. She had a superior air that oozed

337

British aristocracy. Even the absurd double-barrelled name was so typically British, Stefan thought, his lips curling. Oakes-Johnson . . . like a mixture of trees and floor polish.

Nothing pleased Stefan these days. Truth to tell, he was tiring of life in Paris. He was annoyed by the snide glances he got from some quarters, and incensed by a few anti-Nazi slogans that had recently appeared on the college walls where he taught.

He thought constantly about going home to Germany, and the more he thought about it, the more he wanted it. He wanted to be with Helga again. He wanted to be in the Fatherland, where it was a matter of pride to be in the Nazi party, instead of being made to feel like a criminal if it leaked out. And the rumblings of war were making him increasingly ostracised by small groups at the college.

He made up his mind. After Christmas, he would go home. There were German colleges where he could teach in his own language, instead of using French which he didn't like.

Cassie sensed the antagonism between her two friends, and began to wish she hadn't asked Stefan to take them to Versailles. It could all be so awkward if Evelyn began any unfortunate political talk, and Stefan got that cold look on his face that would freeze a plaster saint. To her relief, the visit went off without incident, and the two of them shook hands at Cassie's room, since Stefan wouldn't be seeing her again before she left for home.

'Thank God for that,' Evelyn said with a small shiver. 'He's as nice as apple pie when he wants to be, but I wouldn't trust him an inch, Cass.'

'Wouldn't you?' It was so unlike Evelyn to be so vehement about anyone that Cassie stared in surprise.

'He's typical Nazi material. If he's not one now, he will be, you just wait and see. My grandmother would hate him. She's really set against the Germans.'

'Sometimes I think you people at home are more obsessed with thoughts of war than *we* are, living in the middle of Europe!' She said, half-amused.

'Perhaps.' Evelyn said, lying on her narrow bed and gazing up at the noisy ceiling fan that was meant to keep the room cool and more often ground to a halt when it was most needed. She leaned up on one elbow, her hazel eyes serious, her brown hair falling in neatly ridged waves around her face.

'I suppose you know that Mr Chamberlain flew to Munich for a meeting with Hitler and Mussolini and Monsieur Daladier at the end of September?'

'Of course. Everyone's aware of what's going on. Didn't that allay your fears?'

'Not at all. Daddy's got no patience with the PM. He says he'll believe anything. He reckons the Munich agreement is worthless, and that Neville Chamberlain has his head in the sand if he thinks that Britain and Germany will never go to war with each other again.'

Cassie frowned. 'I have to admit that Harry's paper said much the same thing.'

'Well then!'

'Well what?'

Evelyn looked smug. 'If Harry says it, then it must be true. Didn't you say he only prints the truth?'

Cassie felt a shiver of fear. Through the Munich agreement, poor little Czechoslovakia was going to be dismembered. Though remaining nominally a country in its own right it would virtually have no real strength. Germany, Poland and Hungary would each take a share, but it all seemed inevitable that a great greedy beast was gobbling its way through Europe. The Nazi war-beast. She shook away the fear, and spoke brightly.

'Look, why don't we go out to a little café this evening and have some wine, and forget all about old Adolf? We're in Paris, for God's sake. Let's make the most of it.'

Evelyn was only too glad to follow her lead, since the conversation had suddenly become frighteningly depressing, and she knew she had begun it.

'And tomorrow I want to go shopping. Mummy gave me a generous allowance to buy some new frocks, and I simply can't leave Paris without buying a couple of hats. They're so terribly chic, aren't they? I want to buy you a present too, Cass, to remember this visit by.'

339

'You sound as if it's the last time we'll ever meet! I'll tell you what. Let's buy each other something, as a token of eternal friendship.'

'All right. What a lovely idea.'

They beamed at each other, the nagging worries fading. And much later, in the warm darkness of the room, tucked up in their single beds, the wine they'd consumed mellowing their minds, Cassie spoke sleepily.

'What's it like having a grandmother, Evelyn?'

'What a funny thing to say. You must have had grandparents – two sets, in fact!'

'I suppose I must. I asked my mother about them once, and she never knew my father's people at all, and just clammed up about her own parents, saying they were dead. And somehow the subject never came up again. You know how it is when you get the feeling that something's taboo?'

Evelyn looked sideways towards the hump in the other bed that was Cassie.

'But that's silly. You have every right to know. We can trace our family right back to the Crusades, give or take a few black sheep that we don't mention.'

She couldn't help the unconscious pride in her voice. It was so good to be English, to have roots, strong and firm. You knew that wherever you put your feet, there was a solid foundation beneath you.

'Oh well, it doesn't really matter, I suppose.'

'You can share mine, if you like. Granny, I mean. She's an old love. When you come home for Christmas, come and spend a few days with us, Cass.'

'I'd like that. I really would. Do you mean it?'

'Of course. I'll tell Mummy when I get back. Perhaps you'll want to stay, when you've had a taste of good old English roast beef and Yorkshire pudding, after the oily French stuff they serve up here.'

Cassie laughed. 'I won't. I love it here. I'll probably stay for ever.'

'If the Germans let you,' Evelyn said.

Christmas in England in 1938 was celebrated with an almost

feverish determination to keep everything as normal as possible. Most of the people gathered around Lord Harry Ashworth's table for the traditional Christmas dinner hadn't seen one another for some time, and each one assessed the others with a feeling of surprise, if not shock.

Harry himself was almost dashingly handsome now with his iron-grey hair suiting his rugged features. Bridget, more rounded than she used to be, her hair still black and glossy but with alluring natural silvery streaks at the temples and cut stylishly to emphasise them, wore her age with elegance and lost none of her ethereal beauty because of it.

Ralph had grown surprisingly stout, and Alma positively waddled in the seventh month of pregnancy. But she was perfectly well, she told them all cheerfully, and the doctor had said she was disgustingly healthy to be carrying a child at forty-six years old, and there wasn't a thing to worry about.

Everyone continued to be amazed at Liam. This was his sixteenth birthday, and he was as tall and broad as a man. All the Finleys were tall, as had been the O'Connells, but Liam ... Bridget couldn't get over the way he'd grown and matured. He was still her darling, still reminding her of Michael, and of Austen, her love.

The others exclaimed at Cassie's appearance too. In April she would be twenty-one years old, and she appeared among them now as the complete *Parisienne*, confident and vivacious, perfectly happy in her job, as fulfilled as any unattached girl could be who had chosen to stay that way.

But not for ever, surely. Ralph teased her unmercifully, trying to find out the name of the beau who had given her the little gold cross and chain she wore around her neck.

'I'm sorry to disappoint you all,' Cassie laughed. 'But Evelyn bought it for me when she came to stay with me in October. Isn't it sweet? We wanted to buy each other something, and in the end we bought matching crosses.'

'Oh, but you should have bought something different for each other,' Bridget said. 'They'll hardly seem like presents, will they?'

'Of course they will, Mother,' Cassie said evenly.

'Well, I think it's a jolly nice idea,' Liam championed her.

'Every time you look in the mirror and see your cross, you'll think of Evelyn, and she'll do the same.'

'Exactly.' She flashed a look of thanks at him. Her little brother was really becoming something of a handsome young man, she thought, and would make some lucky girl a good husband in due course. She had never considered it before, nor of making a friend of Liam. But the five years between them seemed of less consequence now than when they were small, and she resolved to write to him more often than she usually did. His letters were more refreshing than Bridget's or Harry's, with their constant reference to war these days. He was always keen to learn about Paris and about her German friend, Stefan, and she'd rarely bothered to answer his letters until weeks later.

'By the way,' her own thoughts reminded her. 'Stefan's gone back to Germany. He's decided not to work in Paris any longer. I think he's homesick.'

'Or it's getting too hot for him,' Harry commented. 'When are you coming home, Cassie?'

'Me? I'm home now, aren't I?' she laughed, and then saw what he meant.

'We've been discussing it, Cassie,' Bridget said quietly. 'And we both think it's time you gave up your job in Paris. It's too dangerous.'

Cassie was suddenly angry. 'How can you say that from your complacent little fireside, without ever knowing what it's like! Paris isn't dangerous. The cafés are still open, the musicians still play on the steps of *Montmartre*, people still go shopping and get married and have babies and do the things they always did. Just like they do here, believe it or not.'

'If it's just like here, then the people must be increasingly anxious. It would be extremely foolish not to be,' Harry said. 'The signs are all there, Cassie, and we want you to come home. This could be the last peaceful Christmas for any of us.'

She saw Alma's hand go to her abdomen, over the unborn child. They'd be all right, Cassie thought. They'd all be safe in Ireland, and Bridget could always go back there if she wanted to. Liam too. But it wasn't in her nature to take the safest way. Not when there was no need.

'I live and work in Paris,' she said deliberately. 'I've made my home there. My friends are there. And what if there is a war? It'll be Germany fighting Britain. Even if they invaded France, they can't touch me. I'm an American citizen.'

She said it with a kind of triumph, and Harry's voice was harsh, the words brutally honest.

'Do you think the Germans will stop to ask for identity papers when they start to overrun French towns? They didn't do it in the last war, and they won't bother in the next. If France is occupied, you'll be classed as an alien, liable to be interned or shot. Believe me, I know what I'm talking about, and so does Ralph. We've seen it all before, Cassie.'

'Stop trying to frighten me,' she gave a nervous laugh. 'You're spoiling Liam's birthday.'

'No, he's not. I hope the war doesn't start until I'm old enough to join the army,' Liam said eagerly. 'Mother's agreed to my leaving school in March and going to work for *Night News*. It would be spiffing to become a war correspondent.'

'I don't want to hear any more talk of war today,' Bridget said sharply, and Cassie knew bitterly that it wasn't on her account that her mother changed this conversation. It was because of the thought of her darling pet going to war . . . but she was forced to admit that she was in full agreement on that.

She too would hate to think of Liam with a rifle in his hand. He was too young, too terribly young to have that light in his eyes that all men seemed to get when they anticipated going into battle. It was frightening and yet poignantly endearing. It went back to man being the hunter, protecting his territory and his womenfolk. In turn, it made Cassie feel oddly protective towards Liam. After all, he was the only brother she had.

'You never told me much about my grandparents, did you? Your parents, I mean.' Cassie said casually to Bridget as she was packing her suitcase to go to Evelyn's. Remembering Evelyn's reference to her granny had prompted the question, and she sensed, rather than saw, her mother's body go rigid.

'What on earth made you think of that?' Bridget said. .

343

Cassie straightened.

'Perhaps it's all this talk of war. Seeing everyone around the Christmas tree, and just wanting to be sure I'm part of a family. It's important, isn't it?'

She was clumsy, awkward. She and Bridget never talked about intimate things. They never got emotional with each other, and Cassie only half-recognised this need to get closer to her mother. If only Bridget would reach out the rest of the way . . .

'My parents died a long time ago,' Bridget said flatly. 'It pains me to speak of them, and I'd rather not.'

'They were Irish, weren't they?'

'Yes.'

'But I was born in America, so you must have lived there as a child. Did your parents emigrate?'

'Yes.'

Cassie became impatient with these monosyllabic answers. 'Oh, Mother, I do have a right to know! They were my flesh and blood after all. Why are you so tight-lipped just because I ask you a simple question? If Liam wanted to know, you'd tell him.'

'He knows what you know. My parents are dead. They died when I was fourteen.'

Cassie was shocked at this bit of knowledge.

'How awful for you. What did you do?'

'I survived. And please – I don't want to say any more. There's nothing more to tell, anyway.'

There was masses, but somehow, even now, Bridget was unable to form the words. They were all in her head, surging around like fishes caught in a whirlpool. Mavreen and Dermot O'Connell were destroyed by the San Francisco earthquake, along with my adored little brother, Michael. My sister Kitty and I survived, and I swore to keep Kitty safe. But I failed, terribly. I let Kitty down. She had an abortion and died, and I married Thomas Finley, your bastard of a father. And you were his child, the one I could never love, because I hated Thomas so much. You took the place of the baby I lost, my lover's child, my Austen's child. And when Liam was born, he reminded me so much of him, that it was

344

like a miracle, so that all the love that was locked up in my heart spilled over for him, leaving none for you. And that's the truth of it, my poor sweet Cassandra Mavreen . . .

'Well, if you won't tell me any more, I may as well finish my packing and go off to Evelyn's. At least I can have a share in her old granny,' Cassie said resentfully.

'I'm sorry, Cassie. I can't produce a family for you out of thin air, like one of poor Norman de Wolfe's old conjuring tricks.'

'No. But you could make me feel part of the one I've got,' Cassie retorted.

Bridget turned abruptly. For a second she'd stepped forward to take her daughter in her arms, but seeing the stiff set of her shoulders, she knew it would be no use. They were both hot with embarrassment. They had grown too far apart, and the opportunity to repair the damage slipped away. And Cassie knew, as she furiously threw her clothes in the suitcase, that she was definitely going back to Paris after this trip. There was no place for her here.

When Hitler marched into defenceless Czechoslovakia without warning in March of 1939, everyone knew that war was just around the corner. Not even the finest pundits could surmise anything less.

'Is this violation the beginning of a hideous tit for tat on the part of a despicable dictator?' screamed the dramatic headlines in Lord Harry Ashworth's *Night News*.

'As long ago as 1919, at the end of the war to end all wars, the Hall of Mirrors at Versailles reflected the silent German delegates listening to the terms of victory on their defeated country. Six countries were to share much of Germany's valuable lands. They were France, Belgium, Czechoslovakia, Poland, Lithuania and Denmark. How long before the rest of these little countries succumb to this march of horror?

'Adolf Hitler joined the German Labour Party in that same year, soon re-named the National Socialist German Labour Party, the party that opposed most fiercely the Versailles Treaty. Few of our politicians read the warnings correctly. Among those who did was Mr Winston Churchill, whose eloquence might well be heeded now.'

There followed a biting account of Hitler's rise to power, and the attitudes of various governments to it. When she read it, Cassie wondered how Harry dared to be so outspoken. But Harry had the weight of his legal advisers behind him. He knew just how far to go and went no farther, and in the months that followed, his frontpage article assumed a measure of prophetic authenticity.

Chapter 26

In the early dawn of Friday, September 1st, Nazi troops marched eastwards into Poland. The governments of Britain and France had already pledged to come to Poland's aid in such an eventuality, and each country was now obliged to send ultimatums to Adolf Hitler demanding the withdrawal of his army from Poland. The deadline was eleven a.m. on Sunday September 3rd.

It was a time when families should be together. That thought was the one most sharply etched in Bridget Finley's mind that Sunday morning. And hers was split in all directions. Cassie was still in Paris, a city that was desperately holding its own breath. Harry had driven into London early that morning, to be at the newspaper offices as soon as any news came through, despite it being the Sabbath. Knowing that the office would be well-manned, Liam had begged to go with him, to get a real taste of crisis journalism. The crack reporters from *Night News* jostled for places in Downing Street along with the silent crowds, waiting for the announcement from the Prime Minister. And Bridget Finley waited alone in Magnolia Cottage, and polished the black bakelite wireless for the tenth time as the clock ticked on towards 11 a.m.

The air seemed very still, as if it too, was waiting. The scent of the dying magnolia blossoms from the garden stifled her. The minutes passed, and finally, at 11.15 a.m. came the news that the Prime Minister was about to speak to the nation. Mr Chamberlain's flat, dour voice seemed to lack all expression in those first pedantic sentences that everyone had dreaded.

'This morning the British Ambassador in Berlin handed the German Government a final Note stating that unless we heard from them by eleven o'clock, that they were prepared at once to withdraw their troops from Poland, a state of war would exist between us.

'I have to tell you now that no such undertaking has been received, and that consequently this country is at war with Germany . . .'

On and on went that droning voice, while Bridget sat as if frozen. However much it was expected, bad news always shocked and stunned, and this was news of the very worst. A word caught her ears, and she forced herself to listen with pounding heart.

'. . . We and France are today, in fulfilment of our obligations, going to the aid of Poland, who is so bravely resisting this wicked and unprovoked attack on her people . . .'

Cassie . . . oh, Cassie . . . why didn't you listen to Harry and me . . .? Bridget heard the rest of the Prime Minister's speech in disjointed little bursts.

'. . . When I have finished speaking certain detailed announcements will be made on behalf of the Government. Give these your closest attention . . .

'. . . You may be taking your part in the fighting services or as a volunteer in one of the branches of civil defence . . .

'. . . You may be engaged in work essential to the prosecution of war, for the maintenance of the life of the people – in factories, in transport, in public utility concerns, or in the supply of other necessaries of life . . .

'. . . Now may God bless you all. May He defend the right. It is the evil things that we shall be fighting against – brute force, bad faith, injustice, oppression and persecution – and against them I am certain that the right will prevail.'

The speech ended. How long Bridget sat hunched in front of the wireless as other voices took over, she couldn't have said. Another sound began to fill her ears. A long, mournful wailing sound that sent her heart plummeting to her feet as she recognised them. Holy Mother of God, air-raid sirens!

Harry had predicted that this was a war that would be fought in the air as well as on the ground. But not so soon . . . not before the British people even had a chance to reel back from what was happening . . . In total panic, because she was alone and very afraid, Bridget made a dive for the small broom cupboard under the stairs, and hid there, trembling and terrified, offering up prayers long since forgotten, begging God to forgive her sins and her wickedness, promising to love her children equally, without ever knowing what she babbled.

It seemed as if she had been in the broom cupboard for hours when she heard the sound of the 'All Clear' siren, and she crept out stiffly, ashamed at her cowardice. She had actually been there for quite a short while, and as she stood up, the telephone rang. She grabbed it, praying that it was Harry or Liam, frantic to know that they were safe.

'Is that you, Bridget ducks?' She heard Marlene de Wolfe's voice from a long way away. 'Gawd, I thought I'd never get through to ya. The operator said all the lines are jammed, just as if I wouldn't know that. Bloody Jerries are trying to scare the living daylights out of us already, ain't they? Sirens going orf all over the bleedin' country, be all accounts.'

'Marlene,' Bridget croaked. Get off the line, she wanted to scream. Harry might be trying to get through. Or Liam. Or Cassie . . . but nothing came out of her dry lips.

'Now you just listen, ducks. You're to pack up yer things at once and come down here to Devon out o' the way of old Adolf's bombs. There's plenty of room wi' me and Ruth, and it's real nice here in Dartmouth –'

'Marlene, it's very sweet of you,' Bridget broke in as soon as she could. 'But I have to stay here. My family must know where I am –'

'They can come too! Me an' Ruth was fretting over all the pictures in the papers of them poor little kids being sent overseas wi' labels stuck on 'em like a lot o' bloody parcels. That's not for our Liam, I said. 'E must come here wiv us. Cassie as well. Poor little devils –'

348

Tears filled Bridget's eyes. 'Marlene, love, they're not children any more. Liam's working with Harry, and Cassie's still in Paris –'

'What!' Bridget held the receiver farther away from her ears at the bellow. 'Is she daft or summat? You must get 'er out, Bridget, quick as lightning. That Hitler bugger will have France next, sure as eggs is eggs.'

Her words sent fear racing through Bridget. 'I will. I was about to call her when you rang me. I must go now, Marlene, but I'll be in touch, I promise.'

She put the phone down quickly. It rang again almost immediately.

'Mrs Finley? I'm speaking from the *Night News* office. Lord Harry asked me to say you're not to worry. The air-raid was a false alarm. It sent plenty of people scurrying for the shelters, but things are getting back to normal now. We're all staying at the office all day and he and Liam will see you when they see you.'

The line went dead before she had a chance to say a word. Bridget had never felt so alone. Or not for a very long time. Not since the silence after the earthquake. She still shuddered with the memory, and pushed it back.

The last war had been very far away from her. She had been safe in America, even with the hated Thomas Finley. This time, she was in the middle of it. If she had any sense, she'd grab at Marlene's offer and flee. Or at the very least, go back to Ireland . . .

But something stronger than fear, stronger than the need to be safe that had always seemed so paramount to her, was telling her to stay put. Hitler wasn't driving her out. This had been her home for a long while now. It was a base for her family, and very gradually the trembling in her bones lessened during the rest of that Sunday as the peace of the English countryside continued undisturbed, at least for the time being.

Cassie's resolution to stay in Paris was eventually taken out of her hands. Three months after the declaration of war, she was still disregarding all her mother's efforts to get her back to

349

England. Even another family Christmas hadn't been enough to make her reconsider. England was the enemy and was just as likely to be bombed, for God's sake! So what was so different about being in France! British troops, guns and tanks, were as much in evidence over there as were their own French soldiers, so, ostrich-like, Cassie maintained that it hardly mattered where she lived, since they were all in it together.

But at the beginning of the new year, the publishing firm of Macon and Girard went into liquidation. For a long time, the two elderly owners had struggled to keep the business going, but now that there was probably going to be a paper shortage on top of everything else, they decided the time was opportune for them to retire gracefully.

'We're both saddened to tell you this,' they said at the meeting of employees. 'But we know you'll understand. We leave shortly for Marseilles, where we have old friends. It will take a few weeks to settle everything here, but it is already in the hands of our company lawyers. Our beloved Paris will naturally be a target for the Germans, and we've no wish to be here when they come. We're too old to fight, my friends, and too proud to surrender. We wish the rest of you much good fortune in whatever you do, and Cassie, we advise you to leave France as soon as possible.'

There was nothing anyone could say. Messieurs Macon and Girard were old and tired and strained, and it all seemed to be a *fait accompli*. But Cassie still resisted, seeking them out when everyone else had been sent home to think about their own futures.

'I want to stay in France,' she stated. 'I have an American passport, and America's not involved in this war. There must be some other work I can do. Can you suggest anything?'

They looked at her sorrowfully. Stubborn, headstrong, beautiful English-American girl, the looks said.

'Go home, Cassie,' Monsieur Macon urged. 'Your presence here only endangers yourself. And possibly others who shelter you.'

'What others?' She was still inclined to laugh this off, until she saw the seriousness in the tired old faces.

'America may yet enter the war as they did the last one. What then? Get out while you can, *chérie*. This is not your country, Cassie.'

Her eyes filled with sudden tears. 'But it's my war. And I think of France as my country. I love it here. Damn it, I've lived in Paris or Switzerland for over five years! I'm as European as you are!'

'Is that what your passport says?' Monsieur Girard said mildly.

'Oh, stupid officialdom!' Frustrated and angry, for the first time Cassie felt that she hated her birthplace. She'd been so happy here. She had never felt a sense of belonging so deeply as she did in Paris. And everyone seemed determined to send her away.

Seeing the troubled looks in the Frenchmen's eyes, she capitulated as if all the wind was let out of her sails, knowing she couldn't win this particular battle. She was what she was.

'I'll go to the American Embassy,' she declared. 'They'll tell me the position.'

She cheered up, having a positive aim. Only to be told by a very junior official in a clipped Yankee voice to get the hell out of here while she could. In a fury, she rattled off a string of expletives in French, which seemed fractionally less insulting than blaspheming in English in this hallowed place.

The junior official's jaw dropped.

'Say, are you French, trying something on?' He said suspiciously. 'Just where'd you get that US passport, little lady? You didn't steal it, did you, and come here expecting us to ship you out all expenses paid, despite that sob-story of wanting to stay on? Hey, just a minute –'

Cassie turned and ran, her heart ready to explode in her chest. Stupid, stupid imbecile of a man in his expensively cut suit that reeked of New York tailoring. She wasn't using devious methods trying to get out. She wanted to stay in!

Her feet didn't slow down until she reached a pavement café and sat down, ordering a cognac, although she didn't usually drink the stuff, swallowing it quickly and banging the glass on the table for another.

'Oui, Mademoiselle. *Tout de suite!*' the proprietor said

351

admiringly, eyeing this tall, elegant girl who tossed back the bitter spirit like a man. *La petite brave*, he commented with twinkling eyes to another customer.

They clearly assumed she was French too, Cassie thought fleetingly. Everyone did who wasn't told anything different. She could easily pass for French. Her eyes began to gleam. All she needed was a French passport . . . but even as the haphazard thoughts raced through her head, she knew it wasn't possible. Who did she know who could provide such a thing? She wasn't in the habit of consorting with forgers and law-breakers. And what was the point, anyway? She didn't have a job any more.

But she did have her languages. She and Stefan had often complimented one another on it . . . He with his so-correct English and French, and she with her impeccable French and German. Her translations for Macon and Girard had been first-class. Because of her linguistic ability she could surely be useful to the war in some way. She finished her drink, ignoring the stinging in her throat and the swimming in her head, and hailed a taxi, asking imperiously for the British Embassy. Once there, she marched inside, and explained her situation.

'Sorry love,' the brusque Englishman answered her perfunctorily. 'We're in the process of packing up here. You need your own Embassy. Best of all, you need transport to get you back home. I'd go while the going's good, if I were you. There'll be precious few boats going to England with room to spare for tourists.'

'Tourists!' She spluttered. The man glanced at her.

'Look, Miss, I'd help you if I could. In fact, you could bunk in with me at any time,' he grinned. 'But none of us will be worth a red cent if the Jerries come marching in, and that's a fact.'

Somehow his very Englishness, and his unhurried, apparently unperturbed manner, struck a sudden chill of fear in her. She turned and went out into the cold January streets. There were few people about late in the afternoon, and darkness was already beginning to fall. Cars had been ordered to cover their headlights to avoid the risk of providing targets

for enemy aircraft, and only tiny slits of dim lights showed
through. Windows, habitually shuttered in France, were even
more heavily battened, and shops and houses looked blank
and dead. Already, there was a sense of impending doom
about Paris, a feeling that it was only a matter of time before it
became a ghost-town.

Cassie faced facts. Abandoning any other ideas, she hurried
back to her room in the old quarter and packed everything
she owned. It was time to leave.

She discovered the truth of the Embassy man's words. There
were long lines of people waiting for passages on the available
boats. If they didn't have current passports, they simply
couldn't leave. Those that did board the ships were mostly
English, American, Canadian, and some French. All running
out, Cassie couldn't help feeling, guilty and ashamed and
helpless . . . but the tension was beginning to get to her. Her
head throbbed appallingly and with it was the feeling that at
any minute she might burst into tears, a temptation she held
rigidly in check.

She finally arrived at Magnolia Cottage, exhausted and
wet through in a downpour of rain, after a nightmare journey
lasting two days. The taxi-driver, to whom she'd paid an
exorbitant fare, wouldn't take her down the narrow lane
leading to the cottage, and she'd had to walk the last half mile.
She banged on the door, and almost fell through it when
Bridget opened it. Cassie's face was streaked with rain, her
dark hair hanging in rats'-tails, her hands chilled to the bone.
But she was home. She gave her mother a crooked grin and
dumped her suitcase on the floor.

'Well, this was what you wanted, wasn't it, Mother?'

'Oh, *Cass.*' Bridget's throat was suddenly full. 'Darling, I'm
so thankful to see you. Why on earth didn't you let us know,
instead of doing this to us again! We could have made
arrangements to meet you at Dover. At the very least I would
have come to meet you at the railway station.'

'It doesn't matter.' Cassie said, her teeth chattering. They
wouldn't seem to stop. Her limbs ached all over, and she felt
extraordinarily weary and light-headed, and it would be the

easiest thing in the world to simply drop where she stood and sleep and sleep and sleep . . .

'God, that fire feels good,' she stuttered on, stretching out her hands towards it. 'I don't know when I've felt so cold. I'd love a cup of tea, with a good swig of brandy in it, Mother. And I'm afraid 'medicinal purposes' is the last thing on my mind right now –'

It was also the last thing she said for a while. To Bridget's horror, Cassie didn't so much collapse on the floor, as dissolve into it like so much jelly, as if all her bones had disintegrated.

When she awoke it was to find herself in a strange high bed, the bedclothes tucked around her so tightly she could hardly breathe. Dark green curtains were pulled around her bed, enclosing her inside. She knew it must be dark outside, because there was a small light shining over her bed. It hurt her eyes to look at it. It hurt her head to try to think. She seemed to be floating somewhere with all her limbs on the move, as if every nerve was doing some macabre dance inside her skin, even though she was so tightly cocooned in the unfamiliar bed. She seemed to be looking out through some sort of opaque film. She felt utter panic, wondering if she was going blind.

She heard the swish of the green curtains, and then the crackle of the opaque substance surrounding her, and a woman in a crisp nurse's uniform put her head inside the small enveloping tent. To Cassie's enormous relief she could see the woman's features clearly, even though she still seemed to be watching it all from a distance, and it was far too much effort to begin asking questions.

A cool hand reached for Cassie's wrist, while the nurse examined her watch. The procedure felt comforting, secure. She stuck a thermometer in Cassie's mouth, examined it and then shook it violently before replacing it in some kind of phial above the bed. Only when the ritual was finished did she speak to her patient.

'Good. So you've come back to us, have you? You gave us all a bit of a fright, my girl.'

'What's – what's wrong with me?'

Cassie couldn't believe she was hearing her own voice.

354

That dull, dragging voice that was little more than a whisper, and surely belonged to an old old woman, and not to her at all . . .

'You've had pneumonia on top of influenza,' the nurse said briskly. 'If you hadn't been brought in when you were, we wouldn't be sitting here having this conversation, so thank your lucky stars and that nice uncle of yours for recognising the danger signs and getting you straight into hospital.'

'What uncle?' She slurred.

The nurse leaned down inside the oxygen tent, smoothing the lank hair back from the girl's white face. She was a real good-looker, even when she was so ill and pinched, and Nurse Loder's normally abrupt manner softened, seeing the bewilderment in the lovely blue eyes.

'Well, now, Miss Cassandra Finley, if I had a gorgeous man like Lord Harry Ashworth for my uncle, I'm darn sure I wouldn't forget him! You'd better not tell him I said so, though, nor your lovely mother and your brother Liam, who've been in to see you every day for the past month and put up with all your ramblings!'

A month! The shock of that gave way to a faint smile on Cassie's lips, seeing the nurse's ploy.

'It's all right. I haven't lost my memory. I know very well who I am. And Harry's not my uncle. He's just a friend of the family.'

The brief explanation totally exhausted her. She let her eyelids droop over her eyes, thankful to drift off again into that half-world where she didn't have to worry about anything. She didn't have to think.

There was a suspect patch on Cassie's lung, the doctor told Bridget briskly. It was probably nothing to worry about, and most likely a relic from the pneumonia, but they wanted to keep an eye on her. They wanted to keep her in the hospital a few more weeks yet.

'It's all so boring!' Cassie said in frustration to Liam, when he came on his regular visit, and she finally felt well enough to begin complaining.

Recovering her health slowly, and her temper very fast, she found the whole experience of enforced lethargy deadly dreary. She was allowed to sit out in what they called the women's day-room on the ground floor of the hospital now, segregated from the men patients in their own day-room. A balcony ran along the whole length of this south-facing side of the hospital, with a dividing partition separating the two factions.

Did they expect instant fornication from a load of old crocks who could hardly totter to the bathroom? She'd tried to shock Nurse Loder, whose bland features had refused to be impressed by such racy talk.

The vista beyond the balcony was pleasantly green and rural. Walking patients strolled the grounds in nightclothes and dressing-gowns when the weather was suitable, or were even allowed to put proper clothes on again. Which seemed to defeat the whole object of keeping men and woman separated, she told her brother in biting terms, since those on the balconies and those walking about could see one another perfectly well.

To Cassie, straight from the gathering storms in Paris, the whole place was nothing less than a wilderness. You'd hardly think there was a war on, except for the occasional uniforms seen on some of the men patients.

'It's worse than being back at La Retraite,' she complained to Liam, well-wrapped up on the balcony in an unexpected spell of early spring sunshine. 'They treat us like children, and just because I said that, don't get the idea that I'm panting to talk to a man!'

'You're talking to me, aren't you? Won't I do?' Liam grinned, used to Cassie's unthinking words.

She put a quick hand on his arm, so strong and muscular now. 'That's different. You're my brother. And I do appreciate you coming to see me so often, Liam. You're the only one I can talk to sensibly. Mother hates hospitals, and we never converse properly, anyway.'

She dismissed Bridget with one sentence. 'Harry's a dear, but he's always too busy to spare more than five minutes, and Evelyn's mother just died, so I can hardly expect her to come calling right now, can I, poor love?'

Liam hugged her arm with quick sympathy.

'It's hell for you, Cass, I can see that. But you'll be home for your birthday, won't you?'

'Good God, I hope so. It's six weeks away yet!'

'Harry's planning something special,' he said conspiratorially. I'm not supposed to say anything, but I thought it would cheer you up to know.'

'Not another surprise party at Ashworthy Hall?' She said, knowing she was being unreasonable and cynical. 'I'll be twenty-two, anyway, and there's nothing to celebrate in that. We had the big bash last year, and it's all downhill from now on.'

Liam laughed. 'I can see you're in a foul mood, but I still love ya, kid! Anyway, it's not Ashworthy Hall this time, but I'm saying no more. See you tomorrow, all right?'

She looked up at him from her chair. It was strange to look up at her little brother, who was becoming more of a man every day. He was gone seventeen now, dark-haired and handsome, with his mother's blue eyes and proud walk. He loved his job at *Night News*, elevated already to junior reporter, and Harry never failed to convey his pride in Liam's progress to his mother and sister.

Once, such praise might have made Cassie feel jealous. But that was long ago, and the rapport between them now was strong and good. And right now, she felt a sudden overwhelming surge of love for Liam, catching hold of his hand as an uncomfortable thought struck her.

'Liam, you won't do anything rash, will you? Like joining up, I mean. Harry needs you, and so do we.'

He gave a quick laugh. 'I won't do anything rash,' he promised, which told her nothing. 'But I'm not prepared to stay tied to Mother's apron-strings for ever, Cass, any more than you were. Look, I'll have to go, before Matron comes round to throw me out.'

Cheekily, he leapt over the balcony rails and into the bushes, before picking himself up and walking off backwards with a mock limp while waving madly, an act which would certainly enrage Matron if she saw him. Cassie felt a prickle of tears at the backs of her eyes. He wouldn't, would he . . .? He was too young for war, too impossibly young . . .

357

She closed her eyes as if to shut out the thought, leaning back in her wicker chair. No one else was in the day-room this particular afternoon, no elderly ladies with their clacking knitting needles, nor was she trying to make sense of those frustrating baskets the physios tried to make them create. What happened to all the bloody half-finished baskets, anyway? Cassie visualised all the physios spending their nights unpicking the unholy messes for the new intake to begin all over again.

Suddenly she heard a laconic and seemingly disembodied voice.

'It won't make the war go away, honey. If the kid wants to enlist, he'll go, and it'll take more than a big sister to stop him, however aggressive she is.'

Cassie's eyes flew open at this unmitigated insult and invasion of her privacy.

'I am not aggressive,' she snapped without thinking, and then stopped abruptly.

'I rest my case,' said the voice, with that silly transatlantic phrase currently being used by Hollywood actors playing sneering lawyers . . .

She clamped her lips shut. She couldn't see who the voice belonged to, but it seemed to be coming from behind the partition between the day-rooms. The damn cheek! Cassie's face was hot with embarrassment and fury in equal measures, realising instantly that the man, whoever he was, must have been listening to every word she and Liam had said to each other. She picked up her bag indignantly, intending to go back to bed.

'Hi,' said the voice. 'Don't go. Have you noticed that everyone else around here seems over ninety? You and I should obviously get together.'

Cassie's head jerked up. The man in the hospital dressing-gown was hanging precariously around the partition separating the two day-rooms. He looked very large. His face was silhouetted against the sunlight, his short dark hair haloed by it, and by the greasy stuff that slicked it down, and was all the rage with the glamour-boys of the Royal Air Force these days.

'You've got a nerve,' she snapped. 'Were you eaves-dropping?'

To her horror, he hauled himself around the partition and over the balcony railing to the women's day-room. The audacity of it took away the anger for a minute, especially as his right leg was in plaster of paris from the ankle to the thigh.

'What do you think you're doing?' She spluttered. 'Matron will skin you alive if she finds you here. It's "out of bounds, don't you know?"' She mimicked Matron's masculine tones perfectly. The man grinned, moving with a hop and a grimace, and easing himself down on the chair next to her.

'What the hell does she think we're going to get up to, with me in plaster, and your brains addled by pneumonia?' He echoed her own thoughts. 'How is it, by the way? Have they cleared your lungs yet?'

Cassie glared.

'Do you know everything that goes on around here?'

'Most of it,' he said cheerfully. 'It comes from being a good listener, so they tell me.'

Cassie would agree with that, though not in quite the way he meant it. She couldn't even tell what he looked like, except that now that she got a good look at him, she could see he looked almost grotesque, because of the huge medicinal plaster across his nose and cheeks, and two decidedly black eyes. His jaw was rugged and square, and his smile was wide, but beneath the clown's appearance, it did nothing for him at all.

'So what happened to you?' She was annoyed with herself for bothering to ask. But at least it relieved the boredom of the day for a few minutes.

'Nothing much,' he said, with the unconcern that told her immediately it had been worse than it sounded. 'I fell out of an aeroplane and landed the wrong way up. Broke my nose and my leg, but they're patching me up OK. I'll be as good as new in a month.'

'You fell out of an aeroplane?' Cassie repeated sceptically. 'What are you, some kind of Hollywood stuntman?'

He gave that wide grin again. 'Not bad, honey, though I

don't quite earn that kind of dough. You could compare it, though.'

'I'm not interested in guessing games. Are you going to tell me or aren't you?' Irritably, she decided that she was obviously still muzzy in the head. She knew she should be able to tell at once who or what he was, but somehow it eluded her.

'I haven't made up my mind yet,' he teased. 'I'm quite enjoying making you sweat.'

Cassie gave him a superior and disgusted look.

'Well, you're not English, that's for sure. Otherwise, you'd know that ladies never sweat. Only horses sweat. Ladies perspire. And it would take more than you to make me even *glow*.'

She stood up, letting her blanket drop to the ground. They reached for it together, and their fingers touched. Cassie snatched hers away at once, but before she could think of another withering remark, she heard the starchy swish of a hospital uniform, and the squeak of regulation hospital shoes on the polished linoleum floor.

Matron's ringing voice was scandalised.

'Flight-lieutenant Buckley, you know you're not allowed in here! Get back to the ward at once. Doctor wants to see you about taking some more X-rays.'

The man hobbled to his feet, giving Cassie a conspiratorial wink and a smile before heaving himself along the wall and out of the room. Matron stood firm until he'd gone, arms folded, shoulders bristling with indignation. And before she turned around again, Cassie had to reorganise her features to get rid of the answering smile.

Chapter 27

'Who's the smart-aleck with the transatlantic accent?' Cassie asked Nurse Loder with studied casualness, sitting out while the nurse made her bed.

'You mean our Canadian airman?' Nurse Loder sighed

360

audibly. 'I can't wait to see what he looks like beneath that nose-job, can you?'

'I'm really not interested –'

'You must be weak in the head as well as everywhere else, then. All the nurses have fallen for him, and why not? He's our first Canadian casualty in the hospital. I daresay we'll get plenty more, though. Americans too. They say thousands of them joined up in the Canadian Air Force as soon as war broke out.'

Cassie picked up her magazine and pretended to read. Canadian, was he? So the accent was genuine.

'You're allowed outside for a stroll today,' the Ward Sister came bustling down to Cassie now. 'Stretch your legs a bit and get the strength back in them, but don't stay out too long. You'll be weaker than you think.'

'I'm quite comfortable here –'

'It's an order, Miss Finley. Patients can't stay bed-bound for ever, and there's plenty of folk who'd be glad of two good legs like yours,' Sister said briskly.

Cassie gave in. Hospital staff were a special breed, she thought grimly, and they always got what they wanted. She put on stockings and shoes beneath the dressing gown, and soon realised that Sister was right. It felt quite odd to put her feet on the soft spring grass, and her legs were quite wobbly. It was almost like teaching herself to walk all over again. She stayed close to the verandah of the day-rooms, as if afraid she'd fall if she ventured too far.

'I wish I had this damned plaster off, then I'd come and give you a hand. We could prop one another up,' came a voice she recognised at once. She jerked up her head, meaning to give Flight-lieutenant Buckley whoever-he-was a taste of her fiercest superior look.

He was leaning over the verandah just above her. He was smiling, but there was such a look of envy in his smile because she was walking and he was not, that Cassie changed her mind about cutting him short.

'If you feel as insecure as I do without your plaster, I'd advise you to keep it on as long as possible,' she retorted instead.

'A fat lot of use I'd be in the cockpit with one leg stuck out the door.'

Cassie paused, glad to take a breather, even to talk to him.

'You're going back then?' She said inanely.

'Does a duck need water? What about you? Do you intend going back to Paris?'

She looked at him in exasperation. It wasn't just him though. She realised by now that this entire hospital was some gigantic grapevine of information.

'I doubt it. I'd be there now if they hadn't chucked me out – well, as good as.' She felt a wave of sadness for the Paris she had known, that would never be the same again.

'So what are you going to do now?' He persisted.

'I don't know.' She was suddenly cross, because she'd been in this never-never land for weeks now, without the need to think, and she still had no idea what her future would be. And she didn't want him to make her think.

'Rich girl, are you?' His tone said she probably didn't need to work, anyway.

'That's none of your business!'

'O.K. You've got tougher bristles than a porcupine, Cassie. Sorry, you don't know my name, do you? It's Joe – Joseph Buckley, native of San Francisco.'

'Nurse Loder said you were Canadian.' As soon as she said it, she was furious at letting him know she'd been talking about him.

'So I am. Born in Canada at my mother's home in Vancouver, but the family home's just north of San Francisco. My Dad's from there, and I was raised there.'

She might have said it was of no interest to her at all. She might have said she too was born in America. She might or might not have said a lot of things, if Joseph Buckley hadn't been called away from the day-room at that minute. He grinned down at her with sudden delight.

'Thank God. They're taking this thing off my nose today. Perhaps I'll start to look and feel human again.'

'Or not,' she couldn't resist saying.

'Bet you ten cents you'll prefer me without the nose-bag,' he challenged.

'Make it sixpence. You're in England now,' she whipped back.

'You're on! See you later, honey.'

She stared at his retreating back, not quite knowing how she had got involved in that little bit of repartee, but realising she had enjoyed it. There was a sparky empathy between them that made her feel more exhilarated than in weeks, and hardly tired at all . . . she soon revised that idea after ten more minutes outside, and was glad to go back indoors, rest for an hour and then finish up the afternoon in the day-room with a few other sitting-up patients.

She saw Joe look cautiously around the partition while she was waiting for supper to arrive.

'Well, how do I look? Do I win my bet?'

She considered. The bruises were still there, and some of the swelling hadn't quite gone down. But he was undoubtedly the best-looking man Cassie had seen in a long while, in a very physical, outdoor kind of way.

'I'd love to say you reminded me of Popeye, but you don't.' It was as far as she'd go in flattering him. 'You win, and I owe you sixpence.'

'Save it, and owe me a dinner instead, my treat, when we're both let out of here.'

'How can I owe it you, if you're paying?'

'Because you'll be doing me the biggest favour, letting me take out the most beautiful girl I've seen this side of the water.'

Cassie's face flamed.

'I'll see. You can come to my birthday tea in April, if you like. Will that take care of the sixpenny debt?'

'Sure thing. That means I'll see you at least twice when we leave here.'

He disappeared around the partition again, leaving her staring at the blank wall. A feeling of warmth was slowly stealing back into her veins these last few days. Ever since meeting Joseph Buckley, in fact. There was something about him . . . something special . . . but she wasn't going to read too much into it. Everyone knew that hospital romances didn't mean anything, and anyway, this was nothing remotely like a hospital romance . . .

*

Bridget and Harry both remarked how much better she looked when they visited her that evening, and she was back in bed again. She spoke triumphantly.

'I've been outside for the first time. It felt really weird to be walking again, but Sister says I can go a bit further every day now.'

Already, she felt the need to stop talking about hospital routine so much, the way patients always did in that small claustrophobic world. She felt the need to get back to normality, whatever that was now.

'By the way, I've asked a friend to my birthday tea,' she said casually. 'That's all right, isn't it? He's an airman.'

'Of course it's all right,' Harry smiled.

'Where's it going to be? Just so he'll know where to go,' she added.

Harry laughed, shaking his head. 'You're not getting me to spoil the surprise like that. Tell me your airman's address and I'll drop him a note.'

'It's here! He's in the men's ward. Why don't you go and meet him, Harry? He's a Flight-lieutenant Joseph Buckley. He doesn't get any visitors, and you'd like him.'

'All right, then you and your mother can get your heads together and talk women's talk,' he said agreeably.

And after he'd gone, the two Finley women talked determinedly about anything but women's talk.

Harry was quiet on the way home after their visit. Bridget could always tell when he had some scheme in his mind, and offered him a penny for his thoughts.

'Seeing Cassie and Joe set me thinking. There will be a lot of other people like them, victims of the war in one way or another, and the hospitals are going to be filled to overflowing. There'll also be a need for more convalescent homes, with casualties coming home from France . . . What do you think about turning part of Ashworthy Hall into a convalescent home, a sort of halfway stage for those not quite well enough to return to the Front?'

'I think you're wonderful to even think of it. But then, you would,' she said huskily.

'Is that a compliment, or do you think I'm being devious to save myself being commandeered into being some kind of stately barracks?' He grinned.

'It's a compliment. And you'll still have your home over-run with servicemen.'

He shrugged. 'It's large enough, and some company will stop me being lonely after a hard day at the office.'

She started to laugh. For somebody who never needed to work at all, he was quite extraordinary. He laughed with her as she told him so.

'Well, you wouldn't marry me and comfort me in my old age, and it's a bit late now to start looking for another wife, so this is the next best thing. I'll get it all organised officially, hire a few nurses and so on, just in case any of the poor chaps have a relapse when they see you around the place –'

'*Me?*' Bridget said sharply.

He glanced at her as they sped back smoothly to Magnolia Cottage in the early evening.

'Why should you be left out of it? We all have to do our bit in this war. Liam's hell-bent on following up every minute of it, like every good journalist. Cassie's only marking time until she can find something useful to do. I'm totally involved with the paper and now this new idea, and that leaves you. What will you say when they ask you what you did in the war?' He teased.

She gave a short laugh. 'How odd. I said almost the same thing to my husband a long time ago. Only I was being sarcastic.'

'So am I,' Harry said. 'You can't sit at home and rusticate, Bridget. You can't hide under the stairs every time a German bomber heads our way, either.'

He couldn't know about that. If it was a guess, it was uncomfortably near the truth.

'What do you suggest I do, then? I'm too old for singing love songs to twenty-year-olds. That's for younger people, though I did have a vague notion that it might be interesting to own a record company myself. To keep myself in the business, so to speak. It's all talk though, and I don't have the money to buy into it – and before you make any daft offers, *no*, thank you.'

He laughed. 'All right. No, what I was going to suggest was that you move back into the west wing of Ashworthy Hall, and become a sort of house-mother to the convalescents who'll come and go. You and Liam and Cassie can be comfortable there. Magnolia Cottage is too vulnerable when the German planes come over.'

'And isn't Ashworthy Hall?' She said, overcome by all he was suggesting. 'It's a bigger target, isn't it?'

'It's better hidden,' he said, and she couldn't argue with that. Surrounded by forests and in a pocket of the Sussex Downs, it wasn't as open as the cottage.

They stopped there now, and in the evening sunlight it was impossible to think there was a war on.

'What do you say, Bridget? Come home, where I know you'll be safe.'

She was touched by his words. 'I can hardly refuse, can I? All right. If you get the convalescent home started, I'll be your house-mother.'

Harry leaned across and kissed her gently.

'I wish you'd agree to all my suggestions so willingly,' he said meaningly. She got out of the car, still laughing at his nonsense, and went indoors to where Liam quickly hid a newspaper under a cushion, knowing how she hated to be reminded that younger and younger men were being called to war. And feeling a restless excitement within himself that very soon he too would be able to go . . . with or without her agreement. The country needed him . . . all the recruitment posters told him so.

'How's Cass?' he said.

'Much better,' Bridget said with a smile. 'She's become friends with an airman, and wants him to come to her birthday tea.'

'That's what they call love in the air, is it?' Liam grinned at his own joke.

'I shouldn't think so. Cassie seems quite clever at keeping the young men at bay!' She said, going into the kitchen to put the kettle on for some tea.

It struck her anew how very like herself Cassie was. In looks, in her ways, in her attitude towards men. Bridget gave a small shiver. The close affinity between them still eluded her, but it didn't change the fact that she wanted Cassie to be happy. She never wanted Cassie to end up with a loveless marriage like her own, nor a sterile life without someone to love. But it had to be the right man. She prayed that her daughter wouldn't settle for anything less.

Lately, Bridget had felt the urgency of telling Cassie the truth about her own inheritance. She owed it to her to tell her what Thomas Finley had left her. For years now, she had balked at it. Not only because just speaking of the man made her ill, but because of how it might affect Liam. His sister would have it all, while Liam had nothing.

But these anxious days when the war was beginning to get into its real stride were making everyone conscious of their own mortality. There were stories of courage and heroism from the Front reported in every newspaper. Families had already been left bereft. Husbands, sons and sweethearts had been killed or maimed. The war hadn't yet made itself felt in Britain, but everyone said it must come. And that meant everyone was vulnerable. Civilians could die . . .

Cassie came home from the hospital at the end of March, pronounced fit as long as she took it easy for another month. Joe had been transferred long before Bridget got a chance to meet him, which her brittle daughter said would make the meeting more interesting when they got together on Cassie's birthday. She had finally coaxed the venue out of Harry. They were taking tea at the Ritz Hotel in London. Joe had started telephoning her at the hospital whenever he could get through, and she'd said that she hoped he was suitably impressed.

'We have impressive hotels in San Francisco too,' he'd said, just as smugly. 'But knowing you, you'll never believe it until you see for yourself.'

'Is that an invitation?'

'It's whatever you want it to be,' he said, which told her nothing at all.

They hadn't had that dinner together yet. It was as if doctors and physios had suddenly conspired to keep them apart, just when they were getting to know one another. Just when their relationship was fresh and new and exciting, and could be on the brink of something more. Perhaps it was just as well, Cassie thought. Too fast, too soon, could be a recipe for disaster.

She remembered Stefan, and still thanked heaven that she hadn't fallen in love with him. She was still fond of his memory, though, even though she would never dare admit it. To be fond of a German – one of the enemy – was tantamount to treason! How ridiculous, when Stefan had just been a pleasant companion, if a little strange, with whom she had once shared a part of her life.

When Evelyn finally went to see her in the hospital, bravely bearing up after her mother's death, she was convinced that Cassie and Joe Buckley were made for one another. Evelyn hadn't met him either, but she had been struck by what she called the stars in Cassie's eyes.

'What romantic twaddle,' Cassie had grinned, and then they both fell about laughing, because it hadn't seemed like twaddle at all, but a distinct possibility that was as yet too tenuous to be put into words.

Bridget knew by now that Joe Buckley was in the Canadian Air Force, stationed 'somewhere in England', as the new war jargon had it, but since Cassie had never been in the habit of confiding in her mother, that was all she knew about him.

On the day Cassie came home to Magnolia Cottage from hospital, so shortly to be vacated once all the alterations at Ashworthy Hall were completed, Bridget drew a deep breath and faced both her children across the chintzy sitting-room. She had insisted that Liam should be there too, and now that the time had come, her hands were damp, her breathing very quick and uneven.

'There's something I want to tell you both. Something about your father.'

'Good God. This must be serious,' Cassie joked. 'I thought that was one of our taboo subjects. You mean we're going to be let in on the family skeletons at last?'

Bridget flinched. Oh, not all of them, my darling. Definitely not all of them!

'I never loved your father, Cassie.'

368

'I don't need you to tell me that.'

'Listen, please, and don't interrupt. Thomas Finley – your father – was much older than me. He died when you were three years old, and didn't know that I was expecting Liam. We left America, and Liam was born in Ireland. That much you know. What you don't know was that he died a wealthy man.'

Cassie sat up straighter, and Liam's eyes flickered with interest. Oh God, this was going to be even harder than she'd thought. Her mouth was dry, and she ran her tongue around her lips.

'Thomas owned a firm called Finley's Canned Goods. He sold it when you were born, Cassie, to spend more time with you. He was besotted with you –'

'It's nice to know somebody loved me,' she muttered, unable to resist the gibe.

'You might vaguely remember his sister, your Aunt Sheilagh, who lived with us. I heard not long ago that she's died.' She stopped again.

'Mother, why don't you just tell us what it is you want us to know?' Liam said. Bridget took a deep breath.

'Thomas left your aunt and me with a pittance. He left the bulk of his money to various charities out of spite. He also left a 10,000 dollar Trust Fund to Cassie, to be realised when she's twenty-five –'

'*What!*'

'I haven't finished, Cassie. It was a large amount that should be even larger by now. It was invested, of course, by our New York lawyer and accountant, but a lot of it was lost during the Wall Street Crash. However, much of it has since recovered, and I've been sent regular audits, which naturally you may see, whenever you wish. At present, the accumulated assets are something over 40,000 dollars.'

'*Phew.* Well done, Cass. You lucky old thing! Spare us a quid when you get the payoff,' Liam said cheekily, grinning all over his face at Cassie's comical expression. What did it matter to him that his sister was wealthy and he was not? He'd never had it so he wouldn't miss it. And besides, he'd always been treated well, wanting for nothing, really. He didn't begrudge Cassie this slice of luck from a father he'd never known.

His sister leapt to her feet, her eyes wild with fury as she looked at her mother.

'How dare you keep me in ignorance all these years! You let me go to La Retraite under sufferance, thinking I was beholden to Harry all those years. You let him pay for me to go to Pooley's, and I was stupidly naive enough to be grateful, even though I always felt like a poor relation alongside the daughters of dukes and millionaires. And all the time, my own father had left me a small fortune. I could have held my head high –'

'You've always done that well enough, my dear! And it's hardly a fortune, Cassie –' Bridget felt the familiar irritation begin to prickle.

'Did you ever have so much?' she blazed.

Bridget was incensed at this show of petulance.

'No, I did not.' She snapped, and suddenly she saw the whole room through a red mist of rage, as the memories came surging back. 'After all the years I lived in misery with that pig of a man, I was left with nothing. I was shackled to him, worse than if I was a slave, and I loathed the ground he walked on. And after all that humiliation, he left me *nothing*.'

'Mother, for God's sake!'

She heard Liam's voice, young and alarmed, and realised what she had done. All the venom she was unable to hide any longer had come pouring out. She hadn't meant it to be like this. She had meant to be calm and dignified, and if Cassie hadn't been so – so bloody ungrateful and vindictive towards her – towards *her*, who'd come out of all this so miserably . . . how *dare* Cassie sit there in judgement. Cassie, who had never had to suffer the perversions of a bastard like Thomas Finley . . .

'I'm not staying here to hear my father abused like this,' Cassie said furiously.

'Abused? You talk of being abused when you know nothing of what my life was like before I took you to Ireland!' Bridget almost sobbed.

'I know nothing, because you chose to tell me nothing,'

Cassie snapped. Her head suddenly began to spin, and she realised how weak she still was. All these revelations had filled her with enough anger to give her momentary strength, but it was fast ebbing away. She sat down abruptly, glaring at her mother. Bridget looked old and defeated, but Cassie couldn't spare her any pity.

All these years she had thought she was Harry Ashworth's pet, dependent on his favouritism. And all these years, she'd had resources of her own. The fact that she couldn't touch them for another three years yet made no difference. Cassie was able to dismiss such an item in an instant.

'Don't blame Mother, Cass. I'm sure she did what she thought was right,' Liam said.

Cassie looked at him. Why wasn't he furious too, she raged. He had nothing, either. And if Bridget had told their father in time that another child was expected, Liam too might have had a Trust Fund.

'I'll give half to you,' she declared. 'It's only fair. He'd have wanted you to have half the money.'

'Don't be daft. You can't go giving away thousands of dollars just like that –'

'Yes I can. It's mine to do as I like with it. And as soon as I'm due to get the money, I'll make over half of it to you. I'll write to the lawyer and tell him of my decision now, then they can organise it in good time.'

Listening to them, Bridget realised she might not have been in the room at all. Cassie totally ignored her, and Liam looked alternately embarrassed and sheepish, and finally pleased.

'Well, if you're sure – if you really mean it –'

Cassie gave a brittle laugh. 'Of course I mean it! The first thing I'll do after my twenty-fifth birthday is to go to New York and collect. We'll both go, Liam. We'll make it a kind of sentimental journey, and look up the place where I was born. We'll have a high old time, and maybe we'll never even come back at all!'

'No, Cassie.' Bridget broke in, agonised. 'I don't want Liam to go to America.'

This time, it was her son who gave her an exasperated look. 'Mother, I'm not a child any more. I can look after myself, whatever ogres you seem to think are over there.'

No, they weren't children any more, either of them, she thought miserably. They had minds and wills of their own, and Bridget felt as vulnerable as when she'd been caught in Thomas Finley's trap. She was still there. He was still able to manipulate her through her children. And she still thought of him with nothing but hate.

'I'm going to my room to rest,' Cassie announced. 'I'd like to see the figures right away, Mother, and to have the address of the lawyer, please.'

She swept out with as much defiance as she could, considering that her legs felt wobbly again, coupled with the fact that she felt the most extraordinary urge to weep on her mother's shoulder and beg her forgiveness for the pain she knew she was causing her. Bridget's face had looked stricken ever since Cassie had railed at her, but it was too late for either of them to pretend a closeness now that had never existed.

Liam put his arm around his mother and squeezed her shoulders in rough sympathy.

'Don't blame her, Mother. She has your quick temper, and if you clash now and then, it doesn't mean she's stopped loving you. All this has been a hell of a shock.'

Bridget's eyes filled with ready tears. She reached up and held the hand on her shoulder.

'Oh darling, what would I do without you?'

'Well, you don't have to think about that, do you?' he said heartily. Too heartily.

Her head was a jumble of thoughts. She was upset and confused. Otherwise, she would have listened more closely to the things Liam didn't say, rather than the things he did. She had suspected for some time that he was excited at the thought of enlisting. But for Bridget, even that knowledge was pushed into the background now. She had seen a different light in his eyes when Cassie told him they'd go to New York together. A light that brought all the ghosts of the past surging forward again. It was the way her father had looked when he spoke of his great dream of going to America.

Cassie knew she needed to regain her strength, otherwise

372

she'd undoubtedly have left Magnolia Cottage and found somewhere else to stay. To Evelyn's perhaps, despite the fact that she was still in mourning for her mother; even down to Devon with that impossible Marlene woman. But it was too comfortable merely to stay where she was and let Bridget care for her, each of them acting with an uneasy politeness towards the other.

Cassie studied the great file of audits from Donaldson in New York, and wrote to him telling him of her wishes. She wrote to Joe Buckley, not telling him, because they didn't know one another well enough yet. She heard back from Joe, whose cheery words tried to overcome the dread he had of not being able to fly again. His leg had been severely broken in several places and wasn't knitting together as it should. His plaster was off, but he had a considerable limp and there was some muscle-wasting. He spoke briefly of having a desk-job and what a come-down it would be. And remembering the Ward Sister's brisk words to herself, she wrote back and told him that having one good leg and one gammy one was better than having no legs at all.

He was coming out to Ashworthy Hall for a few days in April. His new rehabilitation hospital allowed this concession, thinking it kept up their patients' spirits. Harry had generously offered him hospitality, saying it would be good practice for his convalescent home, now quickly taking shape. Bridget and Cassie met Joe at the station on the morning of Cassie's birthday and took him straight to Ashworthy Hall, where Bridget acted the hostess and ordered coffee and biscuits for them all.

'Say! this is some place!' Joe said, awe-struck. 'We don't see anything like this where I come from.'

Cassie laughed. She seemed to have come to life, Bridget thought, since seeing Joe again. It was just as though someone had turned on a light beneath her skin, filling her with a kind of radiance.

'You wait until you see the Ritz,' she chuckled. 'We'll show you, the British know how to do things in style.'

'And you'd better make the most of its delicious cream gateaux this afternoon,' Bridget added. 'If this war goes on much longer, I'm afraid that even the Ritz will have to tighten its belt.'

'I'm really looking forward to seeing it. I've heard about it, of course,' Joe smiled, but all the time he was talking politely to Cassie's mother, his eyes were on Cassie. His mouth spoke such urbane words, but the timbre of his voice betrayed his need to be alone with this golden girl who had stormed into his life with the force of a whirlwind.

Their love affair – if love affair it was destined to be – hadn't yet taken wings. They knew each other so well through the close confines of the hospital wards, and through their letters, but they still hadn't been alone long enough to touch, to kiss, to feel love blossom between them.

'What's your home like, Joe?' Cassie asked him when they were sitting in Harry's plush drawing-room with the aroma of expensive coffee wafting up from the wafer-thin, bone china coffee cups the maid had brought them.

'It's quite a spread,' he admitted. 'My father's in wine. I don't know if I ever told you that, Cassie. The wine industry's expanding rapidly in our area, and our spread is on particularly good grape-growing land. It's what I intend to do myself after the war, start up my own winery.'

'It sounds fascinating,' Bridget said politely. 'But I would have thought Canada was too cold for grapes. I've never heard of Canadian wine.'

He put his cup down in his saucer as Bridget raised hers to her lips.

'I'm sorry. I assumed Cassie might have mentioned that it's my mother's old home that's in Canada. I live in San Francisco – well, just north of it, actually –'

The bone-china cup slid from Bridget's hands and on to her saucer, shattering both. She knew the colour must have left her face because her head reeled so turbulently, and she felt physically sick as she looked at the spots of blood on her hands and skirt.

Chapter 28

To Cassie's delight, Harry's special birthday present to her was an arranged interview with someone at the War Office who was interested in her ability as an interpreter.

'I suggested you could work in Intelligence,' Harry teased over tea and cakes at the Ritz Hotel that afternoon. 'Now, you won't let me down, will you, Cassie? You won't turn out to be a numb-brain after I've put in such a good word for you?'

'I wouldn't dare! I'll give them my best, Harry. Oh, you're a darling to do this for me.'

'You don't know what the job entails yet, but I gather you'll be involved in de-coding procedures, and more than that I'd better not say, considering we keep being told that walls have ears.'

'It's wonderful news, Cass,' Liam enthused.

'Congratulations, Cassie,' Joe said quietly.

'Thanks everybody, but I haven't got the job yet!'

'You will. You can do anything you set out to do,' Joe told her.

Their eyes met and were averted again. But everyone at that table, barring Liam, was aware of the undercurrents between them.

Harry was charmed by them, while Bridget . . . he frowned slightly. He couldn't tell what was wrong with Bridget. Ever since Cassie had driven her and Joe up to town to meet Harry and Liam here, Bridget had worn that tight, carved expression on her face. He'd expected her to like the open Canadian, but she hardly spoke to him except in monosyllables.

'It's the best tonic I could have had, and I feel back to normal already. And I'll be able to come and visit Joe easily at the hospital if I'm working in London,' Cassie said gaily.

'I shan't be there much longer,' he said, and Cassie's eyes sparkled.

'You've heard something, and you weren't going to tell me!'

'This is your day. Why should I spoil it?' Joe said dryly.

'That means you're going to be a pen-pusher. Oh, Joe, it won't be so bad,' she babbled on, knowing how much he would hate it.

'Will you hold on a minute, honey?' Joe said, in a way that Bridget would have expected to have her tossing her head. But this was Joe Buckley, who could say anything and put the stars in her daughter's eyes. 'I'm to take a month's leave, and if my leg's strong enough, they'll let me resume flying duties. If not, I'm to take a course in signal training, and will probably be based in the south of England at the head-quarters of one of the Bomber Commands.'

'That's wonderful – I think. What do you think?' Cassie asked hesitantly.

'Well, it beats being sent back home so soon, now that I've no wish to be far from London. And I guess the grapes will still ripen whether I'm around or not.'

They spoke in coded messages, Bridget thought with alarm. Cassie had already hinted that Joe might be inviting her to go to San Francisco, the scene of Bridget's own worst night-mares, the ones she had managed to suppress for so long. And here was Joseph Buckley, with his charm and charisma, and it didn't take much imagination to know that these two were falling headlong in love with one another. Their eyes said all that their voices did not.

And Liam's eyes too, had been alive with interest at every mention of Joe's activities in the war. Dear God, let it be over soon, Bridget prayed . . .

A month after Cassie's birthday Neville Chamberlain re-signed as Prime Minister, and was succeeded by the Right Honourable Winston Churchill. Cassie had her new job at the

War Office by then and wore a smart new khaki uniform, and Joe got his wish and returned on trial to flying duties. Hopes that with a new government the war would end soon faded every day as the news from Europe became graver.

In June the real battle for France began. Air-raids were heavy and indiscriminate, and newspaper photographs left nothing to the imagination of the terror and destruction being brought to the French people. For Cassie, the most poignant pictures were those of the swastika flag flying from the principal buildings in Paris. She wept for all her old friends, for Monsieur Alphonse, and for the elderly publishers, Macon and Girard, as the German forces swept relentlessly towards the south, conquering all in their way.

Cassie got little information from Joe, now involved in nightly bombing raids over Germany. The occasional telephone call or a brief note, was about all that he could manage. She lived in fear of his being shot down. Fear that was tinged with a guilty thought that at least if he was, then she could have him back again . . .

By July, along with many towns and cities in Britain, London resembled a beleaguered city. Barbed-wire entanglements were erected at strategic points, the streets were barricaded and guarded by Civil Defence workers and Air-Raid Wardens, and all signposts were removed from streets and railway stations. And in August the enemy bombers reached London. Anti-aircraft guns defended the city and the dazzle of enemy planes on fire illuminated the night skies. Croydon airport was hit together with houses in the neighbourhood.

Cassie's fears for Joe were magnified as Harry's newspaper reported everything with brutal accuracy. Liam was becoming a brilliant young reporter, eager to be on the spot no matter what terrors he saw, and recounting them with visual accuracy. He was also secretly counting the days until Christmas when he would be eighteen. No one expected the war to drag on so long, but a year after it had begun, every newspaper reported the grim fact that Hitler now virtually controlled the whole of Europe, except Britain.

*

'Why don't you like Joe?' Harry said abruptly one evening when he and Bridget had finished having dinner together at Ashworthy Hall. The convalescent home was an undoubted success, staffed and funded by the government, and Bridget at last felt useful at being what Harry called the servicemen's house-mother.

'When have I ever said I didn't like him?'

'You don't need to. Whenever Cassie mentions him, you get that ice-box expression on your face that I know only too well, my dear. Cassie's wild about the boy, and I thought you'd be glad that she's found someone at last.'

'I might be, if it wasn't him,' she said, not wanting to put what she felt into words, nor even knowing if she could. 'Oh, it's not Joe in particular, Harry. It's – it's far too complicated to explain.'

'I'm a good listener,' he said obligingly. 'There's nobody here but us, and I'm not letting you out of this room until you tell me what's wrong. I know you and Cassie had a big argument about her inheritance some time ago, but surely you don't think Joe's after her money?'

She laughed at that. 'No, of course not. His family have plenty of their own, by all accounts.'

He spoke softly. 'Why do I have the feeling that whatever bothers you about Joe Buckley is bound up with something else? Bridget, why can't you trust me enough to tell me whatever it is that's haunted you all these years?'

The fire crackled companionably in the hearth, and the lights were turned down low. The blackout curtains at the windows, criss-crossed with tape to keep out any bomb blasts, made the room even cosier. It was an intimate time, a time for telling old secrets, for burying the past, and under Harry's gentle persuasion she felt a growing need to rid herself of it, once and for all. And this man, this dear, understanding man, was perhaps the only one she could tell it to . . .

'You see too much, my love,' she said slowly. 'You always did, but I doubt that you could ever guess what's at the heart of it all. And if Joe lived anywhere else but San Francisco, I'd be glad for Cassie. But not there – anywhere in the world but there –'

At first, the words came painfully as she told him about the fine Pendleton mansion on Nob Hill and the glittering chandelier that her brother Michael had loved so much. About her loving parents and her sister Kitty, whom she had sworn to keep safe all her life. And about the April morning when the ground had started to roll about beneath her feet like giant waves, and great buildings had come tumbling down as if they were made of matchwood, and twisted metal girders had reared up into the air like serpents. And about the gas, and the fires, and the terror . . . and by the end of the telling she was gasping out the rest of it, and Harry was holding her in his arms, knowing she wasn't even aware of him. She was still lost somewhere in that nightmare that had happened more than thirty-four years ago.

'Did you ever tell Ralph and Alma any of this? Or the children?'

'No. The few people who asked me about it when I went to New York wanted to probe into my feelings, and it was like being cut open with a knife. Anyway, it's my pain, not theirs. Why should I burden my family with it?'

'You'd rather hold on to it, then. You don't want to lose it, because it's your crutch, and you can shut out every other emotion that's good and loving, while you hold on to the memory of how terrible it was. Is that it? If so, it tells me a lot about you, Bridget.'

She felt a burst of anger.

'That's not true. You can't understand my need to keep my family safe. If you can't see that, then you don't know me at all, Harry. I thought you wanted to help. I didn't expect an amateur character analysis. Are you saying I *enjoy* the memory of the earthquake?'

'Well, don't you? Doesn't it sublimate the need for a husband or a lover? Doesn't it successfully exclude any man, because the phallic symbolism of one of nature's adventures on a grand scale is far more potent than any mortal could hope to achieve?'

She gasped at his clinical assessment, and her voice shook. 'You're mad! And stop trying to blind me with fancy words. I don't need any man in my life –'

'Every woman needs a man,' Harry said. 'Just as every man needs a woman. You can't defy nature completely, Bridget. The Almighty didn't make us different without some Divine purpose of His own.'

He pulled her to him so suddenly she didn't have time to draw back. His mouth was brutal on hers, his strength sapping hers. She fought him inside herself, even while her arms wrapped themselves around him. Whether it was from gratitude or something more, she didn't yet try to define. All she knew was that just as there had been trauma in telling Cassie about the Trust Fund, there was now the sweetest relief at the telling of this, because at last she was no longer alone.

Despite Harry's peculiar observations that she didn't really follow, someone else now shared her feeling of abomination because of the earthquake. The feeling inside her soared and grew. It was shared now with someone she loved, and had always loved, if not in the same way as the sweet wild love for Austen Hamilton. But that had been a young girl's love, and what she felt for Harry Ashworth was the deep love of a woman for a man . . . and the question flowing through her senses now, was why hadn't she always known it?

She felt Harry put her aside after the savage kiss ended. His voice was harsh.

'No, my dear, I'm not about to seduce you, or try to win you over out of gratitude because I forced you into confiding in me. You've resisted me for too long, and my pride won't let me beg for any favours from a woman, not even from you.'

Her mouth trembled. 'People can change, Harry –'

He put his fingers against her lips. 'And people can sleep on it, and have second thoughts the next day. We're not young and flighty adolescents, rushing into a wartime marriage in order to snatch a few precious hours together. Perhaps when this war's over, we'll sit back and see what we both really want. I can still be stirred by a lovely woman, but we're too sensible to start making mistakes at our age. Or to confuse gratitude with love.'

She wanted to say he was wrong. That her feelings weren't sudden or immature, and that without him she was nothing. But his words stilled hers. Perhaps he was regretting his impulsive action too. In which case, it would be her pride that was in tatters if she begged him to hold her and want her and make love to her . . . the force of her own feelings shook her. She hadn't wanted any man to make love to her since Austen. She had forgotten the sweet, seductive, wonderful sensations that came from loving a man.

She had forgotten so much . . . she swallowed, and told Harry that of course they must be sensible. They were middle-aged and settled, and sometimes friendship was better than love. Ralph had said something like that once. Yet he and Alma now had their own child and were as blissful as two love-birds. And Bridget was discovering a great humbling truth. Love didn't only happen to the young. Whether you were forty or fifty or more, the feelings were exactly the same. The wonder, the insecurity, the need to be near the beloved, the explosive longings . . . none of it was any different. Nor did the frustration of being repulsed become any easier to bear.

'I think I'd better go to bed,' she stuttered, unable to sit here a minute longer with these surging emotions inside her. 'I'm tired, Harry.'

Come with me . . . Stay with me . . .

'Sleep well, my dear. Good-night.'

She walked to the door, and looked back for a second. He was standing by the fireplace, a glass of brandy in his hand, staring down into the flames. He looked what he was. A handsome, rich, highly successful man, and at that moment, incredibly lonely. Bridget went out of the room quickly, before she ran to him and begged him not to leave her alone that night.

A week after Christmas, Liam telephoned his mother from London, saying he'd be home a little late for the New Year's eve celebrations and that he had a surprise for her.

'It's a sort of a New Year present,' he said. 'And you're to promise me you won't be angry.'

'When did a present ever make me angry?' She smiled into the receiver.

'This one might. Cass is collecting Joe from the base. He's had bad news – did you know?'

'Yes,' Bridget said briefly. 'His leg, isn't it? He's been taken off flying duties permanently, and is going to that Bomber Command base he mentioned before.'

'Rotten luck, isn't it? Cass doesn't think so, though. She's over the moon, because she knows he'll be safer than flying over Germany every night, and they'll be able to see one another more often.'

'What time will you get here, Liam? Do you want picking up from the station?'

'No. Harry's hanging on for me, and we'll come down together. Put out the flags and the red carpet, Mother.'

Cassie and Joe got to Ashworthy Hall before the others. Cassie seemed nervous and Joe was more morose than usual. Well, he would be, Bridget thought. It may suit her selfish daughter to have him grounded, but it didn't suit the high-flying Canadian. She revised her thoughts at once. No, Cassie wasn't selfish to want to keep someone she loved safe. It was Bridget's own wish. And it was becoming more and more obvious that these two were in love.

She was becoming edgy herself by the time Liam and Harry arrived for the family celebrations, and the minute they walked into the room, she knew that she should have guessed. Something should have told her. Someone should have prepared her. The glass of sherry in her hand shook as she stared in silence at her tall, dark-haired son in the soldier's uniform.

'Well, Mum?' He only ever called her that if he too was nervous, and now she knew why Cassie had been so fidgety and kept glancing at the clock as if wishing herself somewhere else.

When Bridget said nothing, he crossed the room to her quickly, took the glass from her hand and hugged her.

'This is your surprise,' he whispered. 'Say you're proud of me, Mum. From now on, your son will be reporting news from the Front instead of sitting behind a desk.'

'Oh Liam, how could you? You didn't need to enlist!' She couldn't smile. She couldn't think straight. She was still stunned.

And oh God, she didn't want this! As Liam let her go, she

realised Joe Buckley was shaking his hand as if he was a hero already. Harry too, was pouring more drinks and smiling fatuously. Were all men such blind, stupid creatures to see such glory in going to war . . .?

'Mother, be pleased for him. It's what he wants more than anything,' she heard Cassie's slightly accusing voice say in her ear.

She shrugged away from Cassie She felt so bitter she could hardly speak. They were all traitors, not telling her . . . even Liam . . . she looked into his anxious, eager face, and heard the excitement in his voice, and knew that she couldn't spill out all the bitterness that was in her heart.

'If it's what you want, darling, then I suppose I must accept it,' she said woodenly, and then made an enormous effort. 'And of course, you look perfectly splendid.'

'There, you see? Didn't I tell you she'd take it on the chin?' Liam beamed all round. 'Why don't we all drink a toast to my mother? To the best and sweetest mother that ever lived.'

'Yes, why don't we drink a toast to Liam's mother?' Cassie said mockingly. 'And if these weren't Harry's most expensive glasses, I'd suggest hurling them into the stone fireplace afterwards as a final gesture of something or other that escapes me.'

It didn't escape Bridget. Cassie still hadn't forgiven her for her supposed deceit about the Trust Fund. And Harry thought she was utterly foolish for letting something that happened thirty-four years ago colour her life. Both of them thought her motives unreasonable and selfish. But then, neither of them knew the whole story. They didn't know about Kitty, or Austen, and those were secrets still locked in her heart.

Joseph Buckley readily acknowledged that his roots were on the land, not in the air. He'd volunteered for the Royal Canadian Air Force out of the same pioneering spirit that had inspired his great-grandfather to become one of the 'forty-niners' in the rush for gold beneath the Californian hills. Since then, the generations of Buckleys had prospered, tasted city life in San Francisco and rejected it for the sprawling Spanish-style home built by Joe's grandfather in the north of California.

Joe always told people he came from San Francisco, simply because it was a name they knew. If he mentioned the town of Okaje, they looked blankly, despite the fact that those who lived there knew it for a lush, fertile valley where vineyards flourished, and the profitable wineries made millionaires.

Joe came from a practical stock, so when he was grounded, the initial depression and disappointment were relatively short-lived. He had the kind of temperament that said if you couldn't get what you wanted, you'd just turn second-best into first choice and make the most of it. Especially when second-best in this case meant the chance to see more of a certain young lady.

By now, he knew that there were two things he wanted out of life. One was the chance to make his own name in the wine business, to grow his own grapes and see them through to becoming the clear liquid gold of California wine. The other was Cassandra Finley.

They had been seeing each other for a long while when he'd suggested to his mother that she might care to write to Cassie. She had done so at once, liking the sound of this strong-willed girl who seemed to have done a great deal already in her short life. She appealed to the Buckley style, and obviously to her son.

By now, Cassie and Evelyn Oakes-Johnson had found a small flat together in London, which seemed to Bridget a very foolhardy thing to do in these hazardous times. But she'd given up trying to tell Cassie anything. Evelyn worked in Administration for the Red Cross, an occupation apparently not too demeaning, Bridget thought with rare criticism of Cassie's friend, of whom she was very fond.

'Joe's mother does sound a charming lady,' Cassie told Bridget on one of her evening visits to Ashworthy Hall. 'Would you like to read her letter? She tells me all about where they live –'

'I don't want to read about San Francisco.' She couldn't stop the words. She cursed the block she felt whenever the place was mentioned, but she just couldn't seem to help it.

384

Cassie looked resentful at the sharp reply.

'I can't think why not. They don't live in the city anyway, though it sounds beautiful, all hills and a huge bay with a prison in the middle of it –'

'I know.'

'Do you? Have you been there?'

Cassie shrugged when Bridget didn't answer. Bridget seemed so unreasonable these days, especially since Liam had been sent to the Front. He was a fully-fledged War Correspondent now, working for a National News Agency, and Cassie was very proud of him. Bridget hated it all, of course. And Cassie had never realised how possessive Bridget was of her family, even of her daughter, in a peculiarly resentful way . . .

'Well, anyway,' she persevered. 'Mrs Buckley told me about the huge forests in the area with giant redwood trees, and all the valleys where the grapes grow, and all the old Spanish Missions. Did you know that San Francisco was originally a Spanish settlement?'

'I may have heard it,' Bridget said crossly. 'Cassie, I do think it's a mistake to get too involved with this boy. Wartime produces all kinds of hasty relationships that never last –'

'It depends what you mean by getting involved,' Cassie was defensive at once.' 'If you mean don't fall in love with Joe, it's a bit late for that.'

'Oh, darling, please don't be carried away by a smart uniform and fast talk. He'll only go home and forget you. He may have another girl there already!' She didn't mean to hurt, only to warn, but it came out all wrong.

'No, he won't, Mother, and no, he doesn't. And when this war is over and he goes home, I'm going with him.' She got up to leave in a huff.

Bridget's heart leapt. Cassie was twenty-three years old, and she could no longer control her, if she ever could.

'Has he asked you to marry him?'

'No, but he will,' Cassie said confidently, pecked her mother on the cheek and went serenely out to her small car to drive back to London before the Jerry planes began their nightly jaunts.

Nothing could disturb her for long. Joe's mother was eager to welcome her in to the family. Joe loved her, and she had an independence of which she had hardly dreamed. She had a flat with Evelyn, her interesting job at the War Office which entailed no personal danger but held all the vicarious drama of the war; she had the future security of her legacy, and best of all, she had Joe.

Bridget's unreasonable antagonism towards Joe made no difference to her feelings. It couldn't make her love him more than she already did. Cassie was still over-whelmed at how totally Joe occupied her mind now. Whatever she did, wherever she went, thoughts of Joe were always there. She lived, breathed, and would die for Joe . . .

After Cassie had gone home that evening, Bridget sought out Harry, busy in his study at Ashworthy Hall. The words tumbled out in a rush.

'You can't rule Cassie's life for her, Bridget,' he said. 'We must make our own mistakes, but I'm sure this marriage wouldn't be a mistake. Anybody can see they're made for each other.'

'Perhaps, but you don't understand –'

'I think I do. It's your own selfish nightmare that you're keeping alive that won't allow you to let Cassie go.'

'Selfish!'

'That's the word,' Harry said with infuriating smugness. 'Why don't you tell Cassie about the earthquake, for God's sake? Tell her why you hate the very name San Francisco and finish it once and for all.'

Bridget's nerves tensed. 'You think that would really finish it? Don't you remember what it cost me to tell you?'

'Then perhaps you should talk to someone more qualified to help.'

She flinched. 'A psychiatrist, you mean. No, Harry. It would shame me –'

'Darling, this isn't the Dark Ages! There's nothing shameful in getting help when you need it.'

'I don't need it. I don't even want to discuss it.' She looked

386

at her watch. 'I must go and see the boys. They'll be expecting me.'

She shut off the conversation effectively, and left him frowning at the door, knowing he should do something, but unable to know what. And Bridget hurried along to what the convalescents – the boys – now called their Mess-Hall, a ridiculously mundane name for one of Harry's beautiful sitting-rooms.

There were easy chairs and sofas and a piano, and when one of the transient intakes had discovered that the resident nursing sister could play adequately, and that Bridget could sing beautifully, they had clamoured for regular sing-songs to relieve the tedium of getting properly well. It had now become a nightly ritual, and once, one of the soldiers had looked at Bridget quizzically.

'Pardon me for asking, but didn't you used to be Bridget Finley, the proper singer? I think I heard you sing once at the Corbonna Restaurant with the de Wolfe Follies.'

And she laughed, and said yes, she used to be Bridget Finley, the proper singer . . . She had discovered that her pleasure in singing had shifted once again. She was perfectly content to be doing this, sitting around a piano with a crowd of soldiers missing home, who wanted the old songs, the nostalgic songs and the rousing choruses.

If the younger ones – who looked far too young to be in uniform at all – thought of her as a mother-figure, it no longer bothered Bridget. On the scene now was an attractive young lady called Vera Lynn with a throaty catch in her voice who was entertaining the troops, and had been dubbed 'the Forces' Sweetheart'.

She personified youth and hope for the future, and Bridget was content with her own little band of bellowing songsters. Helping them to temporarily forget their wounds, their night-mares, their lost comrades, their ghastly times at the Front, was a humbling leveller. It put private terrors into perspective, when theirs was so public, so vast . . . If Bridget helped them, she admitted that in an indefinable way, they also helped her.

*

Cassie drove back to London in a fever of resentment against her mother. Bridget understood nothing. She was cold, reserved, uncaring. If she had ever loved a man in her life, then she'd understand something of Cassie's feelings for Joe. But Cassie couldn't believe that her mother knew the first thing about love. She must have fornicated twice in her life to have produced her and Liam, Cassie thought, the crude words suiting her aggressive mood, and that was probably all.

She gripped the steering wheel tighter, cursing the need for these slits of light which was all the government allowed on vehicles, and made it almost impossible to see more than five yards in front of the car. At least she had petrol. She could still make the odd trip home to Ashworthy Hall. Her War Office status allowed her just sufficient to go there under her own steam instead of waiting for a crowded train full of sweaty servicemen. Enough and no more . . . which meant she didn't have to make too many of these uncomfortable duty visits.

She was bursting to get back to the flat. Evelyn had gone home for the weekend to be with her still grieving father, and Joe was off-duty for twenty-four hours. He was coming to the flat, and Cassie was going to cook a meal for them both. She'd got hold of some black market steak at an exorbitant price, found a yellowing cauliflower on a greengrocer's stall, and saved her cheese ration for two weeks to make a sauce. A bottle of wine to dull the senses, and a candlelit table, and they could almost imagine they were back at the Ritz in the heady pre-war days when shelters were just somewhere to hide out of the rain.

She had doggedly thought no further ahead than the dinner. If she thought too far ahead, her hands would shake so much she'd never be able to prepare the food. Joe knew she would be alone in the flat that night, and he didn't have to report for duty again until the following afternoon.

It was the end of November, and the war in Europe had been raging for three years. People were tired, weary of war, of rationing and shortages, boredom mingling with terror in the nightly rush to the air-raid shelters, longing for a different world, and seeing no end to the present one.

And some snatched their happiness where they could, knowing it might be all they had.

Chapter 29

The food was reminiscent of freer, more carefree days, the wine and the candlelight and the flowers Joe brought added to the romantic ambience. And the two of them, too much in love to let this perfect night pass without spending it in each other's arms. Thoughts of right or wrong never entered their heads. There was only the longing, the needing, and most of all the love.

It wasn't in Cassie's nature to be tentative or submissive, but in this, the ultimate intimacy between a man and a woman, the trembling in her limbs was as much through nervousness as desire. She recognised it with something like awe. She loved and wanted this man, and the intensity of her own feelings stunned her.

She fought and lost the battle with her Catholic upbringing. Crowding into her mind came all the red-faced sexual instruction at La Retraite, and the whispered, pseudo-sophisticated discussions of the Pooley girls. And all of it dissolved, as Joseph Buckley reached out for her in an upstairs bedroom of a modest London building, and she felt the warmth of a man's skin against her own for the first time.

Her hands moved inexpertly against Joe's chest, where there was a crisp even covering of hair. She liked the feel of it beneath her fingers. It was strength and power and security. He exuded a faint body-smell that was masculine and exciting and his arms tightened around her. Behind them the candle-flames burned low, creating a warm, sensuous atmosphere. Joe's mouth was kissing hers, and she closed her eyes, wanting this so much, wanting him.

'Don't be afraid, my darling,' Joe whispered against her mouth. 'Don't ever be afraid of me.'

A small, cynical part of her wanted to be very chic and ask

him brightly if he thought she was so inexperienced! But the real, deeply emotional Cassie looked into her lover's eyes and what she saw there stilled the words. Of course she was inexperienced. She wanted to be, for Joe. He was the first, the only one.

The sweet pain when he entered her body was over in a moment, and then came the gradual initiation into something so spectacular that through it all, Cassie wished she could hold the sensations in her mind to tell the world how special it was. And knowing she never would. For this belonged to her and Joe alone. This perfect bliss, this wonder . . . the weight of his body was an added pleasure in a world that had become so fragile. She was safe with Joe. She was filled by him, fulfilled by him, and the glory of knowing he was so moved by her, made tears shine like diamonds on her lashes.

They lay close for a long while after the passion diminished, unwilling to draw apart and become part of the real world again. Somewhere in the night, they heard the distant sound of the All-Clear signal, without ever being aware that an air-raid siren had sounded. Whatever damage German planes had done that night had passed them by, but reluctantly, the sound brought back a semblance of reality.

'I don't think this bed was made for two people,' Cassie grinned eventually, to disguise the sudden small feeling of embarrassment as she wriggled to get more comfortable and found that her skin was temporarily fastened to Joe's.

'I'm not complaining,' he grinned back. 'Though we'll have a bed made for two when we're married.'

The glorious thought almost stopped Cassie asking the question.

'You do intend to marry me then?'

Joe considered. 'I suppose I must, now I've had my wicked way with you.'

She caught her breath, until she realised he was still teasing. Her sapphire eyes glowed, and he too drew his breath at the sight of this dearest girl who meant everything to him. He had come halfway around the world to find her, and if anything could justify a war in one man's mind, for Joe Buckley it was this. He cupped her face in his large capable hands, so he wouldn't miss a fraction of her expression.

'How about next week? We'll get a special licence. No frills, no fancy dress, just the two of us, the registrar, a few witnesses and your folks, of course. I don't intend to antagonise them by eloping with you. But will you settle for that, my Cassandra Mavreen?'

He spoke her name as if it was a caress. She felt his heartbeat against her breast, and knew he wanted this as much as she did.

'I'd settle for a tent as long as I shared it with you, Joe,' she said unsteadily.

Lord Harry Ashworth couldn't pull many strings overseas, but he knew plenty of people who could. Cassie never knew how he managed it in so short a time, but somehow he got Liam a two-day pass plus travelling time to attend his sister's wedding. It was scheduled for Saturday December the 6th. Everything was organised in a terrific rush, but somehow it all got done, and Bridget handed over her own clothes coupons to Cassie for the ice-blue silk dress and matching veiled hat and long gloves she wanted so much.

Bridget held her own feelings rigidly in check, knowing she could do nothing to stop this wedding. She thought it madness to marry in wartime, without other considerations, but Cassie would marry Joe with or without her approval. Everyone else, Liam and Harry and Evelyn Oakes-Johnson, and even the boys at the convalescent home, were charmed by the whole romantic affair.

So Bridget fixed a smile on her face through the entire ceremony and the wedding breakfast at Ashworthy Hall. There were telegrams of congratulations from Ralph and Alma and from Joe's parents, whom he had cabled, and who weren't in the least put out by their son marrying so far from home, and welcomed Cassie into their family.

For now, the newlyweds were moving into Magnolia Cottage, despite Bridget's fears at the risk from enemy bombers passing over Sussex to reach London. Cassie ignored all such warnings, and Bridget gave up arguing, knowing her daughter would simply go right ahead with what she

391

intended, as always! She wouldn't rule Joe . . . but they seemed so well-matched, it hardly mattered.

Eventually the wedding party broke up, and Bridget was temporarily alone. It was good to have a breather, but as she wandered about, slightly disorientated, she caught sight of Liam and Harry with their heads together in the study. They were discussing aspects of the war in their own journalistic jargon. Bridget listened for a few minutes, isolated, out of their male world.

They spoke of the countries at war as if they were pieces on a chess board, she thought with irritation. Blitzed and battered Britain. Defeated France and poor little Poland, swallowed up and forgotten. Troublesome Italy and uneasy Russia. Nazi Germany herding more and more prisoners into the appalling concentration camps. Resentment over when or if America would physically enter the war, apart from her tremendous aid given to the Allies with arms and munitions and food. The threat of the Japanese nation . . .

Bridget couldn't bear to listen any more. She would be glad when tomorrow came. Sunday was a day for relaxing, providing the Germans would let them, enjoying Liam's company and getting over the excitement of a family wedding.

Sunday, December the 7th, began as just an ordinary day, cold and misty in sleepy Sussex. It ended with the terrifying confirmation that the Japanese had bombed Pearl Harbor in the Hawaiian Islands, the main US naval base in the Pacific. The shock news gradually emerged that the battleship *Arizona* had been sunk, three destroyers and a large number of aircraft were lost, and nearly three thousand men killed.

With swiftness and savagery, Japan declared war on Britain and America. In the next few days, Japanese planes were reported over San Francisco and air-raid warnings sounded in faraway New York. Canada and Australia, fearing the worst, prepared themselves for invasion. Finally, on December the 11th, Germany declared war on America. It was war on a worldwide scale for the second time in a lifetime.

*

Cassie shared Joe's fears for his family in California, although he never really expected the US mainland to be seriously threatened. Certainly the cables and letters received from the senior Buckleys in the next weeks were reassuring. There was nothing to worry about. They were all safe. Everyone went about their business in the usual way, and now that America was in the war, they'd soon have the hide off the Huns . . . They sincerely hoped so, because they were dying to meet Cassie, and were planning a big welcome-home celebration for them at the end of the war.

And there was a wedding gift of money already deposited in a new bank account for Mr and Mrs Joseph Buckley, in anticipation of starting up Joe's new winery. Cassie gaped at the figure they mentioned.

'Thank God I never knew you were so rich! You'd have thought I married you for your money and not just your body!'

He laughed, loving her frankness. The official two-day honeymoon was over, but they both got back to the cottage as often as they could, and each time together was a new source of delight.

'No I wouldn't. I knew I'd married a wanton hussy,' he grinned.

'Do you mind?' She demanded provocatively.

It took a while for him to convince her very satisfactorily that he didn't, and then she chuckled.

'Anyway, I might just invest a bit of my own money into the new Buckley winery, if you didn't think it emasculated you.'

Joe laughed with arrogant male confidence.

'Honey, it would take more than a few dollars to emasculate me!'

'How abut 40,000?'

He stopped laughing and looked into her dancing blue eyes. 'You're not serious?'

'Well, no. It's actually only half that amount, because I'm giving half of it to Liam. It's a legacy, and I don't get the loot until I'm twenty-five, but then I collect, and it's a long story, but he should have half of it by rights, anyway.' She spoke glibly, not altogether sure how Joe was going to take this. 'We both kept a few surprises up our sleeves, didn't we?'

To her relief he was grinning again. It was a healthy sum, but it didn't make a ripple on the surface of his own wealthy background.

'And you decided not to tell me, because you thought I might be after *your* money, right?'

'Something like that,' she said airily.

Joe shook his head in mock exasperation, but his voice was rich with amusement.

'Cassie, honey, did anyone ever tell you what a snob you are?'

'Oh, all the time,' she said. 'It beats being humble, doesn't it?'

He caught her in his arms and demanded to know all about this legacy of hers, and she thrilled to the knowledge that their marriage was so good, so perfect, and money was the last thing on their minds in the next hour.

And even when he had to tell her six months later that his latest medical check had revealed that he was fit enough to fly again if he chose, Cassie didn't let the smile slip. Joe wanted this too much for her to act the little martyr and beg him not to go. Besides, she thought of their love as a protective shield that would keep him safe. She sent him back to the war with a cheerful face, and did her crying in private.

She began seeing more of Evelyn again. They went to the cinema occasionally and met once a week in a small tea-room in an unfashionable but relatively safe area of the city. Cassie was surprised to know that Evelyn had struck up an unlikely friendship with Bridget since Cassie's wedding, and went to visit her from time to time.

'She's lonely, Cass,' Evelyn said over tea and buns. 'Oh, I know she has the soldiers to look after, and she enjoys it all tremendously, but she misses you and Liam more than she lets on –'

'She misses Liam, I grant you.'

'And you, idiot! I never realised how interesting she is, Cass. She told me quite a bit about New York last time I saw her.'

'Good God, that's more than she ever told me,' Cassie said, half-annoyed.

'Don't be resentful, darling. I think she's genuinely sorry for me because my own mother died. We both compensate, I suppose. She's a very compassionate woman.'

'Well, that's not a virtue I've ever attributed to my mother,' Cassie retorted.

Evelyn laughed, determined not to get ruffled. 'Other people always see us differently, don't they?'

Then she realised she didn't have Cassie's full attention any more. Cassie was sitting bolt upright in the tea-room, the bun she was about to eat poised halfway to her lips. Her whole body was so tense that Evelyn nearly asked if she was in the grip of *rigor mortis* or something, and then her own gaze went outside the tea-room window.

There was a munitions factory a short distance away. At this time of day the shift changed, and there were always groups of men and girls, exempt from the services because of doing important war work, laughing and chatting on their way home. Cassie and Evelyn never took much notice of the munitions workers in their dreary overalls. They were of a different class from the two young ladies from Pooley's finishing school in Gstaad, after all . . . but today, Evelyn saw what Cassie saw.

There was one good-looking young man, large and blond, surrounded by giggling girls and a few lesser males, all of them chattering together as they disappeared around the corner of the street and were swallowed up in the late afternoon crowds.

'My God, Cassie, wasn't that –'

'Stefan,' she breathed.

'But what's he doing here? He's a *Ger* –'

'Shut *up*, Evelyn,' Cassie snapped. Fortunately the tea-room was packed, and no one heard the quick exchange of words between the two classy girls with their heads close together across the table. They stared at one another, their heads buzzing with all the precautionary notices and posters everywhere. 'Careless Talk Costs Lives'. 'Talk Less . . . You Never Know'. 'Keep Mum, she's not so dumb'.

Everything warning people not to give away information carelessly that could be heard by enemy spies who might be listening . . . And here was this German . . . this *Nazi*, whom

Evelyn had disliked and never really trusted, and who was Cassie's friend. Here in London, apparently working for Britain in an English munitions factory. It didn't take much imagination to see through his little game!

'Cass, we've got to do something,' Evelyn said urgently.

'I know. I'm thinking. Perhaps it wasn't him. It certainly looked like him, but let's be practical about it. How could it have been him?'

She felt utterly thrown. She didn't want it to be Stefan. Oh God, she couldn't bear to think of her friend being a spy. Infiltrating into Britain as so many newspaper articles said they did, working side by side with Britons, gathering up bits of information like scavengers and feeding it back to Nazi headquarters with sometimes devastating consequences . . . dear God, no, not Stefan . . .

'We're in the middle of a war, darling,' Evelyn said brutally. 'Even some of our friends at Pooley's are our enemies now.'

'But he went home from Paris a long time ago. He was a teacher. He was going to be married –'

'He was a German.' Evelyn practically hissed the word. 'He spoke perfect English, and you once told me he could even get away with a cockney accent.'

Cassie's heart thumped. She only had to think of her own ability to know how easy this would all be for someone like Stefan, fluent at languages, charming and friendly when he wanted to be. Who would think of resisting sharing a joke with him in the factory, sharing information, sharing secrets that were unknowingly destined for Berlin?

'I don't know what to do. We can't just knock on the door of the factory and ask if they know they've got a German spy in their employ!'

She had to put it into words, to test it out, and it sounded terrible. She had a horrible vision of some sort of identity parade, and of herself pointing an accusing finger at Stefan, and of his knowing it was her, and that felt terrible too. How did you betray a friend?

'We'll have to tell somebody. We could tell Harry.' Evelyn said, her voice shaking.

'Not yet.' Cassie shook her head. 'We have to be absolutely sure. What if we're wrong? Think how awful it would be to point the finger at a perfectly innocent man. We only saw him for a few seconds, Evelyn. Let's meet here again tomorrow, and we'll keep watch every day until we're certain. Then we'll decide what to do.'

She avoided Evelyn's eyes. She desperately wanted to be wrong. She looked beseechingly into her friend's eyes.

'Promise me you won't do anything on your own. We must both decide, Evelyn. Promise me.'

'All right.' Evelyn gathered up her bag and gloves and stood up to go. 'We'll meet here tomorrow. But Cass, in the end we have to do what's right.'

'I know,' Cassie said in a muffled voice.

All the way home to Magnolia Cottage, her distress turned to raging anger. Friendship was important to Cassie. She valued her friends and was loyal to them. It was the war that had turned Stefan into an enemy, and it was none of their doing. But try telling that to governments!

If they decreed that some nice little foreign shopkeeper was now an enemy, then he was deported or locked up. If they decreed that enemy food imports were now forbidden entry into the country, then you did without. It was the ordinary people who suffered all the time. *They* did without. *They* did the fighting and it was their women who lost their men.

Cassie drew in her breath as she stopped her car at the cottage. It was peaceful in the early evening, before the relentless bombers came over the Channel. Joe was away somewhere on ops again. How would she feel if a few careless words from an munitions worker filtered through to Germany, and made some unknown official chart the very progress of her husband's flight?

How would she feel then, if someone like Stefan, a *spy*, cost Joe's life? Her hands froze on the wheel for long moments before she got out of the car, her heart pounding, as if some gigantic premonition had suddenly turned the blood in her veins to ice.

But it wasn't Joe. She went into the cottage, needing to put the warmth and security of it around her, as if its four walls enclosed a citadel.

Bridget was sitting motionless inside. She looked into her mother's anguished eyes, and she knew.

Bridget had been sitting by the window at Ashworthy Hall, reading the latest letter from Ralph and Alma. The child was thriving, despite the fact that Ireland, although not in the war, still suffered privations. Foodstuffs were rationed, wheat was in short supply, and oats and barley were used in bread-making. Sugar was scarce, and the tea ration was half an ounce per week. Even on Sunday trains had been cut and now that coal had stopped being imported from England, people were having to use turf in their grates as they did in the old days. Not being Irish, Ralph and Alma seemed to find this faintly charming.

'We still don't see why all this is necessary in a neutral country,' Ralph wrote. 'I'm sorry to complain, Bridget, but you would surely feel the same! And you know the indignation that was felt when Dublin was accidentally bombed on one occasion. And why should our newspapers and the wireless and films be censored? We have a right to know about the war, but I'd better not tell you more in case this letter should be censored too, which we're quite sure happens. Our love to you all, Ralph and Alma.'

Bridget wondered just what they thought was happening in England, where bombing was a nightly occurrence! The poor streets of London were a sorry sight, though she only saw them in newspaper pictures. They reminded her all too vividly of the aftermath of the earthquake . . .

She looked up from the letter to see the red Post Office bicycle meandering up the long drive in the afternoon sunshine towards Ashworthy Hall, the messenger boy astride it watching the butterflies around the buddleia bushes, and evidently in a dream.

She watched as he threw the bicycle down on the gravel and strolled towards the main door of the house. In the old days, the butler would soon have seen him off, Bridget thought in amusement, and sent him scurrying round to the servants' entrance. But the butler was on Civil Defence duties that day, and Bridget went to the door herself.

The messenger boy handed her the thin buff envelope with the words 'Post Office Telegram' printed across the top. She went rigid as she saw her own name on the envelope. She slit it open quickly and stared at the stark words, totally unable to take them in.

'Any reply?' The boy said helpfully.

'No. No reply.' She shut the door. She stared at its solid oak panels blankly, then looked down at the telegram again. There was a great roaring in her ears, like the crashing of the sea. The words danced and steadied. Her mind rebelled. Her thoughts screamed out in denial. It wasn't true. There was some mistake. Liam wasn't dead. He couldn't be dead. Not her adored, darling boy . . . it was someone else. They'd got him mixed up with someone else . . .

'Mrs Finley, is something wrong?'

She heard the voice of one of the convalescents. They weren't supposed to be in this part of the house. She turned around. She didn't see his face. All she saw was the khaki uniform of someone who was alive, whose blood still pulsed through his veins, who would love again and fight again, feel pain and joy. She felt a demonic urge to kill this boy who was still alive, while hers was dead.

The anguish inside her swelled and burst, and the cry that came from deep inside her was that of an animal howling for its young. The soldier was frightened. He'd seen men dying in battle, but this was different. This was a woman suffering terribly. She sagged against the door as if she would crumble without its support. The noises coming from her throat were still deep and terrible, and the soldier panicked.

'I'll fetch somebody, Mrs Finley. I'll go for the nurse –'

He fled, and Bridget fought for breath. It seemed as if she had none left. All that she had, she wanted to breathe into Liam, lying somewhere in the mud and filth of a battle-ground, his blood spilling out of him, the life she'd given him emptying away . . . the nightmare images wouldn't leave her, and she was gasping with the pain of it.

She wrenched open the door of Ashworthy Hall and got outside into the clean air of an English summer. All round her the roses were blooming, their scents heavy and violent. Reminding her of Austen, of Liam . . . it wasn't even April, she thought, the anguish sweet and harsh. It should be April, not June. Bad things happened to her in April.

She ran through the lawns and gardens as if demented, desperate to get away from the fragrance that haunted her. She ran until she couldn't run any more, without knowing where she went, without leaving any word, or caring. Nothing mattered any more. Nothing but the one fact drumming through her head. Liam was dead. Liam was dead . . .

It was almost a shock to see Magnolia Cottage in front of her. She didn't remember how she'd got there. Running across the fields without heeding scratches and bruises, then fumbling for the spare key Cassie always left under a flowerpot. Letting herself inside, and feeling the peace and silence of the place enfold her, and then throwing herself prostrate on the floor as if in supplication. And weeping for Liam, her best-loved child, until there were no tears left . . .

'Mother. Oh, Mother, no –'

Cassie's voice cracked as she saw Bridget, sitting so primly on her sofa, like a little carved statue. Bridget was as tall as herself, but right now she looked shrunken, and old. So old.

On the floor at her feet was a crumpled buff-coloured envelope. Cassie hardly needed to take out the coarse official form and read the cruel words.

Bridget looked up at her daughter as if she didn't recognise her.

'They don't mean it, do they? It's not my Liam who's dead, is it? It must be someone else.' She was child-like, begging for reassurance. It was the first time in her life that Cassie had seen her mother so distraught. Yet there was a horrific calm about her. She wasn't crying any more. She was numb, frozen. Cassie burst into noisy sobs.

'They don't make mistakes, Mum. Don't fool yourself into waiting hopefully for Liam to come walking through the door. He won't, not any more. He's dead, Mum.'

She saw her mother's face contort. Cassie couldn't bear it.

But neither could she bear the sight of this strange, cold woman sitting on her sofa with hands loosely in her lap. She looked so very alone. They were mother and daughter, and they were strangers. They needed one another so badly, and the distance between them in that small cosy room might have been an ocean. Cassie leaned down quickly, putting her arms around Bridget's stiff shoulders.

'Mother, you've still got me,' she said in a choked, desperate voice. 'You've got Harry and me and Joe. We all love you. We all loved Liam –' her voice broke, and she felt Bridget's hands patting her back.

'I know, dear,' Bridget said without expression. And then at last her shoulders began to shake, and for long silent minutes they were just two women weeping for the same man, holding each other and drawing comfort from each other. But through it all, Cassie knew it didn't change anything. That was the tragedy of not being loved.

Traumatic days followed, the bringing home of Liam's body, the family burial with all of them standing stiff and formal in their black funeral clothes.

Joe, on compassionate leave, the dear kind support from staff at the Hall and the collective turnout of the convalescent boys, the staff of *Night News*, some army representatives, Marlene travelling up from Devon, Evelyn, white-faced and tearful, Ralph and Alma and the small child from Ireland. Friends and family . . . Bridget clung to Harry, still disbelieving as the priest said the words that committed Liam's body to the ground.

To Cassie's surprise, her mother had ordered a huge heart-shaped floral display of red roses to lay on the grave. It was ostentatious and almost common, and Cassie had hit out and said so before she could stop herself, not understanding, when Bridget always said she disliked the flowers so much.

And then, the night before the burial, the two of them were alone in Bridget's sitting room, going over the arrangements for the next day. She picked up an old book Cassie had never seen before and opened it, handing it to her daughter silently. Between the pages was a dried flower, perfectly preserved.

'Someone I once loved very much gave me that rose, Cassie,' she said, her voice heavy with emotion. 'I know you haven't always understood me, my dear, but Liam was very like him. He wasn't his son, but he should have been, if Austen had lived. Just accept that things aren't always as they appear, Cassie, and try to be tolerant. It's not a gift you possess.'

She couldn't say any more. It was all she could do to try and stem the hurt in this difficult relationship. She knew Cassie was as devastated over Liam's death as herself, but she couldn't go farther in explaining the reason why she had felt this great need to smother Liam with roses. How could she, when she didn't really understand it herself?

For once, Cassie accepted the unsatisfactory explanation and reproof. She knew that intolerance was one of her faults, and felt guilty enough at having lashed out at her mother about the roses at such a time.

'We're all under a strain, Mother,' she said quietly. 'We all have to do what we think is best.'

And on the day after her brother's funeral, she telephoned her friend, Evelyn Oakes-Johnson, and outlined a certain course of action that was best for her. She spoke without emotion, with chilling attention to detail, with a plan that Evelyn thoroughly approved.

And two days later, Lord Harry Ashworth's *Night News* proclaimed a scoop when they printed a photograph of a fair-haired young man called Stefan Hoffmeyer, sent in by an anonymous person who thought the German had been recognised in a certain area of London.

'If seen, apprehend at once,' said the caption. 'Could this spy be working at the next bench to you?'

Someone soon discovered that he was, and there was a brief furore while the spy was taken into custody and dealt with swiftly and privately, and the munitions workers at the factory enjoyed a brief spell of notoriety and 'I Was There' interviews in the newspaper.

And if Harry speculated on just who had sent in the photograph with the French markings on the back, he never said. And Bridget was too wrapped up in her own grief to spare a thought for a name she might have remembered.

For Evelyn, national honour was upheld, and for Cassie, justice was done. A life for a life. Her friend's for her brother's. But underneath, she was still soft enough to weep for them both.

Chapter 30

They got through the weeks and months that followed, simply because they had to. The war didn't stop because Liam Dermot Finley had been killed in action. There were men being killed every day. All the same, in one corner of Sussex, Christmas Day was virtually ignored that year, because it would have been Liam's 19th birthday.

World events overshadowed the spring and summer of 1942. American servicemen, ready and willing for action, were arriving in Britain in droves, and every town boasted its share of billeted GIs.

Every unmarried girl flashed her eyes at these glamorous Yanks, who might or might not come from Hollywood, who chewed gum out of the corners of their mouths, had a slick line in flattery and could come up with the odd packet of nylon stockings or tin of corned beef or packet of American cigarettes.

'No wonder our boys complain of them being over-paid, over-sexed and over here,' grinned Evelyn Oakes-Johnson, in the cinema with Cassie one evening.

They were watching a newsreel now, and half of it was taken up by the way the GIs were being welcomed into English homes to stave off their homesickness.

'Do you think anybody takes in our soldiers like that?' Cassie said resentfully. 'We're getting a few American convalescents at the Hall now, by the way.'

'Really? How does your mother like that?'

They were shushed from behind, and Cassie whispered that she'd tell her afterwards. Seconds later they heard the wail of the air-raid siren and then the screen was blacked out before they were told to leave the cinema as quickly as possible. There were howls of outrage from the rows in front, but Cassie pulled at Evelyn's arm urgently.

'Come on, let's get out before the stampede. Thank God we're near the back.'

Her heart was beating very fast as they emerged into the night. She blinked. No one would think there was a black-out in operation. The enemy planes had arrived suddenly and were making a vicious attack on the capital. The skies were criss-crossed with powerful searchlights picking up the German planes and lighting them up in their beams like silver birds, then doggedly following them across the skies for the ack-ack-guns to blast them out of the sky. Watching it was sickening, disgusting.

They heard a shrill whistling noise, thundering down to earth, and almost next door to the cinema there was an ear-splitting noise as a bomb made a direct hit on a tall building. It collapsed like a pack of cards, before erupting into a great incandescent fireball spitting out remnants of wood and concrete and metal and human debris.

'We'll have to get to a shelter,' Evelyn screamed. 'Come *on*, Cass. We're going to be killed.'

She seemed frozen to the spot for horrified minutes. She had never been this close to death. It was all around them. They could see it, smell it, hear it. Was this how Liam had felt, seconds before he was blasted into oblivion . . . ? The thought seemed to jerk Cassie's senses into movement. They ran, sobbing, towards the nearby underground station, already crowded, already stinking from the sheer volume of people, some of whom used it nightly as their makeshift home, with bedding and possessions filling their own jealously guarded space.

Their teeth chattered uncontrollably. They could hardly believe that farther along the platform people were singing, making jokes, and beyond them, some older people were singing hymns. It was poignant and terrible. It was a different London to the one they knew, these nice Catholic girls who had once been to a finishing school in Gstaad, who had betrayed a friend and probably got him shot . . .

'God, how I hate this bloody war,' Cassie said savagely.

'Don't we all, ducks. We'd all like ter strangle that bloomin' 'itler!' The cockney voice from the bundle of bedding right beside her chuckled. Cassie stepped over it delicately, suddenly realising there was a man and a woman inside, the man snoring noisily, the woman with her head a mass of tortuous metal waving clips.

In a wave of hysteria, she suddenly wondered how they managed – about *it*. There was no privacy. Did such couples do it right here among this mass of bodies, while children along the line of beds sang nursery rhymes and old folk bellowed out hymns? Or was *it* off the agenda, put aside like good thick steaks and oranges and pretty underwear?

'Are you all right, Cassie?' Evelyn peered at her as they fought for a place to stand, since there was nowhere left to sit.

'Yes,' she croaked. 'I was just thinking of Joe, that's all.'

'He'll be all right, darling,' Evelyn said quickly, crossing her fingers tightly as she spoke, because Lord knew what Cassie would do if anything happened to Joe.

'I know.' She heard Cassie begin to laugh. 'I was just wondering how we'd manage if we had to sleep down here like this for many nights, that's all. It would be a trial of concentration!'

They clung together, giggling. It wasn't a topic they normally discussed any more. It was a private and personal thing now, between Cassie and Joe. But tonight, it seemed right to make jokes, to lessen the fear, to try to forget that above them the streets of London were burning and people were dying.

By the time the All-Clear sounded, they were exhausted from the sheer effort of trying to keep up their spirits. How the hell did these people do it, night after night after night . . . they left the underground as soon as they could, disregarding warnings from the people they climbed over that they'd do best to stay put. But the raid was over, and Adolf had vented his spite for tonight. They needed air and space to breathe, and to get away from these stoic, brave Londoners for whom they had a new and throat-clenching respect.

'Let's hope my car's still in one piece,' Cassie muttered as they went out into the night.

The smell of burning was still pungent. The thick choking smoke that hung in the air was reminiscent of London peasoupers, and made any thoughts of breathing clean air vanish from their minds. But at least they were alive and whole, and Cassie felt a sudden fierce thankfulness. It was more important than she had ever considered. To be alive, and to be safe.

'Why don't you come home with me tonight, Evelyn?' she said quickly, wondering how anyone could bear to go on living at the city flat Evelyn now shared with another girl.

'No, thanks. I'm not being pushed out by the damn Germans, Cassie. Thanks all the same. I'll see you soon.'

They parted company, and Cassie drove home to Magnolia Cottage as if someone else was at the wheel. She was so exhausted she could hardly see. It was the first time she had been in the thick of an air-raid, and she counted herself fortunate for that.

What seemed the most appalling thing of all was the horrifying speed with which homes and people could be destroyed. It was of earthquake proportions, she thought, still stunned by it all. She wondered how people could survive such terror and come out of it mentally unscathed.

She almost staggered through the door of the cottage. It seemed hours since she and Evelyn had gone into the cinema that night. It was well past three in the morning, she saw with a shock, and she had to be on duty in less than six hours.

She groaned, pulling off her clothes as she staggered upstairs without putting on a light. She stumbled over an obstacle on the bedroom floor, and cursed loudly. Then her heart nearly leapt into her throat as something in the bed moved, and at the same instant she realised she had nearly tripped over a kit-bag.

'Joe – oh, Joe, my Joe –' she sobbed, falling over herself in her rush to reach his outstretched arms.

He held her close, shushing her, calming her, and all the while whispering endearments and babbling something about a thirty-six hour pass that she hardly registered.

'Baby, baby, it's all right, it's all right,' he kept saying. 'We're together, and that's all that matters. Don't think of anything else.'

'It was so terrible,' she sobbed. 'The bombs and the noise, and all those brave people. And you know what I kept thinking about? It'll shock you.'

'No, it won't, honey. Nothing about you could shock me –' he said.

'This will! I kept wondering how they managed to make love in that beastly smelly underground with no special place of their own. Don't you think that's bloody shameful? What kind of person am I, to think of such a thing, when up above us in the streets, people were *dying*?'

'Don't you think they wonder about it too? I'll bet they find all sorts of ways! There's nothing shameful about love, honey, and if we only had three minutes left to us, I know how I'd want to spend it.'

His calming voice made the violent shaking inside her lessen, and out of nowhere came a wild reckless mood.

'Three minutes? Is that all?'

Joe's laughter was deep and rich against her breasts. She could tell that he was dog-tired too, just as she was, but being together unexpectedly like this produced its own aphrodisiac. It was the last thing either of them had envisaged happening, but right then it was as necessary to both of them as breathing. To make love, here in their own bed, to forget about death and war, and to remember that some things never changed. To reinforce their own familiar pattern of love-making, and to create their own private peace. That was what mattered. That was the best of all.

Bridget had wondered uneasily all through the years just how she would feel on the morning of April 10th, 1943. That was the day that Cassie's Trust Fund became her property, and the appropriate papers would be sent through to an eminent London solicitor from Donaldson in New York for Cassie and Bridget to sign. The investments would be brought up to date, with all the assets clearly shown.

Bridget had never been able to decide exactly when she

would tell Cassie about Thomas Finley's legacy, and there was a certain relief in knowing that she didn't have to reveal everything at this late stage. It should have been done long ago, and she realised that too. The knowledge had come as shock to Cassie, and had been one more thing to alienate them from each other.

She remembered poignantly how generous Liam had been when he had heard the news. It would have been so natural for him to be jealous, to begrudge his sister what was rightfully hers, but there had been none of that. And Cassie too, had been generous in declaring that Liam should have half the money.

'We'll go to New York together to collect,' Cassie had said gaily.

Now they never would. Not together, anyway. And anyway, it hadn't been necessary. Donaldson had written in explicit detail about the formalities involved. She and Cassie were to visit the London solicitor with the outlandish name of Parker-Brown as soon as he informed them the papers were in his chambers. He and his witnesses would deal with everything, and the money that had accrued from the investments would all be put into an English bank, if that was what Miss Finley wished.

Miss Finley had given due notice that it was exactly what she wished. The money was going to be used, not left to fluctuate in stocks and shares, on the whims of city gents and entrepreneurs. And Bridget knew better than to make any suggestions to the contrary.

And now here they were, on a chilly morning at the end of the month, sitting stiffly together in the solicitor's chambers, while his dry voice told them what they had to do. The two women each signed the papers that legally absolved Bridget from her responsibility, and now gave Cassie full control of the money left to her by her father.

'I understand your requests, Miss Finley, but as your legal adviser, it's my bounden duty to advise you that sound investments are the best way of utilising finances,' he said, in the statutory way of using two long words where one short one would do.

'Thank you, but I prefer to put it in the bank,' she said coolly, as though she was used to being handed assets of the accumulated 40,000 dollars, every day.

'*All* of it?' Parker-Brown was clearly affronted at having his advice ignored, and by a young woman with such aplomb. She didn't even look impressed by the amount, he thought in some annoyance.

'No. Half of it,' Cassie said calmly. 'One half is to go into my own account. The other half is to go into my mother's account.'

Bridget gasped, turning her head so sharply towards her daughter that her neck cricked. Her heart began to beat like a drum. Cassie had given her no hint of her intentions.

'No! I don't want your money. It's yours –'

'And by rights it should be yours. If I'd given half to Liam as I intended, and then he'd died, he'd have left his half to you, so it comes to the same thing.' She was clumsy now, knocked off balance by the look in her mother's eyes. She didn't understand it. It was almost – horror.

They heard Parker-Brown clear his throat.

'I think I'd better leave you ladies alone for five minutes while you come to a decision. I can't spare you any longer, I'm afraid –'

Cassie snapped at him, hating his patronising tone towards what he obviously saw as two wrangling women.

'With what I can afford to pay you, you'll give us as long as we like. But I've no doubt that five minutes will be enough.'

He went out, distinctly ruffled at this unexpected flash of temper. And Cassie turned to her mother.

'I want you to have it, Mother. Joe and I have discussed it all, and I won't change my mind. You *earned* it, didn't you?' Her voice shook with passion.

Bridget swallowed. By God, she had earned it. Every touch of Thomas Finley's hands on her body had cost her dear. But she had never expected this. Not from the daughter to whom she had never been able to show love.

That alone filled her with guilt. She wasn't sure if she wanted to weep or not. She hadn't wept since the day they had buried her son. And she couldn't weep now, especially not in front of this elegant girl who always seemed in such control of her life, in sharp comparison with the way Bridget's own had lurched from crisis to crisis.

'That's settled then,' Cassie said, when Bridget seemed unable to answer, and almost simultaneously the solicitor came back into the room, just as if he'd been listening at the keyhole.

In the car afterwards, as Cassie took them back to Sussex, Bridget sat stiffly. It didn't feel right to be beholden to a daughter. It was the wrong order of things. However much Cassie wanted to dress it up with duty being repaid, to Bridget it just didn't feel right.

'Cassie, I simply cannot accept what you're doing,' she said. 'I know it's kind and thoughtful of you –'

'It's not kind. It's justice, Mother. After all you've done for me, I owe it to you.'

Bridget stared at the strong capable hands on the steering-wheel. She was completely unable to tell if there was mockery in the words or not.

'Oh Cassie, have I hurt you so much?'

She saw the fingers tighten over the wheel.

'Does it hurt to pull the wings off a butterfly? Does it hurt to remember that your mother never kissed you good-night when you were little, and how you saw another child being given all the love you ached to have, when you weren't even old enough to understand what was lacking?' She spoke tensely, and Bridget felt her heart turn over.

'So this – gift – is your idea of revenge, is it? To make sure that I never forget that it's some kind of blood money,' Bridget said at last.

'It's not intended that way,' Cassie said impassively. 'I just wanted you to have it, that's all, and Joe thought it was a lovely idea.'

'Joe would, with his vineyards and his Spanish-style home!' Bridget said bitterly. 'What would it mean to people like Joe to hand over 20,000 dollars? He doesn't know what it means to have *nothing*, no food in your belly or a place to call your own. These poor devils blitzed out of their homes know how it feels. And if you think these war-time food rations are meagre, let me tell you –'

She stopped so suddenly that Cassie stared at her in amazement before she had to give all her attention to driving the car.

'Do *you* know about these things, Mother?'

Bridget steadied her rapid breathing. She had been about to spill out all she knew about soup kitchens, and living on other people's charity and wearing dead children's clothes, and the utter bewilderment of a fourteen-year-old skivvy knowing the pain of being homeless and virtually alone in the world.

'I was speaking figuratively,' she said shortly.

'Oh, of course. I should have guessed,' said Cassie, and they drove the rest of the way home in silence.

'Well, I think it's perfectly splendid of Cassie to do this,' Harry said, when she blurted out all that had happened that day.

Bridget gave a deep sigh, accepting the small liqueur he handed her after their evening meal together.

'Am I so out of step with everyone these days?' She asked miserably. 'I can't even accept a gift graciously without seeing some deep dark motive behind it. It might have been different if Cassie had given me some hint beforehand instead of blurting it out in front of that stiff-necked lawyer. Why on earth didn't she tell me what she intended to do?'

'Like you gave her some hint of the Trust Fund before you blurted it all out to her?' Harry said.

She banged her glass down on the table.

'Why must you always be so bloody righteous, Harry?'

'Because I've got more sense than you. Cassie needs to salve her conscience in her own way, and if this helps, then that's all right by me.'

'Everything Cassie does is all right by you! I'm surprised you didn't go to pieces when she met Joe, and snap her up after all.' She started to laugh at her own words, and brushed a hand over her forehead. 'I'm sorry, Harry, I'm in a foul mood tonight, and my head is splitting. I know I'm being rotten company.'

411

'Yes, you are, and if you think I'm going to flatter you and say it doesn't matter, you're wrong. I didn't snap Cassie up, as you so charmingly put it, not because I'm too old for her, but because she's too young for me. And from the way you're acting over this money, you're too young for me too. When are you going to grow up, Bridget?'

She looked at him, open-mouthed. He so rarely lost his temper with her, and she didn't like it.

'And just what did you mean about Cassie salving her conscience?' she remembered the odd words he'd used. 'What has she done that's so terrible?'

'Paid for Liam's life.'

The silence between them was almost brittle, and Bridget hated him at that moment. 'Because of me, you mean? Because I loved him –'

'No, my dear. Not because of you. Must you turn everything so selfishly towards yourself? Perhaps you don't recall the story about the young German spy being caught just after Liam died. His name was Stefan, and he was captured because of a photograph sent to us by an anonymous informant who had known him in happier times.'

'Cassie?' she whispered.

'Cassie,' Harry said. 'She doesn't know that I guessed immediately, and you're never to tell her. I know how good you are at keeping secrets, Bridget, so I'm sure you can keep this one. But perhaps you can imagine what it cost her to betray her friend. If she sees some peculiar kind of justice in giving you what she considers Liam's share in her legacy, take it generously, my dear.'

After she had taken all this in, she nodded slowly. Anything in the newspapers around the time of Liam's death had been so much chaff to her. She remembered none of it. But Cassie had apparently suffered doubly because of what she'd had to do. Her own daughter . . . and Bridget had known nothing about it.

Nevertheless, to Bridget the gift of the money had made the rift between them even wider. It was seemingly unbridge-able.

*

All through that fourth year of the war, the Allies continued to grind away in the fight against the enemy. The Italians surrendered in September, but Hitler's army seemed as implacable as ever, even though their cause became more desperate every day. As the winter dragged on into another spring, there were rumours of an invasion being imminent. Not of battered Britain now, but that of the Allied forces on the Normandy beaches. A wild and windy June 6th was not the best of days for crossing the English Channel, but a scent of victory drove men on to more valorous achievements than they believed themselves capable of doing. The beach-head in Normandy was established, and the invasion forces marched through Belgium and towards the Rhine.

To the echoes of Winston Churchill's rousing speeches, the British people began to cheer, but the exhilaration came too soon. The war was not yet won, and Hilter's new secret weapon, the flying-bombs, soon stilled the cheering voices. There seemed no end to the devil's ingenuity.

Joe's mother wrote desperate letters to Cassie.

'I know it's selfish of me to say so, but I almost wish you and Joe would start a family, my dear. Then you could give up your job at the War Office and come on over to us where you'd be safe. We do worry about you both so much.'

Cassie smiled, reading the words. Starting a family was the last thing she wanted just yet. When the war was over . . . it was the phrase on everyone's lips. It must end soon. Harry's newspaper kept blazoning headlines saying as much, and Harry's newspaper only printed the truth . . .

'How cynical you are these days, my darling,' Joe said to her on one of his rare leaves. He seemed to be on ops all the time now, and their time together was too precious to share more than a fraction of it with her family. They lay on their bed on the Sunday afternoon, knowing that Joe had to report back that night, and putting the knowledge out of their minds for as long as possible.

'I think I was born cynical,' she said ruefully. 'I always talked too much, putting my foot in my mouth and causing trouble. In fact, I can't think of one good reason why anybody should love me, Joe.'

'Neither can I,' he said solemnly, and then his voice deepened. 'Honey, if I shouldn't come back –'

She swivelled her head to look at him, fear darkening her eyes.

'Don't say it. Don't even think it, Joe, *please*. It's such bad luck!' She implored him.

For once he took no notice of her pleas.

'Darling, we've got to be sensible. I've been bloody lucky so far, but anybody's luck can run out. If mine does, I want you to promise me that one day you'll go see my folks. Not to stay permanently if you don't want to, but at least see them. My Mom and Dad already think the world of you, and if – well, if I wasn't here any more, they'd at least feel that they still had a part of me if you went to visit with them. Do that for me?'

'If it ever became necessary, I'd do it with love and pride,' Cassie said, hating this conversation because it seemed to invite disaster. They rarely spoke as seriously as this. And she knew, without being told, that Joe's missions were becoming ever more dangerous, if that were possible.

There were constant newspaper reports of Allied bombing raids over Germany, going deep into enemy country, over Berlin and Essen and Hamburg, destroying munition factories and arsenals and industrial plants. It sounded glorious and wonderful when you read it in newsprint. It was very different knowing it was your man flying the planes that carried the bombs. And Joe never told her where his ops took him. It wasn't his way. It didn't come into the code of the Canadian Air Force.

She had changed. They had all changed, and she longed for the days when you didn't look over your shoulder all the time, when you didn't have to watch every word you said in public places in case a spy might be listening, when you didn't have to betray your friends . . . she bit her lip. Her betrayal of Stefan still weighed heavily on her.

When Joe went back after his short leave, Cassie did something she hadn't done for a very long time. She felt almost guilty at the idea of entering a church and asking an unknown priest to hear her confession, and that in itself was a shaming thing to admit.

414

But seated behind the confessional grille, with only the dark shadowy features in her vision, and the soft, compassionate voice ready to absolve whatever sins she had committed, she found after all, a strange kind of inner peace. She had done what had to be done, and God and this priest forgave her.

Bridget didn't find it so easy to forgive a God who had taken Liam from her. Once again, He had taken everything she loved the most. He left her with nothing. She grieved for Liam as though she grieved for a lover, surrounding herself with photographs and mementoes of him until her sitting-room looked like a shrine to his memory, and at last even Harry became angry with her.

'I just can't stand to see you like this. You're just drifting, Bridget, and I think you should get away for a while. Go to Ireland. Stay with Ralph and Alma. We'll get a replacement in for you while you're gone. You need the break, and the convalescents need a more cheerful face around them!'

The usual idea of a holiday, being carefree, enjoying herself like people were supposed to do, away from everyday cares, was almost ludicruous to her. The pain of losing Liam wouldn't go away just because she was in different surroundings.

'You know I can't. There's a war on. I certainly don't want to inflict myself on Ralph and Alma. They have their own lives, and they hardly want a middle-aged woman moping around all the time.'

'You do admit that you mope around here then?'

Bridget sighed heavily. 'Harry, please don't badger me. I know myself, and I'll recover in my own good time.'

Harry was not content with such vague answers. 'You could start by singing again. You haven't sung a note since Liam died.'

He said the words deliberately, making her face them. 'There are other boys who'd welcome a bit of comfort. They're right here in the Hall, Bridget. You might spare a thought to them instead of saving all your misery for yourself.'

'I don't want to sing. I've lost all the incentive,' she said tightly. 'I couldn't bear it now.'

But still he wouldn't let it go. He kept on at her like a cat with a mouse, and all the time she seemed to be standing back from the duo that was Bridget and Harry, watching them sparring, seeing him goad, seeing her resist. She knew he did it out of kindness and whatever love he felt for her. But she didn't seem to be part of the real world any more, nor did she want to be. If it wasn't such a sin to wish herself dead, she would prefer to be with all those others she had loved.

Her mother and father, Michael, Kitty, Austen . . . Liam . . . she heard a sound in her throat that was like a sob, and knew that Harry's words were beginning to weaken her defences. She didn't want them to. She wanted to stay safe in her own little cocoon of grief. It was bad and it was wrong, but it was all she had left.

Neither Harry nor anyone else could begin to know how she felt when she saw all those other soldiers, sent to the Hall to finish their recovery. Wounded, brave and cheerful, or so morose they merely sat and waited for the days to pass. Some with missing limbs, or half their faces blown away, or shell-shocked . . . but all alive. The bitterness Bridget still felt at the injustice of it all, was still stronger than her enormous capacity for sympathy and understanding. All of that seemed lost in the abyss of her own misery. It shamed her, but it seemed impenetrable.

But when she was alone and her nerves had settled down from yet another verbal battle with Harry, she admitted that perhaps his idea wasn't such a bad one. Perhaps she should go away for a while. It was more than a year since Liam had been killed, and even the people closest to the victims of war had to get on with their lives. Harry did. Cassie and Joe did.

But where could she go? Even as she thought it, she knew where her haven would be. Somewhere where she could depend on finding good old common sense and a no-nonsense approach. She picked up the telephone and asked for the number of the little haberdashery shop in Devon where Marlene de Wolfe lived with her sister.

Chapter 31

At the end of July, Bridget boarded the train for the long journey across England, and finally arrived exhausted at the small country station a few miles inland from the sea. Marlene was there to meet her in a battered old van for which there was a meagre petrol allowance on account of the haberdashery business, even though Marlene's sister Ruth rarely did any delivering of stock.

Bridget saw Marlene at once. She could hardly miss the thatch of flaming red hair and plum-coloured frock among the dingy uniforms of returning heroes, and sensible tweeds of the countrywomen meeting them. She quickly averted her eyes from the sight of a large woman embracing a son with noisy overflowing tears.

'Bridget, am I ever glad ta see ya, ducks!' Marlene wrapped her arms around Bridget, enveloping her in a great hug, before standing back and examining her.

'And not before time, by the looks of it. Me and Ruth are gonna build yer up. You're wasting away! Not that it don't suit ya, mind, and what I wouldn't give to get rid of a bit o' spare flesh! But never mind about that. Where's yer cases? Only one? Good Gawd, have you bin giving all yer clothes cewpons away to that pretty gel of yours? 'Ow is she, by the way? No babe on the way yet?'

She stopped for breath, and Bridget was weak with laughter. Oh, it was so good to be with someone so *normal* as Marlene. Cassie might think her common, but she was a dear, good friend, and she wanted to know everything in ten seconds flat. But they had much longer than that in which to unwind, if Marlene was capable of such a thing, because the government replacement for Bridget's services was now installed at Ashworthy Hall for a whole month.

'Marlene, while we're on our own,' Bridget said, wincing as the old van lurched along the rutted road leading away from the station. 'I want you to know how much I appreciate this – how much it means to me –'

'Ya don't have ter tell me anything, ducks,' Marlene said, grimly hanging on to the wheel. 'I know what you've bin through, and I just wish you'd come to me sooner. Nobody knows better'n me that it takes more'n a pat on the back to get over losing somebody close.'

'Harry lost Fee, but even he didn't seem to understand –' Bridget agreed.

'Oh, men!' Marlene snorted, dismissing the entire race, despite the fact that it was her Norm's demise she was discussing. 'Anyway, there's no comparing, is there? I mean, Harry didn't love Fee in that way, did he? He might have had to do his duty to try and get his son and heir, poor sod, but it was always you he loved, Bridget. Even somebody wearing an eye-patch could see that.'

Bridget smiled at Marlene's quaint turn of phrase. She didn't agree with all that she said, but it comforted her. It comforted her enormously.

Ruth was a facsimile of her sister. They were like peas in a pod, and Bridget couldn't resist a chuckle at the thought of this quiet village housing two loud and flamboyant sisters with dyed red hair and painted faces to hide the cracks, as Marlene used to say cheerfully. One of them was enough for any village, but two . . .

She found, rather to her surprise, that although Marlene and Ruth were treated as novelties, the countryfolk had taken them under their wings. They'd had evacuee children from London, of course, and they considered that these two fading women were no less in need of care and support. Despite the fact that Ruth had lived here for ten years, she was still treated indulgently as 'a forriner from up Lunnon', and Marlene was the comic turn they had sniggered about at first, and finally given an abundance of fond affection.

So when Bridget discovered that Marlene was putting on a

small show at the village hall on Saturday evenings to raise money for comforts for the troops, she wasn't at all surprised. Marlene had the knack of gathering up any talent that she could and utilising it shamelessly.

'I wish my poor old Norm was still 'ere,' she said wistfully as the three of them prepared to go to the village hall on that first Saturday night of Bridget's stay. 'We'd give 'em a magic act and no mistake. I never 'ad the stomach to offer meself to another partner, though –'

'That's a larf, that is,' Ruth shrieked, prodding Marlene's ample girth. 'You always 'ad enough stomach for two, gel. That's as fine a belly as I ever saw, ain't it, Bridget? Any bloke 'ould have ta be pretty 'ard up to take on the likes of you, my gel!'

They were warm and funny and brash, and Bridget loved them both. They helped to heal her wounds by their own simple honesty, without trying, without false platitudes. She knew where she was with them, and that was something she hadn't felt with anybody for a very long time.

She sat through the concert that Saturday night, admiring Marlene's new role as *compère*, applauding with the rest of them as the turns came on. Countryfolk reciting poems, a warbling boy soprano from the local church, an elderly juggler whose knees creaked every time he lunged for his dumb-bells, a Hitler impersonator that had the audience shrieking with laughter, a troupe of ten-year-old Shirley Temple look-alikes prancing across the stage, curls flying, feet tapping, throats hoarse with singing.

And at the end of it, the service hats were passed round for the extra pennies that were added to the modest entrance fee. All of it was donated to the central fund in London that was helping to keep up the morale of British servicemen wherever they were. Marlene's voice thundered out, encouraging, touting for money for 'our needy boys', easily reaching everyone's heart.

Bridget was touched and amazed at the generosity Marlene's eloquence produced. She was no scholar, and her language was sometimes perilously near to fruity for a family audience, but they loved her. They loved what she was doing,

419

and they trusted her. They knew they could, because of the letters of thanks received from the Red Cross and other organisations, proudly pinned up on the wall of the hall for all to see.

Bridget was proud of her too.

'I had no idea you were doing all this,' she said when they went home, weary but happy. 'You never told me, Marlene. Fancy you being such an organiser. Norman would have been so proud of you.'

To her embarrassment, Marlene's eyes filled with tears. Ruth had gone to bed, leaving the two of them alone.

'That's the nicest thing anybody ever said t' me, Bridget. Do you know what I miss the most? Not having anybody to talk to who knew my Norm. Not being able t' laugh about the things he said and did. Ruth only met him the once, even though we was sisters. She didn't care overmuch for theatricals, though I think she's changed her mind now.'

'So she should. And darling, if you want to talk about Norm, I'd be only too happy to listen.'

Marlene's face was pink. 'Well, only if you talk about Liam. We both lost a good 'un, ducks, and we shouldn't ever forget 'em. We shouldn't be afraid to mention their names as if they never existed, which is what some folks'd want us to do.'

Once started, she talked far into the night, about Norman and the fantastic bohemian life they'd once led, being on the road and in digs, and treading the boards, and the excitement of being in the spotlight, the triumphs and disasters, and of how badly she still missed the old bugger, in bed and out of it.

And a year after his death, Bridget talked more freely about Liam than she'd ever done to anyone. Then, slowly and somehow effortlessly, she talked about Kitty, and Austen, and about Thomas Finley and the reason why she had never been able to feel love for Cassie. The words came tumbling out, releasing, hurting and healing at the same time, and at the end of them she realised that she and Marlene had gone through most of a bottle of brandy between them and they were halfway to being roaring drunk, and neither was going to remember very much about any of it in the morning.

'You know what I think, ducks?' Marlene slurred. 'I think you love your Cassie more'n you realise. Why else should you get so mad wiv 'er? You don't get mad wiv people you don't care about. Stands t'reason, dunnit?'

'Oh Marlene, I love you.' Bridget started to laugh, not because she believed her, but at the nonsensical sight of her friend swaying on her feet, her eyes becoming decidedly crossed as she tried to focus on the stairs.

'I luv ya too, but if I don't get this bleedin' corset orf soon, I shall be strangulated. If those bleedin' apples 'n' pears'll stop goin' round for a minnit, I'm gonna try to get up 'em if it kills me, and I'll see ya tomorrer. Sleep tight, and don't let the bed-bugs bite.'

They slept in the next day. Sundays were meant to be for resting, and nobody in this household worried if you wanted to stroll around in your dressing-gown all morning. They managed to keep just a step away from living the bohemian life right in the middle of a sober village community, Bridget thought in amusement. And long before the following Saturday night, Marlene got to work on her.

'Oh no. Definitely not. I couldn't –'

'Why couldn't you? Is there summat wrong wiv yer throat?'

'It's nothing like that. But you know I've given up singing in public, Marlene, and I gave up recording long ago. I found all that far too impersonal –'

'Ooz talking about bleedin' records? It seems to me I've heard all this before, gel. But you can see that everybody's friendly down here. Do it fer me. Fer old times' sake, eh? The crowds'll love ya, and it'll bring in buckets o' dough fer the troops. Wouldn't your Liam be proud of ya for doing it?'

Bridget gave her a straight look. 'They call that hitting below the belt –'

'I know. But I can't think of anywhere else to hit ya. Yer heart's made of stone and your head's full of cotton wool, so right in the gut seemed the best place,' she said.

Bridget stared in surprise at this rare rebuke.

'Well, that's telling me, isn't it?' She said slowly. 'How can you say my heart's made of stone after all that I told you the other night?'

'I can't remember the half of it, ducks, but prove me wrong then.'

'I was going to do that in another way.'

'Oh?'

Bridget's idea had been simmering in her mind all week. Her one-time fancy of buying a recording studio didn't appeal to her. To her, it was as impersonal as the gramophone records themselves. It wasn't vital and alive. It wasn't real show-biz, as Marlene called it. And Marlene was born to the theatrical life. It was a shame she only dabbled in it now. She should be in charge of her own company, the way Norm had been. She could do it blind-folded. Bridget said as much now, testing the water, and Marlene laughed.

'And where would I get the money to start such a thing? My Norm left me a lot o' good memories, but precious little money. A touring comp'ny's a risky business all round, Bridget. Oh, I don't starve, but there ain't any extras. Now, if I had a nice little theatre of me own, that would be a diff'rent matter.' Her eyes gleamed, just thinking about it, and then she shrugged.

'Just listen to me, dreamin' and wallowin', when we're meant to be talking about you singing at the hall on Saturday night, Bridget!'

'Why should it all be a dream? Could you manage your own theatre, Marlene? Do you know the first thing about it?'

'I'd bloody well soon learn. I know enough theatricals to give me all the advice I'd need. But give it a rest, will ya? Yer making me mouth water at the thought, and I'm as likely to get it as seeing a pig fly.'

'I'll finance it, Marlene,' Bridget said.

'*What*? I ain't taking yer money. I never knew you 'ad any, come to that.' Marlene gaped.

'Well, I have. And I want to invest it in something worth-while, not just some big city company that means nothing to me. This way, we'll both benefit. The theatre will belong to me, but you'll have complete control. You'll hire the acts and see to the publicity and so on, and have your finger in every pie, which will suit you down to the ground if I know anything about you. We'll be business partners, Marlene, and there are only two conditions.'

When she'd caught her breath, Marlene grinned, still not believing any of it, still thinking it was some gigantic leg-pull. 'I thought there'd have to be. It's all too good to be true. Come on then, what's the catch?'

'One, that you never ask me to sing in your theatre. That won't be part of the deal.'

'And the other?' Marlene began to wonder at last if it wasn't a game after all, since Bridget looked so serious.

'The other is that it's to be called the Liam Finley Theatre. The money I'll be putting into it would have been his, and I want to do this for him, in his memory. I know he'd have approved.'

That was when Marlene knew that it wasn't all a dream. That her friend Bridget Finley was offering her the chance of a lifetime, and Marlene was never slow when it came to grasping opportunities.

'Done.' She said, thrusing out her hand to shake Bridget's.

The solemnity of the occasion left her just as suddenly. 'Blimey, gel, d'ya realise you've just made me one of the bleedin' ruling classes? Even Norm never had his own theatre. What a turn-up, eh? It still don't stop me asking ya to sing on Saturday night, though. Please, ducks.'

How Marlene got her to say yes, Bridget couldn't think. But in the end she relented, and on the following Saturday night she was singing to a rapt audience, and the nerves that assaulted her before she went on disappeared as she saw the faces of service men among the rows of seats. She might have been singing for Liam, she thought. And he'd have approved of this.

She sang on each of the Saturday night concerts before she boarded the train again to take her back to Sussex. Marlene's enthusiastic thanks were still ringing in her ears. Marlene was ecstatic at the chance to start her own theatre, and Ruth was still telling her to stop running around like a dog with two tails, or she'd catch herself coming back. They were lovely, lovely people, Bridget thought affectionately.

She felt refreshed, renewed, just by being with them, and if she had given something to Marlene, she knew that it had been repaid a hundredfold. They had both come a long way.

'You're doing *what*?' Cassie said, when she told her.

'Investing in a theatre, and Marlene's going to run it,' she said calmly.

'Well, I think you're completely mad. She'll turn it into one of those dreadful end-of-the-pier places. How can you be content with that, after you've had proper training as a singer yourself, Mother?'

'So you do admit I'm a proper singer, do you?' Bridget found she was hugely enjoying this. She'd fully expected opposition from Cassie, and she was getting it.

'Mother, please be serious –'

'I'm perfectly serious. While I was in Devon we went to see a solicitor and land agent, and they're going to find the best place available down there. You made me the gift of the money, darling, and this is what I'm doing with it – well, some of it.'

'It's not what I intended –'

'Oh, were there conditions attached to it?' Bridget enquired. 'You should have told me.'

Cassie looked at her warily. Her mother seemed more quick-witted, more in control of herself than she'd seen her for a long while.

'Of course there weren't conditions attached to it,' she said crossly.

'Good. The money's already been sitting in the bank for more than a year, and it's time it was put to good use. And you may be interested in my own conditions that I put to Marlene. One is that she never asks me to sing in the theatre, because I simply don't want to perform any more –' she didn't miss the faint look of relief flash across Cassie's face – 'and the other is that it's called the Liam Finley Theatre.'

Cassie's face registered a range of emotions, from amazement to a dawning pleasure. And then her emotion threatened to run away with her, and Bridget silently handed her a handkerchief.

'I take it you approve then?'

'How can I not? Yes, of course I approve.'

Why don't you kiss me then, Bridget asked silently? Why can't the two of us reach out and hug one another in these moments that unite us? Why do we both still hold back from showing our true feelings, whatever they are?

'Did you hear the news on the wireless?' Cassie turned away to blow her nose, her voice bright, the mood changing in an instant. 'The D-Day invasion was an entire success, and the Allies have begun the liberation of Western Europe. They've broken through the German defences into the interior of France. Paris has been liberated at last. Isn't it simply wonderful news? I'm so thrilled about Paris. I wonder if Monsieur Alphonse is safe.'

'Yes, it's simply wonderful,' Bridget said, glad for Paris, sad that it took that to put the animation into her daughter's face, rather than seeing her mother home again.

She couldn't blame her. All that she reaped, she had sown . . . or some such phrase, she thought tiredly.

'Have you heard from Joe lately?' She reminded herself to ask.

Cassie nodded. 'Last week. He's well. He says the war can't go on much longer now. Harry says it too. It's in all the newspapers.'

'Yes. They do read newspapers in Devon, Cassie.'

Their conversation seemed to be drying up, as usual. They fenced with one another, finding nothing else to say. Cassie suddenly glanced at her watch, thankful to see the time had passed.

'I must go. Give Harry my love, and I'll probably see you at the weekend. By the way, he says you needn't start work again immediately, but he'll be quite glad to send the other old harridan packing.'

'He didn't really say that, did he?' Bridget laughed.

'Cross my heart and hope to die. He missed you, Mother.'

She flew out, always in a hurry, always with something to do, somewhere to go. She had collected her mother from the station and brought her home, staying just long enough to drink tea with her. So Bridget was still caught up in the half-world of not quite losing the aura of the month's holiday, and not quite fitting back into her usual slot yet. It was an oddly unreal feeling. She would be glad when Harry came home. She had missed him too.

And he at least thought she had done a great and wonderful thing in financing Marlene's theatre and naming it after Liam.

'I didn't do it to be great and wonderful,' she protested.

'Why did you do it?' He enquired. 'It wasn't a spur of the moment thing, knowing you.'

'I hadn't thought of it before I went to Devon,' she said. 'But somehow while I was there everything seemed to fall into place. That money was a bit like an albatross around my neck, Harry. I wanted to be rid of it, yet I knew I had to do something useful with it. I couldn't just do as Thomas Finley did by leaving it all to some anonymous charities. I wanted to *see* it put to good use, not just have it scattered around dogs' homes or whatever.'

'And you're naming it after Liam.'

'Why not? The money belonged to him really. It felt right to do it.'

Harry leaned over and kissed her.

'You're a very special lady, Bridget. I'm glad you've realised at last that if something *feels* right, then it *is* right,' he said gravely.

She looked at him, but it seemed that there was no deep significance in what he said. He had merely spoken words of reassurance and approval that meant nothing more. And it wasn't done for a woman to profess her love for a man unless he said it first. It just wasn't done.

Whatever Hitler's intentions had been in creating a permanently Nazi-occupied Europe, the might of the combined Allied Forces was now pushing him relentlessly back. As the old year merged into the next, hopes were high that surely 1945 would see the end of this war. Surely there wouldn't be another Christmas without the lights going up all over the country.

By Cassie's next birthday, everyone said the end was imminent. Soon afterwards, Cassie had secret hopes of her own, and knew how desperately she wanted to spend the next Christmas in California. She was twenty-seven years old, and she suspected that she was pregnant. Her husband was an airman, still being sent out on dangerous missions over Germany and the continent, and she prayed for his safety constantly.

She told no one of her condition, not even Joe, for fear it would make him worry for her and therefore lessen his concentration in the air. She didn't tell her mother, even though she felt a peculiar kind of empathy with Bridget now. She too, had wanted her child to be born in a certain place for her own reasons. In Bridget's case, it had been Ireland. In Cassie's, it was Okaje, among the lush vineyards north of San Francisco, where her baby would be born safe and free, far away from the holocaust that was Europe.

There was a sort of superstition in Cassie's mind about the baby. It was still totally hers at the moment, growing and breathing inside her. She would share that knowledge with Joe very soon. But only with him, God willing, providing the war ended soon enough for it not to be obvious to everyone.

She prayed that she and Joe could be safe in California before she wrote to tell her mother the news. For one thing, she wasn't sure how Bridget would take it. Would she cry all over her and go all grandmotherly, and embarrass them both? Would she be angry that Cassie was bearing Joe's child at all? She seemed to have got over her dislike of him, but there was still something wrong that Cassie couldn't fathom, and it was that more than anything, that still alienated them as far as Cassie was concerned.

In the end, she did tell someone. The news was simply too wonderful to keep to herself. She had it confirmed by a doctor in London, and couldn't wait to share the news, and she went to her old flat to tell Evelyn. Of course it should be Joe who heard it first, but in the circumstances, she knew he would understand.

'Darling, how exciting!' Evelyn said. 'Though it beats me how you haven't managed it before.'

Cassie blushed. 'None of your business,' she chuckled. 'We've managed it now, and isn't it just marvellous? I hope it'll be a boy for Joe, though I know he'll say he doesn't mind what it is.'

'You mean you haven't told him yet?'

She shook her head, explaining the reasons. They sounded brave and sensible, and all the time she explained them she was conscious of the doubts in her mind. It should be Joe sharing this first moment of telling. It should be Joe's hands holding hers . . .

'Cass, you're so brave. I'd be terrified of having a baby in wartime, or any other time, come to that.'

'Of course you wouldn't. Women have babies every day. And I certainly hope it won't still be wartime when this one's born.'

She put her hand over her stomach, trying to imagine what the baby looked like now. The doctor had shown her a series of pictures of amoeba-like blobs that had gradually turned into recognisable human beings. It had been quite frightening, but totally fascinating and awesome.

'Let's put on the wireless for the news,' Evelyn said. 'Then we can have some tea. You don't have to rush off immediately, do you?'

'Not yet. Where's your girlfriend today?'

'She's visiting her family, so we've got all afternoon to ourselves.' She twiddled with the knobs on the wireless. It was almost time for the news bulletin, to which everyone listened avidly.

There was the usual beginning, with no dramatic announcement to say that hostilities had finally ceased. It was tantalising, infuriating, like waiting for a volcano to erupt. It was as unnerving, in a different way, as the days of expectancy before the war began. The announcer's voice was plummily correct, as if nothing he had to say could ruffle him. Cassie and Evelyn had often wondered if they picked those people especially. The ones who seemed to have nerves of steel – or no feelings at all.

There were stories of heroism and government policy and the continuing interest in the aftermath of President Roosevelt's death earlier in the month, and its effect on the American people.

'Poor old thing. He couldn't even last out to see the end of the war,' Evelyn said sympathetically.

But Cassie was already listening to a late item of news that held her riveted to her chair.

'We've just heard that early this morning three Canadian Air Force planes encountered some German Messerschmitts over Belgium. There was a bitter struggle between them, and several enemy planes were shot down. It is regretted that all three Canadian planes were shot down, and it was unreliably reported that parachutes were seen leaving one plane just before it burst into flames.'

Cassie sat as if frozen. Evelyn switched off the wireless immediately, and knelt down in front of her friend, taking her lifeless hands in hers and gripping them tightly. In an instant, Cassie was as white as if someone had drained all the blood from her. The shock of it made her feel sick and faint.

'Cassie, it doesn't have to be Joe. There are dozens of others it could have been. Just because it was a Canadian plane – for heaven's sake, darling, think positively. We've all heard this kind of news before and never gone to pieces about it. It will be bad for the baby if you do.'

'I know it was Joe. In my heart I know it. And oh, God, the baby!' Cassie stuttered. 'If my Joe – if Joe is dead, he'll never see our baby. He'll never even know. Oh, Evelyn, I was wrong not to tell him before! I did it all wrong! I should have told him. He had a right to know he was going to be a father. Now, perhaps he never will!'

Tears poured down her face, and Evelyn became very alarmed. Cassie was so strong, far stronger than herself, and this was so untypical of her.

'Stop talking about him as if he's dead, will you? He's *not* dead, Cassie. You've got to believe it. You've got to tell yourself over and over. It wasn't Joe. It wasn't Joe. Go on, say it out loud, and keep on saying it and believing it.'

She bullied and coaxed until at last the colour began to come back into Cassie's face, and all the while she uttered the words without conviction. Cassie's voice seemed to be dragged from her throat, but now the desperation was mixed with a strange sort of anger.

'We always said we'd been so lucky so far, but why should it be our luck that held out? Why us? A while ago, Joe was talking to me about mortality in his annoyingly practical way. Now I wonder if he'd had some kind of premonition. If so, he didn't tell me. Perhaps he had a secret to keep as well so as not to worry me.'

The words went on, bitter, emotional, irrational, examining every possibility, trying to find reasons where there were none. She couldn't think properly. She didn't know what was happening, but, in her heart she was already bereft. She already mourned.

'I'll have to go home, Evelyn. I must be there if anyone tries to contact me,' she said, suddenly panicking at the realisation.

'You're not driving anywhere while you're in such a state, darling!'

'I didn't drive today. My car's having something done to it at the garage. Harry brought me. I'll go straight round to his office. He'll take me home. He might have heard something too –'

'Please take it easy, Cass. At least until you find out something definite. And I'm coming with you. I'm not letting you go home alone.'

For a few seconds they clung together, needing each other's strength. Cassie stammered incoherent thanks.

'What the hell are friends for?' Evelyn said roughly, to hide the ache in her own heart. They had been friends for so many years. If Cassie was hurt, she hurt too, and if the worst were true, this would be the deepest pain of all.

'Darling, remember the baby,' she said quickly as Cassie went to rush down the stairs of the tall building. 'You don't want anything to happen to it, and you've got to think of yourself now.'

No, she didn't want to lose the precious baby, especially not now ... when it might be all she had left of Joe. The unspoken words were between them, and Cassie slowed down a little, her eyes dark with fear.

They managed to hail a cruising taxi which hurtled them through streets with fallen masonry and sliced-off buildings, window-frames hanging at crazy angles in the air, roofs like wooden skeletons with all their flesh torn off and only the ribs remaining.

It mildly surprised Cassie that everyone they saw wasn't bursting with the news that had devastated her. But why should they? Such reports came with every news bulletin. Women lost husbands, sons and lovers every day. It was the war. And until one of them personally involved you, it was merely another sad story of bravery and death.

They reached Harry's offices and while Evelyn thrust the fare into the taxi-driver's hands, Cassie rushed on ahead and she had to run to catch up with her. They went through the busily clacking offices, ignoring the curious looks of the staff, and burst into Harry's private office.

'Cassie, what on earth –'

She seemed unable to speak for a second. His startled face told her that the news hadn't reached him. That she was probably magnifying everything because of her condition. There were hundreds of planes in the air. It didn't have to be Joe's that had burst into flames . . . She couldn't think any farther than that. She saw black spots floating in front of her eyes, and then she crashed to the floor at Harry's feet.

Chapter 32

They lifted Cassie onto the leather sofa, and Evelyn rapidly told Harry what had happened. She just managed not to blurt out anything about the baby, though she wondered frantically if she should. Cassie recovered while she was still dithering, and while Harry was occupied on the telephone, making a dozen calls to see what he could find out, Cassie gripped Evelyn's hand.

'You didn't say anything, did you? She whispered fiercely. 'Joe has to know before the rest of them.'

Evelyn felt her heart turn over. There was such a light of desperation in Cassie's eyes, as if her will alone would ensure Joe's safety. And by now, Evelyn too was feeling a horrible

431

presentiment. The air battle must have happened hours ago. Joseph Buckley might have been dead for hours already, even though the information was so new to them. She shuddered, fighting against the ghastly thought.

'Of course I didn't say anything,' she whispered back under the pretence of chaffing Cassie's cold hands. 'If you can't trust your best friend, who can you trust?'

Behind his desk, intent on his latest telephone conversation, Harry's voice suddenly sharpened.

'You're sure? Has it been confirmed? Then what authority gave you the information? Has the Belgian News Agency been on to you? All right, but just get back to me as soon as possible. I have a personal interest in this one.'

This one, this one . . . to any other newspaperman but Harry, this would be just another story. Cassie gave a small moan in her throat, knowing now that however much you thought you were strong and capable, you were always totally unprepared for the worst. She and Joe . . . they had thought their lives together were just beginning. They had believed they were destined to live together, to grow old together and eventually die together, not to have one of them shot out of the sky and blown into a million fragments . . .

'Cassie, darling,' Harry was kneeling beside her, his voice very gentle. 'It's still unconfirmed, but there were positive sightings of three parachutes from one of the Canadian planes. Bomber Command have confirmed that it was Joe's squadron that was involved, and as yet, we've no way of knowing if he was one of the survivors. They can't tell which plane the parachutes came from, but everything's being done to search for the survivors. Whoever they are, they're in Belgian territory, so when they're picked up, they'll be safe, and they'll be flown home as soon as possible.'

'Providing they're alive,' she said.

'Yes, darling. Providing they're alive,' Harry said steadily, knowing he couldn't lie to her. His heart ached for her. She sat upright now, so white and tense and brittle, and so very much like her mother when he had first seen her all those years ago in Dundemanagh when he'd brought a present for Cassie's un-birthday.

432

'What do we do now?' she said dully, needing someone to do her thinking for her.

'We go home. I've asked for any information to be put through to me immediately at the Hall, where I shall be for the rest of the day. I think it's best that any news comes to me first, Cassie,' he said carefully, 'in case it needs to be followed up. And of course I'll phone the cottage immediately I hear anything, unless you want to stay at the Hall and be with your mother.'

'I'd rather be in our home,' Cassie answered. 'It's where Joe will expect me to be.'

'I'm going with her,' Evelyn said quickly, in case he thought the slight to Bridget sounded too awful. 'I shall stay with her as long as necessary. They can do without me for a couple of days at work.'

'Good girl.'

Harry suggested briskly that they go right away, and that Cassie went straight to bed if she felt queasy.

'I'm not ill. Just –' She almost said 'just pregnant' and stopped herself in time.

'I know you're not ill,' Harry soothed. 'But you've had a shock, and it can sometimes knock you off-balance for a while.'

Evelyn wondered if he guessed, but probably not. He got them to Magnolia Cottage as quickly as possible and left them there. He could barely have arrived back at Ashworthy Hall, when the telephone rang at the cottage.

'Oh, darling, Harry's just told me. What do you want me to do – ?'

'Nothing at all, Mother. Except to keep off the telephone so that people can get in touch with Harry when there's any news.'

'Oh Cass,' she heard Evelyn murmur sadly.

She couldn't help it. She simply couldn't cope with her mother right now.

'All right,' Bridget said at last. 'Shall I come and stay at the cottage with you?'

'No thank you. Evelyn's here.'

She put down the phone. She had been unnecessarily cruel.

She knew it, but there was nothing in the world she could have done to stop it. And it was true. She didn't want Bridget. She didn't want to see her mother's beautiful face contorted with distress because of her. This was her pain, hers and Joe's. And the only one she could bear to witness it was Evelyn.

'I'm going to make us some strong tea,' Evelyn said. 'And a sandwich. I'm sure you should eat something. Is there any bread in the house?'

'Yes, but I don't want anything. I couldn't.'

'But the baby might be hungry,' suggested Evelyn. 'You don't want him to turn out a puny little thing, do you? His father wouldn't thank you for that!'

Cassie stared vacantly for a moment as if unable to grasp what Evelyn was saying. And then the hot tears flooded out, streaming down her cheeks in torrents, and Evelyn took her silently in her arms and let it happen, knowing that Cassie's heart was near to breaking.

The telephone rang several times during the evening. Harry's voice told her evenly there was no news yet, but that it didn't mean anything. No news wasn't always bad news, he said encouragingly. He rang again in the early hours of the morning. Neither of the girls had been to bed. They still sat hunched up in their day-clothes, and not even the distant sounds of air-raid sirens could trouble them.

Cassie reached for the phone, her heart palpitating wildly. She croaked Harry's name, sure it would be him.

'Cassie, he's safe. He landed in a thicket of trees, and that damned leg of his copped it again. He's in some Belgian hospital now and they've set his leg in what sounded more like concrete than plaster, and I doubt that he'll be flying again. The other two weren't so lucky. One of them's critical with head and internal injuries, and the other – well, it was just his number on the ticket. But Joe's safe, and he'll be coming home as soon as they say he's fit enough to travel. Do you understand me, Cassie?'

'Yes,' she sobbed, her voice thick and muddy. 'Oh Harry, yes. Oh, thank you. Oh, thank God –'

Evelyn took the phone from her fingers, and heard him tell it all over again. She was weak with relief, and she couldn't imagine how Cassie must be feeling. She was doubled up on the sofa now, and Evelyn felt a sliver of alarm. She thanked Harry quickly, and said yes, she'd be staying on, and she'd get Cassie to call her mother tomorrow.

'Cass, are you all right? It's not the baby, is it?' She said urgently when she'd put down the phone.

'No.' The voice was still thick and exhausted. 'It's just – everything. Thankfulness and relief and a feeling that we don't deserve to be the lucky ones, and prayers I've nearly forgotten going round and round in my head, and not even knowing how I feel any more. I'm just so tired, so terribly tired all of a sudden.'

'How does bed sound, then?' Evelyn smiled for the first time, and the two of them went upstairs together, arms around each other. Evelyn helped Cassie undress and then tucked her up in bed like a mother-hen, and then collapsed exhausted on the bed in the second bedroom without even taking off her clothes.

They kept Joe in the Belgian hospital for several weeks because of the severe leg injuries, and they didn't want to risk any immediate jolting on the journey back to England. But at least Cassie knew that he was alive, and that was the most important thing of all. One of the Air-Force authorities came to see her, saying that it was agreed that Joe should have an honourable discharge and that there was probably a medal in the offing for his part in the action. Cassie arranged to have compassionate leave to look after him as soon as he came home, but everyone kept telling her that it would hardly be necessary. Everyone believed that Germany was poised on the brink of surrendering, and the war would be over for everyone.

She hadn't yet made her own peace with her mother, after rejecting Bridget completely on that terrible April day when Joe had been shot down. She hadn't wanted Bridget then, and she didn't know how to say she wanted her now. She was ashamed at reacting as she had, but to try and apologise would be an embarrassment for them both.

So she had simply glossed over it. She had gone to the Hall

the next day, seeing her mother in the midst of a crowd of cheery servicemen, who said they were glad everything had turned out well for her and her husband. It was easier to talk in a crowd, to smile and be cheerful, and include her mother in the conversation, and successfully keep her at arm's length at the same time.

Cassie didn't know if Bridget was hurt by her attitude or not. She was always so self-contained, so assured, and nothing really seemed to touch her. Only Liam's death had ever really shown Cassie a glimpse of a different side to Bridget, and even then, most of her grief had been kept rigidly private.

Bridget was bewildered and upset by the situation that had developed between them. Of all the times when a mother and daughter should be together, it had been in times of sorrow, and Cassie had shown her cruelly that she hadn't wanted her. It had been so final, that brief sentence on the telephone. Bridget had stared at it for long moments when the line had gone dead, and Harry had taken the receiver from her and replaced it.

And she had turned to him, gabbling that it seemed she wasn't needed anywhere, and he'd taken her in his arms and said it simply wasn't true. But her thoughts had been too deeply involved with Cassie and Joe for her to take any great notice of his words. And how painfully the memories of herself and Austen surged back that night to haunt her.

But Joe had survived, and she had thanked God for it. Nothing else mattered, as long as Cassie and Joe got their chance of happiness. At least she didn't begrudge them that any more, and she couldn't help feeling faintly resentful that Cassie had been as thoughtless as ever towards her that night.

She'd thought they might have weathered it, that Cassie might have spent some time with her, and that this growing estrangement could have been overcome. But after Evelyn went back to her flat, Cassie seemed only to want her own company at the cottage, waiting for Joe to come home.

It was the beginning of May, and the blossoms were bursting on the trees at the beginning of an English summer. And if the cheeky German pilots who flew over the south of England in broad daylight on lone bombing trips as some kind of bravado surge of defiance lately would leave them alone, they might almost think the war was already over.

Bridget made up her mind. She would go and visit Cassie, and take her some flowers from the Hall as a kind of peace offering. The early roses were in bloom, and Bridget steeled her heart against their heady perfume as she picked a great sheaf of them and put them on the back of her car and drove over to Magnolia Cottage in the afternoon.

'Mother, how lovely to see you,' Cassie said more surprised at seeing the roses than anything else.

'Well, if Mohammed won't come to the mountain,' Bridget said dryly.

Cassie flushed. Her waistline was hardly expanding at all yet, but she was sensitive to every remark like that, even though Bridget didn't know about the baby that was miraculously still safe beneath her heart.

'I'm sorry. I've been busy rearranging the furniture so that Joe won't bang his cast every time he moves in here. Come in and have some tea,' she said awkwardly.

'Have you heard when he's coming home?' Bridget said politely.

'In about a week, I think. I shan't really believe it until I see him, though.'

'Well, that's good news, anyway.'

Here they were, making small talk like strangers again, unable to bridge the years of simmering resentment between them. Bridget felt helpless and impotent at the knowledge, but this cool and self-reliant girl never moved one inch to meet her halfway.

Cassie filled a vase with water for the roses. Their scent in the small sitting-room was overpowering. They made Bridget feel faint for a moment. She couldn't think now why she'd picked them. The scent of them was on her fingers, and on her clothes and in her head . . .

She heard the noise of the plane at the same time as Cassie. She jerked up her head, listening.

'It's one of theirs. Their engines have a different note to ours,' Cassie said, unnecessarily.

The sound came nearer, almost overhead, and then there

437

was a shrill whistling as the plane discharged its last remaining bomb before flying home to Germany.

'Get down, Kitty!' Bridget shrieked. She threw herself at Cassie, pushing her to the floor and smothering her with her own body. Seconds later the cottage shook on its foundations, the windows shattered and the door blew in. Splinters of glass flew about the room, followed by great clouds of dust and showers of rubble. The heavy grandfather clock in the corner of the room toppled and fell towards the two prostrate women, and ornaments and pictures and the vase of roses went with it.

'Mother,' Cassie croaked. She spat bits of earth and wood out of her teeth, and ignored the fact that her arms felt cut in a hundred places, as she tried to wriggle free from Bridget's protective weight. 'Are you all right? I can't move. Can you get up? You feel like a ton-weight.'

There was no reply, and she felt sudden fear. She'd attempted to make a joke of it, but there was never any point in making jokes if there was no one around to share them, and Bridget seemed so still, such a deadweight . . . The room was full of choking dust, and Cassie seemed to be trying to peer through a fog. Dimly, she realised that the heavy clock had fallen across them. Her mother had taken the brunt of it. If she hadn't it would have been Cassie . . .

She gave a great sob, twisting frantically to try and shift the clock, trying just as frantically to check if Bridget was still alive. Dear God, she had to be. If she wasn't, Cassie couldn't bear it . . .

Bridget groaned suddenly, and a wave of thankfulness ran through her daughter.

'Oh, Mother, thank God, thank God,' she sobbed. 'I thought you were dead!'

But it was obvious that Bridget could do nothing to help herself at the moment, and somehow Cassie managed to inch the heavy piece of furniture away from them both.

'Can you move at all, Mother?' She stuttered.

She could see that there was a bad cut on Bridget's head, where the blood ran down her cheek. She was chalk-white, her lips almost blue, but at last, very slowly, she began to gaze

438

vacantly about her. Her eyes were dark and unseeing, as if completely unaware of where she was or who was with her. A lone picture fell from the wall with a crash, and Bridget suddenly reached out blindly, clinging wildly to Cassie's arms and the tears gushed out.

'Oh, Kitty, Kitty darling, thank God you're safe. I'd never have forgiven myself if anything had happened to you. Sweet Jesus, but we're the only ones left now, and we have to take care of each other. They've all gone, my poor darling, but I promise you, I *promise you* –'

She felt the sting of someone's hand against her face. It hurt, and so did every part of her as she tried to move, and then began to crawl to the sofa and pull herself onto it with someone's help. Vaguely, she registered that it didn't feel as if any bones were broken, but Cassie didn't need to slap her to prove it . . . the fog clarified a little, at least in her mind.

'Cassie,' she whispered, and the salt tears continued to fall as her daughter stared at her with brimming eyes and trembling mouth, supporting her as she seemed to sway. It was impossible for Bridget to stop the violent shaking. All her nerves seemed to be on fire and tearing her apart.

'Mother, who is Kitty?' The words burst from Cassie's lips, and even now, *especially* now, they screamed out all the past hurts, jealousies, resentments. 'Why do you have to take care of her?'

Bridget closed her eyes against the rushing pain of it. She'd failed to take care of Kitty. And in one illuminating flash she knew that all these years, she'd made Cassie pay. Why had she been so blind not to see it before? It wasn't simply because Cassie had been Thomas Finley's child that she'd refused to give her love. It was because of Bridget's own inadequacy, her failure over Kitty . . . she had let Kitty down so badly, letting her die . . . Bridget had been forced to marry Thomas because of Kitty, and Thomas had left her with a child she hadn't wanted. And Cassie had paid the price of her guilt.

Through the deluge of her thoughts came a single memory. It was Marlene's voice, slurred at the time, but oh, so crystal clear now.

'You know what I think, ducks? I think you love your'

Cassie more'n you realise. Why else should you get so mad wiv 'er? You don't get mad wiv people you don't care about. Stands t'reason, dunnit?'

It suddenly felt as though a great weight was being lifted from her, and to Cassie's amazement, her mother suddenly put her arms around her and held her so tight that she could hardly breathe. They were both battered and bruised, but none of it mattered to Bridget. There would be time later for mending cuts. There were far more important things to be mended.

'Oh Cassie, darling, I do love you. I love you so much, so terribly, terribly much. I've always loved you –'

She couldn't say any more because she felt Cassie's shoulders heaving against her. Her strong, beautiful Cassandra Mavreen, was crying uncontrollably, babbling that she loved Bridget too, and why hadn't they ever told each other before? Why did it have to take a stray German bomber pilot making them think they'd been struck by an earthquake to bring them to their senses?

Cassie felt Bridget's body go very still again. She looked into her face fearfully. Bridget *was* all right, wasn't she . . .?

'Cassie,' she said slowly, 'there's something I want to tell you. Something that's been buried so deep inside me that I couldn't even think of it without feeling ill.'

'Shouldn't it wait until later, Mum? We should get your cut seen to, and we should both see a doctor –'

There weren't just the two of them to be checked over. There was the baby . . .

'I want to tell you now, Cassie, while I have the courage,' Bridget said quietly.

And there, amid the wreckage of their home, Bridget told her daughter about that terrible April morning when the earth had fractured and erupted, when buildings had collapsed like houses made of cards, and San Francisco had burned and died, and along with it, all Bridget's family, except for herself and Kitty.

She told it in a voice thickened by emotion and grief, remembering it all, sharing it and letting it go. It was all so long ago, and she should have let the memories fade. But somehow in suppressing them so much, she had kept them vivid, ready to explode in her mind at any instant.

'Mother, I never knew that anybody could go through such a terrible time,' Cassie whispered. 'What happened to you and Kitty after you went to New York?'

Bridget told her all of it, entrusting her with things she had never told anyone. It was right. It was her heritage. And Cassie's eyes were as wet as her own by the time she had finished. She put her arms around her mother and kissed her, as a daughter, as a friend.

'I'm so proud of you, Mother,' she said in a choking voice. 'You make me feel almost guilty in loving Joe now that I know your reasons for hating San Francisco.'

'Perhaps I won't any more. I can't tell yet,' Bridget said with a small shaky laugh. 'But darling, don't ever feel guilty for loving someone. You and Joe have something very special. I had that once, for a little time.'

'Was it with someone called Austen? You mentioned his name once, and you showed me a dried rose.'

'Yes. Austen.'

They smiled at each other then, not needing to say any more, two women in perfect accord, each knowing the joy and the passion of love. And the silence between them was filled with understanding and harmony for the first time in their lives.

It was broken by the sound of motor hooters and screeching tyres, and then the cottage seemed to be filled with people. Someone had sent for an ambulance, and Harry was there, and some of the staff from the Hall, and most of the convalescent boys who'd insisted on going with them when news of the lone bomber's attack became known.

They all stopped short at the sight of the two Finley women still holding one another and smiling as they sat very close on a rubble and dust-covered sofa.

'Thank God,' Harry gasped. 'Are you both all right? When you didn't phone and we didn't see anything of you, we got damn worried, especially when we found the telephone lines were dead.'

Bridget still had the remnants of tears on her cheeks. She

441

smiled through them. 'We've been sitting here telling stories until we were rescued, Harry. We thought it best not to move in case any bones were broken.'

One of the American convalescents looked at them admiringly as the ambulance people took over.

'Well, if that don't beat all. My God, I've got to hand it to you Britishers,' he said in a Brooklyn twang. 'Your women can beat the pants off the rest of us when it comes to staying cool in a crisis.'

Bridget felt Cassie's hand curl around hers. This Yank would never know how just big a crisis they had overcome that day.

The war in Europe was officially ended on May the 7th, but there had been no fighting for several days before that. Servicemen on both sides were weary of war, longing to get back to wives and children and to begin a new and better life. Cassie Finley moved into Ashworthy Hall, since it was obvious that the damage to the foundations of Magnolia Cottage made it dangerous to go back there.

The cottage would probably have to be demolished, and both the Finley women were saddened at the prospect. There had been happy times and bad times, but now Cassie and Joe as well as Bridget would stay at the Hall for as long as they liked.

Bridget wondered how long it would be for them, and if she'd felt apprehension before at the thought of Cassie going to live near San Francisco, it was doubled now. But she knew at last just why she had felt such fear. It wasn't solely because she expected another earthquake to happen any time. She just wanted to ensure Cassie's safety, as she had wanted to keep Kitty safe, out of love. But no one could or should try to control somebody else's life, no matter where their paths led, and she would have to let Cassie go.

Joe came home with his leg in heavy plaster again, but managing well enough with a stick. He was cheerful and excited and very very grateful to the Belgian folk who'd picked him up after his crash and cared for him so gently until he was taken to hospital.

His spirit had revived after the ordeal, and he was exhilarated to be arriving back in England in time for the victory celebrations, and most of all, to be with his adored wife again. Bonfires and fireworks and street parties were a fitting way to end a war, and for lovers to be reunited, and Ashworthy Hall was decked out with balloons and streamers to welcome home their own personal hero.

And when they had done with all the social activities of his return, and were at last alone, Cassie had something very special to tell him. They sat on the floor, which was the most comfortable place for Joe to stretch out the awkward encumbrance of his leg, and Cassie leaned back against him, the scent of her long black hair in its soft shoulder-length curls sweetly sensuous in his nostrils.

'Joe, when I thought I'd lost you, all kinds of crazy things kept running through my mind. things I wished I'd told you. Things I wished we'd done that I feared we might never get the chance to do. All the wasted years of our lives before I knew you – crazy things like that –'

He kissed the curve of her neck, his mouth warm and gentle on her skin.

'None of it sounds crazy to me, my darling girl,' he said huskily. 'Don't you think I had the same thoughts, shared the same regrets, Cassandra Mavreen? Love makes idiots of us all, honey.'

'Yes, I think perhaps it does,' she agreed softly. 'But there was one thing that kept me sane through that awful time of not knowing if you were alive or dead. One wonderful thing that belongs to you and me and nobody else, my Joe, and I knew I had to be strong –'

She felt his arms tighten around her body and he twisted himself slightly so that he could look full into her face. His hands slid down to the soft swell of her belly, and he hardly needed to ask the question. Her luminous eyes, her full red mouth and the happiness radiating out of her like an aura, told him everything he wanted to know.

'We're going to have a baby?' He said, elated. 'When is it going to be born? How long have you known? Are you all right? My God, honey, are you sure no damage was done to the baby in that bomb thing?'

Cassie began to laugh at his comical expression. He was at once the doting father, the protective husband, the masterful lover she had always dreamed about. She felt warm and cherished and loved, and it was so good, so good . . .

'Joe, I'm fine. The baby's fine. I've known about it for a little while, but I didn't want you to worry, so I waited before telling you. Please don't be angry –'

'I'm not angry. How could I be ever be angry with you, my darling?'

She laughed again. 'Very easily, when I'm in one of my scratchy moods. You don't think that's going to change overnight, do you?' she teased him.

'I hope not, or I shall think I've come home to the wrong woman,' he grinned. 'So put me out of my misery and tell me when I'm going to be a father.'

'Around Christmas-time. I'd love it if it was born on Liam's birthday, but I doubt that I'd be that lucky.'

'I hope not. I always felt sorry for your brother, being born on Christmas Day.'

'Did you? I always envied him having two sets of presents when I only got one,' Cassie smiled, remembering.

'But you got yours in April, didn't you? You didn't miss out, honey.'

She gave him a brilliant smile that took his breath away. 'No, I didn't. I didn't miss out on a thing really, only I didn't always see it, Joe.'

She shifted again, and his hands began caressing her more intimately.

'It seems to me I'm missing out,' he said meaningly. 'How the hell do two war-scarred old crocks manage, when one has a tree-trunk for a leg, and the other has bruises all over and is pregnant?'

'Easily,' said Cassie, having thought the whole thing out long ago, her eyes sparkling and darkening with a desire that matched Joe's. 'Just leave everything to your capable wife, and don't worry about a thing.'

And a long while later, wrapped in one another's arms, Joe sleepily asked his wife how her mother would take the news that her grandchild would be born in California.

'I think she'll take it damn well,' Cassie murmured, with a pride Joe didn't understand but was too exhausted to question. 'Just as she's always taken everything.'

Chapter 33

After she was told the news about the baby and greeting it as joyously as Cassie could have wished, Bridget took the rest of it stoically. She'd known their departure was coming for a long time, and she'd accepted it as inevitable. And at least they wouldn't be going immediately. Joe was still under medical supervision, and his leg had to grow much stronger before they could think of making the long journey to California, and both Bridget and Cassie were glad of these post-war summer months, when each felt they got to know the other properly at last.

But Bridget couldn't help feeling a pang, hearing their excited plans of what their new life was going to be like. Listening to them talk so animatedly was a little like seeing into the future, a good future that Bridget could never share. They would build their own home and their own winery, growing the grapes that Joe loved so much, and begin their own small dynasty.

Their child would run happy and free in the Californian sunshine, and Bridget wouldn't see it. There would only be photographs, and the child would grow up a stranger to its grandmother in faraway England, except for the visits home that Cassie promised faithfully they would make whenever they could.

By the middle of August the convalescent home had been officially closed, the patients sent home, and Ashworthy Hall had resumed its former quiet glory. Magnolia Cottage was surrounded with Keep Out notices, and scheduled to be pulled down at some future date, but there were more important tasks to be done before the demolition of one small

445

cottage in the country whose occupants were settled else-where. The blitz had taken a terrible toll, and whole cities had to be rebuilt first.

And Joseph and Cassandra Buckley were about to start out for a new life in California. Harry and Bridget drove them down to Southampton, with Evelyn squeezed into the car as well as all the luggage, and Marlene and Ruth met them at the dock-side to say good-bye. There had been cards from well-wishers, and from Joe's old service mates, and after all the bustle and farewell parties it was as much as Bridget could do to stem the tears when the last moments came.

In the end, she didn't even try. What was more natural than a mother hugging a daughter, and each crying over the other because they were soon to be six thousand miles apart?

'You'll write often, won't you, Cassie?'

'Every week,' she promised. 'And you'll answer?'

'Every week,' Bridget echoed, and they both laughed, because although the words might sound trite, they said all that was in their hearts. The continuing need to feel close, to be a part of one another's lives.

'And you'll let me know immediately the baby's born? I shall worry until I hear, darling –'

'Well, I hope you won't just sit around worrying for the next four months, Mother! And perhaps, one day –'

'We'll see,' Bridget said quickly, not wanting Cassie to put the question into words. It was still the one small taboo subject between them. Bridget couldn't yet say whether she would ever feel strong enough to go back to San Francisco. To her, it was a giant step that she could even think of such a thing without going cold all over.

'Evelyn's going to come and see me often,' Bridget kept on, trying to smile. 'She says she'll be my substitute daughter.'

'Don't let it go to her head,' Cassie said with mock severity. 'You've only got one daughter, you know.'

'I know,' Bridget said. 'And I love you, Cassie.'

They hugged one another for the last time.

'I love you too, Mum,' Cassie whispered.

Then there were frantic last-minute kisses from everyone, and Joe was whispering in Bridget's ear that she wasn't to

446

worry, and that he'd take care of Cassie always. She believed it implicitly, otherwise she could never have let her daughter go . . . Harry's arm was held tightly around her as the great liner eased its way out into the English Channel with hooters blaring and bands playing. And only when the ship had disappeared from their sight did she finally turn to him blindly, and sob against his chest.

'I've decided I'm not going to sit around and mope,' Bridget declared, after a solid week of doing just that, when nothing Harry said could comfort her, and she had snapped at him a hundred times over nothing, and nearly driven him to distraction.

'Thank God,' he said grimly. 'Do you know just how impossible you've been this last week?'

She gave him a sudden smile. 'Yes. I've been bloody awful, haven't I? But it's going to stop. Marlene called to say the land agents have found a suitable site for the theatre at long last. The land's been released, and I'm going down to Devon to take a look. I'll probably stay a while,' she said carefully.

'I think that's a good idea, darling,' he spoke just as guardedly. 'But I don't think you'll find what you're looking for there.'

'What am I looking for, Harry?'

He gave a short laugh. 'If you don't know yet, then it would be pointless in my telling you. When do you intend leaving?'

'In a couple of days. There's no point in delaying. It's taken ages to get the legal things sorted out, and we want to get everything started as quickly as possible now that there's no risk of the theatre being bombed as soon as it's built!'

'Of course. Do you want me to drive you down, or will you drive yourself? It's a hell of a distance –'

'No. I'd rather take the train, thank you all the same. I can read or doze, and get there reasonably refreshed.'

Harry looked at her thoughtfully.

'You are coming back, I take it?'

'Where else would I go?' Bridget said, an answer that was neither one thing nor the other.

'Will you give Cassie Marlene's address, or shall I send her

447

letters on to you from here?' He enquired, and she realised how wary they were being with one another, as polite as strangers.

'Please send them on. I'll probably only be gone a week or two, and by the time Cassie knew where I was, I'd be back again.'

But she didn't meet his eyes, and both of them wondered if she really would come back to Ashworthy hall. Her theatre would be established in Devon, and she had good friends there, one of whom was her business partner. In Harry's mind it was more than a possibility that she'd decide to stay, and if it was what Bridget wanted, he wasn't ever sure he would try and stop her. In fact, he thought ruefully that he'd like to meet the man who could stop Bridget Finley doing anything she wanted to do.

Marlene told her she looked thinner, and that she could do with a bit of fattening up, making Bridget feel like a prize cow being prepared for market. It wouldn't be easy to fatten anybody up nowdays. Food was still rationed and in short supply, and although they had won the war, it didn't always feel like it when you couldn't get a decent bit of meat for a Sunday dinner, and bananas were still only yellow crescents seen in children's picture-books.

Bridget felt in a kind of limbo. She listened to all that the solicitors and the land agents told her and all that Marlene and Ruth bellowed indignantly about. She understood about contracts and building supplies being short, and that they were going to have to build on the site of a tumbledown place that had its own solid foundations, because it was the only way they could get a permit from the local council.

There were innumerable difficulties to surmount, and she began to wonder if it had been such a marvellous idea after all. Until the day that Marlene told her she had a surprise for her. She took Bridget to a local workshop where a man with paint-spattered overalls beamed at them.

'This is Les Cole, Bridget. I asked him to do some sample signs for the front of the theatre, for your approval. If you don't like any of 'em, just say so. Only I thought it might cheer you up, seeing as you look so down in the dumps when you should be on top of the world! What d'ya think?'

Les Cole was a craftsman. He'd made six miniature signs in wood, and painted on them in different colours and styles were the words 'The Liam Finley Theatre'. Each of them was beautiful, and Bridget felt a lump in her throat at seeing Liam's name so bright and prominent.

'Well?' Marlene said encouragingly.

'I like them all, and you were right to do this, Marlene. It makes it all seem real at last. I'd begun to think it would never happen.'

Les Cole began pointing out various aspects of his work, and it was a pleasure to hear a man with such skill at his finger-tips enthuse so much. Finally Bridget made her choice, and then asked if she could buy two of the miniatures.

'It's my pleasure, Ma'am,' the man said, quoting a ridiculously low price. He wrapped them in brown paper and handed them to her, and promised to start work on the large version so that it would be ready as soon as required.

'What did you want them for?' Marlene asked.

'One for me and one for Cassie,' she said. 'I'll send her the miniature of the one we're going to use, and keep the other one that's very similar to it myself.'

'It'll look a bit cheap among the treasures of Ashworthy Hall, won't it?' Marlene glanced at her sideways. 'Or ain't ya going back there to put that poor man out of his misery? Don't ya think it's time you made up yer mind about Harry, Bridget?'

'I made up my mind about him a long time ago.'

'Why doncher tell him then? For two people who are supposed to be so bleedin' intelligent, you two don't arf take yer time, and you ain't gettin' any younger, if ya don't mind me sayin'. That ain't snow in yer hair, Bridget.'

Bridget laughed. 'Oh, stop it, Marlene. You're a bit long in the tooth yourself to start acting as matchmaker. Harry and I are comfortable enough as we are.'

'Oh yeah? Tell it to the marines, ducks. So when are ya thinking of going back?'

'Do you want to get rid of me?'

'No. I just want ya to find out where ya belong. And it ain't here, Bridget. You can pretend all ya like that yer interested in our little village doings, but yer heart ain't in it. And that's telling ya flat.'

Bridget sighed as Marlene went off to make some lemonade, saying it was too hot a day to argue any longer. Marlene had always seen through her. After two weeks of doing very little, she was finding that the Devon air made her suffocatingly lethargic.

She waited avidly for the weekly letter from Cassie, which Harry sent down to her promptly, and she read it over and over again, as if searching for the tiniest sign of discontent or disillusionment from her daughter.

There was none. Everything was blissful and wonderful. The vineyards were green and stretched as far as the eyes could see. Okaje was far enough away from the city of San Francisco that to drive there took half the morning, and at that point in Cassie's last letter, Bridget's heart had started to thump.

'Joe took me there last week, Mother. I was so curious to see what it looked like, and it's quite breathtaking. Joe's parents told me a bit more about the earthquake, but of course it didn't touch them up here, and I swear that you'd never believe such a disaster had ever happened. The city you knew has been completely rebuilt and is solidly established now, and across the Bay is a beautiful bridge they call the Golden Gate bridge. We drove up through Nob Hill, Mother, and then I lit candles in a church for my grandparents and for Michael and Kitty.'

Bridget felt tears come to her eyes, reading that part of the letter, but Cassie didn't intend her go all soft for long. She plunged into an account of the busy season at the wineries now.

'We're still at Joe's parents until our house is ready, and he's helping with the grape harvest at present. The aroma of the ripened grapes everywhere is heady and glorious, and I'd love you to see the cellars, and to see just what goes into making every glass of wine!'

Cassie also sent her a little booklet about the new San

450

Francisco, looking not so very different from the old, Bridget thought reluctantly, except that it was smarter, more elegant, like a mature woman grown out of a coltish child. It had survived, and survived magnificently. The cable-cars still tortured their way up and down the undulating hills to the Bay and there was that splendid bridge completed two years before the war in Europe began, golden and beautiful, spanning those deep cold waters. She could almost smell the fish from Fisherman's Wharf and the Cannery . . .

Bridget's eyes grew misty. Cassie never said so in as many words, but Bridget knew how much she hoped that in time Bridget would relent and make the trip back. Meanwhile, Cassie went relentlessly on, tantalising her with snippets of information, and putting in a photo or two of the lovely valley area where she and Joe now lived.

It was all a far cry from a hovel on the waterfront where Bridget and Kitty had been taken in, owning nothing but the clothes on their backs.

'I think it's time I went back to Sussex,' Bridget told Marlene, after her stay had lingered on into October. 'We'll be getting fed up with each other's company soon, and you can manage everything perfectly well without me now that all the legal contracts are signed.'

'I'd never get fed up wiv ya, Bridget, but I think yer right. You'll wanter be settled in your own place to get the news of Cassie's babe, and any time ya need me, I'm on the end of the phone, ain't I?'

In her own place? Bridget wondered just what or where that was, as the train rocked back and forth through the green Devon meadows and across country to Sussex. Just how long could she go on living at Ashworthy Hall, using rooms in the west wing at the discretion of a good friend, and never giving anything back? She tried to say as much to Harry when he'd welcomed her back and insisted that they had dinner together that night.

'My dear, you give me back more than you know,' he said steadily. 'You always have. And please don't let's have any more nonsense about going off and finding yourself. This

451

is where you belong.'

She wasn't convinced, but she gave up worrying and arguing, and began instead to get increasingly excited as the weeks went by and Cassie's letters became more erratically worded than ever as the baby's birth came closer. Evelyn called on Bridget often, and the two of them shared the laughter over Cassie's descriptions of her and Joe and the portly Buckley parents all trying to fit into one of the smaller cars now that Cassie was so huge and in her own words resembled 'a beached whale'.

'How long is it now, Mrs Finley?' Evelyn asked, wiping her eyes.

'Less than two weeks,' Bridget said. 'That's if it comes on time. First babies often don't, but if Cassie's as large as she says, I hope for her sake it comes early.'

'I wonder if it will be a boy or a girl.'

'Oh, a boy,' Bridget declared positively. 'Cassie's made up her mind, and it wouldn't dare to be anything else.'

This set them off again, and then Evelyn told Bridget shyly that she'd met a nice young man, and she would very much like to bring him along to meet her.

'I hope you don't mind, but I think of you as the nearest thing to a mother I've got now, and Graham's such a darling. I know you'll like him.'

'Well, at last!' Bridget said, but the words didn't disguise the pleasure at the compliment this very nice girl paid her. She didn't have Cassie, but Evelyn was the next best thing. She gave Evelyn a kiss on the cheek, seeing how pink she had gone.

'Is he special, this Graham of yours?' She asked.

'I think he might be,' Evelyn said, with all the cool sophisticated understatement of Pooley's finishing school girls. And then she capitulated under Bridget's smiling look. 'Oh, Mrs Finley, he's just divine, and I'm sure he's going to ask me to marry him. I know I'm what they call a late-starter, but when it hits you, it really hits you, doesn't it?'

'It really does,' Bridget agreed. She thought quickly. 'Look; why don't you bring him for Christmas Day, and your father and grandmother too, if you'd like to? It's the first

Christmas after the war, and Harry and I would rattle around in this great place. We'd thought of having a quiet Christmas, but it seems all wrong, somehow. Let's make a party of it.'

'Oh, it sounds wonderful, and I know my family would be delighted, but what about – I mean, isn't it –'

'Liam's birthday,' Bridget finished for her. 'Yes, it is, and I know I don't have to tell you that his memory will always be in my heart, my dear. But we can't mourn the past for ever. Life must go on, and all we can do is enjoy what's left to us. It's a precious gift, Evelyn – and if I don't stop being so serious immediately I shall get all maudlin, and we've got too much planning to do to waste time on all that! So will you let me know if you'll all come here for Christmas? I do hope that you will.'

'Of course. And I know we shall be thrilled to accept, Mrs Finley,' Evelyn said softly. 'My father has always wanted to meet you again. I've told him so often what a very special lady you are.'

'Oh, nonsense,' Bridget said, but extraordinarily pleased all the same.

Later, she wondered if she'd taken too much on herself, inviting strangers for Christmas, though she vaguely remembered Evelyn's father from the girls' La Retraite days. To her relief Harry was delighted.

'At last, a good old-fashioned family Christmas again! We'll cut down a fir tree and fetch out all the baubles and tinsel from the attic and decorate it. We'd better buy presents for everyone as well. You can't have Christmas without presents. I'll see about getting something for the table too. I've got my sources, and I might just be able to lay my hands on a goose.'

'Oh Harry, you are wonderful!' Bridget laughed as he rambled on, almost child-like in his enthusiasm. He seemed to have come to life again, and it hadn't even dawned on her until then how tired and drawn he'd been looking lately.

She wondered for a moment if he could be ill, and felt a shock run through her. He was never ill, and if he was . . . she was simply unable to imagine a world without Harry Ashworth in it.

'You should say that more often,' he grinned at her.

'I might start saying it to someone else,' she said mischievously. 'Evelyn says her father's wanted to meet me again for a long time. Wouldn't it be a scream if –'

'No, it wouldn't, Bridget,' he said abruptly, and before she could even open her mouth to reply, he'd gone striding out of the room to the privacy of his study. She stared at the closed door, wondering if it was possible that he was actually jealous at the thought of another man admiring her. After all this time? It was a piquant thought, but not one that Bridget really had any intention of exploiting. She was too old for coquetry, and Evelyn's father would merely be a Christmas guest and treated exactly like all the rest.

But she couldn't deny a feeling of pleasure all the same, whether it was due to the thought of William Oakes-Johnson's eagerness to meet her again, or Lord Harry Ashworth's ruffled retort at hearing of it.

The transatlantic telephone call came late on Christmas Eve. The line was terrible, and Harry rattled the instrument several times as if to clear it. Bridget was in the room with him, and they were putting the finishing touches to the decorations for Christmas Day.

'I can't hear you. Who is this?' Harry bellowed into the phone, and then his face changed. 'Joe? Is that you? Good God, boy, this must be costing a fortune –'

He stopped to listen, and Bridget rushed to his side. He handed the phone to her.

'I think you should be the one to hear this,' he said gently. 'I'll just pour the drinks to celebrate.'

Bridget took the phone, in a fever of apprehension and excitement.

'Joe? Joe, is everything all right?'

'If you mean is a healthy boy weighing seven and a half pounds all right, then yes, I'd say so!' She heard Joe's exuberant voice. 'And before you ask, Cassie's fine. They're both fine – wonderful! She sends you her love, and said I had to call you right away. She's going to write you tomorrow, Bridget.'

'Oh Joe, I'm so happy, and you be sure and give her my love too, and kiss the baby for me, and congratulations to you both.'

'I will. Oh, and I nearly forgot. We're calling him Austen Liam Michael Buckley. It's a hell of a mouthful, but I had to be sure and ask if you approved.'

Bridget tried not to cry into the phone. 'I couldn't approve more. I love you both, Joe, and the baby too.'

She couldn't say any more. She couldn't say his name yet. It was too precious, too dear, too wonderful of Cassie to do this. It linked everything together. Despite the miles, despite the past, they were a real family at last.

When she tried to tell Harry all that she felt, she ended up a mass of blubber on his shoulder, swallowed the celebratory glass of brandy without noticing it, and told him in a wobbly voice that she was going to bed before she made a complete fool of herself. And he let her go, loving her, and thanking God that the baby had been everything that they all wanted.

So Christmas Day was extra-special that year. They all toasted Austen Liam Michael Buckley along with the King, and Evelyn was delighted at Cassie's good timing. Of course, there was never any doubt that clever Cassie would time it right, she told everyone gaily, sparkling more than usual because the young man at her side was so obviously captivated by her. Even her grandmother joined in some of the fun of the party games, and her father clearly thought that his lovely hostess with the clear blue Irish eyes and the dark hair sprinkled with alluring streaks of white, was nothing short of sensational. And as Bridget unconsciously responded to all his flattery, Harry wondered if after all, he had left it all too late.

Days later, Bridget was still in a state of elation about the baby. She had telephoned Marlene and written jubilantly to Ralph and Alma, and waited eagerly for Cassie's first letter to arrive. She had bought dainty baby clothes with her clothes coupons and sent them off to California, trying to imagine how the baby Austen would look in them. Austen . . . she still felt a lump in her throat, knowing that by doing this, Cassie had kept that other Austen alive for her. Her own dear Austen, whose memory had merged into a warm glow of pleasure at last, and held none of the bitter pain.

It was true what she'd told Evelyn. She'd said it as much for herself as for Cassie's friend. Life had to go on, and you couldn't mourn for ever. You just had to do the best you could with what was left . . .

The elation inevitably faded a little, and after a week Bridget began to feel restless, needing to be out of doors on this crisp morning, the first of a new year. It was cold, but not unbearably so. She liked this time of year, when everything was waiting to be renewed, trees and plants that had lain dormant all winter ready to put out feelers of new life. Spring might be a long way away, but to Bridget, the first day of January was the sort of day to be somewhere special, doing something momentous.

She got out her small car, and drove through the sleepy Sussex lanes, free from the threat of enemy warfare now, and sent up a silent prayer that the governments of the world would never let such an atrocity happen again. She found herself on the road to Magnolia Cottage, which was beginning to look neglected and unloved, and on an impulse she stopped the car and sat quite still for a few minutes.

She had wanted to come back here. It had been her home for a long while, and so many important days of her life had passed here. Yet she had never been able to. It was tied up too deeply with her feelings about San Francisco. But nothing moved here now. It was quiet, calm.

And gradually it was almost as if something urged her on. She stepped outside the car and walked slowly towards the gap in the cottage where the front door had been. She moved carefully over the piles of rubble inside and walked into the sitting-room for the first time since that fateful day, all those months ago.

Everything was still the same. Nothing had been cleared out, save the personal possessions Harry had collected, because no one quite knew what to do with the useless pieces. There was no vandalism in the area, so nothing had been touched or stolen. It was a ghost-house, keeping the memories intact. It was like herself.

Bridget looked about her with growing horror, and saw

herself, old , faded, dusty, broken. She had been so young, so vital, and life had changed all that. She was old, a grand-mother, moving into another generation and totally unable to stop the way the years were changing her. She felt a surge of hysteria, so wrapped up in her terror that she didn't hear the other car pull up outside the cottage, and when she heard a voice shouting at her, she stumbled and almost fell among the shattered furniture.

'For God's sake, what are you doing in here? I couldn't believe it when I saw your car. Don't you know it's dangerous?' Harry glowered at her from the entrance, framed by the sharp daylight outside. She looked at him, her dearest friend, whom she loved so much, and couldn't answer.

'Bridget, what's happened?' His voice changed, concerned for her now. 'It's not Cassie or the baby, is it? You haven't had more news – ?'

She shook her head as he crossed to her swiftly. She was a breath away from him, and she wanted – she wanted –

She heard him curse savagely seconds before he pulled her into his arms. She knew that Harry often covered deep emotion with a curse . . .

'Good God, woman, how much longer am I going to have to be responsible for you like this? Am I going to have to stand by and watch you falling for that double-barrelled fellow now, because I warn you, Bridget, I don't think I can. Not any more. I've always been a patient man, but my patience is running out.'

He looked down at her sharply, as aggressive as she'd ever seen him. 'Well? What do you have to say to it?'

'To what? Is this a clumsy proposal of marriage or some-thing?' Now she was as angry as he. The blood was pounding in her ears, and she thought how ludicrous they must look, two middle-aged people standing in the middle of a bombed out cottage, wrangling like a couple of adolescents in love.

But perhaps that was just what they were. Deep inside, beneath all the extra flesh and the wrinkles and the changing hair colour, Bridget knew very well that nothing really changed. Feelings didn't change. The capacity for loving didn't change.

'Well, it's certainly not a proposal for *something*. I'm too old for playing those games.' Harry said. 'So don't you think it's time we got married, Bridget?'

'To comfort each other in our old age, you mean?' She wasn't sure whether he was doing this out of sympathy. If so, she didn't want it. She still had her pride.

'No, it's not out of sympathy, you beautiful stubborn woman! I wouldn't make a mistake a second time, and neither must you, Bridget. We've both made a hash of marrying for the wrong reasons, and this time it has to be for the right reason.'

'And what's that?' Say it, she pleaded, *say* it . . .

'Because I love you more than I've ever loved in my life before,' Harry said roughly. 'I love you so much it tortured me to see you flirting with that Oakes-Johnson fellow. Because I must have you, my darling, and if you think I'm just offering comfort for your old age, then think again. You'll never be old to me, and I want you for my wife in every sense of the word. I want *you*, Bridget.'

She heard all the male authority in his voice, and all the passion of a young stallion was in his body as he held her tight, and to her he would never be old, either. In their hearts they were still fresh, still seventeen . . .

'So, my Bridget? Will you marry me for love?'

She gave a small broken sigh as she leaned against his broad chest and felt the matching beat of his heart against hers.

'Yes,' she said. 'Oh, *yes*, my love.'

He kissed her so hard it sent the blood racing in her veins, and still he held her fast, wanting everything settled before she had a chance to think.

'I think we should go on an extended honeymoon to make up for all the years without each other, my darling. And shall we marry in April, to finally dispel all those old ghosts of yours?'

She took a long, deep breath, knowing that at long last, she didn't need this exorcism.

'Must we wait until then? We've waited too long already.'

'As soon as possible then,' he said, unable to hide his pleasure.

'And about the honeymoon, Harry,' Bridget said. His fingers touched her cheeks and hair as if for the very first time, and his touch awoke a fire in her as though she was a girl in the full bloom of youth. 'Harry, do you think – do I dare – ?'

He saw the longing in her eyes and read her thoughts. 'I think we should both take the chance to visit our grandson, don't you?'

'Our grandson,' Bridget said, tasting the words and finding a new joy in them.

Harry's arms tightened around her again.

'Will you face it with me, Bridget? We'll visit San Francisco together, just once. And then we'll spend as long as you like with our family.'

She had fought a losing battle with her fears all through the years, and looking into his dear, craggy face, she knew that she had finally won.

'Yes,' she said steadfastly. 'I think I can face anything now. After all, I came back to the cottage today, and I didn't even have you with me then.'

'But you have me now,' Harry said. 'Now and always.'